WITHDRAWN
Damaged, Obsolete, or Surplus
Jackson County Library Services

P9-DTL-897

THE SINISTER BOOKSELLERS
OF BATH

ALSO BY GARTH NIX

Shade's Children

The Ragwitch

Across the Wall

To Hold the Bridge

One Beastly Beast

A Confusion of Princes

Newt's Emerald

Angel Mage

The Left-Handed Booksellers of London

THE OLD KINGDOM SERIES

Sabriel

Lirael

Abhorsen

Clariel

Goldenhand

Terciel & Elinor

THE
SINISTER
BOOKSELLERS
OF
BATH

GARTH NIX

 KATHERINE TEGEN BOOKS
An Imprint of HarperCollins Publishers

All the characters in this book are fictitious, and any resemblance
to actual persons, living or dead, is purely coincidental.

Katherine Tegen Books is an imprint of HarperCollins Publishers.

The Sinister Booksellers of Bath
Copyright © 2023 by Garth Nix
All rights reserved. Printed in the United States of America.
No part of this book may be used or reproduced in any manner whatsoever without
written permission except in the case of brief quotations embodied in critical
articles and reviews. For information address HarperCollins Children's Books,
a division of HarperCollins Publishers, 195 Broadway, New York, NY 10007.
www.epicreads.com

Library of Congress Control Number: 2022946698
ISBN 978-0-06-323633-2 (hardcover)—ISBN 978-0-06-331434-4 (int.)

Typography by David Curtis
23 24 25 26 27 LBC 5 4 3 2 1

First Edition

To Anna, Thomas, Edward, and all my family and friends.

And to Katherine Tegen, who deserves a particular dedication upon her retirement from HarperCollins. This book, and many others of mine, might not have been written without Katherine's support and encouragement over many years.

Also to five authors who I first read when I was young, who helped make me a writer, for this book in particular: Joan Aiken, Alan Garner, Susan Cooper, Diana Wynne Jones, and John Masefield.

The epigraphs at the beginning of each chapter are from Brewer's Dictionary of Phrase and Fable, the Cassell and Company edition of 1907.

AS WITH *THE LEFT-HANDED BOOKSELLERS OF LONDON*, THIS STORY TAKES PLACE IN A SLIGHTLY ALTERNATE VERSION OF ENGLAND IN THE YEAR 1983, SO IT IS NOT ENTIRELY AS THOSE WHO WERE ALIVE THEN WILL REMEMBER, OR THOSE WITH A HISTORICAL BENT CAN CHECK UP ON. SIMILARLY, CONTEMPORARY VISITATIONS TO PLACES MENTIONED IN THIS BOOK MAY NOT ACCORD WITH HOW THEY ARE DESCRIBED HERE. WHAT, THEN, IS REAL?

PROLOGUE

THE YOUNG MAN RUNNING PANICKED IN THE DARK INSTINCTIVELY headed towards the Abbey. The streetlights had snapped out a minute before, and he had been suddenly attacked. Something immensely strong had grabbed him in the darkness, lifting him from the bandstand where he'd been slumped trying to work out how drunk he was and what to do since Wednesday night was about to become Thursday morning and everywhere he could get another drink was either closed or wouldn't let him in.

He'd only escaped because he was wearing his coat like a cloak, his arms not in it, and whatever grabbed him had been momentarily confused as he slithered out of the two-pound Oxfam woolly bargain like a lizard leaving its sacrificial tail in a predator's mouth.

He took the steps up and out of the park without slowing

and vaulted the locked gates at the top without pause, heading towards the Abbey because he knew with absolute conviction that whatever was after him was not human, and though he had never thought of himself as religious before and had stopped going to church with his mum when he was twelve, he had experienced a sudden resurgence of faith. The Abbey seemed the only place that might offer him shelter from whatever it was that came so swiftly after him now. So swiftly, and without normal footfalls. Instead it made sharp scraping sounds all too like a butcher's knife being rapidly sharpened on a steel.

The three-quarter moon provided what little light there was, limning the dark shadow of the Abbey ahead with lines of silver. The paving stones were rimed with frost, and slippery underfoot, and he almost fell as he reached the massive corner of the medieval edifice and raced around it and along the southern side. He was now astonishingly sober and incredibly frightened.

"Help!" he screamed into the darkness. "Help! Someone help me!"

It was typical there was no one around to help. Two rozzers had stopped their patrol car to look down at him from Pierrepont Street an hour ago, but they hadn't bothered getting out of their nice warm vehicle and into the cold and drizzle. They'd looked because he was a punk with an orange mohawk and a safety pin through his nose, in a once-good black overcoat splattered with runny drawings in white housepaint, which he thought were anarchist symbols but meant something else entirely. But he was by himself, and a weedy drunken punk slumped on the bandstand in Parade Gardens wasn't a bother to anyone. He'd been glad they'd left him alone, he never wanted any attention from the police, but where were they now?

In his heart he knew the police wouldn't be any help anyway. But he shouted again, not slowing his headlong rush along the side of the Abbey. He had a vague memory the main entrance was right up the other end, and the doors were probably closed anyway. But if he could get there, surely a church would be safe, maybe even the front steps would work, but the thing chasing him was too close, that horrible scraping sound was louder and louder—

A cold hand gripped him and yanked him back. A hand colder than the winter air. This time, he was taken by the neck, not by clothing he could shuck. He tried to free himself, reaching back to break the thing's grip, and thrashed his body with all his strength. But it was not enough, far from enough. He couldn't escape and he couldn't breathe. He kicked back at the thing's legs, pain blossoming in his heels. It felt like he'd kicked the stone walls of the Abbey rather than the creature that held him, but he knew he hadn't.

The grip on his throat eased a little and he managed to get in a gasp of air. His attacker dragged him away from the Abbey, lifting him as if he were no more than a stick of wood, and took him across the Abbey Churchyard. With every step, there came that horrible, scraping sound. *Shk, shk, shk, shk* . . .

They came out of the shadow of the Abbey into the moonlight. The punk twisted his head around enough to see his captor and wished he hadn't. He was held by the neck in an unbreakable grip by something that had the general outward appearance of a woman. One who stood seven feet tall and whose skin was grey and smooth, but weirdly mottled, as if thousands of tiny fossilized shells had been merged together and made into dark marble. Living stone, if that was possible. Her fierce, colorless eyes moved and her mouth twitched, apparently in irritation. She was clad in a simple cross-hatched-patterned dress with a high waist and puffed sleeves, all also of impossibly flexible, moving stone.

She had no feet. Her legs ended in broken stumps at the ankle, jagged breaks, and that was why she made the horrible sharpening noise as she moved, stone upon stone.

The grey stone woman stopped in the full light of the moon and shook out the folded paper she held in her right hand. An old, time-yellowed paper or parchment, the only thing about her that was not stone. It was a map of some kind. For a moment he hoped she might let go of him in order to unfold it properly. But she didn't. She shook the map once, twice, then held it up so the moonlight fell on it, and it began to glow with its own radiance.

As she did so, the punk caught a metallic, sulfurous whiff. For a moment, he thought it somehow came from the illuminated map. Then he heard water gushing and saw wafts of steam rising from the narrow gaps between the paving stones. The stone woman opened her mouth and emitted a growl, the first even faintly human noise she'd made.

"You trespass on my demesne," said another woman, one

the punk couldn't see. There was a lot of steam around now, and the iron stench was strong. Hot water rose up between the flagstones, water stained an orange-red, a sudden flood that streamed around the marble woman's sharp stumps.

Everything became cloaked in steam, and the punk blinked and grimaced, trying to see. But there was only more strangeness, a figure appearing with a face of beaten gold upon a vaguely defined body woven of steam and rusty water. The golden face was curiously familiar. He had seen it somewhere before.

"I have taken my prey and now I will depart," said the stone woman. Her voice was very strange, echoing and distant, as if it came from a hole beneath the ground.

"I did not give you leave to hunt here. You were warned and punished, when last you trespassed on my demesne," said the golden face. Her hair was plaited into a kind of crown and unlike the marble statue, the golden mouth did not move when she spoke, as if it were only a mask for the watery creature behind it. "Besides, he is mine."

The marble statue did not answer.

"I am?" asked the punk.

"Travis Zelley," said the steam-wreathed apparition. "Your mother gave you sixpence to throw in my waters when you came to worship me on your seventh birthday."

"Uh, I did?" squeaked Travis. The only waters he could remember throwing any kind of money into was on a trip to the Roman Baths, just nearby. It came back to him that his mother *had* given him a sixpence. He had wanted to keep it for lollies, but she made him throw it in. A real silver sixpence, it had been a few years before the change to decimal currency and the dull 5p coins. They'd had afternoon tea in the Pump Room afterward. He hadn't thought of it as worshipping anyone. But he suddenly remembered where he'd seen the golden face before. It was a mask on display in the museum part of the Roman Baths.

The stone woman suddenly swung Travis towards the map, throwing him at it as if it were a window. As she let go he felt a moment of elation that he would escape after all, until he found himself falling not to the pavement, but on to grass, somewhere entirely different. It was suddenly bright, so bright he had to shut his eyes for a second. Blinking them open he saw he was somewhere outdoors but surrounded by high walls. It was hot, savagely hot after the cold winter's night he'd been in a moment before.

He started to get up but was forced down again as the stone woman suddenly appeared in front of him. She was hissing in anger. The map she still clutched in her right hand was somehow stretched into thin air as if held by some invisible person opposite her, and as he watched, it tore across the folds and one entire quarter of the map disappeared, rusty water spraying down the statue's arm.

She turned to him, her hand making a terrible claw. She picked him up, stone fingernails ripping through skin, deep to the bone, and shook him, like a terrier with a rat.

"You have cost me more than I care to pay," she said in that eerie, cavernous voice. "The ritual does not demand pain before death, but you shall have it."

Travis started screaming, but there was no one to hear.

The hot waters in the Abbey Churchyard subsided as quickly as they had risen, and there was no steam, no strange figure, no golden head. The streetlights flickered and returned to life. A cold breeze came up and blew rubbish along the streets and lanes, including a piece of heavy, antique paper: the torn-off section of the marble woman's map. It skipped and slid past the Pump Room, blown westward towards Stall Street, where it was arrested by slapping into one of the columns of the colonnade on the far side. Already wet, it stuck there until the early morning, when it was spotted by a street cleaner. She peeled it off, saw it was something unusual, and took it home. She was surprised it dried so well, the rusty water streaks leaving no mark, and greatly pleased when her brother-in-law sold it the next Wednesday from his bric-a-brac market stall in Guinea Lane for ten pounds to one of his regular customers, the bibliophile Sir Richard Wedynk.

CHAPTER ONE

>━┤◆>━O━<◆┤━<

Bath, Saturday, 10th December 1983

Bees. *With the Romans a flight of bees
was considered a bad omen.*

>━┤◆>━O━<◆┤━<

THE SMALL BOOKSHOP IN BATH WAS NOT, IN FACT, SMALL. IT APPEARED
to be no more than a cramped and narrow shop occupying half
the ground floor of a three-story Georgian terrace house, the
other half given over to an equally cramped tobacconist who
sold dubious pipe mixtures of her own devising and cigarettes
from "East of Istanbul." But the Small Bookshop was actually
an outpost of the St. Jacques clan, so there was more to it than
could be seen from outside, both above and below. Even the
tobacconist half was a front, inhabited by a right-handed bookseller whose awful offerings were a ploy to limit customers and
allow her to get on with her researches into the works of Izaak
Walton and obscure enchantments involving fish.

The other fifteen booksellers on the permanent staff of the
Small Bookshop included a dozen of the left-handed variety:

field agents, enforcers, and occasional executioners. They were primarily there to keep an eye on human interactions with the entity the Romans called Sulis Minerva. She inhabited the ever-popular Roman Baths, and when given the correct gifts, properly inscribed, would grant boons of power, particularly to people seeking revenge or retribution. The Baths were visited by tens of thousands of people every year, so it was hard work for the booksellers who monitored the queue going in, keeping watch for Death Cultists and others of that ilk who came to ask Sulis Minerva for the causation of a fatal accident or an astonishingly swift mortal illness. A less careful watch was maintained outside the Bath's opening hours, the constant surveillance replaced by occasional random patrols through the evening and night.

The bookshop was often used as a temporary repository for bulk purchases of secondhand books made in the West Country. "An Auction of the Library of a Distinguished Lady" or "Sale of the Property of a Gentleman, being mostly books" and the like. The books were sorted and cataloged there before being dispatched to the New Bookshop in London, the Mews Bookshop in York, or if they were too arcane to be sold, sent to the Crawley Tunnel Library in Edinburgh, the Salinae mine in Cheshire, or to other secretive St. Jacques establishments.

When a shipment came in from one of these purchases, more right-handed booksellers were drafted into the Small Bookshop to help triage the books before cataloging. The right-handed, while not fighters like the left-handed, were proficient in various arcane arts, including one often mistaken as purely mundane: extensive knowledge of printing, paper, bookbinding, and bookselling through the ages. A book of sorcerous interest might escape *magical* detection by various means, such as being bound in rune-etched bone disguised under buckram; or encased in a field of lunar misdirection by exposure to seventeen new moons in a silver bowl upon one of three particular hills in England (a procedure often spoiled by rain). These methods worked well against general spells of discovery but were of no use if a right-handed bookseller found some incongruous detail of binding, type, title, content, or provenance and looked more deeply.

Vivien St. Jacques, right-handed bookseller, had found just such a discrepancy in a volume of Thomas Moule's maps of English counties. The gilt letters embossed on the spine declared it to be *A Collection of Maps* and the engraved title page went further to say it was "A Collection of Maps by Thomas Moule, Bound for Sir Richard Wedynk by Amos Carlyle of Salisbury in 1954," which was all well and good, Moule's maps of English counties being very nicely done and collectible and Carlyle a well-known and excellent modern bookbinder. But Vivien had noticed a slight bulge in the back of the case and some not particularly expert resewing and gluing of the leather binding, work that would not meet Carlyle's standards, indicating it had been opened up later and something slid in against the board.

She set the volume down on the worktable and looked at it again carefully. She could feel a slight tingling in the thumb of her gloved right hand, which might or might not be related to this book. It could be a general warning, a foretelling of something bad on the horizon.

"Hmmm," she said.

"Got something interesting?" asked Ruby from the neighboring table. She was also a right-handed bookseller, one of the few permanently stationed in the Small Bookshop. She had asked for help to assess the recent purchase of the late Sir Richard Wedynk's library, and Vivien had come from London in answer to the call. Ruby was a decade older than Vivien, in her early thirties, and was notionally in charge, inasmuch as anyone was, the right-handed booksellers tending to work most of the time as a kind of anarchist collective driven by shared interests and responsibilities, setting their own tasks to achieve the generally desired objectives. Though they did take direction from the senior-most, when required, and Great-Aunt Evangeline's word was the final law.

"There's definitely something hidden in the binding," said Vivien. She pushed her chair back and got up, wending her way between the piles of tea chests full of books that had been stacked in lines to allow navigation, over to the essential cupboard that stood by the door to the stairs. Every workroom of the right-handed booksellers had an essential cupboard. Some had more than one. They varied in style, if not in contents. This one was originally an eighteenth-century housekeeper's cupboard, with three individual cupboards above two ranks of drawers.

Vivien touched her white-cotton-gloved right forefinger to the third drawer on the right, which sprang open. She looked into it and frowned.

"Someone hasn't put the dowsing rod back," she said.

"Oh, I've got it," replied Ruby. She held a Y-shaped hazel branch over her head, only the stick and her hand visible above the line of tea chests. "Sorry."

Vivien retraced her path through the narrow way between tea chests, narrowly avoiding tearing her very new Laura Ashley white lawn blouse on a bit of jagged tin that had broken off the corner of one of the plywood boxes. Most of the younger right-handed booksellers would have preferred to pack books in cardboard boxes, but the older ones still insisted they must use the considerable stock of tea chests that perennially shifted back and forth between the various St. Jacques locations like flotsam borne upon the tide.

"Thanks," said Vivien. She took the hazel stick, and holding it in approved dowsing fashion, returned to her own table. When she passed the rod over the book it bucked in her hand, drawn like a very powerful magnet to iron towards the slight lump in the binding. She had to use considerable strength to hold it back and then even hold her breath for a moment to add sorcerous strength in order to turn the stick aside before she let it go, and it became just a forked hazel branch again.

"Something hidden, and powerful," said Vivien. "Can you stand by me for this one, Ruby?"

"Of course!" replied Ruby eagerly. She slid back her chair, got up, and sidled over next to Vivien. "That whole chest has been nothing but editions of *Through the Looking Glass, and What Alice Found There*. Unexciting editions at that. No firsts, not even a later printing, nothing earlier than 1896."

"Pity," said Vivien. "I'll get the gear."

She returned to the essential cupboard to fetch a silver-washed straight razor, two mismatched sets of very long similarly silver-plated tongs that once might have been salad servers, and a vintage silver hatpin. Coming back in a hurry, she did tear her shirt on a tea chest corner, but paid it no attention, all her thoughts now on this mysterious object in the binding of the book. "The Alice fixation suggests Sir Richard had an interest in the esoteric. Was he a known practitioner or anything of that sort?"

"A fringe-dweller, most likely," replied Ruby. She was peering at the book of maps through a jeweler's loupe, her face close to the binding. "A good customer of the bookshop, but as far as we know not actively involved in the Old World. He was vetted in 1965 and again in 1978, cleared of associations. I don't think he was clever enough to keep anything hidden. He must have had his suspicions, but he didn't act upon them."

"No connection with Sulis Minerva?" asked Vivien as she made her way back to the worktable. Ruby lifted a tea chest off a stack that was partially blocking the window, allowing more of the weak winter sunlight to come through. There was a six-bulb chandelier above, so plenty of illumination, but they both knew the sun was a better source to see things that were hidden, or if it came to that, as a protection against things inimical that prospered in the dark.

"He has never been observed entering the Baths," she said. "If he was a real follower he couldn't keep away. Though there are some other adits of her power, I very much doubt he frequented them. He was what he seemed, a nauseatingly rich, amiable old buffer who never worked his whole life and just collected books."

"So, this is an anomaly," said Vivien. "Let's see what we've got."

Taking up the straight razor, she carefully cut a slit in the leather binding at the top of the back case, then used the tongs to lift the leather up a little.

"Looks like a folded page has been slid in here," she said. "Old paper. Older than the book."

Her right thumb was twitching now, uncontrollably. Outside, the wintry clouds parted a little and a beam of actual, honest-to-goodness sunshine came through the window, making the previously unseen motes of dust twinkle. But it only lasted for a few seconds before the clouds closed up again and the sunshine disappeared as if turned off with a switch.

"It's powerful," added Vivien. "Saturated with sorcery. An entity's, I think, not a human practitioner's. We'd better get one of the sinisters up here."

"I'll call down," replied Ruby. "I'm not sure who's available right now. Ibrahim and Polly have gone to escort the next shipment from Sir Richard's library, and there's a full shift watching the Baths."

She hurried over to the intercom mounted on the wall next to the door and pressed the orange button. It squawked for a second, then a testy woman's voice answered.

"Yes? What?"

"Ruby here, Delphine. In the sorting room. Can you send up a leftie or two? Vivien's found something sorcerous in one of the books."

"I'll see who's available."

There was a hatch set in the wall between the tobacconist and the bookstore. Vivien and Ruby heard footsteps, the hatch being slid open, Delphine calling out and some indistinct reply.

"One of you layabouts is needed upstairs, in the sorting room. Yes, you'll do. What? I don't care if you're not rostered on. Up you go."

The footsteps came closer, then Delphine's cigarette-rasped voice issued a curt, "Done."

The intercom clicked off.

"Any preliminary ideas?" asked Ruby, returning to the work-table. They both stared at the book, which was facedown, the slit in the back binding towards them.

"Not yet," replied Vivien. She took up the long tweezers in her right hand and closed and opened them a few times, the points clicking. Ruby held her own right hand six inches above the book, palm down, and inhaled deeply.

Ruby exhaled.

"You're right about the sorcery. But I'm not sure you're correct about it being an entity's magic. I'd say it was a joint effort, some mortal practitioner drawing the map and providing the focus, an Old One supplying the power. Not an entity I know. Something old and cold and hard."

Vivien nodded. She tilted her head, listening to the sound of someone coming up the stairs, taking them very swiftly, leaping up three or four or even five at a time, in heavy shoes or boots.

"Our left-handed helper comes," said Ruby drily.

"Hmmm," said Vivien. There was something familiar about the style of the stair ascent, a wholly unnecessary rapidity and joie de vivre in simply trying to leap as many steps as possible in one go. So while she was not expecting this particular left-handed bookseller, she was not surprised when the door was flung open to reveal an exceptionally stylish young woman, albeit one exceptionally stylish for circa 1816.

This stunning apparition wore a fox fur tippet over a high-waisted morning dress of pale-blue Italian taffeta with golden ribbons at the neck and wrists, a single white kid leather glove on the left hand, and a straw hat also beribboned in gold, atop a lace coif. The ensemble's historical accuracy was somewhat spoiled by the addition of a surprisingly large carpetbag and the toes of black Dr. Marten boots peeking out from under the almost floor-length dress.

Thanks to their somewhat "shape-shiftery nature," the booksellers could and did change gender from time to time, but at present, this Regency arrival was male, and was in fact Vivien's younger brother, Merlin. He simply liked clothes of all kinds, and let his fancy take him where it would. Vivien was physically very similar, and obviously his sister, but she lacked whatever it was that made (nearly) all eyes look first to Merlin, and Vivien preferred it that way.

"When in Bath," said Merlin, interpreting Ruby's enquiring

look at his clothes. "I made four pounds fifty posing for photographs with American tourists on the way up from Manvers Street. If I'd brought a Polaroid camera I could retire after a few days, I'd say they'd be good for two pounds a pic, at least. Surprised there's still so many around at this time of year. Tourists, I mean."

"They come for Christmas and hope for snow," said Ruby. "They might get it this year."

"Are you Jane or one of her characters?" asked Vivien. "And where did you get that dress?"

"I'm Elizabeth Bennet, of course," said Merlin. "The dress is from the BBC, the miniseries *Pride and Prejudice* from a few years back. You know, with Elizabeth Garvie. I've made friends with one of the wardrobe department assistants. This was Garvie's dress halfway through episode two."

"That carpetbag is much too big and ahistorical," said Ruby. "Should be a reticule."

"I know," replied Merlin with a shrug. "But those tourists don't, or they don't care. Besides, a reticule would be far too small."

He set the bag down on the end of the table and opened it. Shrugging off the tippet, he folded it carefully and tucked it in one end of the bag that contained, among other things, his favored .357 Magnum Smython and two speedloaders; a turned lignum vitae truncheon from William IV's time, marked with the royal arms; a parrying dagger reputed to have belonged to Sir Philip Sidney, the blade later plated with silver; his current reading material, a Penguin paperback of *Cold Comfort Farm* by Stella Gibbons, the 1977 edition with the generally scorned cover; a day-old Chelsea bun wrapped in waxed paper; two wire coat hangers; and a variety of other small useful odds and ends.

"Why are you in Bath?" asked Vivien. "I thought you had the weekend off."

"I do, or did," replied Merlin. He hesitated, then added, "Susan's visiting her mother. I thought I might pop over and see her later."

Merlin and Vivien had met Susan Arkshaw earlier in the year, and they'd been involved with her in deep matters that led to the binding of a powerful and malevolent entity, the unmasking of a traitor among the booksellers, and the discovery that Susan's father was the Old Man of Coniston. An Ancient Sovereign, as the most powerful entities of the Old World were known. All three had become friends, and Merlin and Susan more, though their relationship had recently run into stormy waters. Susan's mother lived near Bath, though Susan herself was now a student at the Slade School of Art and so spent most of her time in London.

"I thought you two were taking a break?" asked Vivien. "Or something."

Prior to Susan, Merlin's relationships had tended towards the spectacular and short-lived, usually ending without recrimination on either side. Merlin gravitated to those as outwardly attractive as himself, similar bright comets whose orbits crossed in a flurry of sparks and spun onwards to new collisions without looking back.

"Susan thought we should go slow for a while," said Merlin stiffly. He was evidently unused to still being with the same person after several months, and with the concept of even temporary rejection. "She wants to concentrate on her studies, so we're only going out once a week. I haven't seen her since Wednesday!"

"As it's only Saturday you seem to have not grasped the once-a-week thing," said Vivien. "Does she know you're going to 'drop in' on her at her mum's?"

"I didn't expect I'd miss her so much," said Merlin, not answering the question. "It is quite aggravating. And I am waiting until the afternoon."

"This is all very interesting," said Ruby brightly. "But however dull I'm finding my current tea chest of books, I do have to get through it, and together we have many more after it, so perhaps we could investigate this sorcery-laden paper and move on?"

"Suits me," said Merlin. "What are you expecting?"

"We don't know," said Vivien.

Merlin sniffed, hiked his dress up above his knees, pulled hidden elastic loops to keep it there, and took the lignum vitae truncheon out of his bag, throwing it up to spin twice before he caught it in his left hand and made some swishing motions in the air, missing a tea chest by a masterly sixteenth of an inch.

"Ready?" asked Vivien.

"Ready, aye, ready," confirmed Ruby. She stepped back a pace, raised her right hand, took in a deep breath, and held it. This was a necessary precursor to the use of right-handed magic, and a limitation, because the magic would only endure as long as the bookseller could hold their breath. Nearly all of the right-handed were swimmers and divers, and those that weren't practiced holding their breath in the depths of their generally claw-footed baths.

Merlin looked questioningly at Vivien.

"Ruby's father was an admiral," said his sister before taking her own breath. She held it and, lifting the tongs, pulled the paper out of the binding. She placed it on the table and took up the other pair of tongs. Using both pairs with dexterous skill, she unfolded the heavy, ivory parchment to reveal a map, or a portion of one. Unfolded, it was obvious it had been torn away from a larger whole.

"A garden," said Merlin. "Eighteenth century? Or a little later?"

Vivien nodded, using the tongs to place four six-ounce bronze weights purloined from a post office decades ago on each corner of the map fragment.

The map, which was a quarter or perhaps an eighth of the original, was hand-drawn in meticulous detail. It showed a portion of a wonderful garden, designed by the likes of Humphry Repton. There was a small fraction of a moated great house to the north, most of it lost beyond the tear. A bridge over the moat connected the house to a broad avenue that led to a freestanding tower that was labeled in perfect copperplate "Clock Tower." From the tower the avenue continued due south to a large ornamental lake, which had a kidney-shaped island,

and on it a Grecian structure labeled "Temple of Diana." The bridge to the island was also drawn in detail and labeled "Pont Saint-Bénézet" and looked to be a one-tenth scale replica of the famous bridge at Avignon. The eastern side of the avenue was wooded, and labeled as "Wolf Wood." To the west of the avenue there was a walled kitchen garden in one corner, with a row of beehives by the wall; and a much larger garden surrounded by high hedges, accessed by a masonry gate labeled "Egyptian Gate," which from the drawing looked to be a hodgepodge of orientalist ideas. Rows of flower beds ran east to west, all drawn as being in full bloom, possibly with roses though it would need close inspection with Ruby's loupe to see what they were. South of the flower beds, but still within the hedge walls, there was a maze that appeared to be made of brick or stone walls overgrown with climbing roses or something similar, but most likely roses, as it was labeled "Rose Court Maze."

"There's rather an abundance of statues along that avenue," said Merlin. "Odd ones."

Vivien exhaled, letting her preparatory magic slowly leave her. Her right thumb had settled down to a low vibration, no longer full-on twitching. The map was sorcerous, but it was quiescent. There was no immediate threat. She leaned closer.

"Statues of heraldic beasts," she said. "Including the unusual ones. A hippalectryon, pismire, musimon. I don't know what that tusked thing with the camel body and the serpent's tail is—"

"An ypotryll," said Ruby, letting her own breath out with a sigh of relief. "A veritable parade of heraldic statues. I've never heard of such an extensive collection. Is it a real place do you think, or a plan that was never executed?"

"I don't recognize it," replied Vivien, frowning. "And I haven't read about such a garden."

As she spoke, the clouds outside split again, and the sun caught the chance, streaming in through the window. Golden dust motes danced once more, and everything on the map on the worktable became sharper and more defined, as if it had only just been completed, the ink still shiny and drying. Summer spread across the room, borne on a warm breeze, carrying the scent of new-mown grass and gillyflowers, and the mellow languid evensong of several blackbirds. The two right-handed booksellers stepped back, sucking in urgent breaths.

"A bee!" exclaimed Merlin.

"No!" shrieked Vivien, reaching for his arm, but it was too late. Merlin caught the bee in his right hand, fingers cupped around it to keep it safe before putting it outside. But as the bee landed on his palm, the map shone even more brightly. Merlin and the captured bee disappeared and the map began to crumble at the edges, vanishing as if it were millennia older and unable to withstand the open air without turning to dust.

Vivien, in the middle of recapturing her breath, snatched up the silver hatpin and drove it through the top right corner of the map into the table. Ruby laid her gloved right hand on the bottom left corner and pushed down hard with her fingers. In those two places, the dissipation stopped, the map was held in place and its internal light dimmed. But in the other two corners it continued to ebb away into nothing, until Vivien weighted each one down with a pair of silver tongs. Finally, she laid the straight razor down across the corner in front of Ruby's fingers. The other bookseller slowly lifted her hand and exhaled.

The clouds closed up and the sunshine disappeared. But the map still emitted its own golden summer light, even if it was now subdued.

"It's still active," snapped Ruby. "We need to properly pin it down *now*!"

"Yep," said Vivien. She dashed to the essential cupboard and opened a drawer, taking out a black varnished seventeenth-century papier-mâché box that was full of silver-plated iron tacks as old as the box. Rushing back she spilled a pile of tacks on the table and she and Ruby fixed the map in place, using their right thumbs to drive tacks in every inch along the edges.

The map was smaller now. The great house was completely gone, as was nearly all the moat, and the lake in the south reduced to halfway across the island, the Temple of Diana bisected. The eastern wood's label now read "Wolf Wo" and in the west, the kitchen garden was a third smaller and the larger garden was reduced to a narrow swath next to the western edge of the maze.

"I can see Merlin," said Ruby. "He's in the center of the maze."

Vivien bent close and peered at the map. She could just make out a beautifully drawn, very tiny Merlin, not even an eighth of an inch high.

"He's moving," she said with surprise. "Very, very slowly. I don't know much about these translocation maps. Is it normal to see movement?"

"When it's active, it's effectively a window," replied Ruby. Merlin was moving, but it was so slight it was more like the tiny figure was shivering. "One way, at least. He is *slow*. There must be quite some time dislocation between here and there."

"I'd better go in after him," said Vivien. She started to reach out with her bare left hand, but Ruby stopped her.

"No. You'll be trapped there as well."

"What? We can walk out—"

"No. It's not anywhere," said Ruby. "I felt it when I was holding the map here, and you can see it from Merlin's movement, or lack of it. This is a real place, but it's been taken out of our world. Time is running *much* slower there. You'd need another translocation map to get out."

"So I'll take one with me," said Vivien impatiently.

"We haven't got any maps of that kind here," replied Ruby. "We'll need to get one sent up from London, or perhaps Thorn House. We don't have to be hasty. I'd say an hour here is only a few minutes there. We have to call this in, see if anyone has any good ideas. I'm not a map expert either—"

She was interrupted by the sudden clanging of a fire alarm bell on the stairs outside, followed a second later by a sickeningly loud crash that made the whole house shake.

The fire alarm bell was not for fires.

"General Quarters!" shouted Ruby. "All hands to repel boarders."

She started towards the door, stopped, and looked back at Vivien, who was still standing by the map.

"All hands," she said gently. "The map can't go anywhere.

Only minutes will pass for Merlin. Come on!"

Vivien followed her to the door. A cacophony of shouting and what sounded like sledgehammers smashing stone echoed up the stairs, with the occasional ringing ricochet of metal rebounding instead of breaking whatever it struck.

Behind them, on the map, in slow time, a tiny Merlin moved a fraction of a step in the heart of the maze.

CHAPTER TWO

Bath, Saturday, 10th December 1983

Lion. In heraldry any lion not rampant is called a lion leopard.

BY THE TIME VIVIEN AND RUBY REACHED THE GROUND FLOOR AND the bookshop proper, the smashing, ringing sounds had ceased. They leaped in from the foot of the stairs to see a dozen broken pieces of a stone lion on the floor, just inside the threshold. With no other evidence of intrusion, Vivien and Ruby presumed this now dismembered statue was responsible. Somehow.

One of the pieces was a maned head, which had been separated from its body by a two-handed swing from Cameron, a left-handed bookseller. He was now trying to straighten the wrought-iron bar that had done the business, so it could be slotted back into its place as one of the levers used to turn the massive screw of the antique bookbinder's press that took pride of place in the front left-hand corner of the shop, a dim mass of dark iron behind the smoke-grimed windows, which had intentionally not been cleaned since 1911.

Fortunately, the statue-smashing had taken place largely in the doorway, and most of the shop's valuable stock was in three rows of too close-together shelves farther back, with the cashier's desk in between. The desk had been gouged by a piece of flying stone, and the Persian carpet on the floor—a fine vintage Kerman—was regrettably torn in several places. But otherwise both books and shop were intact.

Not so the front door. As was usual for the booksellers' secure buildings, this had been heavy oak discreetly reinforced with an inner steel plate and set in a two-inch steel frame. Now it hung awry from only one of the six reinforced hinges that had once supported it, the consequence of a two-ton stone lion smashing into it at some speed. A cold breeze was blowing through the open doorway, carrying biting particles of sleet with it, entirely banishing the warmth of the ancient radiators, which had taken the first two weeks of winter to build up to something only several degrees under a comfortable temperature.

"No more living stone lions in sight," announced Stephanie, another left-handed bookseller, as she stepped back through the doorway. She held the other turning bar from the press, also bent. Given that it was hardened iron designed to have great pressure exerted on it to turn the screw of the press, it must have taken enormous force to bend. More than would usually be needed to shatter stone. "But there is a curious bobby ambling this way."

"I think this is Purbeck marble," said Ruby, inspecting a broken-off paw. "See the distinctive mottled shell pattern, and it's a greyish sort of white. Curious. An eighteenth-century statue, I'd say, not done very well. It's been underwater from the look of this algae, and the stone has deteriorated. Anyone recognize the statue?"

"Looks like one of those lions that used to be up in Hedgemead Park," said Cameron. He was fifty-ish, handsome, and rather resembled Sidney Poitier. His parents had come from the Bahamas, but Cameron grew up a Scot and spoke with a Clydeside accent and dressed like an absent-minded professor in flannel pants, once-good shirts that were too big for him and always had the tail out, and one or more hand-knitted cardigans with multiple pockets. Currently he wore three cardigans, two brown and one green. He was permanently assigned to the Small Bookshop and dealt with most of the customers, who presumed it was his own shop. "Off Lansdown Road. But they disappeared a while back. Stolen, which was no mean feat, since they had to weigh several tons apiece."

He gave up trying to straighten the bar and slid it as far as it would go into its position through the axle of the press's screw.

"Gave us a wee bit of a surprise," he said. "The wards only flared a few seconds before it smashed the door down. And they didn't stop it."

"The wards are cast to repel living things of evil intent," said Ruby. "And dead things of evil intent. But not animated stone of limited intelligence, or at least not this kind, whatever it is. An oversight to be addressed, now I think of it. I'll bring it up at the next staff meeting."

"That's what this was? A statue given movement, if not

life?" asked Stephanie. "It did seem kind of stupid. It didn't fight back at all, just charged through the door and kept trying to get to the stairs."

Stephanie was younger than Vivien, a recent graduate from Wooten Hall. A quicksilver, elfin young woman who ran everywhere at high speed, she always wore Adidas tracksuits and carried a backpack, doubtless even more full of weapons than Cameron's over-stretched cardigan pockets and whatever he carried under the spreading tail of his oversized shirt. Stephanie's tracksuit of choice today was teal with orange and black stripes. It seemed to serve the same purpose as wartime dazzle camouflage, at least out in the street.

For the purposes of actually selling books, Stephanie assumed the role of Cameron's granddaughter who was "helping out," as many of her presumed older siblings and cousins had done before. Cameron was often asked about particular left-handed booksellers who had once had temporary duty in the shop, and he was believed to have an enormous and widespread family comprising many races and combinations thereof. This was actually true, but not in the way ordinary people thought.

"I think so," said Vivien. "We'll have to investigate. How close is that bobby?"

Stephanie stepped out past the hanging door, and quickly back in and to the left, kneeling down to place the iron bar she held on the floor against the wall.

"Here," she said wryly, standing quickly again as a large, puffing constable of the Avon and Somerset Police came up the steps and stood in the doorway, rocking on his heels in unconscious mimicry of the stereotype. His overcoat was sodden from the sleet, and his face was somewhat shadowed by his custodian helmet, which was slightly too big and had rocked forward as he rocked back.

"Good morning," he said, his overall dampness, the tilted helmet, and his considerably younger than expected voice all rather lessening the impression of authority he hoped to achieve. "My name is P.C. Wren and I have reason to believe that a crime has been committed—"

The booksellers bit their lips and there was the suggestion of a chuckle that made the constable falter.

"P.C. Wren?" asked Ruby. "Really?"

The constable sighed, and the dream of promotion came to him again. As "Sergeant Wren" he would not suffer from literary types being amused that he had effectively introduced himself as the author of *Beau Geste*. Of course, this was a bookshop, he should have known to have said "Constable Wren" and not introduced the deadly "P.C."

"As I was saying," he said stolidly, "I have reason to believe a crime has been committed. . . ."

He paused and looked over the broken pieces of statue and the shattered door.

"Though mebbe not the crime I thought it was," he said. He lifted his chin strap forward with his chin into his mouth and nervously sucked on it for a second before he realized what he was doing and stopped. "At eleven oh six I observed a pantomime lion proceeding along the street and suspecting an unlicensed street performer I—"

"I'll stop you there, constable," said Cameron. He took out a slim black wallet from a cardigan pocket and flicked it open to show the warrant card inside. "Have a read of that, and then you'll need to call Inspector Torrant at your Broadbury Road station, not via radio."

Constable Wren looked at Cameron dubiously, but he examined the card with care. His expression slowly became even more wooden, and he did not look at the pieces of statue or the broken door again, instead staring at a point in space roughly a foot in front of his nose.

"I see. Inspector Torrant," he said. "I've heard of her."

He gestured at the brick-sized Burndept personal radio that hung down the front of his overcoat on a nylon strap. "Can't use my radio anyway. It's on the fritz. Got too wet, I reckon."

Cameron gestured to the phone on the desk, a black Bakelite unit of World War Two vintage, next to the cash register that was even older, purely mechanical, and made a terrifyingly loud chime whenever the drawer was opened, invariably making customers jump.

The police officer strode majestically over to the phone and called the station, his attempted air of regal unconcern lost when he got the wrong number and had to call again, one large finger fumbling on the rotary dial.

"Mr. Cutts the Butcher," whispered Ruby, but she spoke so low only the booksellers with their uncanny hearing caught it, and they did not smile as the constable could see them. One joke at his expense seemed plenty.

"Sarge? It's Wren. I'm at the Small Bookshop, corner of George and Bartlett Streets. Yes, that's what I said. I see . . . well, there was a pantomime lion . . . no, forget that . . . anyway, there's a gentleman here, got a warrant card from the funnies, says I'm to call Inspector Torrant—"

He stopped talking and listened, noticeably coming even straighter to attention, with no more rocking on the heels. When the sergeant at the other end stopped speaking, Wren carefully laid the handset down as if he feared to wake a cross baby.

"I'm to stand outside," he mumbled. "And look the other way. Sergeant Lucas will call Inspector Torrant."

"Very good," said Cameron. "Thank you, constable."

The policeman exited, looking to neither left nor right. Stephanie wrestled the massive door—which must have weighed three hundred pounds or more—up and leaned it back in place.

"Lucky we didn't have any customers in," she said. "I don't suppose any of you knows what's going on?"

"We have an inkling," said Vivien. "It concerns a translocation map we just discovered in a book upstairs. It connects with the garden of a great house that has been taken out of time. A garden with a very large number of statues. Including a couple of lions that look rather like this one."

"We can't say for sure they're connected yet," said Ruby. "Though I agree it is likely, and in fact I suspect this lion here was tasked with retrieving the map. When we woke the map, so the lion woke. I wonder where it was? When did the lions disappear from Hedgemead Park, Cameron?"

The left-handed bookseller scratched his nose with his gloved left hand. A white cotton glove, suitable for an antiquarian bookseller.

"Seventy-seven," he said thoughtfully. "Around this time, come to think of it. A little closer to Christmas."

"You said there were two," remarked Stephanie. "So there's presumably another one just like this out there somewhere. Uh, we're supposed to call this in to London, aren't we?"

"Yes. Una and Great-Aunt Evangeline need to be advised," said Vivien. "But most important we need to get the closest translocation map here so we can go and get Merlin."

"Where is Merlin?" asked Stephanie and Cameron together.

"Translocated," replied Vivien. "He touched a bee that came out of the map we've got upstairs. So, he's in that garden. Which is not in our world."

"And you can't get out of there without a map that will bring you back," said Cameron knowingly. "Ach, that's annoying. We used to have two such maps here, one to a castle in Devon and the other a rather beautiful stretch of the Wear. Not separated from the world, places in our time and space. But the clever-clogs wanted those maps in London for a study of some sort. They were sent away last year."

"Aunts Zoë and Helen?" asked Vivien.

Cameron nodded. The two even-handed booksellers mentioned were experts in paper conservation and other dark library arts, both of the mundane kind and the more esoteric.

"I'll call them after Evangeline."

"Use Delphine's phone," said Cameron. "I'll call London."

"I'm already on the line to London Exchange, 'cause unlike some I know the proper procedures and don't hang about," said Delphine's voice from the partly open hatch through to the tobacconist's shop. "Evangeline isn't at either bookshop. She's at a booksellers' conference in Brighton."

"We're having a conference in Brighton?" asked Ruby. "No one told me—"

"No, regular bookselling," said Delphine. "Hosted by 'The Bookseller.' 'Ho, Ho, Ho, How to Boost Your Christmas Sales' or something like that. A junket, with occasional chunks of usefulness."

Vivien made a face.

"Doesn't sound very appealing," she said. "I'll come through."

She headed back through the bookshelves to the connecting door at the rear of the shop, Cameron's penetrating voice following her.

"We should prepare for further incursions," said Cameron. "You keep an eye on the street, Stephanie. Ibrahim and Polly should be back within the hour. Delphine, since you're so hot on procedure I guess you've already alerted the sentry post at the Baths?"

"'Course I have," said Delphine, sniffing. "Advika wants to know if she should send anyone back, and to let you know there was a minor disturbance about five minutes ago, three of Sulis Minerva's acolytes popped out of the Baths and stared about the place before going back in. So the Sovereign sensed something was up."

"Interesting," said Vivien. "So Sulis Minerva knew when

the map became active, and the stone lion, I guess, even though we're out of her demesne."

Delphine looked at her with amusement.

"You haven't been here long, have you? Sulis Minerva may not have power beyond the spring, but she knows what's going on in the whole valley."

Vivien acknowledged this with a nod, and joined Delphine behind the counter of the tobacconist's, doing her best not to breathe in the unique atmosphere of rich tobacco and stale cigar smoke mixed with Delphine's perfume, which she apparently made herself. It smelled rather like wet dog mixed with talc, possibly another tactic to discourage customers. There were four phones there, kept out of sight behind the counter. Delphine was balancing a handset on each shoulder and a third handset was laid down with someone's voice burbling out of it.

Delphine pointed at the third phone, the one emitting the burbling, anxious voice. "That's the New Bookshop. Jake is the duty officer."

Vivien frowned. All the right-handed booksellers had a tendency to absent-mindedness on matters apart from the pursuit of their current intellectual interests. Uncle Jake had rather a larger dose of this than usual, making him not someone you wanted to talk to when urgent things needed to be done. She picked up the phone.

"Uncle Jake? Vivien here. We need a translocation map sent to the Small Bookshop as swiftly as possible. One that points to somewhere close by, if possible . . . what . . . well Zoë and Helen have two maps that came from here. . . ."

Next to Vivien, Delphine was speaking to the Baths sentry post on one phone and to Una at the Old Bookshop on the other. Una was the new commander of the left-handed booksellers, following the treachery and death of Merrihew, who had led the sinister moiety of the St. Jacques for more than a hundred years.

"Una's sending Sabah and Diarmuid up on the 2:21," shouted Delphine, so everyone in both shops could hear her, and if the building's walls weren't so thick probably everyone on the street as well. "And Sairey's coming from Thorn House on her Triumph."

"How can you not have the key to that cabinet?" asked Vivien in frustration. "You're the duty officer in the New Bookshop, Jake! Who else is there? Can you get them, please?"

She cradled the handset to her chest and called out.

"Half the bloody staff of both bookshops have gone to that conference in Brighton, Zoë and Helen are in New York for a meeting at the Met on silverfish prevention, and Jake can't remember where he left the duty officer's keys."

The phone warbled with a different, more determined voice. She lifted the handset to her ear with an energetic shrug from her shoulder.

"Eric! Thank heavens. We need a translocation map fairly urgently . . . what? Are you sure? Okay, I'll try Thorn House."

She tapped the cradle twice, without returning the handset.

"Exchange? Put me through to Thorn House. Alpha."

Waiting for the call, she turned to shout through the hatch.

"All the translocation maps have gone to the secure storage under the Old Bookshop for whatever Zoë and Helen are working on, but with them absent no one knows exactly where the maps are. Kersten's going down to check the log. And apparently Evangeline is giving a keynote at that blasted conference and can't be interrupted. Oh, wait, Thorn House is . . ."

She listened to whoever it was with an expression of growing frustration.

"Okay, thanks."

Vivien hung up.

"Great-Aunt Beatrice and Aunt Rachel have gone rock climbing somewhere and they're the only ones who would know off the top off their heads whether there are any translocation maps at Thorn House. Guido is looking through the library register but that will take hours. I'm going back up to see where Merlin is and what's happening."

"I'll come, too," said Ruby through the hatch. "Remember you are *not* to go through without a map yourself."

Vivien didn't answer, because that was exactly what she was thinking of doing. But she was also thinking of alternative sources for a translocation map. They weren't a particular area of study for her, but she remembered the basic lessons on their making, use, and care.

She met Ruby on the stairs. As they ascended quickly, but with nothing like the pace of Merlin, a thought came into Vivien's head. The beginning of an idea, at least.

"Ruby," she said. "I recall the two key things for making a translocation map are the prepared paper and an intensely strong connection with a place. So they have typically been made by entities for their own demesnes, sometimes with mortal help, and by our even-handed types who have long been in one place. Is that right?"

"Yes, that's correct," replied Ruby. "And the third thing is—"

"Do you have any of the paper here?" interrupted Vivien as they reached the landing at the top of the house.

"No," said Ruby, slowing to allow Vivien to go ahead of her into the workroom.

"Damn!" swore Vivien. "There goes that idea."

"But the millboard we use to rebind the most troublesome books is basically the same thing," continued Ruby. "Sorcerously, that is. It's made to contain and hold magic. We use it for binding and containment spells, but it would work just the same for translocation."

"You mean the boards from Rubyven Mill?" said Vivien. "They're jet black. The drawing would have to be reversed out; it would be even more difficult."

"Nah, silver ink," said Ruby. "We've got plenty of that. But you still need that strong connection to place, like an entity has for their demesne. I doubt anyone here has that, or the drawing talent, and not to mention there's the issue of—"

Ruby had to shout after Vivien, because the other bookseller had spun about on the spot and was leaping down the stairs with the similar multistep abandon as her brother had come up them, calling out she had to use the telephone again, most urgently!

CHAPTER THREE

Labyrinth. *A mass of buildings or garden-walks, so complicated as to puzzle strangers to extricate themselves. Said to be so called from Lab'yris, an Egyptian monarch of the twelfth dynasty.*

MERLIN OPENED HIS HAND. THE BEE BUZZED IMPORTANTLY AWAY, spiraling up into the summer sky. Which should not be there without the roof of the Small Bookshop between him and the blue expanse, and it certainly shouldn't be summer anyway.

"That was stupid of me," muttered the left-handed bookseller to himself. Hefting the William IV truncheon, he slowly turned on the spot, taking stock of his surroundings.

He was in the center courtyard of the maze he'd seen on the map, but it was not quite as he had seen it in the drawing. The eight-foot-high walls were not brick, but constructed from far larger blocks of some kind of greyish mottled marble and the climbing roses that crowded the walls and lay in thick bunches all over the top of the walls were not plants at all, but also sculpted from that same stone. Very fine carving, which was inherently suspicious, for if it was carried through on all the walls of the maze it had to represent the work of decades by a master sculptor and numerous apprentices.

Merlin had appeared next to a sundial of sculpted stone set on a plinth, both sculpted from the same kind of marble as the walls. The gnomon was bronze, untarnished with verdigris, and its long shadow sloped across to the incised Roman numeral twelve.

There was grass underfoot, well-kept turf. It had been mown or scythed recently. From a quick survey it appeared largely untrodden, or at least no one had passed by recently. Though his eye instantly noted something out of place near the single exit from the courtyard, a door-sized gap in the wall. There was a small, square object on the grass. A wallet or purse.

He didn't go and check it out immediately. Instead he stayed where he was, slowly looking up at the sky, and at the walls, and the sculpted roses. The rose canes that climbed the walls featured an unusually large number of thorns, and the thorns were bigger than he'd seen on any natural roses. They had much the same effect as festooning the walls with barbed wire, making them difficult to climb. Though Merlin could ascend without too much injury, he judged. But only if the roses were simply stone sculptures. He had the suspicion they were something more. To test it, he walked over to the wall, not too close, and, extending his arm, rapped the nearest rose with the end of his truncheon. He was unsurprised when the stone flower snapped at the club, revealing rows of hidden teeth that were themselves tiny thorns, and the canes lashed out and tried to wrest the truncheon from his grasp. He dragged it back, frowning at the scratch marks that now scored the previously perfectly varnish.

"How very unwelcoming," he said to the flower, and carefully walked over to the exit from the square, being sure not to get too close to any of the walls and their thorny accoutrements.

The small object on the lawn was a man's wallet. A tatty thing of vinyl doing a bad job of pretending to be leather. Merlin examined it closely, down on one knee, before picking it up. It took a little effort to open it. The dark stain on the underside indicated it had been lying in a pool of blood, which had leeched away into the grass over time, but left the wallet stuck together. He had at first thought it was stuffed with money, specifically fivers, but when he managed to extract the blood-sodden mass it turned out to be papers cut from a color magazine to the size of five-pound notes.

From a copy or copies of "Look and Learn" in fact, one at least seven or eight years old, because Merlin remembered the particular "Trigan Empire" cartoon from the few panels he could make out through the stains. Apart from the fake money, which might impress someone very gullible in a dark room and no one else, there was a bloodstained photograph of a woman and a child; and a folded-up piece of paper that was so thick with dried blood it would need an expert to pry it apart. From the little he could make out, it looked like it was some sort of court document, perhaps a summons.

He put everything back inside and tucked the wallet away in one of the hidden pockets under his dress.

"Left or right?" Merlin muttered to himself. The exit led into a classical narrow maze corridor that about thirty yards farther along ended in a T-intersection. He had looked at the map for several seconds, and ought to be able to remember the layout of the maze, but the memory remained stubbornly foggy. A magical effect, he thought, which would make sense. Unwanted arrivals via the translocation map or some other means would be trapped in the maze until they could be dealt with at leisure.

Merlin considered who might be dealing with who and reached under his dress to draw the .25 Beretta he wore in a garter holster on his thigh when in Austen apparel. Holding the pistol in his right hand and the truncheon in his left, he advanced along the corridor.

At the T-intersection, he knelt and, using the end of the truncheon, scored an arrow in the turf to mark his choice, before continuing on. The left path had no intersections for a long time, but turned at right angles twice, once to the left and then to the right. Merlin walked slowly, pausing every now and then to mark the grass, look behind and to study the walls. As far as he could tell, the maze was static, there were no walls moving behind him or changing the way ahead.

He'd hoped to use the sun to help him work out his relative position amidst the turns, but it was almost directly above and didn't seem to be moving at all. The whole place had an unearthly feel about it, the sleepy heat of a perpetual summer, fixed in a brief moment of time. Though Merlin's arrival had upset the equilibrium of the place, he felt sure of that.

The lane turned again and ended in a small court with three exits, one ahead, one to the left, and one to the right. Merlin chose the left path, marked the turf again and continued on. The sun certainly wasn't moving, he was sure now. His watch—a World War Two vintage Vertex previously hidden under a ruffled sleeve—indicated half an hour had elapsed since his arrival, and it was still directly overhead. He stopped to take off his bonnet, because it was too hot, but kept the lace coif on against the sun. Fortunately he had not chosen to go full Regency in terms of his underwear, and the fur tippet was back in his bag in the workroom of the Small Bookshop.

Something moved atop the wall. Merlin's right hand flashed up, Beretta at the ready, but he didn't fire. A pale grey cat was slinking along, stepping carefully over the thorny canes. The roses didn't attack it, or move at all.

"A stone cat," said Merlin. "Hello, puss."

He lowered the Beretta, as it would do little more than knock small chips off the cat, which was the same grey stone as the walls, and though it moved fluidly in excellent imitation of a real cat, it wasn't quite perfect. There was something wrong with the size of its head and paws; they weren't quite right. He wished he had his .357 Magnum Smython, which would shatter the smug stone cat, though it might take a few shots. Till then, he had the truncheon in his good left hand.

The cat followed him along the top of the wall, occasionally leaping across to the other wall. But it did not try to get too close. A watcher, for certain. Merlin kept an eye on it. As far as he could tell, the cat was an animated sculpture—he could see the chisel marks and it had no whiskers—which was quite out of his experience of various cats or catlike entities from the

Old World he had previously encountered. An Ancient Sovereign was clearly responsible, one of great power to breathe life into stone, or perhaps if not exactly life, at least movement and some intelligence.

There were a few entities he could think of who could do something of that sort, and others who might inhabit a statue themselves. But of that list, all were long dormant, in the category the booksellers listed in the *Index* as "Quiescent One" and there would have been a general alarm, many mimeographed warning notes sent around the St. Jacques establishments, and general blather if one was waking up. They were not the sort that would rise at a single ceremony or ritual, it would take days if not weeks and there would be portents of their coming.

No, thought Merlin. The entity here was something that had successfully remained hidden from the booksellers. This was some sort of bolt-hole or refuge for it, a secret to be preserved at all costs. Which naturally would include the death of any nosy parkers like Merlin St. Jacques.

He continued on, being careful to mark his turns, both failures and successes.

Forty minutes later, after having to backtrack four times, which certainly would not have occurred to a left-handed bookseller in any ordinary maze, he found the final exit and went out.

The maze was set within the grounds of a garden bounded by tall, thick hedges, carefully trimmed. The hedges were very tall, sixteen feet high, and so thick as to be entirely opaque. They looked quite normal, as did the three long flower beds ahead, stretching east to west. The closest bed was planted with gillyflowers in riotous profusion—pinks, Sweet Williams, and carnations—but the other two were somewhat starker, with staked roses. White roses, but these were alive, not carved from stone. In the northeast corner, there was a gate in the Egyptian Revival style, two obelisk gateposts on either side of stone doors, the whole surmounted by a rather squat pyramid, all in the same pale grey marble as the maze.

Visible above and beyond the gate was a clock tower a hundred yards away. A square, fairly squat tower perhaps sixty feet high. It, too, was built from the grey stone, though the pinnacle at the top was copper-sheathed, with a gilded knob.

A clockface dominated the southern side of the tower, though the western side was solid stone and Merlin couldn't see the other two sides. Two-thirds of the way up, it was black metal, easily fifteen feet in diameter. The chapters of the clock were silver Roman numerals and there was a golden sun on the hour hand and a silver moon on the minute hand. Presently the clock indicated the time was one minute to noon. Which was interesting, as the sundial had indicated it was just past noon, though Merlin wasn't sure how accurate sundials were.

There was a smaller dial within the main one, and it did not indicate the hours but was crowded by all the letters of the alphabet starting at "A" in the twelve position and going all the way around, set very close together. It had a single hand, a sharp, narrow pointer like a bodkin-tipped arrow. It was pointing just past the "Z" back up at the top of the dial, not quite yet arrived at the "A."

Below the clockface was an open archway, with a figure

about to emerge. Merlin's eyes narrowed as he looked at it. The figure wasn't a clockwork automaton like Father Time, a saint, or an angel, as you would expect. It wasn't going to turn an hourglass or flap its wings, offer a benediction, or perform any other clockwork movement.

This was because it was a human corpse, lashed upright to the post intended for an automaton. A young man, thought Merlin. Not long dead, or at least a very well-preserved corpse. He had an orange mohawk, a large safety pin through what was left of his nose, and he wore jeans and a patterned T-shirt . . . or not patterned . . . after a longer study, Merlin realized it was probably a huge bloodstain.

There was a strange haze behind the clock tower, a shimmering mirage that brought the blue of the sky down and blurred whatever lay beyond. There was the suggestion of some large building, but that was all. Merlin supposed it was the effect of the torn map. Only what was on the part of the map in the workroom existed in the same place, reality, dimension, or whatever it was. One of the right-handed could tell him, no doubt, but it didn't matter right now.

He started off towards the Egyptian Gate, and the stone cat chose this moment to attack.

Merlin had expected it, the watcher become guard at the last moment, and he was ready. As it sprang from the wall he spun around and met the cat's leap with a roundhouse swing of the lignum vitae truncheon, the densest of woods meeting stone with a crack like thunder.

No ordinary human hand could have stood the shock of that

impact, but the truncheon did not waver in Merlin's kid-gloved left hand. He struck again as the cat rebounded from the grass and tried to claw at his knees, stone talons ripping his dress and at least one managing to get through to cut skin beneath.

But the cat had been cracked by that first blow, a crooked line propagating between shoulder and head. Merlin rained blows down upon it as he skipped backwards, the cat lunging after him, swiping and biting. It was completely silent, the sorcerous power that gave it movement not extending to lungs and throat. Merlin could even see where its mouth ended in blank stone as it snapped at him.

He could feel blood dripping down his leg, or possibly even flowing, which was a bad sign. The cat lunged again, and this time Merlin thrust the baton down its throat instead of swinging for the cracked neck.

It had been purely instinct to try to keep it farther back, but for whatever reason, it worked. The cat's lower jaw came off and fell away. As it looked down at the fallen piece, Merlin withdrew the truncheon and swung it down again right between the eyes. There was a double crack as both truncheon and stone head broke, the truncheon in half and the cat's head into three pieces.

It immediately stiffened and fell over, animated no more. It was just a broken cat statue.

Merlin looked around for any other immediate threats. Not seeing any, he sat down and hiked up his dress. His right leg was bloody from the knee down, and there was a deep gash to the side of the patella. He sighed and, reaching into his sleeve, took out a silver vial of Sipper saliva, the healing agent made from the spit of the Old World entities who were definitely not vampires. Grimacing, he poured the evil-smelling, foul-tasting contents of the vial into his mouth, whished it around, and then with a minor contortion spat it onto his wounded knee. The fluid that came out from his mouth burned with a cold heat, blue-green flames licking around the wound, and under them the blood began to congeal.

To complete the first aid process, Merlin took a wickedly sharp Fairbairn-Sykes fighting knife from the sheath built into his right boot and cut a length of cloth from the linen lining of his dress, and used it to bandage the wound. Finished, he stood up and tested his leg. The bandage made his knee a little stiff, but he thought it would be fine. As long as he avoided any acrobatics, head-high kicks, or the like, the wound would stay closed.

He looked around again, checking for threats. Nothing was moving. The air was hot and still. Behind him the maze stood stolid and threatening, the stone roses strangely ugly en masse. Merlin noted the Egyptian Gate was closed and wondered if the garden walls of brick would also have some hidden safeguard.

The pieces of the stone cat and his broken truncheon lay a few feet away. Merlin picked up the truncheon and eyed the splintered end. He thought for a moment, got out his previously discarded bonnet, and used it to pick up the biggest piece of the broken cat's head. Tying this inside the bonnet, he twisted the bonnet ribbons together to make a single cord that he slid through the splintered end of the truncheon and knotted on one end. It wasn't secure, but he reached under his dress again to another hidden pocket and took out a reel of pink legal tape and used this to lash the broken ends of the truncheon together, effectively making a short flail or mace-and-chain.

He swung it a few times, cut more legal tape to continue the sheer lashing from the splintered end of the truncheon all the way down to the other, unbroken end. Swinging it again, he felt sure it would be good to deliver at least a few dozen solid blows before it all came apart. He had nothing else that would work against animated statues.

"I tripped on some ice and tore the dress," he said to the air, while practicing his most rueful expression, one that had been known to make small puppies cry in sympathy. But he knew there was no way he was going to be able to explain the damage to the outfit to his friend at the BBC Costume Store, and thus a bright future of unbridled clothing access had suddenly dimmed.

"I was in Bath, everyone loved the costume, but they were too enthusiastic trying to touch the fabric and all, so in order to *save* the dress I had to run away from them and it was icy . . ." he started again, but his heart wasn't in it. This wasn't Bath, and he had to work out how to get the hell out of wherever it was as soon as possible. Apologies to BBC costume assistants would need to be worked out later.

CHAPTER FOUR

⊱ ⊰

Bath, Saturday, 10th December 1983

Stone Still. *Perfectly still; with no more motion than a stone.*

⊱ ⊰

SUSAN CLIMBED OUT OF HER MOTHER'S MUSTARD-YELLOW 1971 MINI on George Street, outside the building with "Old Post Office" on its facade, a point of contention for local historians, as it had never been a post office. The street was deserted save for a handful of people braving the occasional burst of sleet, the closest an older couple under one enormous umbrella that had clearly already gone inside out at least once and been imperfectly rehoisted. They were pretending not be fascinated by the Small Bookshop across the road at the corner of the narrow lane that was Bartlett Street. This was because three police officers were loitering outside it, who were also trying to look as if nothing was going on and failing miserably, as no one sensible would be standing around outside in the current weather without good reason.

"Are you sure you want to go there? There are *police*," said Susan's mother, Jassmine, leaning out of the driver's-side window. No easy feat as the winder was broken so it would only go halfway down and she was wearing a vast Russian fur hat roughly the size of a Grenadier Guard's bearskin cap. The overall effect was as if a furry, talking animal was in charge of the vehicle. An animal with a deep suspicion of authority figures.

"Vivien said they're expecting me," said Susan unenthusiastically. She yawned, a consequence of the troubled sleep that had been bothering her for days. "It'll be all right."

"If you say so," said Jassmine dubiously. "Don't be late for tea."

The furry creature withdrew through the window, and the Mini roared off, the hole in its muffler characteristically letting out a series of bangs that sounded a bit too like gunshots and made the three uniformed police officers jump, stare after the departing Mini, and then look back at Susan.

She started towards them, heading diagonally across the road, bracing herself for the potential suspicion the police quite often had for someone who was both young and dressed unconventionally. She hoped Vivien would emerge swiftly and circumvent it.

At Jassmine's insistence, since the weather was already bad and forecast to turn even more sleety and cold, she was wearing her mother's favorite bad weather outer layer, a knee-length flying coat possibly from the First World War. The untreated sheepskin had at some point been not so much dyed as painted a bright red that had faded unevenly into shades of pink, and the fleece inside, once bleached white, had turned a color resembling infected snot. A lime-green hand-knitted beanie with a CND badge pinned to it was a memento of the protest at Greenham Common earlier that year, which Susan had taken part in along with her mother. Under the coat she was wearing an oversized black wool jumper, rather frayed at the wrists, over her favorite blue boiler suit, courtesy of the booksellers, and her feet were warm and dry in hand-knitted socks and oxblood Doc Martens.

"You can't go in the bookshop, miss," said the senior-most police officer, a sergeant. Her sharp, bony face was wet from standing out in the sleet, and she had thin mascara trails bleeding from the corners of her eyes, which made her look rather like Alice Cooper and so much more threatening that her colleagues, who were already frightened of her, had been afraid to tell her it had happened.

"I'm expected," said Susan. She pointed. "They called me in."

"Oh," said the sergeant, stiffening. "You're one of them."

"Um, that depends on what you mean," replied Susan cautiously. It was hard to know what the police sergeant might already know, and she had been warned numerous times to never discuss the business of the booksellers, her own unique nature, or even the very existence of the Old World with anyone who didn't already know about it. This made some conversations very difficult.

"Box five hundred," muttered the police officer behind the sergeant, earning him a sharp runny mascara glance. "Sorry, Sarge."

"I can't say," said Susan truthfully, with some relief. If they thought she was just someone from the security services, that was easier and safer for all concerned.

"Susan! Thank you for coming so quickly!"

Vivien looked out the front door of the bookshop, which was being held open or actually held up by a young tracksuit-clad woman, whose gloved left hand and ridiculous strength gave away her identity.

The sergeant and the other two officers looked away, as if Susan had vanished. She noted they did not turn around to gaze at the bookshop, but very intentionally directed their eyes everywhere else. Across the street, up and down the street, up at the sky. Just never behind, never towards the bookshop.

"I'd have preferred not to get involved in whatever you have going on, to be frank," said Susan, skipping up the two steps. "But you said it involved *Merlin*—"

"I'll brief you inside," replied Vivien. She had noted the shoulders of the police sergeant twitching as Susan had said "Merlin" and all three of them had sidled a bit farther away. They didn't want to know whatever that was about. It certainly sounded like a code word.

The tracksuited woman wrestled the door back in place behind Susan as she stepped in.

"Hi, I'm Stephanie," she said. "You probably didn't notice me at the time, but I was up at Totteridge with the crew when you sorted out that bastard Holly."

"Oh, yeah I was a bit distracted," said Susan. "Hello."

"And I'm Cameron," said the older left-handed bookseller, a man of many cardigans, who was on his knees sweeping up small bits of broken stone that had evidently been forcibly separated from the larger bits of a huge stone lion that was stacked against the massive bookbinding press that dominated the front of the shop. "I missed that bit of excitement. I'm pretty much permanently stationed here in the *backwaters* of Bath."

Stephanie groaned, Vivien pretended not to have heard, and Susan gave a dutiful smile.

"Are those coppers still outside?" asked Cameron.

"Three of them now, including a sergeant," confirmed Stephanie. "Apparently they have been instructed to wait for Inspector Torrant and to keep the public out of harm's way, that is to say out of here."

"I hope they don't get themselves in harm's way," said Cameron. "Which they will if there's another stone lion about, or something else. At least Ibrahim and Polly are guarding the back now, and Sairey should be here soon."

Susan looked at Vivien and raised one questioning eyebrow, an effect mostly lost because her hat was pulled down too low, a consequence of too vigorously renewing her usual buzz cut, which was not ideal in winter and her head felt permanently cold.

"You know I don't want to get involved in bookseller stuff again. So what's this about Merlin being in danger and needing *my* help?"

"I'll explain," said Vivien hurriedly. "Come on upstairs."

"Is Merlin there?" asked Susan, following her to the staircase.

It was a drab, ordinary kind of shop stair, not at all interesting like the New Bookshop in London, and Susan was disappointed at the lack of artworks on the walls. Which were themselves disappointing, as they featured peeling once-cream wallpaper of a distinctly 1950s economy tone. "I thought he was in London."

"Kind of yes to your first question and no he isn't in London. He came down here this morning."

"'Kind of yes?' Why did he come to Bath? He told me he had the weekend off and was going to visit some friend who had a lot of clothes for him to try on."

"He got dragged into something," said Vivien, with the long practice of a sister who avoided involvement in her brother's love affairs. Or any other affairs, if she could help it. "You'll have to ask Merlin. The thing is, we need your help to get him back."

Susan stopped on the step below.

"Get him back from where?"

Vivien looked back down at her. Despite the events of the previous May, the general imperturbability she had displayed, and her very unusual heritage as a child of Ancient Sovereign and mortal, Susan had not been exposed very much to the Old World since, by her choice. She had started her studies at the Slade School of Art, and Merlin had taken care—because he had been expressly asked to do so—to keep to the ordinary world on their dates and not expose Susan to any more arcane or mythic experiences.

"Um, I'm not sure how to explain," began Vivien. "There are maps that are deeply connected to the places they depict, so much so that someone can travel via the map to that place . . . er . . . a place that might not be in the same general world or time as everything else, a kind of bubble of another reality—"

Susan nodded as if she understood perfectly.

"Oh. Well, I found one of these maps this morning bound into a book, and when we were taking it out, a connection formed and a bee flew out and Merlin caught it to put it out the window but that was enough to take him into the garden. I should have said the map is of a garden—"

"Yes," said Susan. "Just like 'The Serial Garden,' the Joan Aiken story. One of her Armitage ones. I mean the map in that was turned into a 3D model you had to cut out from a cereal packet and put together to work, but the principle is—"

"I don't know that one," said Vivien. "I love her novels. *Black Hearts in Battersea* is probably my favorite, but I have a fondness for *The Cuckoo Tree* and also *Midnight Is a Place*—"

She stopped herself.

"Children's writers! I mean she probably thought she was just making it up, but we'll have to investigate her again in case she has come across an actual translocation map. I know she was vetted a few years back. They are always so much work! Anyway, it doesn't matter. You understand about the map. Basically, anyway."

She started up the stairs again. Susan followed, noting that for all their ordinariness, this staircase had one similarity with the other bookshops of the St. Jacques she had seen. From the street she would have sworn the building only had three stories counting the attic with the dormer windows, but they had already gone up four floors and there were two to go.

"Merlin's got himself stuck," Vivien said over her shoulder. "There's bound to be a way out but it's invariably very well hidden in this sort of situation. So, the usual thing is for someone to go in with another translocation map and everyone uses that to come back out."

"And this hasn't happened because?"

"We don't have a map here and unfortunately things are a bit snarled up in London and elsewhere and we can't get one until tomorrow or maybe very late tonight. Which we didn't think was going to be a problem but now time is starting to speed up."

"What?"

"For Merlin, I mean. Here we are. Be careful of the tea chests. The edges bite. Stupid old crates. Ruby, this is Susan. The Old Man of Coniston's daughter, you know."

"Oh yes, good to meet you," said Ruby. But she didn't look at Susan. All her attention was on the faintly glowing map that was nailed to the worktable with silver tacks. She was observing it closely through a large magnifying glass held in her left hand, while she held her right hand palm down a few inches above the map, as if testing the heat from a frying pan.

"It's definitely speeding up in there," she said. "I estimate it was about twenty-four to one soon after Merlin went in and got it going again, and now it's four to one. At this rate it will equalize in less than three hours. Our time, I mean."

"Where's Merlin?" asked Vivien.

"Just about to leave the maze," said Ruby, peering through the glass again. "There's some sort of animal, a cat or a dog, keeping pace with him, on top of the wall. Hard to tell its intentions, but he's left it alone."

"By four to one do you mean fifteen minutes there is equivalent to an hour here?" asked Susan. "An hour there is four hours here?"

"Yes, of course," replied Ruby. "But like I said, it is speeding up."

"What happens when the time equalizes?"

Ruby did look at her this time, her expression being one of someone who has just remembered that their visitor had a personal stake in Merlin's well-being beyond the technical temporal aspects of the situation.

"Oh, well I'm not a specialist, but I suspect the whole bubble will burst, as it were," she said. "The slow or stopped time is draining out of that little pocket, and it's not sustainable, no matter how much magic has been invested to keep it separate. This open part of the map is like a hole in a bucket. Very interesting, as a matter of fact. Worth looking into, no one has done any real research as far as I know—"

"What will happen *to Merlin*?" interrupted Susan.

"Oh. If he's there at that point, he'll die," said Ruby. "But before then we could close off this map, which would essentially close the hole in the bucket, and time there would slow down once again to a full stop, the status quo preserved in that little reality."

"Leaving Merlin trapped there," said Vivien drily.

"So how can I help?" asked Susan. "You said you needed me, Vivien."

"The thing is," said Vivien. "Well, the thing is . . . while we don't have a translocation map, we do have the special paper you need to make one, or at least we have a version of it, and I think *you* could make one."

"Me? I wouldn't even know where to start!"

"Much of it is in the preparation of the paper, which is already done," said Vivien. "Then the creator must focus intently on a place they are deeply connected to, and draw it, willing the connection."

"If it's that simple why aren't there thousands of these maps around?" asked Susan skeptically.

"The creator does need to have innate power," explained Vivien. "Some have been made by entities of the Old World, invariably of their own demesne, and others by right-handed or even-handed booksellers of places they have inhabited for several decades or more."

"And there have been a few made by mortal practitioners, usually towards the end of their lives," said Ruby chattily. "Roger Crab the hermit, he made one for an island in the small lake in Ickenham, that's another map Zoë and Helen have got—"

"But I don't have any innate power!" exclaimed Susan.

"Daughter of an Ancient Sovereign, who has been immersed in the Bronze Cauldron?" said Vivien. "Of course you do. Also, I've seen your drawings. They are always so vibrant, so real and alive."

Susan thought about this, her face troubled. She had largely coped with the events of the last summer by putting them behind her, focusing on art school, her new life in London, and, she realized, a conscious effort to be as ordinary as possible. But as the year had drawn to a close, she was becoming more and more aware that "as ordinary as possible" would only go so far. She had started to dream almost every night about the Old Man of Coniston. The mountain and surrounds, and the entity who was her father. Intensely detailed dreams where she was somehow aware of everything that was happening within the bounds of the demesne and could focus in on anything she chose. She could see into the thoughts of the people who lived there, the rawer emotions of the birds and animals, the movement of air and water, the deep subterranean reaches. Wherever she wanted to go, she went, to the top of the mountain or deep into the stone below. Whatever she wanted to know, she knew.

Behind all this, she felt her father waking, beginning to rise from the deep slumber he had chosen after they had released him from Southaw's binding. He would wake at the turn of the year, he had said. What that meant for Susan she didn't know, but she felt it would be very significant. Something was going to happen, she sensed the imminence of some vast change.

The new year had seemed far away back then, something Susan could ignore. And she had ignored it, but it was getting harder and harder. She knew now that come New Year's Eve, she would be atop the mountain, waiting for her father to rise from his rest, and while she hoped she would come back down again simply as Susan Arkshaw, art student, she didn't know if that would be possible.

Now there was this, another step into the Old World, to make something magical. She was torn because she wanted to do it, of course to help Merlin but also because she loved the idea of drawing a magical map that could transport her to wherever she desired. But that, too, might mean she was choosing a path from which she could not return, and Susan did not want to abandon her normal life. It flashed through her mind once again to wonder how the booksellers managed, living as they did always between the Old World and the New.

"There is another . . . er . . . complication," said Vivien, with some embarrassment. "I'd forgotten, but Ruby reminded me. You see, these maps can't be drawn here."

"In the bookshop?" asked Susan.

"No, here as in the ordinary world," said Vivien. "They have to be made elsewhere. Like in Silvermere, or some other place out of the ordinary way of time. In this case, it seems most straightforward for it to be—"

She pointed at the map.

"In that garden. We go in, find Merlin, and you draw a map to get us out. Before the time difference equalizes."

"I see," said Susan. "Where is the paper? And what do I draw with?"

"I've got everything in Merlin's bag," said Vivien eagerly, indicating the large carpetbag on the corner of the desk. "The board is unfortunately black, but we've silver ink, and Ruby has filled three fountain pens and put in a silver pencil and sharpener."

"I see," said Susan slowly. "Isn't there someone else you could get to draw your map? Surely one of your—"

She stopped as they heard rapid footsteps on the stairs, someone rocketing up them at speed. A second later the fire alarm bell chattered and the intercom bellowed, "Intruders on the roof!"

Susan, Vivien, and Ruby looked up. There was a heavy thump overhead, followed by a sharp crack, and a great cloud of suddenly freed soot blew out of the long-disused fireplace at the end of the room, fortunately behind a wall of closed tea chests. A moment later, there was the sound of stone screeching on stone.

"Something's coming down the chimney," said Ruby unnecessarily. She stood up and raised her right hand, drawing in a very deep breath.

"Grab Merlin's bag," said Vivien as she snatched a small velvet bag—smaller than a cigarette packet—from the table and shoved it in her jeans pocket. "Link arms."

Susan grabbed the bag and put her right hand through Vivien's left, their elbows locking.

Cameron and another left-handed bookseller Susan hadn't met charged into the room. Cameron held the slightly bent iron bar from the press, and a massively muscled woman in a mud-spattered boiler suit like Susan's with a biker's leather vest over it, wielded a bricklayer's hammer in each hand.

"Bloody gargoyles now," said Cameron, in the tone of someone decrying the weather. "Stone dragons the size of dogs with long gutter mouths. There's two on the roof and one at the back door."

"We're going," said Vivien.

"What, now?" asked Susan.

"They've come for the map," said Vivien. "I doubt they'll get it, but we can't take a chance it'll be damaged or taken away. We need to go now or Merlin might be lost forever."

"Here, take this," said the muscular woman, handing over one of her hammers. Susan took it clumsily, her arm still through Vivien's. The latter, being a right-handed bookseller, had made no move to take something intended to be used as a weapon. "For Merlin. Tell him hi from his Aunt Sairey."

More soot exploded from the fireplace, and the stone screeching intensified.

"You fix 'em in place when they break in, Ruby," said Cameron. "We'll smash 'em."

Ruby nodded, still holding her breath. Sairey spun her remaining hammer in the air and caught it in her left hand, indicating who she was, though she wore heavy motorcycle gauntlets on both hands. She grinned and flexed her shoulders like a boxer stepping into the ring.

"In the 'Serial Garden' Mark had to hum or sing a tune to get into it," said Susan. "Do we have to sing or—"

"No," replied Vivien, and touched the map.

CHAPTER FIVE

Somewhere, Somewhen

Gate-posts. *The post on which the gate hangs and swings is called the "hanging-post"; that against which it shuts is called the "banging post."*

SUMMER HEAT HIT SUSAN, AND THE HARSH GLARE OF NOONDAY SUN-shine. She had to half close her eyes and look down. There was lush green grass under her feet, and she felt momentarily dizzy from the sudden change in light and temperature.

"We got here at least," said Vivien, unlinking their arms. She revolved on the spot, turning a slow circle, pausing to stare at a sundial that was indicating about half past twelve, before coming back to her starting point. She took the velvet bag out of her pocket and opened it, taking out a small silver camera. Lifting it to her eye she took shots of the walls and the roses, the sundial, and the sky before returning the camera to the bag and the bag into her pocket. "Now to catch up with Merlin."

Susan jumped as Vivien unexpectedly lifted her head and bellowed far louder than would seem possible from a slight young woman. The powerful lungs of a right-handed bookseller were given free rein.

"View halloo!"

A second later her call was answered from somewhere beyond the maze walls, not far away, by a lesser, but also strident shout, in a very similar voice, a kind of sibling echo.

"Yoicks! Tally-ho! Beware the roses and my turf cuts will give you direction!"

"Still alive," said Vivien. "And in good voice. Come on."

She strode to the exit from the central court, with Susan following, feeling rather like a railway porter, Merlin's surprisingly heavy bag in one hand and the bricklayer's hammer in the other. She was also immediately far too hot in her long sheepskin coat, but she didn't want to pause to take it off and lose Vivien, who was moving fast.

"What was that about roses?" she gasped, catching up to Vivien.

Vivien looked askance at the sculpted flowers and thorny canes that rioted over the walls, took in a swift breath and held it for a few seconds before she scowled and puffed out her breath with disdain.

"More animated stone," she said. "Dormant until touched or someone tries to climb a wall and then they'll go for you like a moray eel. No thought or discretion, just aggression. Crude but powerful. The entity behind all this must have invested all of their strength here. Or found some other way to keep it going. . . ."

Vivien's voice trailed off and her mouth tightened in distaste, as if what she had just said came with the sudden recognition of an unwelcome and horrible truth. She started to walk even faster, only pausing at the intersections to study Merlin's marks in the grass.

"It's interesting the map does not accurately reflect the maze," said Vivien. "I wouldn't have thought that was possible, given the nature of the connection. There's a whole other layer of obfuscating sorcery. The maze is designed to trap an unexpected visitor, presumably until the entity behind this place can come along and bag them."

"And . . . er . . . is this likely to happen soon?" asked Susan.

"I don't know," replied Vivien. "With our part of the map torn off from a greater whole, it's likely everything is out of whack here. It's even possible the entity who made it can't get back themselves, though that may be wishful thinking. There are probably other connections, not necessarily via an ensorcelled map. We need to find out more."

"We need to get Merlin and get out," said Susan feelingly. "Presuming I *can* make us a map of our own."

"I'm sure you can," said Vivien confidently. "We go right here. There's Merlin's mark. And yes, we should be concentrating on getting out of here in a hurry. I was letting my curiosity get the better of me."

A few minutes later, having the advantage of Merlin's scratches on the turf, they emerged from the maze. Merlin was sitting on the grass with his legs out in front of him, dress hiked up, tightening a bandage around his knee. He looked up, and a small ripple of surprise at seeing Susan flashed across his face.

"A ploy for sympathy, I see," said Vivien, but she knelt down to take a look at the bandaged wound. Susan and Merlin exchanged oddly shy glances. Things had been a bit strained between them ever since Susan had said she wanted to focus on her studies more and Merlin had asked did this mean she wanted to see him less and she had not been able to immediately answer, because it was a complicated question tied up with her instinctive desire to have less to do with the Old World, and the booksellers who were so deeply connected to it, while at the same time not wanting to drive Merlin himself away.

"From your aunt Sairey," said Susan, handing him the bricklayer's hammer. "And I brought your bag. Nice dress, pity about the bloodstains and everything. Are you okay?"

"Thank you," said Merlin, taking the hammer. He gestured to the "stone in a bonnet" mace and chain. "As you can see, I improvised a statue-smashing weapon, but this will be better. And I am okay. This is just a cat scratch."

"One with stone claws," said Vivien, glancing at the other bits and pieces of stone cat strewn near the maze entrance. "You've treated this with Sipper spit already?"

"Yes, sister," said Merlin. He looked at Susan. "I don't want you to ever feel unwelcome, but surely you didn't need to come here, too, Susan? It could be a bit sticky getting out of the place."

"I *am* the way out of here," said Susan. "At least I'm supposed to draw a map that will get us out. Shall I start?"

"Oh," said Merlin. He glanced at Vivien. "I see. Do you think—"

"Yes," said Vivien firmly. "I do think. Susan has the connection, the inherent power, and the drawing ability. The card and the pens are in Merlin's bag, Susan. You should get started. I'm not sure how much time we have."

"Time?" asked Merlin. He sounded unusually apprehensive. "Can you sense the entity behind this place? Are they here?"

"Not yet," said Vivien, though she couldn't help but look around. "Not as far as I know. Hopefully it doesn't know we're here. But this place has been held out of time, and it's equalizing now, bleeding out through the map in the Small Bookshop. If that completes, this little bubble will pop. And so will we."

"So how long have we got?"

"A few hours, I'd guess," said Vivien.

"The arrival of the entity is the greater threat," said Merlin, swiftly getting up. "We need to be somewhere more defensible, where Susan can work. The clock tower, I think. I want to take a look at it anyway."

"You want to check out the body that should be a clockwork figure?" asked Vivien, staring up at the tower.

"Yes," said Merlin. "A relatively recent murder, I think. Since the war, at least. Jeans and a T-shirt."

He didn't need to say that this was very much bookseller business. The booksellers' raison d'être was to police the Old World and protect mortals from predatory entities and dangerous magic, and occasionally the other way around as well.

Susan looked at the clock tower properly for the first time. She hadn't noticed the body before, but now that it had been pointed out, it was easy to see that it wasn't inactive clockwork but a corpse slumped in death.

"Susan, on second thought, you take this hammer," said Merlin. He handed her the tool, then bent and picked up his makeshift ball and chain. "Can you carry my bag?"

Susan nodded and picked it up. Merlin set off, walking with only the slightest limp from his wounded knee, Susan and Vivien following a few steps behind.

"*En avant, mes braves*," said Vivien.

At questioning looks from both Merlin and Susan, she added, "*Beau Geste*. We met P.C. Wren this morning."

This led to further explanation about what had happened at the Small Bookshop after Merlin's departure, up to their own exit ahead of gargoyles.

"That probably means the entity is still there, or was, which is good for us," said Merlin. "And they are desperate to get the map."

"What will happen if the gargoyles do manage to grab it?" asked Susan.

"They won't," said Merlin confidently. "Not with Sairey and Cameron and the others there."

They reached the Egyptian Gate, which was closed, two large leaves of rough-worked stone fitting very tightly together. There was no obvious handle, knob, or lock. Merlin tapped one side tentatively with the truncheon end of his cat-head weapon, without result. "Some kind of marble, isn't it? Everything is the same sort of stone. The maze walls, the carved roses, the cat . . ."

"And the lion back at the bookshop," added Vivien. "Ruby said it was Purbeck marble. That kind of shelly composition is characteristic, apparently."

"From the Isle of Purbeck," said Merlin thoughtfully. He transferred the mace and chain to his right hand and pushed on the stone door with his left. It didn't budge. "Hardy country. Wessex. I can't recall any particular malevolent entities from the *Index* being located there. Can you, Vivien?"

"Not offhand," said Vivien. "I remember there's one of the Wessex dragons in the pebble bar, but it's been quiescent since Saxon times, and we'd know if it had woken for sure. I'd say whatever Purbeck entity is behind all this has managed to evade our notice, has never been recorded. I will be looking very carefully into the matter as soon as we get back."

"Yes. Getting back. I'm going to have to climb over the hedge," said Merlin. "This gate must open from the other side."

"No," said Vivien thoughtfully. "I doubt it has any mechanism, as such. The entity has power over stone, can give it movement, if not true life. I suspect the gate will work the same way."

Merlin stepped back and scratched his head under the lace coif. Even he was sweating under that summer sun, which had finally slipped a little down the sky but not enough to make a difference to the heat.

"What do you suggest?" he asked.

"I can try to wake it myself," said Vivien. "Enough to crack open, at least, so we can push it or squeeze through."

She stripped off her glove, laid her luminous silver right hand against the stone gate, and took a very deep breath. Nothing happened for at least thirty seconds, then with a sound like eggshells being trodden on, the gate cracked open and the leaf under Vivien's hand began to slide backwards. She took a small step forward, maintaining contact, and then another. Not quite pushing the stone, more following it up. When the gap was wide enough to slip through she lifted her hand and gulped in air, before replacing her glove.

"That was hard work. I couldn't have done it if the spark wasn't already there. It has the memory of movement in it."

Merlin went through the gap, mace and chain ready. Susan followed, then Vivien, still recovering her breath, as if she had just done a hundred-yard sprint.

They could now see the lower part of the clock tower, the avenue lined with heraldic statues going down to the lake, and part of Wolf Wood to the east, though as to the north, the sky came down into a blue fuzzy blur, far closer than any normal horizon.

So far, it was all as depicted in the map. But there was something else they had not seen in that drawing, and surely could not have missed. There was a seventeenth-century four-poster bed, without a canopy, at the foot of the tower, directly below the clockface. An old lady was curled up asleep on the bed, above the covers. A little old lady in a full-length nainsook nightgown with many ruffles and flounces and a voluminous green-ribboned mobcap that was twice the size of her head.

Susan noticed that after an initial glance at the old lady, Merlin was far more interested in the statues. He watched them warily, as if he expected to see them suddenly leap off their plinths and attack.

"The statues are the same grey-white stone," he said. "Purbeck marble again."

"They're badly executed," said Susan critically. "I mean, the proportions are out of whack. Their legs are too long, or short, and that one's head is too big."

"Their artistic merit doesn't really matter if they come alive and attack us," replied Merlin.

"It's not the statues that worry me right now. That old lady wasn't on the map," said Vivien. "But I don't think she's an entity. . . . This is all very strange."

"And it's ridiculously hot," added Susan. She bent her head to wipe her face on the coat she had now draped over her shoulder, but it didn't really help. "It's like a hothouse, one all closed up, as if there isn't enough air."

"There might only be a finite supply of air here, come to think of it," said Vivien thoughtfully. "Another reason to get out as swiftly as we can."

"To the tower, then," said Merlin. "So Susan can start drawing. We can check out the little old lady on the way."

He set off towards the tower, the others following. All of them were walking more quickly now, as if Susan's suggestion that there wasn't enough air had taken root.

The bed was positioned a few feet in front of the tower door. The door was not stone but heavy oak, with a massive iron keyhole. Merlin did a quick lap around the tower to see if there were any other entrances, while Vivien approached the bed with Susan close at her heels.

She'd thought the old lady must be dead, but on closer inspection, she was alive. Her chest slowly rose and fell, and her mouth twitched slightly. She was simply very deeply asleep.

"Don't touch the bed, or anything on it," said Vivien. She extended her right hand towards the sleeping woman, her thumb violently twitching as if it was being stimulated by electric shocks. "This is the focus of the whole place."

"The bed?" asked Susan.

"The woman," replied Vivien, and took in a deep breath. She became motionless, and her thumb stilled. Merlin came running back around to the front of the tower.

"That's the only door," he said. "There's only the one clock-face, too, on this side, which is unusual. And no windows at all, just that archway below the clockface with that corpse instead of a clockwork figure."

"Vivien says this woman is the focus of the whole place," said Susan.

"Sleeping Beauty," said Merlin. "The garden is too well-kept, but there is a thorny motif going on."

"She's a bit old for that tale," said Susan dubiously. The woman looked to be in her seventies, perhaps even older. She was quite beautiful, though only part of her face was visible to

Susan, what with the huge mobcap and the lady's head being enveloped in the massive goose feather pillow, one of three piled on the head of the bed.

"I wouldn't take the story you know as authoritative," said Merlin. "I'm going to open that door."

He took his carpetbag from Susan and limped over to the tower.

Vivien exhaled and took her camera out again, taking careful shots of the bed, the old woman, the clockface on the tower, the body below it in the archway, and the avenue of statues, while she talked to Susan.

"Fairy tales are often extremely mixed-up versions of something real or that really occurred in the Old World," she said. "But in this case, I think this has happened the other way around. An Ancient Sovereign has created this place in imitation of the story. Probably the Perrault version, though it could be the Grimm. I think this garden dates from the first quarter of the nineteenth century, so that is possible. If whoever it was read the first German edition, I believe *Kinder- und Hausmärchen* was 1812—"

"But why?" interrupted Susan, fearing a longer dissertation on Grimm editions. "And who is the woman?"

"I don't know who she is, but I do know one thing. She's like you," said Vivien. "A very rare individual indeed."

"What?" asked Susan.

"She is also the child of a mortal and an Ancient Sovereign."

"Oh," said Susan blankly. "But why is she asleep?"

"I don't know," said Vivien, replacing her camera. She frowned. "There's something wrong with her. Physically I mean, some lurking illness. Cancer, maybe. But she's also much older than she looks, at least a hundred. I mean, she was at least a hundred when she was put to sleep here. She hasn't aged since, because no time has passed. This whole place was taken out of time, and it was done for her. The working is centered right here. A tremendous outpouring of power, sustained over centuries, which is very troubling."

"I agree," called out Merlin from where he was working on the lock of the tower door with a contraption made from one of the wire coat hangers out of his bag. "The sooner we get out of here, the better. I've almost got this. Correction. I have got this."

They all heard the click of the lock turning, and the squeal as the gate was pushed open.

The old woman heard it, too. Her eyes flashed open and she sat up. Susan jumped back, but Vivien held her ground.

"Mother!" called out the old woman, raising her arms. Her sleepy eyes focused on Vivien, becoming sharp. "Oh! Who are you? Mother!"

The last word was a scream that seemed to reverberate everywhere, as if the blue sky above was actually the very high, reflective ceiling of an opera house. When the scream stopped, the silence after it was also theatrical, the silence of an expectant audience holding its breath.

Into this silence, there came an answering howl from the east, where the Wolf Wood disappeared into the blurred horizon. It was the scream of a ferocious wind, and sure enough, a freezing blast of air sent branches flailing and leaves flying. It blew fiercely across the avenue and ruffled the hedge walls of the inner garden as it screamed over and around them, but the wind did not touch the bed and its ancient inhabitant, and Susan, Vivien, and Merlin were also spared.

"Mother," said the old woman again, this time in contented welcome. But she was not talking about the wind.

On the heels of the wintry blast came a vast, reaching hand of airborne dust or dense, concentrated fog. It came high over the treetops, swift as the wind, each finger the size of the tower, the hand as a whole completely blotting out the eastern sky.

"Inside!" yelled Merlin. He pushed the door fully open and hustled Vivien and then Susan in. Through the doorway, they looked back to see the hand coming down, each finger and thumb alighting on a statue in the avenue. As they touched, the dusty digits flowed into the stone and were absorbed by it, and within seconds the hand was no more.

A moment later, the touched statues shivered and as one turned towards the tower and stepped down from their plinths. The closest was a hippalectryon, which was all too like a Pegasus gone wrong. Its front half was a horse, but the rear parts those of a giant rooster, complete with spurred legs, and its wings were a chicken's writ large. Behind it was a relatively normal-looking lion, only it was much bigger and its paws were wrong, as if the sculptor hadn't ever seen a real lion. Then came the astonishingly ugly ypotryll, a creature with a boar's head featuring oversized tusks, the body of a dromedary with a disproportionately high and narrow hump, the legs of an ox, and trailing behind it a long, scaly tail that ended in a sting the size of a First World War sword bayonet. Caracoling next to it was a unicorn, also wrong in its proportions, its head too small for the horn it sported; behind the unicorn came a pismire, which was basically a giant stone ant, though this one sported a small crown upon its head and its legs were too long and they all had an extra joint.

"The one with wings can't fly, can it?" asked Susan.

"They're still stone, albeit animated," said Merlin, who was wrestling the door shut. He slammed it closed, leaving them in almost complete darkness. "So I don't think so. Head upstairs, I'm going to wedge this door."

"You go," said Vivien. "I can fix it in place better than any wedge."

"Okay, Gandalf," said Merlin. "You hold the door. Susan, we'll go up and you can get drawing."

"I can't see a thing," said Susan, relatively calmly. "So that would be difficult."

"Really?" asked Merlin. "I'd have thought you'd be able to see in the—"

"Well, I can't!" snapped Susan.

"Sorry," said Merlin. The booksellers *could* see well in the dark. They were often in it. Susan heard him rummaging in his bag. "I've got a candle. Here, Viv, you light it."

Vivien drew in a short breath and blew upon the candle, a

spark leaping from her mouth. A tall flame sprang up from the wick, and with it, a stupefying scent of vanilla and cinnamon, which would have been fine separately and less strong, but combined in this candle were almost a chemical weapon. It was about the size of a gin bottle and had a love heart design repeated around the top.

"What the hell, Merlin?" exclaimed Vivien, coughing and stepping back. "That absolutely reeks!"

"It was a gift," said Merlin defensively. "I've had it for ages."

He passed the candle to Susan, who turned her face aside in an attempt to avoid the wafting scent. Vivien cleared her throat and inhaled again, this time much more seriously, and laid her right hand against the door. She had hardly done so before it was struck an almighty blow, and the whole tower shook.

"Up!" urged Merlin. "Up!"

Susan ran to the stair and up it, unable to think of the unfortunate choice Merlin had made calling Vivien "Gandalf." Now all she could think of was "we cannot get out," which would be true if she couldn't draw the map they needed, and she really doubted she could, and the tower shook again and she heard the door groan and crack and Merlin was very close behind, urging her on.

CHAPTER SIX

>─┤◆>─○─<◆─┤─<

Somewhere, Somewhen, and Elsewhere

Statue. *It was Pygmalion who fell in love
with a statue he had himself made.*

>─┤◆>─○─<◆─┤─<

SUSAN STUMBLED OFF THE TOP STEP ON TO THE NEXT FLOOR AND
stopped. Merlin almost ran into her and had to steady himself
against the wall.

"Susan! Keep going!"

In answer Susan lifted the candle high and stepped forward
to let Merlin come up next to her. The ceiling of this floor was
much lower, and there was only a ladder going up through an
open trapdoor in the corner, rather than a proper stair. Apart
from the narrow pool of light from the candle, it was intensely
dark.

But the candlelight was enough to see the bodies stacked up
in the middle of the room. Three rows, each of eight bodies,
the middle row stacked perpendicular to the others. They were
all young, men and women, and remarkably well-preserved,

though their pallid faces and rigor, not to mention the indignity of how they were arranged like firewood made it clear they were dead, not sleeping like the old woman, even though they had no obvious wounds.

Those on the bottom row wore clothing typical of the Georgian period. Two of the women still had bonnets tied under their chins. The middle row started that way at one end and then the clothes became Victorian halfway through, a style that persisted in the next row until it, too, changed. There were several men in uniform, one in a scarlet coat, two in the khaki of the First World War or thereabouts, and another a policeman from the 1920s.

The bodies in the top row came from later, including a woman in a naval uniform of the Second World War, a Wren; the younger woman next to her wore the dowdy, rationed clothes of the late forties; then a Teddy boy in something close to a zoot suit; he had only one shoe on, a suede creeper.

Next to the three neat rows of corpses, there was another body laid down all by herself, the start of a new line. A hippie, a flower child in a tie-dyed summer dress of orange and sky blue. Her feet were bare, there were badly drawn henna symbols up both arms, and she held an oversized card in her closed hand.

Another boom came from below, and the tower shook once more.

"Go up! Go up!" urged Merlin, pushing Susan. "Get drawing. There's nothing we can do for these people. Give me the hammer."

Susan broke out of her moment of shocked stillness and

handed him the hammer, which he put in the bag, before she ran to the ladder. She almost dropped the candle on herself climbing one-handed, but managed not to, and sprang out on the next floor. This room also had a low ceiling, but there was the archway where the mohawked corpse slumped on the post, and the sunshine was streaming in. Rails on the floor and some scattered toothy wheels showed there had once been proper clockwork here, and presumably harmless automatons, but it had all been removed to make room for the horrid display of the dead body.

There was another ladder in the corner, but Susan ignored it. She needed the light. Not looking at the dead punk on the post, she moved to the archway and sat down cross-legged in the sunshine. She was a foot or so back from the edge, so she couldn't see what was happening directly underneath. From the shaking and the concussive booms the statues were taking it in turns to throw themselves against the door. But whatever Vivien had done was still holding. Though she heard cracking sounds, there was not the sudden smashing noise that would announce their entry into the tower.

"I need the board and the pens," said Susan, looking back. But it wasn't Merlin who came up through the hatch, it was Vivien, who now had Merlin's bag. She dashed over to Susan, dropped it next to her, and flung it open, swiftly handing over a thick, black board and two fountain pens, a Waterman Le Man Rhapsody Caviar and a Pilot F Milano. Susan uncapped them and tested both quickly on the edge of the board, drawing several lines with each, including using it with the nib backwards, to see how they performed.

"Where's Merlin?" she asked, capping the Waterman and shoving it in a pencil pocket of her boiler suit, choosing the Pilot F as the better to draw with.

"He'll be here in a sec," said Vivien. "Don't worry about him. Concentrate on the drawing, focus on the place, feel your connection. I'll help you with that. I can . . . um . . . block out things for you. Merlin will keep us safe. Put everything else out of your mind."

"I'll try," said Susan. She bent her head and looked at the black board and drew four decisive lines to make a frame. Then she began to properly draw the scene that sprang into her mind, the safest place she could think of, and with it came the memory of how that place looked and smelled and felt, every small detail that made it what it was. She only faintly heard Vivien take a breath and hardly noticed at all when the bookseller gripped her shoulder, but as she did so, the world narrowed around Susan. She could no longer hear the battering attempts at entry below, or feel the heat of the sun, or anything. There was only the black board and the silver lines, and the place she was drawing with all her heart and soul.

She didn't hear Merlin rush up, lie down on the floor, and reach down to break the top four rungs of the ladder with his left hand, snapping the heavy oak planks with his inhuman strength, though admittedly with great effort. That done he ran to his bag and took out the Smython, and holding on to the post that held the dead mohawked man, he leaned out and fired six shots straight down, in rapid succession. Not with the success he hoped, for while he reloaded using a speedloader with practiced ease, he didn't try any more shots, placing the revolver back in the bag. He considered his mace and chain for a moment, then took up the bricklayer's hammer.

As he lifted it out, a massive crash below announced that the statues had broken through. Vivien had effectively made the door become part of the wall, using the strength of the stone around it, but even that could not hold out against repeated battering. Merlin had seen while shooting at them that most of the statues had suffered as well, losing horns and limbs and parts of their mythological bodies. The unicorn was totally out of action, its head snapped in half, but the Ancient Sovereign animating it had simply inhabited the next closest statue along the avenue, so now there was a minotaur lumbering up to join the fray. It wielded a stone battle-ax, which made it even more dangerous than the other statues.

They would be delayed by the missing rungs, Merlin knew, but possibly not for long. They might even be able to stand on each other's heads or something. And he hadn't seen the pismire, which he hoped did not have an ant's ability to climb a vertical wall, though if it could, he supposed it would already be up here.

He hefted the bricklayer's hammer and stood ready. Susan was sketching frantically, a scene emerging in silver on black. It looked like a little stream in woodland, presumably somewhere on the lower slopes of the Old Man of Coniston, maybe near the lake.

He hoped it would work. They needed to get back to start tracking down the Ancient Sovereign behind this place, who was evidently a serial killer. Mythic entities who murdered people were not to be tolerated. This was no case of self-defense or accident, or even misunderstanding, as when entities thought people wanted to become a sacrifice. Or when they actually did want to be a sacrifice.

He looked over at the young man on the post. Unlike the other bodies below, he *did* have visible wounds. Merlin frowned deeply, considering the damage. The young man had been tortured before death, he thought. He took note of his clothes, jeans and a T-shirt that looked like a promotional freebie from some small business, though the logo and name were so bloodstained he couldn't quite make them out. The jeans had many holes and numerous safety pins, none of them where they were of any use, purely for the look of it. The rear pocket flapped, mostly torn away, and Merlin thought he had most likely found the owner of the wallet he had picked up in the maze.

All these details, and those he had seen below, plus the few things he had managed to snatch from the other bodies, would be of vital importance in the investigation. If they could work out who the people were, and when they had disappeared, it would be very useful—

Merlin stopped thinking and lunged at the trapdoor, bringing the bricklayer's hammer down on the little crown atop the pismire's head. As expected, the giant ant was the best climber and had easily got past the missing rungs of the ladder.

It snapped at him with its sharp mandibles, but he dodged

aside and brought the hammer down on the little crown again. Cracks propagated across the pismire's head as it lunged again, getting halfway through the hatch. Merlin landed another blow in exactly the same place and this time the head shattered into five pieces.

But the pismire continued to thrust up through the trapdoor, its front legs striking at Merlin. He smashed one off where it joined the thorax, but still it came on until he managed to crack another and it fell on one side, scrabbling wildly. Merlin methodically broke off the legs on the other side, the hammer rising and falling with incredible force.

Too much force, for when he brought the hammer down between the pismire's head and thorax, the haft snapped and the head of the hammer flew off and bounced against the wall.

"Tarnation," muttered Merlin. He tried kicking the still wiggling creature down through the hole, but it kept coming on, propelled by its last two legs. He caught a glimpse of the minotaur behind it. As soon as the pismire was clear, the bull-headed monster would be up and through, swinging that battle-ax.

"Viv!" he yelled, dashing to the corner to pick up a heavy cast-iron sprocket, which he held in his left hand, fingers curled inside, making it into an unorthodox circular cestus. "We have to go!"

Vivien didn't answer. She was still holding her breath, and Susan wasn't finished with the drawing.

Merlin delivered a shattering left hook to one of the pismire's remaining rear legs, sending the limb flying. But it managed to push itself fully into the room and across just enough of the floor to clear the hatch. The minotaur sprang up in its wake. Its shoulders were only marginally narrower than the trapdoor, and Merlin regretted the entryway wasn't smaller, or the minotaur larger.

Even so, the creature took a precious half minute to get through, time enough for Merlin to backtrack to his bag, drop the cogwheel and take up both the Smython and his mace and chain. Vivien stood immobile next to Susan, her right hand on her shoulder. Susan's pen still flew across the black board.

Merlin fired carefully, aiming all six shots at the minotaur's right elbow as it struggled to get through the trapdoor. Chips of stone flew, and ricochets bounced about, fortunately none back towards the arched window. The arm was definitely cracked, but not enough to break it off, and then the minotaur was through and charging at him. Merlin charged, too, ducking under a horizontal swipe of the battle-ax as he swung his cat-head mace and chain at the minotaur's arm. He shouted at it as he struck, eager to focus all its attention on him.

But it didn't work. Instead it lumbered towards the defenseless Susan and Vivien, raising its axe. Merlin flung his mace and chain aside and grabbed the creature's arm. This time, already weakened by the gunshots, the joint broke, the minotaur's forearm and the axe coming away in Merlin's grasp. Instantly, he swung arm and weapon with an overhand swing, aiming between the creature's horns, even as the minotaur lowered its head, intent on goring Susan and Vivien in their unprotected backs.

The stone axe broke with the force of the blow, and Merlin was left holding only a piece of the monster's arm. The minotaur reeled back, teetering on one hooved foot. Merlin threw the piece of arm at it, jumped high and delivered a double kick with the heels of his Doc Martens, pushing it away from Susan and Vivien. It fell heavily and one horn snapped off.

Merlin grabbed the cogwheel from the floor. Holding it in both hands he brought it down on the minotaur's head again. It still struggled to get up, but Merlin kept hitting it until with a resounding crack its head shattered into rubble and it was only a broken statue, still as stone should be.

But another creature was climbing up. The lion, which was slightly too large to fit through the trapdoor, was splintering the frame as it forced its way through. Merlin could hear other statues below, and doubtless more would be coming from the avenue. The Ancient Sovereign could animate five at a time and would keep sending them.

"Viv!" shouted Merlin. "We really, really have to go!"

"Okay," said Vivien mildly. She inhaled gratefully as she stood up, helping Susan rise at the same time. The latter held the board in her hand, no longer a black expanse of nothing, but a beautiful sylvan scene drawn in silver. A tiny sandy islet with a high boulder on one end and pebbled shores, in the middle of a narrow stream, with willows on one shore and alders on the other, and the hint of drier meadows beyond.

The drawing shed its own light, the silver brighter than any ink.

"Hold it up, Susan," said Vivien quickly. "Shut your eyes and imagine the place again. Don't open them until I tell you. Merlin, come here. We need to touch it together, your left hand and my right."

Merlin was so fast he almost teleported next to them, snatching up his bag on the way. He looked at Vivien and saw she wasn't sure this was going to work. Behind them the lion wriggled its hindquarters through the trapdoor.

Vivien and Merlin touched the map together as the lion cleared the trapdoor and swung around towards them, its ungainly rear paws scrabbling away broken pieces of pismire or minotaur as it readied itself to spring.

"Open your eyes! See your place!" shouted Vivien.

CHAPTER SEVEN

><+>-O-<+><

Slightly North of Bath, Late Saturday, 10th December 1983

Queen Regnant. *A queen who holds the crown in her own right, in contradistinction to a Queen Consort, who is queen only because her husband is king.*

><+>-O-<+><

IT WAS DARK AND COLD AND DAMP. SUSAN FELT SOMETHING COLD fall in her left eye. She yelped before catching on that it was rain, or a snowflake. A moment later she was violently shoved to the ground and she felt a rush of displaced air over her head. Something whizzed past and there was an almighty splash.

"Stay down," snapped Merlin.

"Give me the map," said Vivien, who was on Susan's other side, also on the ground. "Merlin, is it—"

Merlin didn't answer immediately. Susan heard him moving ahead of her, sand and pebbles crunching for half a dozen steps, and then him coming back.

"It's okay," said Merlin. "It's mere stone again."

"What's going on?" asked Susan, unable to suppress the tremor in her voice. She held up the map and felt Vivien take it.

There was no silver light from it; it was just part of the blackness all around. "I can't see a thing. Again."

"The lion followed us through," said Merlin. He helped Susan up. "But the animating power of the Ancient Sovereign did not. Thank heavens."

"Where are we?" asked Vivien. "It doesn't . . . feel right for Coniston."

"Oh," said Susan. She knelt again, dragging Merlin with her, and felt the ground. As she expected, it was sandy, with small pebbles, and she drew in a sudden, choking breath of relief to have this confirmed, even as she realized she already knew where she was from the familiar sound of the brook burbling past on either side of them. "It's my island. You said to draw somewhere I felt safe and know really well and this just came to mind. More than the mountain. I mean I know that, too, but it's Dad's, not really mine at all. This is my own place. I used to come here almost every day. I still do when I'm at home. My island."

"This is the brook that goes past your mother's house?" asked Merlin. "It's not much of an island."

"It's a perfectly perfect island! We're about a hundred yards upstream of the house," said Susan. She was starting to see more, just the hint of shapes, Merlin and Vivien and the slightly brighter sky. The snow was very light, just a few flakes landing on her upturned face and bare hands every now and then. But the night was cold.

"Oh shit," said Susan suddenly. "I dropped Mum's favorite coat back there. In the tower. She'll kill me."

Vivien and Merlin laughed. After a moment Susan joined in. It was all slightly strained laughter, born from the sudden relief of survival.

"I've got another candle here," said Merlin. Susan heard him open his bag, and the puff of Vivien's breath. A flame sprang up, cupped in Vivien's hands. The candle this time was a squat novelty item, a begging Dalmatian with the wick in its open mouth. It was not scented.

"I won't even ask," said Vivien. Protecting the candle from the falling snow, she held it up. In its weak light, Susan saw they were indeed on her island, a little sand and pebbled spit that was preserved from erosion by a massive boulder at the upstream end, the visible part six feet high and a dozen feet long. There was a small hollow in the top of the boulder, and Susan used to sit there for hours, imagining herself a queen, ruler of her tiny island country and the brook, watching the birds and the fish and crayfish, and every now and then, a passing otter.

"This feels like an entity's demesne," said Vivien slowly. "And yet it doesn't. You continue to surprise me, Susan."

"It's just . . . just mine," said Susan. "Though technically it belongs to the Parment family—it's their fields on both sides of the brook. But they've always left this stretch of the stream alone. Old Mrs. Parment used to come down here sometimes when I was little. I think she was worried I'd drown. She thought Mum didn't look after me properly. But she never made me go home. She'd just chat from the bank and give me cake and go away again. I wonder what the Parments are going to make of that!"

She pointed at the hindquarters of the stone lion, emerging from the brook like the stern of a sinking ship. Its leap had carried it headfirst deep into the silted bed of the brook. In the flickering candlelight it looked like a bizarre art installation, a modern artist making a point about English lions and willful ignorance, or something like that.

"We'll get it taken away," said Merlin. "Though that's not going to be easy. Our right-handed folk will want to look at it, for sure. I daresay it'll be the only unbroken statue of our new enemy."

"I'm going to take a look at it now," said Vivien. "You take this, Susan, and start for home. You're already turning a bit blue around the edges."

She offered the candle, which immediately went out, struck by a snowflake or snuffed out by the light breeze that sent the snow swirling.

"Are you sure you can't see in the dark?" asked Merlin.

"Of course I can't," said Susan crossly. "How many times do I have to tell you?"

"All right, I'll guide you," said Merlin. He held her elbow for a moment, felt her shivering, and added, "Hold still a second."

Susan heard the carpetbag clasps click open and shut, then the fox fur tippet was clasped around her neck and smoothed over her shoulders, bringing welcome warmth.

"Let's go," said Merlin. "Don't linger, Viv."

"I won't," said Vivien. "But I think we should be safe enough now. I can feel no trace of the entity nearby."

Merlin stopped. "Maybe I should smash this statue to pieces anyway, to be on the safe side?"

"No," said Vivien thoughtfully. Susan could hear a sloshing as she waded into the brook. "It might be useful to have a complete statue to investigate. I'm making an educated guess, but I'd say she works with the particular stone in two ways. One is to invest a little of her power in a statue and give it some sort of limited orders, because the stone can't think as such. Like the stone lion who came into the bookshop. I reckon years ago she set it to wait for any sign of the map and to go and retrieve it. The second way is to directly inhabit the statue, or statues, as we saw at the tower. But the lion here was violently torn from her control when we went through the map, it has no remnant of her power. It's safe. She won't even know where it is."

"She?" asked Merlin.

"The old woman called for her mother, and she came," replied Vivien.

They were all silent for a moment.

"You sure I can't just smash it?" wheedled Merlin. "There's a few big stones around. I can use one of those."

A fresh gust of wind spun the snow about them, and Susan shivered violently.

"No," said Vivien. "Get Susan home, get her warm, and put the kettle on. I'll make absolutely sure no remnant power lingers in the statue."

"You okay to wade, Susan, or shall I carry you across?" asked Merlin.

"There's a submerged log," said Susan, "over near my thro . . . the boulder. . . . It makes a bridge. The water should only be a few inches over it this time of year."

"Ah, I see it," said Merlin. He laid his hands on her shoulders and steered her forward for a dozen steps or so. "Stop, you're almost there. Put your foot forward. You feel it?"

"Got it," said Susan. She walked forward easily, surprising Merlin, who had to catch up. He was holding her shoulders lightly, just with his fingertips, but Susan found she didn't need the guidance. She knew exactly where the sunken bridge ended, and the height of the step up to the riverbank, where the narrow path meandered through the alders. She also was able to see more than she expected. Some light from the unseen moon was reflecting under the clouds, or something like that.

"This reminds me of when we first met," she said as they walked on. She could feel his left hand even through his glove and her fur tippet, it was so much warmer than his right. "Is this an old straight track?"

"No," said Merlin. "And I'm happy to say there isn't a Shuck pacing alongside either. The only entities about, as far as I can tell, are your friends. The one under the hill, the other in the brook downstream, and those ravens who are not ravens in the great chestnut above the house. But they are less active now than they were when I was last here. In fact I would say they are on the verge of sleep. Still watching, mind you, but not restless."

"What keeps entities awake, anyway? Or active?"

"Many different things," said Merlin. "Worship, sacrifice,

attention of various kinds. Particular events or conjunctions. Sometimes just circumstance. Some wake—or slumber—for reasons forever beyond our ken."

They walked on in silence, until the glowing windows of the farmhouse kitchen came into view beyond the fringe of alders and the blurring filter of falling snow. Light spilled from the windows of Jassmine's nearby studio—a repurposed barn—as well, enough so that Susan could see quite well.

"I'm sorry you got drawn into this," said Merlin. Susan glanced back at him and saw he was anxious, not a look she often saw on his face. "No pun intended, unfortunately. I'm not feeling particularly clever."

Susan stopped and turned fully around, so she stood very close to him, and they put their arms around each other and drew close.

"Is your leg okay?" she asked anxiously. "You're not bleeding—"

"It is bleeding," admitted Merlin. "But not too much. I think the cut got reopened when I kicked the minotaur."

"I'm sorry I missed that," said Susan.

"I wish you'd missed all of it," said Merlin. He sighed. "I was stupid to catch the bee, and even then, Vivien should never have called you in. I *know* you don't want to be involved in bookseller business—"

"It's not exactly I don't want to be," said Susan quietly, talking to Merlin's collarbone, shown off very nicely by the square-cut bodice of his gown. He didn't even have goose pimples, despite the cold. "I'm afraid of being seduced by it. By the Old World and magic, I mean. It's so attractive, but I mustn't lose any more of my normal self to it, no more than I must. Oh, I know because I am my father's daughter I can never really be an ordinary person again, but I want to be, as much as possible."

"I see," said Merlin, holding her tighter. "And I'm a part of the Old World, too."

"Yes," said Susan. "And I don't want to lose *you*! I just need to find a way to keep everything . . . even . . . I suppose. In balance. Only seeing you once a week is part of that, only I hadn't really figured that out for myself until just now. It was my subconscious I suppose. I'm making a mess of this, aren't I?"

"No," said Merlin. "It is something I . . . all of us St. Jacques . . . have to deal with as well."

He hesitated, then said quietly, "Some booksellers have abjured their powers and become fully mortal. It is rarely done, and it is not easy, but it is possible."

"I didn't know you could do that!" exclaimed Susan. Thinking quickly she added, "I don't want *you* to do that, mind. After all, I can't give up my own heritage. I mean, I presume I can't. . . ."

"You'd have to ask some of our elder folk," said Merlin softly. "Or the Grail-Keeper in Silvermere. Or your father, I suppose, though I doubt he'd be sympathetic to the notion. I don't know."

"What don't you know?" asked Vivien, coming up behind. Susan started, but Merlin had already heard her approaching. "Besides almost everything? And why aren't you inside already making me a nice cup of tea?"

"We stopped for a moment to chat," said Susan, covering up Merlin's mouth as he was about to insult his sister in return. He kissed Susan's palm instead. She let her hand fall and turned around. She could see well enough now to lead the way. "Come on. I hope Mum isn't cross I wasn't home for tea. What time is it anyway?"

Merlin looked at the night sky, said, "Eight thirty-five p.m.," remembered he was wearing a watch, and checked the dial of his Vertex. "No, I'm wrong. Eight thirty-four."

"So there was still quite a time difference," said Vivien thoughtfully. "I expect the Ancient Sovereign now has closed off the section of the map we had, so that garden and the house and everything will go all back into stasis again. And we won't be able to get back in. At least not that way."

"Why would you want to go back?" asked Susan.

"We need to investigate," said Merlin. "Twenty-six deaths by my count. Most likely murders. And that last one, tied up on the clockwork figure rail? He was tortured before he died."

"Oh," said Susan. "That's horrible. Even more horrible."

"There's a lot to look into," said Vivien. "We need to get back to the Small Bookshop as soon as possible. Do you think we could borrow your mum's car?"

"While I'm sure she'd lend it, it won't help you," replied Susan. She gestured in the air, making the snowflakes swirl about her hands. "If this has been going on all afternoon, the Mini won't make it up Drifton Hill. Or down it, for that matter."

"Won't it be plowed or gritted or whatever?" asked Merlin.

"Londoner," said Susan. "It's a local road. If the snow's heavy the council will plow it in a few days at best. Or the Parments might do it, they've got a plow they put on one of their big tractors. But they usually only do from their farm west to Shire Hill, not in our direction."

"We'll get Cameron to send a Land Rover," said Vivien. "Give us time for a cup of tea and a snack. And I'll take another look at that cut, Merlin."

"I think it's stopped bleeding again," said Merlin. "But thanks. And thank you for coming to get me out of that place. Both of you."

They walked on across the lawn, which was already a few inches deep in snow. Susan was about to open the heavy kitchen door when Merlin stopped her.

"Wait. There's voices," he said. "Sounds like some sort of mass incantation!"

"I can't hear anything," whispered Susan.

"I can," said Vivien dubiously. "Very faint. I don't think it's—"

"It's not from the house," said Merlin, turning his head like a dog alerted to a suspicious sound. "It's coming from your mum's studio."

He put down the bag, opened it, and took out the Smython. Swiftly reloading, he held it ready and started towards the barn Jassmine used as her painting workshop. But as soon as he was close enough to look in the window, he stopped, and a few seconds later did an about-turn and came back, returning the revolver to his bag and snapping it shut.

"What?" asked Susan.

"Radio," said Merlin sheepishly. "Flying Pickets. 'Only You.'"

"That song is *everywhere*," said Vivien.

"Yeah, Mum must hear it ten times a day at the moment," said Susan. "She likes to have the radio on. Was she painting?"

"Yes," replied Merlin. "A very large canvas, something quite abstract. She was actually *throwing* paint at it, totally oblivious to anything else."

"She'll be hours, then. Come on, let's get inside. I'm freezing."

After ditching their footgear in favor of various non-matching slippers from the box in the boot room, and toweling their hair and faces dry with new and fluffy towels hung there for this purpose (surprising Vivien and Merlin, who'd expected the usual old ragged ones with the paint stains), they emerged into the welcome warmth of the kitchen, thanks to the AGA. As always coming in from a cold night, it was almost too warm at first.

Susan returned the fur tippet to Merlin, filled the kettle, and put it on the hob, while Vivien went along the corridor to the sitting room to find the phone—which Jassmine often buried under cushions on the lounge—to call the Small Bookshop. Merlin asked if he could borrow some of her clothes, and after Susan had stopped laughing she agreed he could have whatever might fit him, which since he was both taller and slighter than her, would be not much.

"I'm sure I can find something," said Merlin, looking down at his torn and now very dirty dress. He climbed the stair in the corner, instinctively ducking his head at the turn. The farmhouse had originally been built in medieval times and though updated in various parts, the low ceilings on the stairs were a danger to anyone of even medium height.

Left in the kitchen alone, Susan determined from the state of the washing up—the breakfast dishes still waiting, with no additions—and the larder that Jassmine had forgotten all about tea and supper and had probably been painting ever since she got back from Bath.

She set out the butter dish; a wheel of cave-aged cheddar in its wax armor; a wholemeal loaf Jassmine had baked the day before; two not very tasty tomatoes and half a lettuce from the big Sainsbury's in Chippenham; a jar of Branston pickle; some Dijon mustard; and five bite-sized (if you had a very large mouth) pork pies that came from the Parment Farm shop up the road. Susan's mother must have bought them on the way home and then forgotten to eat any.

Vivien returned from her mission first, which was unsurprising as Merlin's involved clothes. She took the offered mug of tea with a glad cry and pulled a stool up to the kitchen counter to attack the food.

"They sorted out those gargoyles," she said. "Cameron said they were hunting the last one when whatever animated it left and it became simple stone again, slid off the roof, and shattered into a dozen pieces. Luckily it was up the back, only lefties below, no public, and they were quick enough to get out of the way. I guess that's when the Ancient Sovereign came into the garden after us."

"Have they identified it? The entity I mean?"

"Not yet. But the Small Bookshop is a hornet's nest right

now, Una's just arrived with more sinisters and Great-Aunt Evangeline got in from Brighton at about six with a bunch of senior aunts and uncles from the right-handed side. Everyone's taking it very seriously. And that was before I told them about the bodies in the tower. Gosh, these pork pies are good with the pickle. And what kind of tea is this? It's great."

"A blend a friend of mum's sends from Sri Lanka," said Susan. "An admirer from the past, I think. It doesn't have a label or anything. We get a kind of small bale of it twice a year. I used to wonder if it was actually used to smuggle drugs to Mum. Before I knew it wasn't drugs that made her mind go peculiar."

Jassmine's unusual thought processes and absent-mindedness were classic symptoms of close and personal exposure to a powerful mythic entity, in this case Susan's father. Not everyone was affected in this way, but it was common. Susan had been told by Vivien that it could have been even worse. Ordinary mortals exposed to the entities or Old World environments sometimes dropped dead from heart failure, developed medical conditions that defied modern diagnosis, or had very serious mental health issues.

Merlin came down when Susan and Vivien were on their second cups of tea and debating whether to save him any pork pies or not. His appearance caused Susan to blink and Vivien to laugh and mutter "It's a Dexy's Midnight Runner" under her breath, which was easily heard by her sibling, who ignored it with visible effort.

He was wearing a cream pullover and a pair of tan bib and

brace overalls that were too big for him across the hips and too short in the trouser department, revealing at least four inches of sock above his slippered feet.

Susan got up and made herself busy making a new pot of tea. Merlin sat on a stool, his overall pants riding up even more.

"It is mortification enough to have to wear this," he said. "Without any comments from you, Vivien."

"Fair enough," said his sister. She hummed a little "too loo rye ay," but stopped when she saw Merlin was really rather upset.

"You got through to Cameron?" asked Merlin. He saw Vivien about to reach for the last pork pie and forestalled her with a lightning snatch. "Piglet. How many of these have you already eaten?"

"Hardly any, and yes, I got through to Cameron," said Vivien. "All is serene right now, but Una and Evangeline have chosen to personally take charge, and they want us back immediately. There's a police Land Rover coming to pick us up. I guess it'll be here in about half an hour, maybe longer if the snow is worse than it looks."

Merlin said something incomprehensible, as he was chewing vigorously on the pork pie. Susan poured him a mug of tea, to which he added three sugars and a lot of milk.

"Speaking of piglets, I couldn't understand what you just grunted out with your mouth full," said Vivien.

"Do they want Susan to come in?" asked Merlin.

Vivien looked across at Susan. "Cameron didn't say. I guess it's up to you, Susan. Do you want to come in with us or stay here?"

Susan frowned down at her cup, thinking. She felt herself at a turning point. Caught up in bookseller business again, but this time it had nothing to do with her. She didn't need to be involved.

"It is up to you," said Merlin. "At this point, anyway."

Susan looked up from her tea.

"What would happen if I were just a regular person who'd got involved in this?" she asked.

"Well, you wouldn't have been involved," said Vivien. "I only asked you because I knew you could make a translocation map. No ordinary mortal could do that."

Susan looked at Merlin, who was unusually silent. He met her gaze and slowly said, "I know what you mean. I suppose we'd make you come with us, and then have to work out what to do with you. And it probably wouldn't be anything good. But you're not ordinary, Susan. You're unique and special, in many different ways. You do have the choice. This, and . . . and everything else. But there are also consequences that are unavoidable."

Susan nodded slowly and took a sip of her tea. It was too hot and burned her tongue, which was annoying.

"Have you still got my map?"

"Um, yes," said Vivien, tapping her blouse. It made a cardboardy thud, indicating she had shoved the map under it. "I was going to tell you . . . it's better you don't keep it. We should make sure it's safe. I was very confident you'd be able to make a good translocation map—and you did—but there's often a case of diminishing returns with this sort of thing. Quite literally, in that if you try to use it again it might not work properly and you wouldn't get back to your little island in the brook but might end up somewhere else entirely. Or nowhere. Which would be . . ."

"Worse than death," said Merlin. "Being sort of alive forever, trapped. Probably. We don't really know."

"Okay," said Susan. She nodded decisively. "You keep the map."

"And will you come back with us to Bath tonight?" asked Merlin.

Susan hesitated.

"I only have tomorrow with Mum anyway. I've got a seat booked on the 2:16 from Chippenham."

"Do you have to go back to Town?" asked Vivien.

"I have been told that 'no matter what other institutions may do, the Slade insists on students attending the last week of term,'" said Susan. "I have a painting and an artist's statement to finish, anyway."

"But you're here for Christmas, aren't you?" asked Merlin. They had briefly discussed whether they could get together over the Christmas break, so he knew Susan was planning to spend it here with her mother. He had hoped to get some time off to be with her, but it was the busiest time of the year for the St. Jacques, the bookshops would be heaving with customers right up until the last minute on Christmas Eve; and it was also very busy for their other activities, with the winter solstice a time of change in the mythic world, of doors opening and closing, of bindings being broken and remade.

"I am, but Mum has invited at least five friends, possibly more, so we won't have any time together when I come back next weekend. And we're making Christmas puddings tomorrow. Mum always misses Stir-Up Sunday and does it later."

"It might not be safe for you to stay here by yourself," said Merlin. He looked at Vivien. "Are you sure that Ancient Sovereign won't know where the lion statue is? Or could track Susan from where we came back?"

"You know I can't be *absolutely* certain," said Vivien testily as she made an end-run around Merlin's blocking hand to nab the wedge of cheddar he'd just cut.

"What if the entity does find and reanimate that lion?"

Vivien was quiet for a moment, but it was because she was trying to swallow the imperfectly chewed cheese.

"You're probably as safe here as anywhere," she said finally to Susan. "Safer. Those guardians of the earth, air, and water your father set to guard you are not trifling entities."

"I *can* feel their presence," agreed Susan. "I suppose they'd at least give me warning."

"They'd do more than that," said Vivien with conviction. She hesitated, then added, "And if they failed for some reason against something like that stone lion, or some other danger, you do have powers of your own. In fact, it would be sensible to prepare yourself to use them."

Susan followed Vivien's glance to the large blue-and-white delft saltshaker.

"Salt and steel and blood," said Susan slowly. "To bind someone . . . or something . . . to my service. I told you I don't want to do that. Besides, would it even work on stone? I thought you said an open wound . . ."

"Blood to blood is swiftest," said Vivien. "But as long as you make contact it will work. At the least it would disrupt the entity's control, and if she was inhabiting it herself, you might even be able to overcome her. Do you remember what you need to say?"

"Yes," said Susan shortly.

She remembered. *I am your master. You will serve me.*

"It's only a precaution," said Merlin, understanding her reluctance. "If you always carry a knife and some salt you probably won't have to use them. It's kind of like an umbrella and rain. Here, I've got just the knife for you."

He rummaged in his bag and pulled out a 1930s army-issue clasp knife in mint condition, black bexoid grips gleaming. He opened it to demonstrate the marlinspike, can opener, and, most important, the blade, which was impressively sharp.

"It looks like the regular issue," explained Merlin, "but this one was made by Harshton and Hoole. The knife is astonishingly sharp and both it and the marlinspike are washed in silver. The can opener is quite handy, too. Please, I want you to take it. Keep it on you. Just in case."

"And some salt," said Vivien. She glanced around, saw a large Ship brand matchbox on the windowsill and grabbed it. Emptying the matches out, she filled it with salt from the shaker and set it down on the table in front of Susan.

"And in case of some more mundane enemies, you can have this," Merlin added, dipping into his bag again. He pulled out a nickel-finished Colt Cobra short-barreled .38 revolver. "It's very similar to the Smith and Wesson Model 10 you fired at the range with me."

Merlin had taken Susan to the Metropolitan Police's range at Lippitts Hill twice, in the dead of night when it catered to "other services," usually MI5 or MI6. The booksellers had their own ranges at Thorn House and elsewhere, but the police facility was closer to London.

"I don't want a gun," said Susan, shaking her head. "I don't want to shoot anyone, and anyway it's all been statues so far and it would be useless for that. Why do you think there might be mundane enemies anyway? Aren't you both overreacting?"

"We don't know," said Vivien.

"That's the trouble," said Merlin. He didn't return the .38 to the bag, instead slipping it into the bib pocket of his overalls. "This Ancient Sovereign is unknown to us, clearly very powerful, and a killer. Maybe it's vindictive. Maybe it has mortal worshippers or subjects. Until we can identify it and sort it out, you might be in danger."

"Why me in particular? What about you?"

"Well, not just you in particular," said Merlin. "The thing is, she might be able to work out who we are because we were in her special garden. I don't know how it works but—"

"Because you never paid attention at Wooten," interrupted

Vivien. "Simplistically, the entity will remember our essential natures, which cannot be easily disguised or hidden, so would be able to recognize us as the trespassers. But only if we were in her presence, so I don't think we need to worry for the moment."

"But it is possible," continued Merlin. "If that Old One tracks me or Vivien down, that's okay, it could even be handy. But if she finds you—"

"I just want to spend some time with my mum," protested Susan. "And finish my first term at the Slade! That's all. I want to be allowed to get on with . . . with normal things!"

"I know," said Merlin regretfully. "I wish we could make it so. I wish *I* could. But we can't. We can only help you make your life as normal as possible under the—"

He stopped talking and tilted his head to listen, though once again Susan couldn't hear anything. "A vehicle just turned off the road and is coming down the track. A Land Rover. Our ride back to Bath, I imagine. Look, if you won't come with us tonight, can I take you back to London tomorrow afternoon? Don't just go on the train by yourself. The snow shouldn't be a problem, I've got Emilia's Range Rover back in Bath."

"You have?" asked Vivien in surprise. "Does she *know* you've got it? I mean, after her Jensen—"

"Yes, she knows," said Merlin testily.

"I guess I'll need a lift to the station at least," said Susan slowly. She was thinking about what he had said. "As normal as possible" was not a comforting situation to be in. But anything else was probably a pipe dream. "Thanks."

"Don't leave the vicinity of the house," said Merlin. "Promise me. Just in case."

"I have no intention of going anywhere," said Susan. "Except into the bath. That is, a hot bath in this house. While you go to Bath. Take care."

Merlin slid his stool back, stuffed another piece of cheddar in his mouth, chewed it twice, and swallowed before swooping around to kiss and hug Susan. Despite the cheddar breath, she kissed him back and held him for a moment.

"I'll pick you up around twelve, okay?"

Susan nodded.

"Come on, Eileen," said Vivien from the door. She opened it, and the cold from the boot room invaded the kitchen. Merlin growled and followed, shutting the inner door behind him.

CHAPTER EIGHT

North of Bath, Sunday, 11th December 1983

Ball. *To open the ball. To lead off the first dance
at a ball. (Italian, ballaro, to dance.)*

DEEP, DEEP BENEATH THE MOUNTAIN THAT MORTALS CALLED THE
Old Man of Coniston, Susan Arkshaw wandered, slipping
through stone like a ghost, cupping molten copper in her hands,
lifting with ease the heaviest hammer the Knockers had in their
workshops, to work the iron they drew up from even deeper in
the ground. The Knockers gathered around her, watching her
work, nodding with every blow of hammer on hot iron, hammer
on anvil, the rhythm of the forge. She was many miles below the
surface, but she was comfortable there, it was her place, where
she was meant to be—

"Susan. Wake up."

Susan woke, in darkness, though it had been light under
the earth. She was disoriented for a moment, before she came
awake enough to reach across, switch on her bedside light, and

look around. She was unsure why she'd woken. It took a few seconds of sleepy, thick-witted thought to remember someone had called out to her. But the house was quiet, and there was no one in her room.

She went to the window and looked out. It was very dark outside, but in the spill of light from her window she could see snow falling. Light snow, almost ambling its way from sky to ground, snowflakes drifting sideways and even whisking upward from time to time before they fell again.

As she watched the snow fall, Susan was surprised to find she could make out more detail than she expected. The outline of the studio barn, the silhouette of the massive chestnut where the ravens roosted. Perhaps the sky was clearing, she thought, but it couldn't be, as the snow continued to come down.

Susan frowned, walked back to her bed, and turned off the light. Even with it out, she could see the basic shapes of the room, as if everything were sketched in charcoal, all bold lines and quick fill. But she shouldn't be able to; she knew it was the middle of the night and fully dark.

Then she remembered her dream of Coniston, of being in the tunnels and diggings made by mortal copper miners and before them, by the Knockers and other things of the deep earth. She had been able to see there, in the same sort of way, everything in shades of grey.

This was what Merlin had meant in the tower, Susan realized. He had expected her to be able to see in the dark, as the child of the Old Man of Coniston. It was another aspect of the inheritance she both desired and feared.

Susan returned to the window and opened it to the chill night air and occasional incursion of snow. She knew who had called to her now, and she looked over to the brook.

The entity that inhabited the water stood on the bank. Taller and larger than when Susan had seen it before, it was at least ten feet tall today. Made from weed and swirling water and sticks of willow, its torso had a new addition, a corselet of river pebbles, wet and shiny as steel. Its head, usually appearing as a tubular basket of woven alder roots, was obscured by a massive helmet of swirling water and river sand. The entity was girded as if for battle.

But if there had been a battle, the brook creature had won. Its long arms of braided willow withies held the stone lion that had pursued them from the tower. Despite the fact that the statue must weigh several tons, the brook creature clearly had no difficulty lifting it, and in fact must have carried the statue down from the island upstream. Gazing at the entity, Susan for the first time realized it was not a creature simply of the gentle, murmuring stream that usually flowed past the house, it also had the torrential power of a "one in five hundred year" flood that could wreak total destruction for miles.

Susan opened her mouth to ask it why on earth it had brought the lion there, but shut it without speaking a word, as she heard and felt the low rumble of earth moving. When she looked across, the stone dragon was coming out from under the hill. Though it wasn't actually a dragon. It was hard to say what it was, save a massive outcrop of stone that from the right angle and with the element of fear, could be taken for a giant reptile.

Susan was not afraid of it, or of the brook entity. She felt, as much as knew, that they would not harm her, that her father's compact with them still held good. Perhaps they would help her anyway, regardless, like old friends.

The brook creature stepped out of the stream and sloshed across the paved area, lifting the stone lion high. Susan noticed the water pouring from its arms had gouged deep grooves in the lion's hide—the Purbeck marble of fossilized shellfish did not stand up well to high-pressure water.

The hill creature came to meet it, a cavern analogous to a mouth yawning wide. The brook entity lifted the stone lion high and threw it in. The opening closed and there was a muffled, distant grinding sound. Like coffee beans being ground, but grittier.

"Thank you," said Susan.

"I watch and ward," said the thing from the brook. It turned and strode towards the stream. This time, it did not diminish to leave a trail of flood debris, but waded into the water, gradually becoming one with it. It was still on guard.

"You are stone," said Susan to the hill creature, though she could see little of it now, just a ridge of dark rock thrusting up through the grass, like the dorsal fin of a shark, on a much larger scale. "Who is the entity who made the stone lion move? What is her name? Where can she be found?"

"I know not," came a deep rumble from far below, so deep Susan wasn't sure if she heard it with her ears or understood it in some other way. "This stone was once a multitude of small living things, it was born of the sea and time and pressure. It did not come from the deep fires, it is not of my kin. I know not. I watch and ward."

The ridge of stone sank into the earth and the turf closed above it, not entirely meeting up, which would perhaps be taken for a sign of a minor slippage of the hill if anyone saw it. But they probably wouldn't, for it would be covered in snow again by first light.

Susan felt the presence of the two entities dim. She could sense the raven entity watching, too, or the ravens. She was never sure if it was one special raven or all of them together who made up the mythic creature who lived in the chestnut. It was curious, watchful, and as always more alert than the other two. But it wasn't indicating any threat or approaching danger. She heard it call, too, in its hoarse, drawn-out raven caw.

"We watch and ward."

Susan shut the window and went back to bed, shivering as she pulled sheet, blankets, and quilt tightly against herself. Within a minute she was asleep again, and as before with her guardian entities, the experience she'd just had drifted from memory into dream and back again, before settling uncertainly somewhere in between.

Susan woke the second time to the sound of a ringing phone downstairs. It was still dark. She had no idea of the time until she stretched out a hand to turn the clock radio's face to a readable position and saw the bright-red LED numbers telling her it was 7:22, and groaned. Hardly anyone called her mother, because they knew Jassmine rarely answered the phone. A call this early on a Sunday morning was bound to be for Susan, and given recent events it was certain to be a bookseller, probably Merlin.

Slipping on a pair of fleecy tracksuit pants under the over-sized T-shirt she slept in, but without bothering with slippers, Susan gingerly trod down the cold stone steps and hurried into the living room. The telephone, thanks to Vivien using it the night before, was sitting on a corner of the lounge rather than buried under a cushion. Susan picked up the handset and said crankily, "What?"

"Is that Susan?" asked a woman. Her patrician, authoritative voice sounded vaguely familiar to Susan, but not enough to know who she was.

"Yes, it is, and why are you calling me this early on a Sunday morning?"

"My apologies, Susan. This is Evangeline St. Jacques."

"Oh," replied Susan. Merlin and Vivien's Great-Aunt Evangeline, who had healed Susan's collarbone after it was broken diving into the Copper Cauldron, and who was now the head of the right-handed booksellers. A sudden fear struck the young woman. "Is Merlin . . . are Merlin and Vivien okay?"

"Yes, they are fine," said Evangeline. "My great-nephew and great-niece have told me you don't wish to be involved in our current problem in Bath, and they didn't want me to call you.

They are embarrassed. I am not easily embarrassed. We need your help, Susan."

"My help?" asked Susan. She was still waking up. "Look, I realize I was needed to go after Merlin but—"

"Yes, and we are very grateful for that. But as is often the case, the reward for a good deed is more work. You see, we need to ask Sulis Minerva some questions, and she has said she will only speak to you."

"Sulis Minerva? The Ancient Sovereign of the Roman Baths? I was told to stay away from her demesne! You told me. I mean, Vivien told me, but said it was from higher up."

"Yes, we did think it best you be kept away from Ancient Sovereigns in general," said Evangeline. "And Sulis Minerva can be quite tricky and, given her many followers, is very powerful. It is fortunate she is constrained by proximity to her spring. Or at least her avatar is so constrained, she is able to extend her thoughts and senses more widely. She knows you were at the Small Bookshop yesterday, and she knows something about who is behind the animated statues. But she won't tell us. She'll only speak to you."

"Why me?"

"We don't know. She has some connection with your father. It is possible she might owe him a debt. This may be from the time he was courting your mother and visited Bath, or from longer ago, perhaps even in Roman times or earlier still. Ancient Sovereigns have complicated relationships with each other, as allies or enemies, or via shared interests or similarities of mythic power or responsibilities, and they often trade favors. Sometimes these are related to mortals or mortal concerns. In any case, it seems she is well disposed towards you and she will answer the questions we want you to ask."

Susan smiled as she listened to Evangeline. The right-handed booksellers simply couldn't help themselves explaining things, often in excruciating detail. In this case, it was handy, and Susan wanted to know more.

"She won't answer you directly?"

"No. We are always somewhat at odds, because we watch her visitors and cull the troublesome. She considers this to be lèse-majesté. We could compel her, but it would be difficult and dangerous, and there would be complications for the fabric of the city and the ordinary folk of Bath we'd rather avoid. So will you help us?"

"Will I be in danger?" asked Susan.

"Not from Sulis Minerva," replied Evangeline. "She has sworn no harm will come to you from her or her followers, should you visit. As with many Ancient Sovereigns her word is quite literally her bond. We would be very grateful—"

"Okay, okay," said Susan. She sighed. "I'll talk to her. But I have to be back in London by tonight."

"We'll make sure you get back in time," said Evangeline. "I'll have a police Land Rover sent to pick you up."

"Not Merlin?" asked Susan, feeling a slight pang. "He offered, I mean he was going to come later today but—"

"I have instructed Merlin to rest his wounded leg," said

Evangeline. "As with most of our left-handed family, he is inclined to keep going when he should be lying down. There is a relatively low probability you are at risk from the entity you encountered in the encysted garden."

"A *relatively* low probability? What does that mean?"

"I'm sure you'll be safe," soothed Evangeline. "Now then. Inspector Torrant, our local liaison, is going to come and get you herself. She is a very broad-shouldered, imposing woman; you'll recognize her easily. The Land Rover will be a marked police vehicle."

"The snow—"

"The gritters and plows have been out all night. There should be little difficulty," said Evangeline. "I look forward to seeing you soon."

Susan put the phone down.

"Little difficulty," she muttered. "Relatively low probability! Slightly weaselly words! And *encysted* sounds horrible."

She went into the kitchen and put the kettle on, then looked out the window. The lights from Jassmine's studio were out. Susan felt a sudden fear steal her breath, and swiftly went to the stairs at the other end of the house that led up to her mother's room, not noticing the cold stone underfoot this time, and peered around the slightly open door. She was relieved to catch sight of Jassmine in her four-poster bed with the red velvet curtains. Her mother was curled up and, on closer inspection, Susan saw the slight rise and fall of her chest under the covers.

She retreated back to the kitchen and sat in thought until the kettle started to whistle. She removed it from the hob before its astonishingly powerful whistle could wake Jassmine, made tea and marmalade toast, using the last of the good homemade orange marmalade that had more than a dash of Campari in it. A little later she boiled an egg as well and ate it with more toast, cut into soldiers.

Still clean from her very long bath of the night before, Susan dressed in M&S underwear her mother had unsuccessfully tie-dyed so it looked like weird camo; a faded men's red flannel shirt with press stud buttons from a country-and-western singer friend of Jassmine's; black tights; and then over it all a 1950s silk ski suit her mother had reluctantly parted with from her wardrobe the winter before. It was a faded gold color and had a large hood that folded back down to become an impressive collar. Since Susan almost never wore the hood up, she added a very dark and earthy mud-colored herringbone Harris Tweed Stornoway cap to keep her shorn head warm. Woolen socks went over the tights and her ubiquitous Doc Martens awaited in the boot room. The final touch was to pick up her toothbrush from the bathroom. That was all she took between her student accommodation in London and home. She had enough clothes in both places.

Downstairs, after a brief hesitation, Susan put the folding knife in a pocket of the ski suit. She picked up the matchbox full of salt, frowned at the pile of loose matches on the kitchen table, took out the silver cigarette case she always carried—the one that had been made for her father—and transferred the salt to that, before repacking the matchbox with the spilled matches. After another moment's thought, she put the matches in a pocket as well, and added a three-inch stub of a beeswax candle from the collection under the sink.

She was thinking about what else she might need when she heard the sound of a vehicle slowly negotiating the driveway down from the road, crunching new ice over snow. Headlights flickered across the kitchen window as the car turned around in the large parking area outside another of the repurposed barns, this one the garage for the Mini.

Susan looked out the window. It wasn't snowing anymore, but at least half the portion of sky she could see was covered in low, thick grey clouds that were slowly moving to cover the whole, so more snow would be coming. There was a distant glow in the sky to indicate the sun was rising, though it would not be seen down here for a while, or perhaps not at all given the encroaching clouds.

A Somerset & Avon Police Land Rover, the van style with no rear windows, parked facing back up the drive, the engine running and lights on. The driver got out and stretched. Her arms were huge, and she was about twice as broad across the shoulders as Susan. Her three-quarter-length black nylon raincoat with white "Police" markings would have made two raincoats for most people. She had jet-black hair and brown skin. It had to be Inspector Torrant.

"What do *they* want?" hissed a suspicious voice behind Susan, making her jump. Jassmine had emerged. Out from under the covers it was clear she was still wearing her painting clothes, and her hands were spattered with rainbow drops. "Let's pretend we aren't here! Come upstairs."

"It's okay," said Susan soothingly. "She's just here to give me a lift into town. The booksellers need me again."

Jassmine frowned and didn't say anything for a full second.

"Don't let anyone see you, then," she said. "They'll think you're a snitch."

"No, they won't," said Susan.

"They won't if no one sees you."

"Okay, Mum, I'll keep a low profile," said Susan with a sigh. "And I'll probably go straight on from Bath back to London. But I'll see you next Friday, or Saturday morning at the latest."

"If you don't end up locked away in some secret prison," said Jassmine.

"I won't, Mum," said Susan. She reached out for a hug, and they held each other tight for a few seconds. Some of the paint on Jassmine was not entirely dry and came off on Susan's ski suit, but neither of them minded.

Susan hesitated, then added, "You be careful, too. Maybe don't go anywhere until I get back. Stay close to home."

"I have work," said Jassmine simply. Whether this was in agreement or a statement that she wouldn't be going anywhere until her painting or paintings were finished, Susan didn't know. But it would have to do.

There was a cautious "not to wake anyone who wasn't already up" knock on the outer door. Susan kissed Jassmine on the cheek and nipped into the boot room, shutting the door quickly to keep in the heat.

"We were going to make puddings!" shouted Jassmine through the door.

"Sorry," yelled Susan back as she put on her Docs. She turned to the outer door and called out, "I'll be out in a minute, Inspector!"

When she'd laced her boots, Susan sorted through the umbrellas that were piled up in the corner, selecting a Brigg & Sons oak and black silk number from the 1920s that might have been her great-grandmother's. Jassmine had once referred to it as "grandmama's prodding stick" but as per usual later on would not answer direct questions about its provenance. In any case, it was an impressively solid umbrella and could also be used as a walking stick, or with its heavy bronze ferrule, as a weapon.

The air was very crisp outside. Torrant was marching up and down the path, swinging her arms, billows of frosty breath coming from her mouth. She stopped as Susan came out, turned towards her, and smiled. It was a professional sort of smile and didn't touch her eyes.

"Miss Arkshaw. I'm Inspector Torrant, here to take you into Bath."

"Thank you, Inspector," said Susan. "I hope it isn't too much of an inconvenience."

"Not at all," said Torrant. "To tell you the truth I was happy to come out. Never seen so many of your lot on my patch, I was feeling a bit claustrophobic. Not to mention paranoid."

"My lot?" asked Susan as they walked over to the Land Rover. "You mean the . . ."

"Booksellers," confirmed Torrant. She opened the passenger door for Susan to get in before walking around the front and climbing in her side, the whole vehicle rocking as she did so. "Seat belt on, please. I apologize for the so-called heating. It's warm enough but smells like exhaust fumes, so we'll need to keep the windows open a crack."

"I'm not one of the booksellers," said Susan, keen to make this clear. She slid the umbrella down next to the door where she could grab it easily. She looked behind but there was a solid partition between the front seats and the rear, with a sliding panel, which was closed. "I'm just helping with something."

"So Cameron told me," said Torrant. "Which is not something I've come across before with our bookseller friends. A consultant! They'll be hiring public relations people next. So you're a curiosity. That's one of the reasons I was happy to take on this driving job. I wanted to have a look at you."

She put the car in gear with some effort, cursed the venerable age of the vehicle, and they began to slowly crawl up the driveway to the road, which was actually narrower than the driveway, little more than a narrow lane cut into the side of the hill higher up.

"I see," said Susan.

"I also didn't want to put one of my officers at risk," said Torrant. She craned her head forward to look both ways before turning right into Drifton Hill. It would have been surprising to see another vehicle on a snowy Sunday morning on an ungritted single lane road, but you never knew.

"At risk?" asked Susan. "Is there something specific you're supposed to warn me about?"

"Not that anyone's told me," said Torrant. They continued the slow crawl, with the occasional squeal of a wheel slipping. The Land Rover was in four-wheel drive mode, and it needed to be to get up the slope. The snow was only three or four inches deep, but there was a good layer of ice on top. "But then they don't go in for sharing information, much. All I know is the booksellers wanted an armed officer to escort you, which is a mite suggestive."

Susan couldn't help glancing across. If Torrant had a firearm, it was under her massive raincoat.

As they neared the top of the rise, the radio under the dash crackled and a badly distorted voice said something Susan couldn't understand. Torrant picked up the handset and spoke into it.

"Bath Central, this is Whisky One-One, I have the package and we are en route, Stage One. Over."

The distorted voice spoke again. This time Susan understood it to say, "Roger. Confirm Stage One. Out."

Torrant replaced the handset.

"I'm a package, am I?" asked Susan.

"People listen to our radio sometimes," said Torrant. "We're on an alternative frequency but still best not to say too much."

"All part of that low probability of me being at risk, I guess," said Susan.

"Who said that?" asked Torrant.

Susan was about to answer, but she stopped herself. After a minute or so, Torrant spoke again.

"So, what exactly is it you do for the booksellers? Consultant-wise?"

"If you don't already know, I can't say," said Susan.

Torrant laughed and shook her head.

"Guess I asked for that one. We had better continue in dignified silence."

It was easier going once they topped the hill, and though the road was still called Drifton Hill, it was mostly flat, a single lane running between low stone walls and snow-covered fields. They had yet to meet any other vehicles.

Just before they reached the intersection with Shire Hill that later became Tormarton Road, it started to snow again. Torrant sighed and turned the wipers on, which mostly smeared melting snow across the windscreen rather than cleaning it. With the snow increasing and the clouds lowering, the visibility dropped to less than a hundred yards and they had to slow down.

"Still got the original wiper blades I reckon, from about 1970," said Torrant as they turned southward. Shire Hill was a slightly more important road and for a short stretch here was even two lanes wide. Or to be fair, more like one and three-quarter lanes wide. "Budget cuts. Can't afford anything as supposedly nonessential as wiper blades."

Torrant picked up the handset as they picked up speed. There was still no traffic.

"Bath Central, Whisky One-One, Stage Two. Confirm. Over."
The radio crackled.

"Roger, confirm Stage Two. Over."

"Thanks. Whisky One-One out."

"You seem very cautious if there's nothing to be cautious about," said Susan.

"Just routine," said Torrant. "If something happens to us, it'll be too late, of course, but they'll have a better idea of where to start looking for our bodies."

"Do you know Inspector Greene?" asked Susan. "Special Branch?"

"Mira Greene? Of course. She rocked up late last night, with some of her oppos."

"What? To Bath?" asked Susan. "Why? She's Metropolitan Police."

"Now it's my turn to say if you don't already know I can't tell you," said Torrant. "Except I will anyway. Her lot, Section M, have national responsibilities, like Special Branch in general. Home Office says all of us turnip-heads and yokels have to cooperate, bend our necks and so forth when they come trumpeting out of London to show us how it's done."

"And you resent it," said Susan.

"Nah," said Torrant. She sounded more serious. "I'm actually grateful when they take over anything to do with the book-sellers. I don't want us to be involved if we can avoid it. And I certainly don't envy Mira Greene her job. She's lasted longer than most in it."

"What do you mean?"

"There's quite a few former heads of Section M in padded rooms," said Torrant. "Or on memorial plaques. Far more even than anti-terrorism or EOD or other pointy-end stuff."

"EOD?"

"Explosive ordnance disposal. Bomb disposal. So you get the idea."

Torrant rubbed her elbow against the window to clear it, since it had fogged up, and Susan saw it was to get a better look through to her wing mirror. Susan did the same on her side and saw the flare of headlights behind them.

"Car coming up behind," she said. She glanced at the mirror again. The vehicle behind wasn't closing rapidly or anything, it was just following normally. But Susan still felt suddenly tense, even though she told herself not to be ridiculous. How many times had she gone into Bath, driving herself or being driven, and not given a moment's particular thought to the cars behind or ahead, except as part of the overall traffic?

"A lorry," said Torrant. She didn't seem concerned. "Old Bedford, I reckon."

The lorry followed them, not too close, down Tormarton Road and stayed behind when they turned right into the A420 at Marshfield, where Torrant radioed in to Bath Central again. There was a little more traffic on this road, all driving carefully, even more so when Torrant flicked a switch and the dome light above them began to light up the falling snow with lurid flashes of blue.

"Keeps everyone on their toes," said Torrant.

Susan noticed the inspector kept a careful eye on her mirror as well as on the vehicles ahead. When they reached the Cold Ashton roundabout and turned on to the A46 and the lorry that had been behind them didn't follow but kept straight on, Susan felt a sense of relief, though as far as she could tell Torrant had no reaction.

The A46 had been plowed and gritted earlier, and it was busy enough that the salt had been well dispersed, so it had only a thin layer of snow from the fall that had just begun. They picked up speed a little, despite there being more traffic. Torrant kept the blue dome light flashing.

Usually there would be a good view out to the west, but right now there was only the grey blur of low cloud and snow falling. Susan's legs were too warm from the Land Rover's inefficient heater, and almost too cold above the waist, with the wind whistling in the one-inch gap she'd left in the window as instructed, so as not to asphyxiate from the engine fumes. Theoretically this should have helped defrost the windows, but it didn't seem to, and if there was any hot air coming out of the car's weird add-on demisting vents it was not enough. Torrant kept wiping the windscreen with her arm and leaning forward to try to see better, the wipers outside not helping much either.

Susan was just beginning to think there was absolutely no reason to be anxious when they swept around a bend on a slight incline before the road began to descend towards Bath. There was a stone house built close to the road and as they approached,

121

three men suddenly came out from behind it, each pushing a wheelbarrow. They were clad in blue overalls with woolen jumpers on top, which was fairly typical for manual workers, but also wore long white leather aprons adorned with strange symbols, which was not.

Their wheelbarrows held large stone balls, like medieval cannonballs, twice the size of a basketball. All at once, the three of them upended their barrows and sent the balls rolling down the road, like bowling balls headed for the pins, with the Land Rover as the kingpin.

CHAPTER NINE

Close to Bath, Sunday, 11th December 1983

Purbeck. *Noted for a marble used in ecclesiastical ornaments.*

TORRANT CURSED, DOUBLE DECLUTCHED TO DROP DOWN A GEAR, pumped the brakes, and drove off the road to the left, as far as she could up the hillside without rolling the Land Rover over. The vehicle fishtailed on the icy verge, bucked over the drain, and then they were fully off the road with the left-hand wheels four feet higher than the right, the van at a terrifying angle. For a moment Susan thought all three of the massive stone bowling balls would miss, but the third one hit a pothole and veered off enough to head straight at them—

"Brace yourself! Bend your knees!" shouted Torrant, gripping the sash of her seat belt and leaning back. Susan copied her.

A moment later there was a horrendous bang, the shriek of crumpling metal, and the Land Rover slammed backwards, Torrant having taken her foot off the brake so the vehicle could move and absorb the momentum. It slid back a dozen yards, slewed across the gutter, rocked frighteningly close to overturning but didn't, and stopped.

Torrant banged the partition behind her twice and shouted, "Out! Out!" before unbuckling her seat belt and heaving the door open, moving much faster than Susan had thought she could. As the inspector jumped out, she drew a Browning Hi-Power pistol through a slit in the right-hand side of her raincoat and knelt behind the open door, peeking around it to shout up the road, "Armed Police! Stop and raise your hands!"

The inspector was answered by a shot that drilled through the window above her, showering her with glass. She snapped off two shots in reply and there was a scream of pain.

Susan bailed out of her side, grabbing the umbrella on the way. Leaving the door wide open she dropped prone and crawled into the gutter. Looking under the vehicle she could see one of the apron-wearing men was down on the road, now the source of a spreading river of bright-red blood, stark against the snow. A revolver lay near his open hand. The other two had taken cover, one in the same drain as Susan about forty yards farther up the road and slightly around the bend, the other behind the concrete end post of a crash barrier on the western side. Both had revolvers.

"We just want the girl!" shouted the man in the gutter. "Give us the girl and save yourself! We got help coming! You don't stand a chance!"

"Armed Police! Drop your weapons and come out into the

road with your hands over your head!" shouted Torrant again.

Susan heard the tailgate of the Land Rover crash open and heard a slithering on crushed snow. She whirled around, ready to lunge with her umbrella, but stopped herself at the last moment.

"Déjà vu," said Merlin, crawling around the left rear wheel to join her in the gutter. He was dressed in upmarket gumboots, hunting tweed plus fours, and a jacket with leather shoulder reinforcement, and carried a very large, long, and obviously heavy rifle on his back, holding it with the unusual monopod at the end of the barrel hooked over his shoulder. He rolled on his side, brushed some snow from his front, and maneuvered the weapon around, pushing it forward and bringing the butt to his shoulder. From there, he could fire under the vehicle at targets up the road, or at least at their lower extremities.

The tracksuit-clad Stephanie followed him, leopard-crawling with a Remington 870 Police Magnum pump-action shotgun cradled in her arms. She smiled at Susan and slithered around them and up the hillside, edging towards the curve so she could get a shot down at the two opponents.

Merlin moved the rifle slightly and chambered a round, the massive bolt clicking ominously.

"Tell 'em to surrender again, Inspector!" he shouted at Torrant. "Last warning!"

His voice was very loud, and disquieting to the aproned ambushers, who'd evidently thought Susan was only accompanied by a single officer.

"Ted?" shouted the one by the barrier, a host of nervous

questions contained in that one word. "What do we—"

In answer, the one in the drain—presumably Ted—rose up and charged along it, firing at Torrant, his shots high and wild, only one round striking the doorframe at the very top, ricocheting off with a spark and clang. His companion started shooting, too, his shots close enough to make Torrant drop prone.

Merlin fired at the charging man. There was a deafening boom and the man fell, screaming, the massive bullet taking off his right leg at the knee. A second later, two rapid shotgun blasts followed, Stephanie working the pump action so fast the distinctive ratchet click was lost in the second shot, and the man behind the end post who'd shouted for Ted was flung down into the snow and loose gravel by the roadside.

"What is that?" asked Susan, pointing at the rifle. Her voice sounded weird to her, barely audible over the ringing in her ears.

"Boys anti-tank rifle," said Merlin, chambering another round. He did not look at Susan, eyes intent on the road ahead under the car. "We were expecting animated statues, not Masons."

"You were in the back?" asked Susan.

"Of course," said Merlin. He raised his voice. "Steph?"

"All visible enemies down!" Stephanie answered from somewhere up the hillside and farther ahead.

"Stay low, Susan," instructed Merlin. "Steph, cover!"

He edged back from the rifle, rose to a crouch, and rushed forward to the man he'd shot. A knife appeared in Merlin's hand and for an awful moment Susan thought he was going to finish off the fallen attacker. But he cut the top strap from the man's apron and used it as a tourniquet. As he did so, the man swore at him and tried to land several ineffectual blows, but the effort was too much and he'd lost too much blood. Merlin merely fended him off until he fainted.

Torrant was up again and she was talking on the radio, her voice louder than normal, giving rapid orders.

Merlin picked up the attacker's revolver and brought it back to the Land Rover, throwing it in the passenger's side. He looked across at Torrant.

"He going to live?" asked Torrant.

"Maybe," said Merlin somberly. "Ambulance on the way?"

"Two ambulances and three armed response cars are en route, under ten minutes away. Uniform are stopping northbound traffic at Upper Swainswick, and my trail car should be here inside two minutes."

"You saw the aprons?" asked Merlin.

"Yeah," said Torrant sourly. "It explains a few things. Like how they knew we were coming. So much for your magical sensing bullshit when an informer can do the job."

"You've probably got fewer Freemasons than the Met," said Merlin consolingly. "And I doubt these are any of the regular kind anyway."

He pointed at the dead man. He had fallen on his back and his apron was clearly visible, the symbols of the square and compass stitched in gold, along with what at first glance looked like a Tudor rose, but on this one several petals were replaced with very large thorns.

"That rose thing is not your usual Freemason symbol. A rose cross maybe, but not that. Ties in with our hostile Ancient Sovereign, though."

Torrant shook her head.

"I didn't even think about the Masons being a problem," she said. "The ones I know for sure belong make no secret of it these days, and I've never been told they're involved in your weird shit. Are they?"

"Not the mainstream ones," said Merlin. "But there are a few unusual lodges. I should have thought of it. Freemasonry started among stonemasons centuries ago, after all. We'd better be careful. How about your tail car crew? Could they be Masons?"

"Too young, I reckon. The young ones don't join," said Torrant.

"Just be on guard," said Merlin. "And be suspicious of inter-ference, overt or otherwise. Who's the highest-ranking Mason you know?"

"There's a Superintendent Ledworth. He's got a photo on his desk of him in an apron, not trying to hide it or anything," said Torrant. "But he's Bristol local policing now. He wouldn't have any grounds to interfere, it'd be too obvious. One of the assistant chief constables *might* be a Mason—"

"Vehicle coming from the south!" shouted Steph.

Torrant swore, got up, holstered her weapon, and ran around the back of the Land Rover. Grabbing a stack of lurid orange traffic cones she sprinted up the road, past the body that sprawled right in the middle, the wounded assailant in the ditch, and the dead Mason by the guardrail, the one Stephanie had shot. Twenty yards past all that, at the bend, she dropped cones in a line across the road and stood off to one side, waving her left hand with her right hand holding the pistol behind her back. Snow swirled around her in little whirlwinds as she waved.

A white van came around the corner a fraction too fast for the conditions. The driver saw the cones, the body on the road, and the crashed police Land Rover. They slammed on the brakes, immediately skidded through the cones, and lost control. Torrant jumped aside as the van fishtailed wildly and slid off the road and smacked into the guardrail with a sickening crash. The windscreen shattered as the driver was flung out and down the even more precipitous western side of the hill.

The motor kept running, engine howling and wheels spinning, till Torrant raced over, opened the driver's door, reached in, and turned the ignition off.

In the sudden silence, Susan heard a siren coming from the north. She started to turn to look, but at that moment Merlin suddenly flung himself down next to her and grabbed the anti-tank rifle, swinging it around to point up the hillside, his back against the Land Rover.

Something large and very heavy came hurtling down the slope, smashing through bushes and undergrowth, sending snow-encrusted branches and foliage flying.

Merlin fired, worked the bolt, fired again. Stephanie came running, firing from the hip, again and again. The crack of the rifle and the boom of the shotgun echoed over Susan's head as she crawled down the drain and then rose up and turned, her umbrella held high. Whatever happened, she was not going to be killed lying down in a ditch.

A discolored, lichen-covered stone griffin lurched out of the bushes. One of its rear legs was missing, blown off by the Boys AT rifle, and there were divots all over its body from the shotgun solid slugs. But it still came on, heading straight for Susan. Merlin fired again as it passed, there was an almighty crack and stone chips spalled back, spattering him like shrapnel, but the creature ignored it and pressed on.

Stephanie dropped her shotgun, unable to get a clear shot, and raced up to grab the creature's tail. But even with her left-handed strength she couldn't hold the creature back. It dragged the bookseller forward, her heels scraping deep lines in the slush.

Susan flung open her umbrella and shoved it at the thing's head. It tried to reach around and grab Susan with its massive front paws, but she stepped back, leaving the umbrella between them. The griffin's massive eagle beak and lion talons closed on black silk and steel ribs and it tried to shake the umbrella free but instead got tangled up in a mare's nest of bent steel ribs and silk.

Confused by the umbrella and held back by Stephanie, the griffin was open to a more medieval attack. Merlin took a crowbar from the back of the Land Rover, stepped forward, lifted it high, and brought the pointy end down vertically between the creature's eyes. Its head split in two, cracks propagated from there all the way along its spine, and it fell in several jagged pieces and moved no more.

A Police Range Rover pulled up twenty yards behind them, lights flashing, the siren blaring out a last plaintive wail before it stopped. Two officers got out, pistols held down at their sides, and stood behind the open doors, staring at the shattered statue. They would have seen the whole attack.

Torrant did not give them time to wonder what the hell it was they actually saw.

"Jackson! Get a double line of cones and a sign across the road fifty yards back. Hazlet, grab some rope and a first aid kit and get yourself over the side here, there's a hurt civilian somewhere down the hill."

Stephanie walked back and picked up her shotgun, reloading it with solid slugs from her ubiquitous backpack. Merlin picked up the Boys and put it in the back of the Land Rover, replacing the five-shot magazine with a new loaded one from a green ammunition box. Susan, looking over his shoulder, saw several similar boxes, one marked "US Army Grenade Hand Offensive MK3A2" and there was also a wooden farm crate full of short crow and pry bars and some bricklayer's hammers. Merlin and Stephanie had come prepared.

"Why didn't you tell me you were in the—" Susan started to say. "Oh, you're hurt!"

Merlin had tiny cuts all over the left side of his face and throat from flying chips of stone. He'd turned his head just in time to save his eyes. He shook a large and ridiculously white handkerchief out of the breast pocket of his jacket and dabbed at his face, inspecting the dots of blood on the cloth afterward. "Nothing serious. Were you worried I'd lose my looks?"

"Don't be silly," snapped Susan. "And don't try to avoid the subject."

"I wanted to come and fetch you myself," he said. "But Una and Great-Aunt Evangeline thought it better to lay a trap by sending what appeared to be one police officer. We had to hide in case anyone was watching you being picked up."

"How would anyone know to watch for *me*?"

Merlin looked embarrassed.

"Your sheepskin coat you left behind in the tower," he said. "I should have thought of it, but we do often tend to forget the mundane. It might have had your mum's name on it, or some other indication that could lead to you."

"Yes," said Susan. She felt a sudden chill, and not from the snow and ice all around. But it did remind her to brush the snow off the front of her suit, which was surprisingly waterproof. Part of her mind was thinking "the silk must be treated with something" as she continued. "There were some letters or bills in one of the pockets. Mum does tend to stuff them in whatever she's been wearing."

"Sorry," said Merlin. "I mean, I do think you were safe at home, and your mum will be, too, with the guardians. There's two booksellers en route to watch over the place, by the way, just in case. But with us needing you to come in anyway . . . setting a trap seemed a good idea."

Susan was silent for a moment, suddenly remembering the dream she'd had, which was not a dream. The brook guardian and the creature from under the hill, disposing of the statue.

"I would definitely have been safe at home," she said slowly. "But I suppose I was going to leave anyway, later today. You could have told me once we got going."

She could feel the beginning of shock coming on, and she was suddenly very cold. There were two dead men close by, another probably dying, and the driver thrown from the van might well be dead, too. There was all that blood on the snow . . . the snow that was coming down thicker and faster now, and the cloud had lowered to the treetops, adding to the sense of desolation and loss.

"I really am sorry," said Merlin. He looked it. "Operationally it made more sense. You couldn't inadvertently give us away if you didn't know. Look, I'm going to walk you over to the other police car, where you can be warm. Come on."

"I just want everything to be normal," said Susan absently. Merlin took her arm and led her away down the road. Unnoticed by Susan, Stephanie followed half a dozen paces behind, shotgun ready.

It was warm in the Range Rover, the engine was running and the heater blowing hot air that didn't smell of old oil and insufficiently burnt petrol. Merlin sat her in the back seat. Susan leaned back and rubbed her shoulder, which was slightly sore from the sash belt when she'd been thrown forward from the stone ball impact. She'd have a bruise, but considering what might have happened, she felt very lucky.

"Maybe shut your eyes for a moment," said Merlin gently. "I'll be back in a minute. I have to talk to Torrant. We'll get you going very soon, down to Bath. I doubt there'll be any more trouble. Stephanie will be on guard here, outside, okay?"

"Yes, I'm okay," said Susan irritably. "Don't fuss. You know I've been through worse."

"I know," said Merlin. "But sometimes adding even a little to what you've already been through is too much. And it always seems worse when it's close to home."

"I'm okay," repeated Susan. But she closed her eyes.

She didn't go to sleep. That was impossible. But she fell into a weird kind of frozen state where her mind kept replaying the events of the last few minutes. The stone balls rolling down, the impact with the car, the Masons attacking, Merlin firing, the griffin attack. . . .

Susan opened her eyes. The griffin had seemed vaguely familiar. It was clearly the same grey stone as the statues in the "encysted" garden, Purbeck marble, even though it was discolored and stained. She thought she had seen it somewhere before, though it had been holding something. . . .

She opened the door and stepped out. Stephanie was next to her in an instant.

"You okay?"

"Yeah, I'm okay," said Susan tersely. "I need to look at the pieces of the griffin. I've seen that statue—or one like it—somewhere before."

She walked over to the crashed Land Rover. The pieces of the griffin sculpture were strewn over the road behind it. Susan carefully avoided looking any farther, to the dead men who lay where they fell. It was easier not to see because the snow was falling so thick and fast. She could hear multiple sirens coming from the south.

The griffin's head was in several parts, but it was the lion paws that she wanted to see. She picked one up and turned it over. She'd half expected to find a slot behind the claws, as if something was meant to go in there, for the paws to hold. But there was no slot.

"Something interesting?" asked Merlin, appearing behind her. Susan jumped, and felt a jolt of fear. She hadn't heard him approach. What if he'd been an enemy, she thought? But then Stephanie was nearby, standing guard.

"No," said Susan. "I thought it looked familiar. Maybe a study for the eventual finished work or maybe a rejected commission for the griffin on top of the Sir Bevil Grenville monument. But it's not that similar. This one is bigger and the paws are wrong. Have you seen the monument? Up on Lansdown Hill?"

"I haven't," said Merlin.

"I guess if you're making a heraldic griffin, there are bound to be similarities," said Susan. "If it was the same artist, that might be a useful clue. But I don't think it is."

"Vivien and Ruby and some other of our right-handed folk are working along those lines already," said Merlin. "Trying to find out where that house and garden were, and who might have sculpted heraldic animals in Purbeck marble, which apparently wasn't used for full-size sculptures very much. More decorative elements in churches and so on. So those statues were very unusual for that, as well as being all a bit askew."

"More than a bit, some of them," said Susan thoughtfully. "But all in the same way, the basic proportions of limbs to body being wrong. There's an associate professor of sculpture at the Slade who gave one of the introductory lectures that had a lot of history of sculpture in it. I wonder if she might know of an eighteenth- or early-nineteenth-century sculptor who couldn't get proportions right . . . or chose not to. It could be intentional, now I think about it. Like drawing grotesques. Anyway, I could ask her tomorrow. If she's in, of course. Half of the staff have already gone on holiday; it's only the students they're making stay through the week. Maybe only first years, come to think of it. Anyway, I could ask."

"It might be best to leave it to us for now," said Merlin. "We hadn't thought a long-hidden entity would have much to do with mortals, but clearly from these Masons, we were wrong about that. An Ancient Sovereign with power over stone might have connections with modern-day sculptors, too."

"In London?"

"Maybe," replied Merlin. "I don't know. The right-handed kin have been busy. Hopefully they'll tell us more at the briefing."

"Great," said Susan. "So even in London I might not be safe from it? And why does it want me in particular? You heard what they said, 'Give us the girl.'"

Merlin was silent for a moment.

"You are very special, you know," he said quietly. "In many ways. In this case it is probably you being the first mythic-mortal child born in almost two hundred years. That may be of particular interest to this entity, given the old woman in the garden is also the mortal child of an Ancient Sovereign. It may be mere curiosity, or it might be something more . . . more malign."

"Malign?"

"As Coniston's daughter, you have enormous mythic potential, magnified by your connection with the Copper Cauldron," said Merlin. "You have power or the potentiality of power that you might come to wield yourself, but also others might seek to use. Possibly in the same way Southaw usurped your father's magic. We had hoped to keep your existence secret from the Old World, but this entity will know your nature now, from your visit to its garden."

"And Sulis Minerva obviously knows, too," said Susan. She shivered.

"Sulis Minerva probably always knew, because she would have seen or sensed you many times in the past, particularly when you were at school in Bath," said Merlin. "But for all her vanity, she can be trusted. Let's get out of the cold and get on."

He started leading her to the car and added cheerfully, "And Sulis Minerva might tell you everything we need to know, and we can nip this problematic entity in the bud."

"Is that likely?" asked Susan.

"Probably not," said Merlin. "But you never know."

Susan nodded thoughtfully and trudged back to get in the Range Rover. A few minutes later, Merlin opened the tailgate, and he and a police officer loaded the Boys anti-tank rifle, the ammunition boxes, and the crate of steel bars from the Land Rover into the back. He opened one of the ammunition boxes and took out his familiar tie-dyed yak hair shoulder bag, checked its contents, and slung it over his shoulder.

"We'll be off in a jiffy," said Merlin. He closed the tailgate and came and sat in the back with Susan, while Stephanie got in front to ride shotgun. Literally, the Remington was held upright between her knees, with the young police driver trying her best not to stare side-eyed at both the weapon and the wielder.

"Inspector Torrant said to take you to the side door of the Empire Hotel, sir," she said as she put the Range Rover in gear and they edged forward. "On the Grand Parade. Is that right?"

"Yes, thank you, Constable," replied Merlin.

They drove past the wrecked Land Rover, which was still emitting a thin column of steam from its crushed front end, skirted around the crashed van and the beginning of the rescue operation to recover the driver on the hill below, and then wove between two more police Land Rovers, two ambulances, a police Rover 3500, and a cluster of several armed police officers who were watching some of their unarmed colleagues set up more lines of traffic cones and a "Road Closed" warning sign.

"The Empire Hotel?" asked Susan, frowning. "That's the navy place on the river, isn't it? Why are we going there?"

"It is an Admiralty building," confirmed Merlin. "They've lent us—masquerading as MI5—and Torrant's people some space to set up an Incident Room. We need to talk to Great-Aunt Evangeline there first, before you go see Sulis Minerva. And our old friend Inspector Greene will be there, too. That reminds me, she wants us *all* to appear to be MI5 to the Navy and any locals who might crop up, including you. Here."

He reached into an inside pocket and took out a small leather wallet, handing it to Susan. She flipped it open and saw her own passport photograph on a card that identified her as a civilian consultant to the Home Office, but did not give her name.

She grimaced as she put it in a pocket of her ski suit, with the cigarette case of salt. This was yet another power that could take her away from the straightforward life of an art student she still faintly hoped to have. But she had to acknowledge to herself it was no more than wishful thinking. The best she could hope for was what Merlin had said before "as normal a life as possible." How much *would* be possible remained to be seen.

CHAPTER TEN

Bath, Sunday, 11th December 1983

Bath. *There, go to Bath with you! Don't talk nonsense. Insane persons used to be sent to Bath for the benefit of its mineral waters.*

THE SNOW WAS FALLING THICK AND FAST IN CENTRAL BATH, AND THE steeper streets were very slippery and difficult despite having been gritted the night before. There was already at least one snowplow at work and all the streetlights were still on despite it being ten in the morning, not that they helped much. There was very little traffic, but a surprisingly large number of pedestrians still out and about. Susan wondered if they were tourists, because surely all sensible Bathonians were holed up at home on this snowy Sunday morning, and would stay there unless the weather improved.

The Empire Hotel was an imposing building of curiously mixed architecture, with different roof sections: a castellated tower on one end, a peaked house in the middle, and the two lesser peaks of a cottage, apparently to represent the upper, middle, and lower classes. Taken over by the Admiralty in the Second World War, they'd never handed it back. Though far from the sea, it did occupy an enviable position on the banks of the Avon, just down from Pulteney Bridge, opposite the weir. Possibly this riverine location lent enough of a nautical air for the navy to be reluctant to give it up.

The Range Rover pulled up on the Grand Parade opposite a side door at the northern end of the building. But only Merlin and Susan got out, Stephanie and the police driver taking the various weapons and munitions on to the Small Bookshop. The bells in the Abbey were ringing, as they always did on a Sunday between the two main morning services, the snow muffling and redirecting the sound. It was hard to tell where the peals came from. It sounded as if there were bells all around.

"Can't have an MI5 type walking in here with a Boys anti-tank rifle and a box of hand grenades," said Merlin. He waved at Stephanie as the Land Rover crawled away, and they crossed the road to the building. "Don't worry, we'll be safe enough. There's a bunch of our people here. And Sulis Minerva would doubtless take a dim view of any other entity trespassing on her demesne."

"Here?" asked Susan, as they reached the door and Merlin knocked on it. "I thought her demesne was only the immediate surrounds of the Roman Baths?"

"Where her water runs, so also goes her power," said Merlin. He pointed south. "The Great Roman Drain runs through Parade Gardens to join the Avon. We could probably see the steam from the outflow if we looked over the railing, just past that second tree."

"Is there an Ancient Sovereign of the Avon?" asked Susan.

Merlin shook his head.

"There are dozens of lesser entities along the Avon and its tributaries, but they sank into deep slumber at the beginning of the industrial revolution, and most have never risen since. Goram and Vincent in the Avon Gorge were the most powerful, but the building of the Clifton Suspension Bridge locked them in iron. They cannot stir while it stands. These days, Sulis Minerva is by far the most active entity of the Old World in the region. All the visitors to the Baths must keep her awake. Come on!"

His last words were addressed to the door. He knocked again, louder, and this time was rewarded by some sort of mumbling behind it, before it slowly yawned open. An elderly commissionaire in a blue coat with the fouled anchor of the Admiralty embroidered in gold on his breast pocket and a row of World War Two campaign ribbons above it looked out. Susan could see a grinning, fortyish left-handed bookseller behind him, one she'd briefly met before but had forgotten her name. She was in uniform as a Royal Navy petty officer and carried a Sterling submachine gun.

"Yes?" asked the commissionaire.

"We're expected," said Merlin, holding up his warrant card. "Can we come in out of the snow?"

"I need to see identification from both of you," said the man.

Susan fumbled out her new ID and showed it to him, blinking as snow fell in her eyes.

"Come in, then," said the commissionaire. "I'll just write you in the book."

"No you won't," said Merlin, ushering Susan inside and closing the door behind himself. It wasn't much warmer inside. He looked over at the other left-handed bookseller. "Haven't you sorted this out already, Hawkins?"

"Yes sir," snapped "Hawkins." She turned to the commissionaire, who had retreated into a sort of cubby near the door and was preparing to write in a large, red leather-bound ledger. "Just put down 'Commander Bond.'"

"Again?" grumbled the commissionaire. He pointed his end-chewed Bic at Susan. "What about her?"

"That is Commander Bond," said Hawkins.

"Well, who is he?" asked the commissionaire.

"He is also Commander Bond."

"You can't all be Commander Bond! That's the fourth one today, and there's been two Admiral Nelsons!"

"And my name is Smith," said Hawkins. "Your point is?"

"Smith? But you said Hawkins before. . . . I'm going to inform Captain Leamington about this!"

He reached for the wall-mounted phone but hesitated as Hawkins shook her head.

"You can tell him all about it when you see him tomorrow morning," said the left-handed bookseller. "If you like. I suppose you don't want this job anyway. And Strangeways has a lovely wing for people who violate the Official Secrets Act. Restful, I hear."

The commissionaire took his hand off the phone and started

writing "Commander Bond" in his book. Twice.

Merlin sighed.

"So where are we?"

"Through that door, along the corridor to the far end," said Hawkins. "The Jutland Conference Room."

"Inauspicious," replied Merlin. "A draw, at best."

"Famous victory, you mean," said Hawkins, opening the door and indicating for them to go ahead. "As far as the navy is concerned."

"Is she really in the navy?" asked Susan, as Hawkins's door shut behind them. "And is Hawkins or Smith her real name? Shouldn't she be a St. Jacques like the rest of you?"

"Kelly is a St. Jacques, of course," said Merlin. "And she is really in the navy, though she's a reservist now. Her bookseller father died when she was little and her mother—whose surname was Hawkins—moved away and broke contact with the family. So Kelly didn't dip her hands in the Grail at seven like we usually do. It's a more complicated story, but basically she didn't realize what she was or could be until she'd done twenty years in the navy and made Chief Petty Officer, and a bit after that she came to the Grail. It doesn't always work later, but it did for Kelly. We call people like that Lost Cousins. It doesn't happen often, and doesn't always end well. They dream, you see, and then if they do make it back and the Grail refuses them . . . it is pretty horrible."

"It would be," replied Susan. "Kind of the worst of both worlds."

Merlin shot her a sympathetic glance but didn't say anything. She was thinking of her own situation, they both knew.

Susan dodged the glance, looking away from him and along the corridor, which was painted battleship grey, probably several decades ago. The floor was linoleum and had been worn smooth down the middle. She glanced through the glass quarter-windows of the offices they passed. They were all empty and dim, the lights either off or not working.

"This place seems rather empty," she said, just to say something.

"The whole building doesn't get used much these days, or so I was told," said Merlin. "Probably why they were okay to lend us space for an incident room. By the bye, there may be some police here not cleared for our side of things, so best to see who's there and what gets mentioned or *not* before bringing up anything . . . er . . . exotic. Here we are."

The door at the end of the corridor was solid oak and a faded sign proclaimed in gilt letters "Jutland Conference Ro m." The second "o" in "room" was missing.

Merlin knocked. A moment later, the door was opened by the left-handed bookseller Diarmuid, who it took Susan a moment to recognize as he wasn't in his motorcycle courier book delivery leathers and fluorescent vest, instead wearing an inexpensive, rumpled suit with a knotted tie at half-mast, the standard look of the junior plainclothes police officer, complete with a revolver in a shoulder holster, inadequately concealed.

Behind Diarmuid was a large room crowded with people and

activity. It had no windows and no other door.

In the far-right corner there was a telephone exchange frame festooned with cables that went down into the floor, and extended to a dozen telephones mostly gathered at one end of the central table, each phone freshly labeled with a handwritten name. A woman in overalls with the upside down "L" and two dots insignia of British Telecom was mucking about with more cables next to the exchange frame. She was possibly an even-handed bookseller or more likely simply someone who just happened to be wearing gloves on both hands.

In the far-left corner, there was another table laden with three different radio sets and a chunky keyboard in front of a flickering green screen video display unit that currently showed in chunky, pixelated letters ten inches high "PNC," indicating it was a terminal connected to the Police National Computer. A wide variety of cables and antenna leads led from the various electronic devices up into the ceiling through what looked a newly cut hole the size of a dinner plate. A naval leading seaman with the lightning bolt and wings insignia of a radio operator and a uniformed Metropolitan Police sergeant tended to the terminal and radios, both had headsets on and their backs to the room.

One long wall was plastered with photographs of people, clothes, objects, and places, among them some large blown-up color photographs that Susan immediately recognized as being the shots Vivien had taken in the strange, dislocated garden. For a moment she was surprised they'd come out, it seemed wrong somehow that something so ordinary as photographs should work somewhere that existed out of the general run of time. But there they were, the maze, the sundial, the gardens, the tower, the statues, the old lady, the corpse below the clockface . . . all in reasonable definition, bright with the summer light. Most of the other photographs were official-looking, police exhibits and passport or driver's license photos, some in black and white.

In stark relief to the variety of the photos, there were several rows of plain white pages just stuck up with almost nothing on them, save a number from 1 to 26 in the top right corner and the last two, numbers 25 and 26, also had names written on them, large and bold, but followed by a question mark.

The names were "Lucinda Yourcenar?" and "Travis Zelley?"

The long table down the center of the room, in addition to the telephones at the far end, was covered with more photographs, files, maps, reference books, and at the closer end, a microfiche reader. There was also Susan's map, pinned with silver tacks to a wooden board with silver wire stretched between those tacks across it in a zigzag fashion reminiscent of a cat's cradle; and a sawn-out piece of the worktable from the Small Bookshop, with the antique garden map also comprehensively tacked down and crossed with silver wire.

There were seven people around the table, sitting or standing. All but one looked around as Susan and Merlin entered.

Most of them she knew. There was Evangeline, and Vivien, both right-handed booksellers; Inspector Greene, hard-faced and impassive as usual, in her familiar leather jacket; Una, the new leader of the left-handed booksellers, unfamiliarly dressed in a tailored dark-green pants suit to look the part of a senior police officer; and Aunt Zoë, the white-haired even-handed art restoration expert, who spun her wheelchair around and rolled towards the new arrivals. The others waved (Vivien), scowled (Una), stared unemotionally (Greene), or inclined her head slightly (Evangeline).

The sixth person, a right-handed bookseller Susan didn't know, kept listening to one of the phones, with another held ready in his other hand, and the seventh, also an unknown right-handed bookseller, continued to ignore the new arrivals, his gaze intent on a volume of Pevsner's *Buildings of England* that he was cross-referencing with an unfolded Ordnance Survey map. The other forty-five volumes of Pevsner were piled on the table in ramparts around him, interspersed with piles of other O.S. maps.

"Merlin! Susan! How nice to see you," called out Zoë as she wheeled to a stop in front of them.

Merlin bent down and kissed her on the cheek.

"I thought you were in New York for a conference? With Aunt Helen."

"One word," said Zoë. "Concorde. It was fun, if a little cramped. Helen stayed on for the conference. We flipped a coin and as per usual, she won."

"Yes, welcome, both of you," said Evangeline. "Thank you particularly, Susan, for coming in to help. We have only about half an hour before your appointment with Sulis Minerva, so let's get on with things. We need to know what you know, and you need to know what we have found out. I understand there was trouble coming in? Inspector Torrant radioed in a brief report, but if you wouldn't mind filling us in on the details, Merlin?"

Merlin glanced over at the two radio operators and the telephone technician.

"Oh, don't mind them," said Evangeline breezily. "They won't remember anything they hear here."

Susan looked at the three people in question, and only then noticed how unnaturally they went on with their tasks. They hadn't looked around at all when she and Merlin came in, they didn't show any sign of being aware anyone else was in the room. Presumably Evangeline had done some right-handed magic to blank out their minds or keep them focused only on their immediate tasks. Not for the first time she was reminded how ruthless the booksellers could be if they believed it to be necessary.

"I didn't get a good look at the beginning of the trouble," continued Merlin, drawing out a seat and offering it to Susan, who sat down, before he took a chair for himself. "I was in the back of the Land Rover. Susan?"

After a moment's hesitation, Susan described what had happened when the Masons attacked. Greene took notes in shorthand, but the others simply listened. When Susan stopped talking, Merlin started to fill in a few more details she'd not mentioned, including the thorny rose symbol on the Mason's aprons.

"A secret lodge," said Evangeline. "Not one we have recorded, which is always concerning. Torrant also radioed in that they found a four-ton lorry parked behind that house, belonging to a 'Jenkins & Co. Monumental Masons' in Chippenham. Their workplace will be raided in the next hour or so by Torrant's opposite number in the Wiltshire Police, with a good number of our people along, left- and right-handed."

"Speaking of Masons, I was disturbed by their demand that we hand over Susan in particular," said Merlin. "Do you know what that was about?"

"We have some suspicions," replied Evangeline. "Let us fill you in on where we are up to here. Vivien, you can start."

Vivien stood up and crossed to the wall of photos and other exhibits. Though she was clean and in fresh clothes—blue slacks and a white shirt that looked like police issue—she looked a little tired to Susan, who presumed she had not slept all night.

"Okay, to begin with, we still don't know where this house and garden were, before they were taken out of time," she said. She pointed to the right-handed bookseller who was flicking through Pevsner's, ignoring everyone else. "Cousin Clement is working on that. He is certain from the style that it was built in the late eighteenth or early nineteenth century, probably between 1790 and 1820, and removed from this world not much later, otherwise he'd already know about it, and this accords with some other information. Whatever contemporary records there are will probably report total destruction by fire or a storm or the like, once they're found. One useful clue Ruby and I didn't spot on the map, but Clement has pointed out, is down in the right-hand corner, the suggestion of an embankment and cross-hatching that may indicate a canal, or the private extension of a canal.

"Given all the construction is of Purbeck marble, which is very unusual, we initially concentrated on the Isle of Purbeck, and Dorset in general. Samples of the shattered lion and the gargoyles have been sent to the Sedgwick Museum in Oxford to see if their source can be identified. A very preliminary response from the only geologist we could get to come in last night has come back that they are of a rare, very fine quality of grey-white Purbeck marble. More information may be forthcoming.

"So most probably Dorset, but as yet no definite leads on the house and garden, nor have we been able to identify the sculptor. Aunt Zoë, you may have more on this?"

"Perhaps," said Zoë. "An inkling, no more. Looking at the sculptures, I was struck by the malformed nature of the beasts, particularly the limbs and appendages being out of proportion. At first glance, this gives the impression the sculptor was inept. However, closer study shows that they are all out of proportion in exactly the same ratio. This would be enormously difficult to achieve, so the sculptor was not inept, but very skilled and deliberate, perhaps with a fondness for the grotesque or had some reason to make them anatomically unbalanced. I have been looking for such a combination, in the late eighteenth and early nineteenth centuries, so far without success. However, this is also a clue. Who could have been so skilled, and yet unknown, in that time? It was probably a woman. My research continues along that line, and we have five of our people scouring records and periodicals of the time for any references to such a sculptor."

"I thought the griffin that attacked us this morning was by the same sculptor," said Susan. "The same oddity of proportion, but well executed. I briefly thought it might be the same sculptor who made the griffin on the Bevil Grenville monument. But I don't think so."

"No, that is earlier," said Zoë. "But well done to think of it."

"I was also wondering if the Old One could have made the statues herself?" asked Susan.

"I don't think so," said Vivien, and Zoë shook her head, adding, "The malign Old Ones don't create, even for fell purposes, and she is certainly malign. They co-opt others to make things."

"Besides, we think the spell of the garden is a collaboration between a learned mortal and an entity either captive to that person, or allied with it," said Zoë. "Particularly given the old woman in the bed, who is a mortal offspring of the entity."

"A 'learned mortal'?" asked Susan. "What does that mean?"

"A wizard," said Zoë. "Almost certainly now dead, thank goodness. But they set in motion a most horrific spell."

"Which brings us to the bodies," said Evangeline. "I have seen something of this nature once before, though it was not so ultimately successful, being interrupted early on. Stopped by the late Merrihew, as it happens, so I have some slight regret she is no longer with us to offer her knowledge of this particular magic."

"I don't regret it," said Susan, with Merlin and Vivien echoing her.

Evangeline inclined her head.

"You have cause. In any case, what you observed appears to be a spell of human sacrifice, or rather a ritual hunt ending in sacrifice, the deaths in this manner providing the power to take the house and garden out of time and keep it there, with the internal time either stopped or enormously slowed. This is a very powerful, difficult, and dangerous spell, and the mortal wizard must have given their own life to set it in motion. It has since then been maintained by the Ancient Sovereign, the spell's continuance requiring the ritual hunt and death every six years, from its beginning, which we have calculated was 1821."

"How do you know that?" asked Merlin.

"We'll get to that detail in a moment," said Evangeline.

"But why do it at all?' asked Susan. "I mean if the wizard *died* to cast the spell, what would be the point?"

Evangeline looked at Zoë.

"This is not definitive," said the white-haired woman. "But we think it is all about the woman in the bed. Though Vivien put her age at over a hundred, this is not an excessive age for a child of a mortal and Ancient Sovereign. But she was sick, which is unusual, though not impossible. Most likely she has one of the rare cancers that can afflict even such beings. Us too, for that matter.

"So we have a child of a wizard and an Ancient Sovereign, very precious to both, not least because to engender such a child would have been very difficult, something not done lightly. So they both must have decided to put her out of time, where the disease would not worsen, and so she would not die. The mortal parent would die in so doing, but it is not unusual for a parent to sacrifice themselves to save their child."

"But she wouldn't really be alive!" protested Susan. "Just stuck like a fly in amber. So why bother?"

Zoë looked at Evangeline, who nodded.

"Keeping her from dying is likely only the first part of their plan," said Zoë. "The second part would be to cure her, and make her young again."

"How?" asked Susan. "Is that even possible?"

"Another kind of sacrifice would be needed," said Zoë. "A variation on the spell already in place, but requiring the ritual hunting and death of a much rarer individual."

"Like who . . ." Susan started to say, before she caught on.

"No," she whispered, remembering Merlin and Vivien telling her how she was the first offspring of an Ancient Sovereign and mortal to be born since the early nineteenth century. The only one they knew of in the current time.

"Unfortunately, yes," said Zoë. "Ordinary, or rather nearly ordinary mortals have been enough to sustain the encysted house and garden with a hunted, ritual death every six years. But to do more, the Ancient Sovereign needs to sacrifice someone far more powerful, but also still mortal. You, in other words, the only child of Old One and mortal we know of, probably gifted with even greater potential power by your immersion in the Copper Cauldron."

"Shit," said Merlin.

"Given the nature of the chosen ritual, the timing, and the

victims we have identified so far," said Zoë. "It seems likely the wizard who set all this in motion consulted a prophetic entity to predict your eventual birth, or rather the birth of someone who would make this possible, and all their plans proceeded from this prophesy."

"Please . . . explain," said Susan.

CHAPTER ELEVEN

Bath, Sunday, 11th December 1983

Alphabet. *This is the only word compounded of letters only. The Greek alpha (a) beta (b) ; our ABC (book), etc.*

"LET'S GIVE YOU ALL THE NECESSARY BACKGROUND. THE RITUAL HAS an alphabetic structure," said Evangeline. "That extra hand on the clockface indicates this, and it is further confirmed by what we know of the victims so far. Inspector Greene?"

Mira Greene did not bother to stand up. She pushed her chair back and pointed at the twenty-six mostly blank pages stuck to the wall.

"Thanks to Merlin picking up a wallet and some other odds and ends, we're confident we've identified two of the victims. Both were registered as missing persons. The most recent, Travis Zelley, was last seen very close to here, in fact, in Parade Gardens on December 21, 1977—"

"The winter solstice," interrupted Evangeline. She had a natural lecturer's voice and treated her audience much as a professor might address some reasonably intelligent but not particularly well-prepared students. "This is significant. The formal structure of the spell is alphabetical, but much of the power behind it comes from the *hunting* of the victim, using a form of sympathetic magic to capture a tiny fraction of the power of a very deep magic indeed, which for our purposes today we will call the Wild Hunt. This is extraordinarily dangerous, and most often would result in total failure and the . . . er . . . *taking away* of all concerned. The hunt can only occur when there is a thinning of the boundaries between the Old World and the New, when the Wild Hunt readies to ride, though fortunately it is generally prevented from doing so. However, at this time some of the power of the hunt can be accessed at great risk, as clearly has been done. The killing is the culmination of the ritual, and it must be done at the stroke of midnight on the night of the solstice. But first there must be the hunt."

"Yeah," continued Greene. "Anyway, Zelley was nineteen years old, a punk with an orange mohawk, not employed, living at home with his mother. She reported him missing the next day, but there was no active search for several days. Bit of bias from the local constabulary there, him being an unemployed, self-professed anarchist with a couple of priors for shoplifting and so on, and in fact a paper Merlin found in his wallet was a summons for another minor offence. Anyway, eventually it turned out two officers on patrol had seen him in Parade Gardens shortly before midnight but no one saw him alive thereafter, anywhere, ever again. His overcoat *was* found, but not straightaway. Zelley's mother spotted a homeless man wearing it about ten days later. The man swore he had picked it up in the street, and had not seen Zelley's body or anything. This was believed to be true by the investigating officer as the man had a good alibi. There were no bloodstains on the coat, though the collar had been torn off."

"This is the overcoat," said Vivien, who since she was standing by the wall, took on the role of pointing out individual photographs. The overcoat had been photographed spread flat on a whiteboard, with some textual annotations about the collar, the date it was processed, and the exhibit number. The only unusual thing about the coat was that it was covered in odd symbols, daubed in runny white paint.

"What are those symbols?" asked Susan.

"Meaningless, for the most part," said Vivien. She leaned in and indicated the right sleeve. "Except for these three, which are glyphs devised by John Dee to represent particular Ancient Sovereigns. Dee, by the way, *was* an actual wizard. He was . . . er . . . definitely rendered harmless late in his life by some of our ancestors, so he is not the wizard we are looking into."

"Why did Zelley have those symbols on his sleeve?" asked Susan, frowning.

"We think he simply liked the look of them," said Vivien. She nodded at Greene. "Mira spoke to Travis's mum this morning."

"She said he copied all the signs on his overcoat from an old book he 'borrowed from the library and forgot to take back,'" continued Greene. "She'd got rid of it since, unfortunately, and couldn't remember anything about it except it was old. So we don't know the title. Evidently some sort of esoteric tome."

"Did you tell her that her son was dead?" asked Merlin.

"No," said Greene flatly. "And we won't, until and unless we can retrieve his body and absolutely confirm his identity. Which it seems we can't do."

"Not unless we can find another way into that garden," said Zoë. "The portion of the map we have has been severed from the place, possibly by the nature of your exit via Susan's map. This may be temporary, so we've kept it locked down, but the entity will have other means of entry and exit."

"The important thing here is that Zelley unintentionally marked himself as being aware of the Old World," said Evangeline impatiently. "That is what I meant by 'nearly ordinary mortals' because our second identified victim had a similar connection. Inspector?"

"The previous victim we believe to be Lucinda Yourcenar. Last seen December 19, 1971, a few days before the winter solstice, in Keynsham, at the station. She was twenty-four, an itinerant sort of hippie who did a fortune-telling act-cum-scam at various railway stations along the Great Western main line, particularly in the lead up to Christmas. You know, cross my palm with some rustling paper money, never mind the silver, it's the modern way. She was quite convincing by all accounts and so may actually have had some minor prophetic talent. The description fits, and Merlin grabbed a piece of cardboard from her hand that turned out to be a hand-drawn tarot card, which we consider further confirmation. Though it is a pity you couldn't get some photographs of the stacked-up bodies, Vivien."

"We were a bit busy trying to escape a bunch of killer statues at that stage," said Vivien.

"What about the others?" asked Susan.

"We're checking missing persons around the winter solstice every six years back from 1977 as far as we have records, concentrating on Somerset, Wiltshire, and Gloucestershire," said Greene. "Not all missing person data is in the PNC—the Police National Computer—so it's not straightforward."

"We have also set some of our people to assist in this," added Zoë. "Who are cross-checking with our own records and the PRO, HMC, Somerset House, and so forth. Or will be tomorrow."

"We have two possibilities for the presumed 1965 victim," said Greene. "Given the alphabetical surname issue, by far the most likely is a Kostas Xenophon, twenty-three years old, who worked for a candle-making firm in Bristol. We haven't located the full report yet, it's on microfiche in some warehouse of files from the former Bath and Somerset Constabulary. Torrant has rousted out a retired station sergeant to search for it. But the basic details to hand fit the frame: Xenophon disappeared on the evening of the winter solstice, December 22, 1965. He was last seen leaving the Lock Keeper pub, which is on an island in the Avon at Keynsham, going to the car park. His own vehicle was left there. No witnesses and no traces of foul play in or around the car. If he had some sort of Old World connection or suggestion of one, we don't know what it was—"

"Candle-making," interrupted Evangeline. "A fairly obvious connection, I would have thought. There is a great deal of ritual magic in particular that involves candles."

"If you say so," muttered Greene.

"I do say so," said Evangeline. "Xenophon, Yourcenar, and Zelley. The alphabetical structure made clear. It is now six years since the last victim. It has gone full circle and must begin again."

She looked directly at Susan.

"The next murder, in a few weeks, will be someone with a surname starting with 'A,' Susan Arkshaw. A new beginning for the ritual, a new life for the demi-mortal who sleeps in that garden. Twenty-six people ritually murdered over one hundred and fifty-six years to keep the wizard's daughter alive long enough to steal your life and magic and return to this world and time."

She paused before adding breezily, "Not that we will let this happen, of course. The entity and its offspring will be brought to answer for their crimes and will be prevented from committing any more murders."

"Okay," said Susan slowly. "That sounds good. But . . . um . . . how?"

"We will identify the stone entity," said Evangeline. "Discover its locus and bind it to first answer our questions and then we will force it into a deep slumber, as we did with Southaw. That will break the ritual spell that keeps that house and garden out of time, and it will cease to exist. The demi-mortal will be expunged with it."

"Meaning she'll die?" asked Greene.

"You might consider it an equivalent in this case," said Evangeline.

"Sounds a bit extra-legal to me," said Greene. "After all, she isn't a murderer herself, is she?"

"We don't know," replied Evangeline. "She was probably involved in setting this in motion and certainly must have known what was planned. It is bookseller business, not a police matter."

"Murder is police business," said Greene stubbornly.

"Not in this case," said Evangeline.

She matched the inspector's gaze. Greene held it for a few seconds before looking away and said no more.

"So how is the identifying and discovering going so far?" asked Susan into the silence.

"We have deployed a great many people to seek information, even so far as sending Thurston to ask Grandmother, which he did not want to do," said Evangeline. She sniffed, "It will be good for him."

"Even if Grandmother is not helpful, Sulis Minerva must know of this entity, given the last sighting of Travis Zelley was so close to her demesne. I hope she will give us its name and locus. It is annoying she will only talk to you, Susan, but even so it will doubtless provide us with a swifter resolution than otherwise might be the case. But even if she does not, I am confident we will soon know all we need to in order to take executive action."

"The bells have stopped," said Diarmuid, from the door. Susan hadn't heard the Abbey bells once she was inside, but she was used to the booksellers' acute hearing.

"Then it is time for your appointment with Sulis Minerva," said Evangeline to Susan. "You know what we need to get from her. The name and locus of the Purbeck marble entity is essential, but glean anything else you can about her and her child, whether it seems relevant to you or not. *We* will assay its worth. So try hard to remember everything she tells you."

"I'll do my best," said Susan, feeling like a young schoolgirl being berated by an over-keen headmistress before an interschool debating challenge or the like.

"Merlin, Diarmuid, you'll escort Susan to the Baths," said Una. "Advika, Sabah, Sairey, and Polly are watching from the sentry post. It's unlikely there'll be trouble, but I trust you will be *extremely* alert. Sulis Minerva has given her word you'll be safe, Susan. Who's got the tablet?"

"Uh, I have," said Diarmuid. He reached inside his suit and took out a lead tablet the size of a pocket diary.

"Give it to Susan," said Una. "You read Latin?"

"No," replied Susan, taking the tablet, which had been inscribed in chiseled capitals with a message or phrase in Latin above a simple ideogram of a fist closed around a thumb. "I mean I know a few words. What does *pollice compresso favor iudicabatur* mean?"

"It's basically an expression of goodwill," said Vivien. "Our weapons will be sheathed."

"The tablet grants you safe passage in Sulis Minerva's demesne," said Una. "You don't need it, her word is good, but she likes the tradition."

"Okay," said Susan. She looked down at the tablet, but not

to read the words. She could feel the alloy, sense its making, knew how old it was.

"There's copper from Coniston in this, a little under eight parts in a hundred," she said slowly. "Ninety-two percent lead, from some hills to the southwest. The Mendips, I guess. It was made long ago, sixteen hundred and twenty years. How do I know this?"

"You are your father's daughter," said Una. There was something a little scary in the way she said this, something in her tone that made Susan shiver inside. But she had always found Una scary.

"I'm coming, too," said Vivien quickly. She took a dark-green overcoat with bronze buttons off the back of a chair and shrugged it on. "So as to make sure my left-handed kin don't get lost crossing the road."

"Thank heavens for that," said Diarmuid. "I was worried."

He opened the door and was about to step out when Una called him back.

"Diarmuid! Put on a coat. And act as if you can feel the cold!"

"Yes, ma'am," mumbled Diarmuid. He grabbed a very faded, crumpled, seen-better-days tan Burberry trench coat from a pile of jackets and outerwear in the corner of the room and put it on.

"I'll want that back," said Clement, looking up from his Pevsner's. "Should have brought your own. Jackanapes!"

In the corridor, Diarmuid looked at Merlin.

"She didn't tell *you* to put on a coat, class favorite."

"That is because Aunt Una recognizes the thermal qualities

of a Harris Tweed Fife shooting suit in the heaviest weight," said Merlin smugly. "Unlike you."

"Clotheshorse," retorted Diarmuid.

"I can say no more to that than to repeat Cousin Clement's apt description," replied Merlin. "Jackanapes."

They grinned at each other and led the way. Susan and Vivien exchanged a look that encapsulated in a moment their similar affection and exasperation towards Merlin, held in differing ratio by girlfriend and sibling.

There was a brief delay in the antechamber, where the aged attendant wanted them to sign out individually, only to be thwarted by Kelly Hawkins-Smith-St. Jacques, who waved every-one on and solved the signing out issue by taking the end-chewed Bic from the commissionaire and writing "Gone" in big letters next to the list of Commanders Bond and Admirals Nelson.

The weather had changed outside. It was no longer snowing, but it was considerably colder, and a thick fog had rolled across, so the very air was white and visibility was down to only a few yards. Susan shivered as the chill, wet air rolled across her, sharp on her face.

Merlin stopped, keeping Susan behind him in the doorway, while Diarmuid peered to the left and right, his hand inside his jacket. Vivien edged around Susan and took in a deep breath of the cold, foggy air. She held it for about ten seconds and exhaled.

"It is an unnatural fog, and the chill has been conjured, too, but there is nothing else untoward about it. It is of Sulis Minerva's making. The fog doesn't extend very far, only for a few hundred yards around the Baths."

"I guess she desires her audience with Susan to be as private as possible," said Merlin.

They walked alongside the building, then cut through the little park once known as Orange Grove, but since World War Two named Alkmaar Garden after the twinned town in the Netherlands. The snow was thicker here, not swept off pavements or plowed away, and Susan was glad of her good socks and tights and well-dubbined boots. Unsurprisingly, there were now few pedestrians about. At least visible ones. Everything was very quiet.

"Advika and Co. won't be able to see a thing in this," said Diarmuid as they crossed the road and the east wall of the Abbey loomed ahead, a dark mass in the fog. He waved his arms to send tendrils of fog spiraling about. "We should have brought a radio."

Merlin reached into the right side of his shooting jacket and pulled out a Pye PF8. Just like the ones used by Bodie and Doyle in *The Professionals*, which was why he'd chosen it over the PF5000 that had greater range and power and was what most of the other left-handed booksellers used. The PF8 simply looked better, even if it could be mistaken for an oversized electric razor.

"Advika? This is Merlin. We're entering the churchyard now, turning the corner of the East Wall."

The radio crackled.

"Yeah. We can't see a thing from here. I've sent Sairey and Polly to watch the main entrance, they'll be in earshot. Inspector

Torrant is there with some uniforms, keeping people away. Not that there's too many out and about now. Too bloody cold and foggy. Oh, I can relay to Torrant if you need me to. Over."

"Thanks," replied Merlin. "Out."

He put the radio away and winked at Diarmuid.

"All right, all right," said the other left-handed bookseller. "I had to come up here in a hurry this morning, you know. Wait!"

They all stopped. Merlin moved to Susan's left, and Vivien came up close behind her. There were footsteps ahead. Merlin's hand went into his tie-dyed bag, and Diarmuid's under his jacket.

Two fuzzy human shapes appeared in the fog, coming towards them, slowly resolving into actual humans, a middle-aged man and woman hurrying along, both heavily garbed in coats, scarves, hats, and gloves.

"The police have shut the Baths," exclaimed the woman as they drew closer. She had a distinctive American accent, from New Jersey perhaps. "A suspected gas leak! I hope you're not going there!"

"No, ma'am," said Diarmuid, who was closest to them. "Wouldn't think of it."

"It's very inconvenient," said the woman crossly.

"We'll go tomorrow," soothed the man, who was also American, but his voice was midwestern. "Let's get back to our warm hotel! Have a nice day, folks."

"You too," said Merlin smoothly. As he spoke, the man turned his head and looked at him sharply, focusing his previously abstracted attention. He frowned, shook his head, and walked on, but as they disappeared into the fog he spoke to his wife in what was clearly meant to be a confidential aside, but was heard by the booksellers and even Susan.

"That guy in the tweed suit, he could be the twin brother of that Jane Austen we took the photo with yesterday!"

This disarming comment did not disarm the two left-handed booksellers, who remained on the alert with hands on weapons until they heard the footsteps take the turn around the corner of the Abbey.

"Probably what they seem to be," said Merlin. "Onward."

"Are we going in a side entrance?" asked Susan as they left the Abbey behind and struck through the fog across the paved yard. She could see the glow of light from the big Georgian lamp above the door in the north wall of the Baths ahead, and another fuzzy silhouette coming around from the western side, which was extremely broad and so was probably Torrant. Diarmuid and Merlin obviously thought so, too, because they didn't stop.

"*You're* going in a side entrance," said Vivien. "We're staying out. You'll be met by Dr. Alexandra Prester. She's the Director of Avon Museums, including the Roman Baths, but more important she's the high priestess of Sulis Minerva. Her right-hand woman."

"Does everyone who works at the Baths know about . . . about the Old One here, and the Old World?" asked Susan.

"Oh, no," replied Vivien. "Hardly any of them, I'd think."

"Don't worry, everyone not in the know will have been cleared out by the supposed gas leak," said Merlin. "Good thought from Torrant."

As if summoned by her name, the fuzzy but solid shape of Inspector Torrant closed with them as they neared the side entrance. She was windmilling her arms to clear the fog ahead of herself, though all it really did was make interesting spirals.

The side door was an unprepossessing entry reached by four broad steps, part of the mostly eighteenth- or nineteenth-century superstructure of the Baths. The lamp above the right-hand corner of the doorway was huge but failed to shed much light. What it did manage to emit gave the fog an eerie glow.

"Hullo again, Susan," said Torrant. "Booksellers."

"Hello, Inspector," replied Susan. Her breath came out in a little fog of its own, mixing with the greater mist about them.

"We've cordoned off the Baths entirely, Merlin," said Torrant. "My initial story was a gas leak in the Pump Room kitchen, but I've had to change it to a bomb threat because Avon Fire naturally responded and the only area commander briefed for weird shit is off sick. So now it's a bomb threat, code words, the lot. Everyone is holding back while we wait for the Met bomb squad up from London or army EOD from Ashchurch. But the whole thing will blow up in my face, pardon the expression, as soon as they get here and don't find anything. Which is to say whatever you're up to, try make it quick."

"It shouldn't take long," said Vivien. "Not for us, anyway. It may seem only a few minutes. Longer for Susan, though."

"I don't want to know," replied Torrant. She turned on her heel and strode off into the fog towards the main entrance to the Roman Baths, around the corner.

"Only a few minutes?" asked Susan.

"For us. The Baths will be Sulis Minerva's temple while she receives you, and so somewhat out of time," replied Vivien.

"Like the May Fair with the goblins," said Merlin. "But safer."

"And here's Dr. Prester," said Vivien.

The lantern light was suddenly augmented by a shaft of flickering red light that grew as the door swung open. A tall woman in a long, rather shapeless lilac dress knotted at the shoulders and far too lightweight for the weather, stood in the doorway. She was in her late forties or early fifties, with dark skin and jet black hair, which was long and fell loose on her shoulders, though constrained at the temples by the circlet she wore, which was gold, of six woven-together serpents who gripped each other's tails, their eyes tiny sapphires and emeralds. The flickering red light came from the burning torch she bore in her left hand, its piney, resinous flames surely dangerous to the ceiling above.

"Welcome, Daughter of Coniston," she said, her voice clear and strong, as if she were addressing a multitude, not a quartet six feet away at the bottom of the steps. "Sulis Minerva awaits you, and I confirm your safe passage here. No hand will be raised against you and no harm will come to you. Do you say likewise to Sulis Minerva? You will not raise your hand against her, or exert your powers against us?"

"Um, of course, I . . . er . . . I am a friend," said Susan.

"You are thrice welcome," replied Dr. Prester. She touched her forehead, sternum, and navel with two fingers from her right hand, then beckoned. "Come in."

Merlin gripped Susan's elbow lightly, holding her back for a moment, and addressed Dr. Prester.

"We welcome the safe conduct," he said easily. "But could you also confirm we'll have Susan back safe and sound in a timely manner? None of your lost days, months, years? No fairy hill business?"

"That is presumed in the welcome," replied Dr. Prester. "But yes, our honored guest will be with you again before the Abbey clock strikes twelve."

"Best to be careful," muttered Merlin in Susan's ear. "Vivien's comment to Torrant reminded me. Be on your guard."

He stepped back, and Susan stepped forward, up and through the door, and suddenly she was not in any part of the Roman Baths she or any other modern visitor had ever seen before, and it was clear why the flaming torch presented no danger to the ceiling.

CHAPTER TWELVE

⊱━◈━◯━◈━⊰

Aquae Sulis, Date Uncertain

Sovereign. *A strangely misspelled word, the last syllable being mistaken for the word* reign.

⊱━◈━◯━◈━⊰

BEYOND THE DOOR THERE WERE NO WALLS AND NO CEILING. THEY were outside, it was not winter, and it was deep night. Susan could see a clear, starlit sky, and the air was no longer bitingly cold on her face. Though it wasn't warm, it felt like a cool autumn day. In the light of Dr. Prester's torch she could see they stood on a well-paved road that was lined on both sides with Doric columns, only two or three feet taller than Susan, each one topped with a small gilded figure, all owls in different postures.

To either side of the road, there were rows and rows of larger than normal olive trees, the fringe of some vast grove that eventually disappeared into formless shadow in the night. Susan looked at the closest tree, which bore a great quantity of fruit, black or very dark-green olives dangling in thick bunches. It was further confirmation that wherever they were, it was not really

Bath but some mythic concept of it, Sulis Minerva's dream or idea of what it should be. Olive trees might grow in Somerset, but not to that size, nor did they deliver fruit in such abundance.

The road didn't go very far, only twenty yards or so, to an impressive gate of six fluted columns more than twenty feet high that supported a pediment carved with the head of a Gorgon surrounded by cavorting dolphins. This pediment seemed to be illuminated from within, for the whole thing had a soft silvery glow that was not from star- or moonlight, torch or oil lamp.

Through that gateway the ground descended. Susan saw terraced levels and realized there was some sort of sunken Roman theater ahead.

"After you," said Dr. Prester.

Susan walked along the road and through the gate. She paused there for a moment. The theater had a dozen terraced levels, but the center was not a stage or gladiatorial arena. It was the hot spring, civilized and contained by Roman engineering into a perfect circle some fifteen yards in diameter, the sides paved with marble edged in a narrow mosaic bordered with strips of beaten gold. Steam rose from the spring, and the waters roiled and bubbled.

There was no one else around, no one sitting on the honey-gold Bath stone terraces. Only the stars in the night sky above and the turbulent water below. It was very quiet save for the surprisingly prosaic washing-machine-like noise of the spring.

"Sulis Minerva awaits you," said Dr. Prester. She sat down on the topmost terrace. "Go down. Cast the tablet into the waters."

There was no separate stairway. Susan simply stepped down each terrace until she reached the paved area around the pool, stopping short of the mosaic, which she saw depicted a turquoise sea where dolphins and owls co-habited happily among underwater olive trees and jaunty crabs.

She could feel the warmth of the spring, and the iron stench was strong, but weirdly not unpleasant, not a rotten egg smell at all. Wisps of steam curled in spirals from the center of the pool, but only there, presumably where it was hottest.

Susan took the lead plaque out of the pocket of her ski suit and threw it in, aiming for the very center where the steam rose. But it did not land with a splash. There was a sudden eruption of steam and water, and in its midst a tall figure burst up, extending one slender hand to snatch the tablet from the air.

It could only be Sulis Minerva. She was like the brook entity, being made of dense, swirling water, but her eyes shone like great diamonds, her watery skin was clothed in a toga-like robe composed of steam and starlight, and Susan felt a great aura of power and majesty about her. It was hard to properly look at her. Ever after Susan was unable to describe the face and features of Sulis Minerva, save that she appeared as a tall woman with coiled up hair, though that, too, was only shaped of water.

"Welcome, Daughter of Coniston," said Sulis Minerva. She continued to rise up above the pool, supported on a swirling column that hid her feet, if she had any. She was at least nine feet tall herself, and the column was of an equal height, so Susan had to crane her head back to look up at her.

"Greetings, Sulis Minerva," said Susan. She tried to sound

cool and confident, not over-awed by the massive being so high above her, in the middle of her sacred spring, the center of her power. But she was, and she had to fight hard against an almost overwhelming desire to kneel.

Sulis Minerva smiled, lips of sculpted water—no crayfish tails here—parting to reveal perfect pearly teeth. She touched her forehead, sternum, navel and made a brushing gesture with both hands. As she did, she began to diminish in size and the column shrank, until the aqueous woman was about Susan's height and stood on the surface of the pool, though the water closed over her ankles, so her feet or the possible lack thereof remained a mystery.

"Thank you ever so much for visiting," she said conversationally. Susan was slightly surprised the Old One sounded like a BBC presenter. She had half expected her to sound Italian or even to speak in Latin, with Dr. Prester throwing translations from the top tier. "Please note I am not wearing the mask, so this is *quite* an informal chat."

Susan blinked, unsure of what not wearing the mask implied or what mask the Ancient Sovereign was talking about.

"Uh, great. It's good to be here."

"Would you like tea? A savory biscuit?" asked Sulis Minerva.

"Uh, no, thank you," replied Susan. She knew she had to be careful accepting food or drink in such a place, or anywhere from the hands of an Old One. She hesitated, then said, "I think we have urgent matters to discuss. A murderous entity you may know."

"Hmm. Yes," said Sulis Minerva. She wrinkled her nose in

distaste, an interesting movement as her watery flesh had the same solidity as jelly and the wrinkle continued across her cheeks and around behind her ears. "The Stone Lady. She stole from me."

"Stole? Uh, what—"

"A worshipper, consecrated by a gift of silver when he was seven," continued Sulis Minerva. Steam came from her nose and out of her ears as she continued, little puffs of angry cloud. "Travis Zelley. Snatched on my doorstep. She must pay for that."

"The Stone Lady, that is her name?" asked Susan.

"One of them," said Sulis Minerva. "Some called her Gwyre."

"Gwyre," repeated Susan, committing this to memory. "Can you tell me where her locus is?"

"She is of the stone that once was teeming with life, life from the sea, small shelly things," she said. "She was born long ago, sunk between layers of lesser stone. The little people found her, scratched away the lesser stone, and worshipped her in that place. Later, much later, the wizard found her again, and took her stone from the earth. Later still their daughter made three figures from it: maiden, matron, crone. Her locus was that strand of stone. Then it was invested in the three statues, and there it lies, though she has some remnant power within *all* pieces of that original stone, no matter how small."

"Do you know where those three statues are?" asked Susan.

Sulis Minerva shrugged. Several lead tablets flew out of her shoulders and splashed into the water around her.

"I think the Maiden was lost to her, long ago, perhaps at sea. Few powers could harm it, fewer still break it forever. She would have used the Maiden if she could, when she came here to capture my Travis Zelley. She was the most nimble of the three. As for the Matron . . ."

She smiled, showing her teeth again.

"My mortal servants found the Matron years before poor Travis was lost, after Gwyre first trespassed here. Many were slain in the battle, but in the end they were victorious. However, they could not break her, nor bring her here without those obnoxious booksellers interfering. So they set her feet in bronze and sank her in a lake, the sea being too far for me to oversee their actions. I thought this enough, but she broke herself free and came hunting again, trespassing again, tripping sparks from her shortened legs to take my poor Zelley. Where the Matron is now, I do not know, save that when my people last found her, she was traveling on the straight river. Hoping I would not notice her skulking past. Bah!"

"The canal? Here in Bath? The Kennet and Avon Canal?" asked Susan. She remembered Vivien's comment about a canal extension in the corner of the map.

"Indeed, the canal," said Sulis Minerva, inclining her head in agreement. "My servants caught her where the canal crosses Sydney Gardens."

"And the Crone?"

"The Crone must be bigger, slower, and heavier," said Sulis Minerva. "Containing the greatest proportion of the original stone. I have never seen that shape of Gwyre, nor have those of my people who range farther than my waters."

"What about her house and garden, that the Stone Lady took out of time?" asked Susan. "Do you know where that was?"

"Not in the valley of my spring," replied Sulis Minerva. She smiled again, teasingly, and was silent.

"But you know something?" asked Susan, hoping this was the right approach.

"I know a great deal," said Sulis Minerva. "About all manner of things."

"About this house of Gwyre's in particular?" prompted Susan.

"It was called Alphabet House," said Sulis Minerva. "The wizard made it, mostly using the lesser marble that had cradled Gwyre. Not the sculptures, which had to be made of the original stuff of the Stone Lady. In any case, the wizard was not a sculptor, you see. The wizard's father was, and later the daughter."

"She? The wizard was a woman? Wait, how did she and the Stone Lady have a child?"

Sulis Minerva laughed, laughter bubbling out of her like the waters of the spring.

"You are too much the sheltered mortal, Daughter of Coniston. The wizard bore the child. Gwyre is called "Lady Stone" by her choice, but in nature could not be called female or male. She inhabited some poor mortal man or men to serve as the engine of their desire. The man would live for a day or two with Gwyre resident within him, time enough to engender a babe before his blood turned to powder and his flesh to stone."

"I didn't know Ancient Sovereigns could do that," muttered Susan. She had an urge to shiver, but she didn't, being careful to show no weakness. "Inhabit other people, I mean."

"Some few have that power, but never without detriment, nor for long," said Sulis Minerva. "Many others have mortal forms they can assume, as your own father and your existence can attest."

Susan nodded slowly. Questions thronged in her mind. How did her father come to have a mortal form in the first place? Did he somehow conjure it? But these were questions to ask him, or perhaps not. She wasn't sure she wanted to know the answer. And there were other, more pressing questions to ask right now.

"Alphabet House," said Susan. "How do you know about it? And do you know where it is, even if it is not in your valley?"

"The stone was carried on the Avon, and thence along the canal," said Sulis Minerva. "How could I *not* know? The boats came from the west, and the wizard paid the Giants to allow its passage, probably in a coin your bookseller friends would not approve. But where eastward the stone ended its journey, I do not know, save it went beyond the valley and so out of my ken."

"How do you know what the house was called?" asked Susan.

"The builders, too, came by the river from the west, and returned thence," said Sulis Minerva after a moment. "And the architect lingered here and drank of my waters. His name was Joseph, Joseph Gwilt."

"But you didn't learn from him where this Alphabet House was located?" asked Susan. She had the strong feeling Sulis Minerva knew far more, and was toying with her, though she didn't know why. A natural mischievousness perhaps . . .

"He was a Mason of the thorny rose, sworn to Gwyre's service," said Sulis Minerva. "Besides, in those days the Stone Lady had yet to trouble me. He was simply a minion of another, passing by."

"So you have no idea where this Alphabet House was?"

"Of course I have an idea!" retorted the Ancient Sovereign. "It is simple. The stone could not be taken far from the canal. Somewhere east of here, near river or canal."

"That covers an awful lot of ground," said Susan. "Is there anything that might narrow it down?"

"I have told you what I know," said Sulis Minerva pettishly.

"What was the wizard's name?" asked Susan. "And the daughter's, for that matter."

"So many questions! But I will answer, in the hope that you will remember this kindness, and good may repay good."

"That seems a sensible principle," said Susan cautiously. "The names?"

"The wizard was called Everilda Gibbons. I knew her well. In her younger years, she sought knowledge from many places, and would bring me gifts. She was not troublesome until later, when she found the Gwyre stone, and told her father of it, thinking to give it to him as a gift, as he was a sculptor of some fame. She had long sought his affection and acknowledgment, being a bastard daughter, born from a mistress, not his wife. He had always refuted the claim, but she hoped the wonders of the Gwyre stone would finally sway the matter in her favor. But it did not. He died soon after, and perhaps in grief or perhaps in resentment, or perhaps already under the influence of Gwyre, Everilda determined to have a child who would be as great a sculptor as her father, and who would work the wondrous stone she had discovered. The father, as I have said, would have been in form some mortal man, but the essence that engendered the child was Gwyre's."

"And the child's name?"

"I am not sure I ever knew it," said Sulis Minerva evasively. "I only heard of her existence from visitors to my spring. But she was indeed a sculptor of great talent."

"Did you know Everilda died casting a spell to remove Alphabet House and the daughter out of time?" asked Susan. "I guess if the daughter was already a hundred or so this would have been much later. Everilda herself must have been ancient. A spell founded on the death of a mortal every six years?"

"So the booksellers told me," replied Sulis Minerva. She did not appear bothered by the mention of dead mortals. "When they came prying and peering, asking what I knew of the Stone Lady."

"Why did you not tell them?" asked Susan. "Why only tell me?"

"I wanted to see you," said Sulis Minerva. "I did not want to see booksellers. They are a pestilential lot, interfering and managing, usually in matters best left alone. Particularly if those matters are of my purview."

"Why did you want to see me?" asked Susan. There was more going on here than Sulis Minerva being annoyed by the booksellers. She could feel it, sense the attention of the entity. Sulis Minerva did not really care about the Stone Lady, or the murders of mortals. Her glittering, diamond eyes watched Susan with an attentiveness that was unclear. Susan did not think it was predatory, but it still bothered her, to be so watched.

"I wanted to see you for two reasons. The first is simple. I was curious to see a child of an Ancient Sovereign and mortal. There have been so few, and none for centuries. Or if there have, the booksellers have killed them. Did you know that, Daughter of Coniston? Your bookseller friends slay the likes of you."

"They have done so in the past, yes," said Susan. "My friends told me. Not anymore."

"Not anymore," whispered Sulis Minerva, almost to herself. "Perhaps that is true, or has yet to be fully put to the test. Did you know they call their powers the High Magic, and those of others Wild or Low?"

"No," said Susan.

"They are merely words, but they say much about the St. Jacques," said Sulis Minerva. "There is no real difference between their magic and, for example, mine own. And have you considered that they themselves are demi-mortals, albeit made, not born. The killing of the offspring of mortal and Old One is no more than rivalry. They can brook no others like themselves."

"They chose not to kill me," said Susan. She was troubled by Sulis Minerva's words, but she trusted the booksellers. At least she trusted Merlin and Vivien, and some of the others. She was sure they would be with her, if some other booksellers wanted her dead, as Merlin and Vivien had stood against Merrihew.

"Not yet, anyway," said Sulis Minerva. She sighed, a long heartfelt sigh. "I hope I am wrong, but I suspect the matter has not been permanently decided, it has merely been delayed; and there will be even more reason for the booksellers to fear you in the days and years ahead."

"Fear me? The booksellers have nothing to fear from me. I don't want my father's power or anything like that. I am an artist. I want to learn and grow as an artist, live as a . . . a straightforward ordinary person, a mortal, that is all."

"You are already not a straightforward ordinary person," said Sulis Minerva. "What exactly you will become remains to be seen."

Susan didn't want to talk about that.

"You said you had two reasons why you wanted to see me."

Sulis Minerva nodded slowly, her head wobbling strangely on her neck, too fluid, scarily inhuman.

"The second reason is because I have been keeping something for you. Here."

She reached inside herself. One watery hand entered her stomach in an effortless merge, as if reaching into a bowl of water. She drew out a reddish-gold bracer and threw it to Susan, who instinctively caught it. As her fingers closed, she instantly knew the bracer was bronze, specifically an alloy of Coniston copper and Cornish tin, with a small amount of silver and lead, the latter two from the Mendips. But more than that, the bracer had been made in concert by her father and someone else, another Ancient Sovereign of a similar kind, and it was an object of great power, a power to augment an Old One's natural ability to make an oath binding, when it was freely entered into by both parties.

"I don't want it," she said automatically, holding the bracer away from herself as if it were potentially toxic, out over the pool. It was heavy, designed to be worn on the forearm, in the Roman military fashion. She had at first glance thought it was plain bronze, carefully polished, but now she saw there was a figure etched into the metal. It took her a moment to work out it depicted a bear. Not a heraldic bear rampant. Rather it was a bear sitting on its haunches, holding a piece of honeycomb above its mouth, with three ludicrously oversized drops of honey falling into its jaws. Not Winnie-the-Pooh, for it was a full-sized, fully toothed and clawed bear, but there was a kind of Pooh-like sensibility about it. There was a sense of humor there, a dangerous beast pacified by honey and made harmless. Not at all the sort of thing you would expect to see on a military-style bracer.

"It is yours and has been since your birth," said Sulis Minerva. "*I* do not give it to you. I was entrusted to hold it, no more, until you claimed it. I advise you to keep it hidden from the booksellers. They cannot abide others to have such things and would take it for themselves."

Susan still held the bracer out towards the Sovereign. She did want it. She wanted it so much. It would feel absolutely right upon her arm, and with it she could do great good. Ensure fair and equitable agreements between mortals, between entities, between entities and mortals. But it would also change her, she knew. It would accelerate whatever was happening anyway, the power of Coniston that was growing within her. It would be another step away from being human.

"I do not want it now," said Susan steadily. "I ask you to keep it for me, as you have done."

She threw the bracer back, flipping it up high. For a moment it seemed Sulis Minerva would not catch it, but then one long arm blurred in motion, spray flying as she moved. The Ancient Sovereign snatched the bracer from the air, popped it in her mouth, swallowed it, and then made Susan jump by belching very loudly.

"You surprise and interest me," said Sulis Minerva. "I hope you will call again, *Susan*."

"I will, I hope," said Susan. "Thank you."

She noted the significance of Sulis Minerva using her first name rather than "Daughter of Coniston" and also that this was a clear dismissal. The audience was over.

Sulis Minerva raised her arms high and slowly sank beneath the surface, until only her right hand remained. This hand she waved languidly in the style favored by Queen Elizabeth, finishing a complete revolution of the wrist before she sank completely below the roiling waters of the spring, a great gout of steam punctuating her departure.

Susan laughed and trod back up the terraced levels to where Dr. Prester was sitting. The Director of Avon Museums had an open manila folder on her lap, fountain pen in her hand, and was making marginal notes on the topmost document inside.

"Paperwork," she said, shutting the folder and capping her pen before she got up. "It never ends. Particularly in local government. Ah well, I suppose it could be worse. If I were a Roman functionary, I'd be up to my ears in wax tablets and working on my stylus technique. Come on, I'll show you out. We have to go back a different way, through the grove. That door you came in through will have moved."

CHAPTER THIRTEEN

⤞•⬦•○•⬦•⤝

Bath, Sunday, 11th December 1983

Sally Lunn. A tea-cake; so called from Sally Lunn, the pastrycook of Bath, who used to cry them about in a basket at the close of the eighteenth century.

⤞•⬦•○•⬦•⤝

SUSAN STEPPED BACK OUT INTO THE CHILLY FOG. SHE HEARD THE door close behind her but did not look back. Merlin, Vivien, and Diarmuid seemed to her to have hardly moved, if at all, still the same tableau of figures wreathed in white. Though now they were all wearing blue-black beanies with bright yellow "Police" written on the front.

Merlin glanced at his watch.

"Fourteen minutes, thirty seconds," he said. "For us, at least. I hope it was a productive meeting?"

"It was much longer," said Susan. "I think."

She blinked several times, feeling a little dazed, and watched strands of fog writhing above Merlin's head. Her nose suddenly felt very cold. "She answered some of my questions. We'd better get back and tell the others."

"Good news on that front," said Merlin, pointing. "Evangeline and Una have repaired to Sally Lunn's Eating House. Taken it over in the interest of national security as being close to the scene but not too close, but in actuality in response to the terrible Admiralty tea and the lack of decent comestibles. This whole terrorist bomb idea of Torrant's has grown in the making. She's running around trying to downplay it now, but it's too late. All of central Bath is locked down and police are converging in droves from neighboring forces and the Met. Can you hear the helicopter?"

"Yes," said Susan. She hadn't paid it any attention, but now she could hear the deep rattle of a helicopter, coming closer and then fading away as it circled somewhere above the fog. She shivered. "I hope I don't have to go in it. Or any other helicopter."

She, Merlin, and Vivien had survived one helicopter accident. She never wanted to fly in one again.

"It wasn't that bad," said Merlin.

"We *crashed*," said Susan.

"And survived," said Merlin cheerfully. He took one of the police beanies out of his bag and handed it to her, taking her hat. "Wear this. It's to help avoid friendly-fire incidents. Move slowly and keep your arms up and away from your body, in case we come across any armed police. There shouldn't be any within the perimeter, but with this fog and lots of different forces involved, you never know."

Susan put on the beanie and unrolled the sides down over her ears, which were more chilled than she'd thought. She regretted not putting the hood of her ski suit up before, over her hat, when they were walking over from the Empire Hotel. It was so close it hadn't seemed worthwhile, but it felt like a lot of heat had been leeched out of her body; she was tired and cold. Though possibly that was a side effect of visiting Sulis Minerva's spring. The steaming heat from there hadn't lasted.

"Tea and buns," said Vivien firmly. "I can see you need them. It isn't easy crossing to and from a place like you've just visited."

She took Susan's elbow and led her away, Merlin going ahead and Diarmuid slipping back to guard the rear, even though it was only a matter of tens of yards to the tea shop that was reputedly home to the emblematic Sally Lunn bun but was actually more likely the work of a clever 1930s marketer.

They left the Abbey Churchyard, heading into Abbey Street. The enormous plane tree in Abbey Gardens loomed up ahead of them, a true giant in the fog. Susan glanced back at it curiously as they turned away into the narrow alley of Church Street.

"Is that tree a locus for an entity?" she asked. "Like Southaw's yew?"

"No," replied Vivien. "It's just a tree. It isn't old enough, only a few hundred years. Besides, Sulis Minerva would never allow another entity so close."

Sally Lunn's was only a little farther along, a narrow terrace building with a curved bay window. Susan had been there only once before, and hadn't particularly liked the eponymous buns, but she was grateful they were heading somewhere warm where she could have a cup of tea. Sulis Minerva had given her a lot to think about.

A police officer with an H&K MP5 and CPO Kelly Hawkins with her Sterling SMG were standing sentry outside the tea shop, both watching Merlin's party approaching through the fog. They didn't lower their weapons until Merlin stopped about ten feet away and spoke.

"The reprobates return, Kelly," he said. "I take it the big bosses are still inside?"

"They are," replied Kelly. "Stuffing themselves, no doubt."

"We'll join in, then," said Merlin. "All quiet on the Western Front?"

"So far," replied Hawkins. The police officer smiled thinly. Hawkins did not introduce him, nor did he seem to want to know who the new arrivals were. Merlin led the way inside, the others following. Susan paused for a moment to glance in the bay window, which had a cheerful toy picnic set up—a bunch of dolls and stuffed toys arrayed around some Wedgwood china and what were probably Plaster of Paris Sally Lunn buns.

The entire upstairs floor had been colonized by the booksellers, who had moved half the tables away; taken over the shop's telephone, which Evangeline was issuing orders into; and spread maps, books, and documents over the remaining tables, except for the occasional spot where there were cups or mugs of tea and plates that mostly did not have Sally Lunn buns on them but other tasty foodstuffs.

Not all the people from the incident room were there, presumably they were still working away back in the Empire Hotel, but there were more left-handed booksellers in a huddle around

Una, and several police officers with Inspector Greene, all of them holding various radios. Greene was talking on a radio twice the size of Merlin's PF8, which had a long whip aerial that kept swiping the ceiling. The voices coming back over the radios were loud, confused, and confusing, and overlapped each other. There were many instructions to "clear this channel" and "urgent traffic only" and constant repetitions of "say again" all of which seemed to be entirely ignored. It was very noisy.

Susan collapsed at a table near the door, took off her beanie, and unzipped her ski suit. It was too hot inside after the chill outside—the classic dilemma of central heating—but the warmth was welcome and the whole place smelled deliciously of baking. Vivien sat down next to Susan. Merlin collared a waiter, who had the same vacant stare as the radio operators Susan had seen earlier at the Empire Hotel. He took their order for tea, coffee, buns, sandwiches, pastries, and muffins while his eyes seemed to be focused on an empty space somewhere above Susan's head.

"Evangeline blanking people's minds again?" asked Susan as the waiter retreated.

"She is a little too fond of it," admitted Merlin. "He won't come to any harm. It'll just seem like a really busy day for him, with the details a bit blurred."

Evangeline, perhaps hearing her name, handed the phone to a right-handed bookseller, who started talking in her place, and came over to Susan's table, as did Una and Greene, the latter handing her radio to her silver-haired associate. The cacophony continued, the general gist being that the bomb scare was over and everyone could stand down, but this didn't appear to be getting through to all parties or they wanted more information or specific instructions, or they were senior officers who just liked hearing their own voices.

There weren't enough chairs at Susan's table. Una glared at one of her cohorts, who dragged another table across and joined it on, and added chairs.

"So," said Evangeline, sitting down and assuming a regal posture. "We have made some progress. Clement is ninety percent certain he has identified the house and garden from the map, it was called—"

"Alphabet House," interrupted Susan, unable to resist.

"Indeed," said Evangeline. "That is confirmation. I take it Sulis Minerva has been forthcoming?"

"I think so," said Susan. "She said Alphabet House was built of lesser Purbeck marble, not the entity's stone, but from the layers around it, and the stone was shipped up the Avon and then the Kennet and Avon Canal, beyond Bath. She didn't know where exactly, though."

"Claude has located it near Bradford-on-Avon, based on a reference to 'an Alphabetickal House' in some correspondence about the manuscript of *Evelina* between Fanny Burney and her publisher Thomas Lowndes. It also mentions the 'curious statues.' However, we have not yet found it on a map, nor pinpointed its exact position. It is useful to know the stone came up the canal."

She turned to the bookseller on the telephone, raising her

voice. "Prahdeep, tell Claude the stone came up the Kennet and Avon Canal, the cut on the map is probably an extension, since filled in."

Prahdeep nodded his head and kept talking.

"I think that has narrowed it down sufficiently for us to find it soon," said Evangeline. "What else did Sulis Minerva tell you, Susan?"

Susan told them what she had learned about Gwyre, a.k.a. the "Stone Lady," and Alphabet House, the wizard Everilda Gibbons, and their daughter. She did not mention the bronze bracer, or Sulis Minerva's warning about the booksellers still being a danger to Susan herself.

"Everilda Gibbons," mused Evangeline. "Illegitimate daughter of Grinling Gibbons. I do recall she was a known practitioner, but not a proscribed one. My mother had some dealings with her, she kept us apprised of certain entities in Dorset. Keeping us sweet while she was up to no good, no doubt."

Once again she turned to Prahdeep and issued a string of instructions for researches to be made into Everilda Gibbons, her children, and anything else that might be related, and also to tell Claude to look for a quarry or remnant in the Isle of Purbeck relating to "Gwyre."

Susan listened to her and wondered exactly how old the right-handed bookseller was. She had presumed Evangeline was a young woman around the time of Waterloo, because she had said Merrihew had "stolen her lover." But neither of them were necessarily young then, Susan had just presumed that. So

Evangeline was several hundred years old at least, maybe even older. Which was a disturbing thought. Susan had thought of the booksellers as basically people with some special powers, but perhaps they were more akin to the entities of the Old World than she'd realized. Living for such a long time would surely distance you from contemporary life and ordinary people.

That might be something that would apply to her, too, Susan considered. Maybe she would live for a really long time? How would that change her? It was a lot to think about. Maybe she would simply become part of Coniston. To sink into the stone, like falling into a comfortable bed. She could almost feel the mountain welcoming her—

"Susan? Did you hear that?" asked Merlin excitedly.

Susan opened her eyes, not having realized she'd shut them, and in fact must have phased out for a minute or two. A lot had happened that day and somehow it was still not quite lunchtime. But there was now tea and a Sally Lunn bun in front of her. Susan took a quick gulp of her tea and a mouthful of bun and looked at Merlin as if she'd been paying attention all the time, and tried to say so, but a mouthful of bun impeded this and obviously Merlin wouldn't believe her anyway.

"You didn't, did you?" asked Merlin.

"Mmmph," replied Susan, trying to swallow.

"Now everyone's paying attention," said Una. "Pauline has just reported in from Chippenham. Three more Masons were arrested at their yard, but most important the Matron form of Gwyre was there and has been neutralized. Two of my people were injured, but only broken bones and so forth, and Inspector Green's Sergeant Lalonde has been hospitalized with concussion, but she is doing well. I think this is a very positive step forward."

Susan finished swallowing. "What does neutralized mean?"

"The statue could not be broken at first, but my sinisters held it down while the right-handed forced the inhabiting essence of the entity to retreat elsewhere. To Alphabet House, most likely, or possibly into the Crone form. Once it was gone, the stone was broken into small pieces and packed in hazardous waste containers that will be shipped away to a place where we keep such things. So there should now only be the one primary form Gwyre can use for the ritual hunt: the Crone. Presuming Sulis Minerva was correct about the Maiden. Which we will check up on, as far as possible."

"This increases your safety, Susan," Evangeline cut in smoothly. "And we will take further measures to ensure it, of course."

"Like what exactly?" asked Susan.

Evangeline did not immediately answer, instead daintily sipping her tea. Hers was in a proper cup, with a saucer. A vintage Royal Doulton Leonora pattern from the 1930s, Susan noted.

"I do have a particular interest in staying alive, you know," said Susan.

"Quite," replied Evangeline. "Merlin will be in charge of your close security, but we are speaking to the significant, woken Ancient Sovereigns of London to . . . request . . . them to watch for any attempt from this Lady Stone to enter the metropolis or exert her power there, to alert us if she does, and to bar her way. Most of them would gainsay her anyway, from natural animosity, but if we make it clear it is our wish, even the more neutral entities will repel her from their demesnes. This is being done now, and I expect we will have the necessary agreements in place before you return to London this afternoon, as I believe you intend?"

"Yes," said Susan. "What does close security mean?"

"You will need to be guarded until after the winter solstice, or until we have found and neutralized Gwyre's Crone form and destroyed Alphabet House," said Evangeline.

"Okay," said Susan. "But I have things I need to do; I'm not going to hide away somewhere. I have to go to the Slade, I have my work at the Twice-Crowned Swan, and so on."

"You should be able to do all that," said Merlin. "We'll just be keeping an eye on you. And . . . uh . . . it would be good if you could move into a safe house until after the solstice."

"Milner Place?" asked Susan somberly. She'd been kidnapped from there by goblins and a Fenris wolf, and the landlady, Mrs. London, had been killed.

"No," interjected Inspector Greene. She sounded quite enthusiastic, which was unusual for someone who wore cynicism as easily as her ubiquitous leather jacket. "We've got a new safe house for the likes of you. Freestanding, to avoid problems with adjoining roofs and goblins climbing over them. Just off Abbey Road, St. John's Wood. Pretty posh."

"A rather larger investment than we'd intended. Though the

Milner Square property did sell at a good price, this new one was at least twice as much," complained Evangeline. "However, I suppose it does have a fine library, and we got the books included."

"You know a lot more now about what can happen," said Greene to Susan. "Too late to go home now, like I once advised you to do. Move into the safe house, accept the protection. I'll have officers assigned as well, in case this Stone Lady has more of those Masons around the place."

"You'd better vet your officers again," said Merlin. "I'm concerned about Freemasons who may not belong to Gwyre's special lodge but who might help them out of Masonic solidarity or whatever, not knowing what is really at stake."

"I'll be careful who I send," said Greene. She grimaced. "It is a fair point. There *are* a lot of Freemasons in the Met, and in the Home Office, too. Someone might think it would be easy to get Susan arrested and taken to some suburban nick and disappeared from there, for example. It has been done. That's another reason why you'll need some of my people around. Better they clue in any Freemason police who try anything than have your lot kill them."

"Great," said Susan. "So I'm going to be surrounded by left-handed booksellers and plainclothes police? Everyone's going to think I've turned into Lady Di."

Greene shuddered. "I'm still getting over the bloody royal wedding. We got roped in for that, too, along with every poor fool in blue who didn't have a murder or something better land on their doorstep that morning to give them an excuse to miss it. Crowd control is not my forte, I can tell you. But in your case, we'll try very hard to be discreet, and I'm sure whoever Merlin puts on the job will be, too, right?"

"Of course," said Merlin. "It'll only be me, and probably four other sinisters, and Vivien if you don't mind, and say three more right-handed—"

"Definitely Lady Di!" protested Susan. "Not something I've been aiming for."

"It'll only be till the winter solstice," said Merlin. "A week and a bit."

"The overtime's going to kill my budget," complained Greene. She looked hopefully at Evangeline. "Unless you might like to cough up a special imprest?"

"Our budget for cooperating with Special Branch has been *completely* exhausted buying and outfitting the new safe house," said Evangeline. "Do you have any idea how much it cost to line every window and door with silver? Not to mention the time invested in the wards. I had ten of my best people working on them for a week—"

"Evangeline," interrupted Una. "Perhaps save it for the fiscal committee?"

"Hmph, yes," said Evangeline. "Sometimes I think we should put Thurston back in charge. He liked the fiscal committee meetings."

Una sniffed, a slight motion that encapsulated everyone's feelings about Thurston. His lax leadership of the right-handed booksellers had let Merrihew, the former chief of the left-handed, take overall charge and enter into a highly illegal and insidious partnership with the malevolent Ancient Sovereign called Southaw. Many terrible things had happened as a result, including the murder of Merlin and Vivien's mother and the imprisonment of Susan's father. So his was not a name to conjure with.

Evangeline, belatedly realizing this, hastily changed the subject.

"You might not need protection for a week. It could only be a few days," she said. "We've made excellent progress already. Who knows, perhaps we'll have this Gwyre entity sorted out quick as look at you."

Susan nodded wearily. "I hope so. I am keen to live as normal a life as possible."

No one said anything to that, which was in itself an answer.

"More tea?" Vivien asked Susan. "Yours is probably a bit cold."

Susan gratefully accepted a top up from the pot. She sipped it and ate the rest of her bun and then an egg and cress sandwich, hardly listening as the conversations continued on around her, and the booksellers and the police kept talking on their radios and the responses came back amidst crackles and whines and pinging noises and guarded discussions and messengers running in and out and the tunnel-visioned waiting staff weaved through it all with buns and sandwiches, tea, coffee, and hot chocolate. Susan noticed Greene surreptitiously take one of the hot chocolates and pretend it was coffee.

Amidst the noise and generally self-important bustle, Merlin leaned in close to Susan's ear and spoke to her softly.

"Do you want to leave now? We can be at the safe house in three hours or so, once we get on the M4. It's stopped snowing in the west and it never really started past Reading. They've just had a bit of sleet and rain."

"I'd like to go back to my crappy room in my share house," said Susan. "But I realize that's not sensible."

"The new safe house has a proper bath," said Merlin. "And a really good hot water system. And it's heated. Properly, I mean."

"Hmmm, that is actually more tempting than it should be," admitted Susan. She shared a run-down terrace house in King's Cross with three or sometimes four other art students, depending on if they could get someone prepared to sleep in what had once been a larder, and it only had a shower, no bath, and a hot water system that was economical by virtue of only ever supplying enough hot water for one person to have a fifteen-minute shower once a day. They boiled water on the stove to wash the dishes, and often, themselves. It also had no heating at all and was known among themselves as the "Ice Palace."

"I can go and get your things once you settle in," said Merlin. "Your sketchbooks and everything."

"It would be good to get away from all this, only . . ." said Susan. She sighed and looked ruefully at Merlin. "Only going back to London won't really get me out of all this, will it?"

"You'll be safe," said Merlin. "We'll make sure. Getting there, too."

"That's not really what I meant," said Susan. "But I do want to get out of here."

"Okay," said Merlin. He raised his voice. "I'm going to take Susan to London now, unless anyone has a good reason why we need to delay? Vivien, you want to come with us? Una, who can we have for cover?"

Una and Evangeline both looked rather miffed that Merlin had decided to leave without waiting to be told to go. Evangeline was the first to reply.

"You should wait until we have heard back that all agreements are in place," she said.

"Better to arrive in daylight," countered Merlin. "We can get updated on the way."

"I need to head back, too, with my people," said Greene. "Torrant and her locals can run the Incident Room here until we close the case, which sounds like it shouldn't take too long. We can go in convoy."

"You can have Diarmuid and whoever is at the Small Bookshop who needs to get back to London, Merlin," said Una. "Let me rephrase that. Anyone at the Small Bookshop who is supposed to be back in London. Cameron can liaise with Torrant on whatever needs to be done locally. It can be a Small Bookshop operation. I'm going on to Wooten anyway, later tonight. They want me to teach an improvised weapons seminar tomorrow."

"I remember that one," said Merlin. "Who knew a clothes peg could be so dangerous? Or as I learned to my profit recently, a Regency bonnet?"

"I am pleased you remember one of my lessons at least, Merlin," said Una. "Perhaps there is hope for you yet."

"Thank you, Aunt Una," said Merlin. "I like to think so."

"Though I still find it hard to believe Emilia has lent you her Range Rover," continued Una. "After what happened to her Jensen."

"That was an operational necessity!" protested Merlin. "She forgave me. Eventually."

"Then I suggest you go and get Emilia's extremely precious vehicle. You can pick up Susan from the Empire Hotel. We'll all go back there now and let the ordinary folk in for their buns. And into the Baths, presuming the bomb threat has subsided."

"I think it will be a little while before everything is opened up," said Greene. "Poor Torrant is going to be explaining that particular shout for the next year or so, I'd say."

"Maybe *we* should blow something up to support her," said Una thoughtfully. "Torrant has been useful to us here. Not the Baths, of course. Nothing too close to Sulis Minerva."

"Uh, I don't think that's necessary, or a good idea," said Greene hurriedly. "There are bomb threats all the time—the IRA, the INLA, Bader-Meinhoff, you name it. Very few of them are the real thing. No need to have any more bombs, real or threatened. Plenty to go around, and Torrant's tough enough to cope with criticism. Really, there is no need to blow anything up."

"I concur," said Evangeline sharply. "Really, Una, you are letting your enthusiasm get away with you."

Una smiled, but it was hard to tell if she had been joking.

"I'll get the car," said Merlin. "It's over at the Manvers Street police station. I won't be more than fifteen minutes. Diarmuid, stay close to Susan. See you shortly."

He dashed away down the narrow stairs, leaping down half a dozen at a time.

"This has all been very satisfactory," declared Evangeline. She reached across and patted Susan's hand. "You see, you have absolutely nothing to worry about, Susan!"

CHAPTER FOURTEEN

⊷⧫⊶ ○ ⊷⧫⊶

Bath and London, Sunday, 11th December 1983

Lud's Town. *London; so-called from
Lud, a mythical king of Britain.*

⊷⧫⊶ ○ ⊷⧫⊶

THE CONVOY BACK TO LONDON ENDED UP BEING RATHER LARGE AND, Susan felt, very conspicuous. Greene said she was in a hurry, so it was led by a Met Police Rover SD1-V8 with lights flashing but no siren; followed by Greene's unmarked Jaguar XJ12; another Police Rover SD1; then Cousin Emilia's astonishingly bright silver Range Rover, which Merlin explained had been custom outfitted for a Saudi sheik who then reneged on the deal, which explained its metallic silver finish, walnut paneling, camel leather seats with built-in heating, and armored glass windows. If that wasn't enough, there was a gold Ford Capri Mk3 full of booksellers following, and behind it a nondescript blue Ford Transit of the unrequired Met bomb squad who had arrived in Bath just in time to turn around and go back to London again; and bringing up the rear was a Met Police Triumph 2.5PI until this broke down just outside Swindon and its disgruntled occupants got left behind.

"I do feel like Lady Di," said Susan, who was sitting in the extremely comfortable back seat of the sheik's Range Rover, with Vivien next to her. Merlin was driving, and Diarmuid riding shotgun. Once again, literally, he had either the actual Remington 870 Stephanie had carried, or an identical model. "Not something I've ever wanted, I can tell you. Princess Di, I suppose she is now. Poor thing."

"You don't think she's happy to be a princess?" asked Vivien.

"I think she's got storybook princesses confused with real life," said Susan. She thought for a moment, then asked, "Do the royals have any idea about the Old World?"

"No, and everyone tries to keep it that way," said Vivien. "The Duke of Windsor did start down that road at one point, consorting with some fringe-dwelling individuals who had ties to a Death Cult associated with the Beast of Camden. They were removed from the scene and the Duke was discouraged from further enquiries into what he thought of as 'the occult.' This was when he was the Prince of Wales, and he was quite young. Well before Wallis Simpson, his abdication, and all that."

"Did you never want to be a princess?" asked Merlin. "Even when you were little?"

"No," said Susan. "I always was much more interested in being a witch. And now I suppose I sort of am one. A witch, I mean."

"You're not a witch," said Vivien. "I mean, we use witch and wizard interchangeably, pretty much, regardless of gender.

But it means a *mortal* practitioner of magic, someone who has *learned* how to use the powers of the Old World."

"It is very strange to think I am not entirely mortal," mused Susan. "Will I live a really long time? Or what?

"A very long time, most likely," said Vivien. "But like us, you *are* still a mortal. A human. You can get sick, though far fewer illnesses will affect you seriously. It's likely you will still be vulnerable to some rare cancers, as we are. Gwyre's daughter in Alphabet House probably has one of those. And you can be killed. That is the big difference between us and the entities of the Old World. They can be quietened, banished, bound . . . but not killed."

"Though they can suffer a near-enough fate," said Merlin.

Susan thought about this for several miles, mixed in with other thoughts about what she had become, or was becoming.

"Is there life after death?" she asked. "I mean a heaven or hell, or anything like that?"

No one answered for almost a minute. Merlin cleared his throat, but it was Vivien who spoke.

"We don't know. There may be. There are places not of this earth that have some of the characteristics of a heaven or hell, and they can be visited, though not without extreme difficulty. The inhabitants of these places might be incarnations or the next . . . step, I suppose, of people who were alive here. But they may only be responding to who the observer wants them to be. I mean, two people might talk to one and both will swear they were talking to their own dead mother. There are a number of

Ancient Sovereigns who guard the gateways to these realms. They are generally among the most difficult to find or deal with, and as they never actively interfere with mortals or mortal concerns, we have little to do with them."

"I am certainly mortal in one regard," said Susan. "I am totally knackered and am going to sleep. Wake me up when we get there."

She shut her eyes and leaned back into the plush camel leather seat. For a few minutes sleep would not come, though she truly felt absolutely exhausted, worn out by the events of what felt like an incredibly long day, though it was still only the early afternoon. But eventually the weariness overcame the fears and doubts and troubles that spun about in Susan's mind, of what she was becoming, Sulis Minerva's warnings, the bronze bracer . . . all were banished by sweet sleep.

Until the dream came. As so often in the past weeks, Susan found herself atop the mountain, the Old Man of Coniston, with the winter winds howling around her. But she did not feel cold, and within seconds she was sinking into the stone, as if it were water. But it was not frightening, not like sinking into quicksand or the like. She simply became one with the stone, losing her body while still retaining her sense of herself.

Deeper and deeper she sank, passing through mine shafts and natural caverns, deeper and deeper until she was miles below the surface and she drifted down from the ceiling of a truly enormous cavern, bigger than Wembley Stadium. It was lit by fire, lurid red light filling the great space, and as she drifted down, Susan saw the fire came from a single long trench of lava, channeled and embanked to flow in a line across the floor of the cavern, and next to it ran a subterranean river that flowed in from one side of the cavern and disappeared down a sinkhole on the other.

Hundreds of smiths worked the lava trench, wielding long tongs to hold metal to the fire, or lift crucibles that glowed cherry red, and these they took to stone worktables nearby, or to pound upon vast iron anvils, or to pits of sand for casting, or to quenching in the dark waters of the river.

They were not human. Susan knew them to be Knockers, mythic entities themselves, but of a lesser kind than her father, and sworn to his service. When in corporeal form, as they were now, necessary for their work, they were basically humanoid, but short and narrow-waisted, with long arms and legs, and their skin was crocodilian, hide resistant to fire and blows. Their faces were similar to a human's, but with outthrust jaws and recessed eyes, shielded by protective forehead ridges of bone, and they did not have hair, but wore iron caps of their own making.

Susan alighted by the lava flow. She could feel the heat now, but not the true, terrible force of it; it was more like the comfy warmth of a fireside at a safe remove. The Knockers nearby who were not busy with their craft saluted her, with a gesture like grasping a thrown coin. She noted their hands had six fingers, each of three joints, all the better for their clever work.

Two Knockers lifted a massive, heavy crucible from the fiery river using their long tongs and brought it towards Susan. It was clearly very heavy, and two more Knockers joined them, extending their own tongs to grip it by the lip. The four of them edged closer, with sparks flying up from the crucible in gouts of red and silver. Susan still felt only a comfortable heat and was not perturbed until the Knockers suddenly tilted it forward and a great wave of molten metal poured out straight towards her.

She tried to jump away but someone was holding her in a tight embrace, keeping her fixed to the spot. She snapped her head around and saw it was her father, as she had seen him last, copper-haired, Nehru jacket and all.

"We have power over metal in all its forms, daughter," he said. "Remember that."

Then the molten metal splashed over her and Susan was never sure if she would have suffered excruciating pain or not because she woke up.

"Ow!" she said, massaging her neck.

"Sorry about that," said Merlin, thinking she'd woken because they'd stopped rather more suddenly than was comfortable. "Traffic."

Red rear and brake lights stretched for miles ahead on the motorway, across all lanes, undulating up and down, diffused by the rain or light sleet that was falling.

"Where are we?" asked Susan, looking around.

"About a mile short of Junction Five," said Merlin. "Shouldn't be too long."

"With this jam?"

"Greene said she was in a hurry to get back," said Merlin. "So I expect—"

Ahead of them, the lead vehicle of the convoy blipped its

siren on. After a few seconds this rose to its regular full-scale donkey bray and the Rover turned on to the empty hard shoulder and began to accelerate, though only up to fifty mph. Not the seventy or eighty mph they had maintained before. The other cars followed in turn, all the police vehicles turning on their lights and sirens.

"Princess Di," muttered Susan, and closed her eyes again.

The convoy split up at Edgware Road, with only Greene's unmarked Jaguar, Merlin's Range Rover, and the other booksellers' Capri continuing on to the safe house in St. John's Wood. Susan slept again, but this time did not dream, or didn't remember doing so. She woke when the car stopped and the engine was turned off.

"We're here," said Vivien softly.

Susan looked out the window. It was already dark but the cul de sac was well-lit. They were parked directly in front of a large white Georgian house. There were other freestanding, large houses of various eras to either side, and behind them, where the cul de sac joined the road, there were two undistinguished seven-story Edwardian blocks of flats.

"We'll just check all is okay and then you can go in, Susan," said Merlin. Chill air came in when he opened the door, but it was not currently raining, sleeting, or snowing here. There was the usual faint odor of the city, of vehicle exhausts and industry, and of hundreds of thousands if not millions of domestic fires, many still burning coal that was only notionally smokeless, despite the Clean Air Act of 1968.

Ahead of them, Greene and her people were getting out of the Jaguar, and other booksellers from the Capri, behind. Merlin closed the car door, leaving Susan and Vivien together in the half-dark, the light from the nearest streetlamp falling only across the front seats.

"Are you okay?" asked Vivien.

Susan took a moment to answer.

"Not really, no," she said. "It isn't just what has happened in the last two days, either. More that it's made me have to think about some stuff I didn't want to think about, that I was putting off."

She fell silent. After a minute or two, Vivien spoke.

"How's the Slade?"

"It's good," said Susan. "I like working in the studio there, and they mostly just let us get on with our work, with the occasional lecture and so on thrown in, almost as an afterthought it seems sometimes. Everyone is an artist. The teaching staff are all creating their own work, too. That is a bit of a double-edged sword if you do need help, of course, since some of them hate being interrupted. But the students pretty much all want to be there, and we help each other. I think I've probably learned as much from just working with my peers, or more, than I've actually been taught. But that's good. It's very different to school. How's your business degree?"

"I like it, though a lot of people would probably find it dull," said Vivien. "I'm already annoying the uncles and aunts at the Old Bookshop with ideas on how to improve our business."

The Old Bookshop was one of two bookshops run by the St. Jacques clan in London. Despite its name—which referred to the age of the building—it sold new books and was a thoroughly modern store in Charing Cross Road. Though evidently not modern enough for Vivien.

"What about the New Bookshop?"

The New Bookshop in Mayfair sold secondhand books, rarities, and collectibles from a Georgian mansion that you might easily pass without ever knowing it contained a retail store of any kind, unless you caught a glimpse of the discreet brass plate.

"No, that's a dead loss," said Vivien, smiling. "Nothing will ever change there. But I might be able to get some computers into the Old Bookshop, things like that. I have an IBM PC at home, you know, a personal computer."

"I've seen a few," said Susan. "My friend Lenny has an Apple II. I've played *Ultima* on it. It's a good game—"

"Games! I'm talking serious business software," said Vivien. "There's an application called Lotus 1-2-3. It does this matrix thing called a spreadsheet, a way to sort and cross-reference and calculate data! It just came out last year. We can get all our stock movements and sales on it and do away with the handwritten ledgers, which are insane, they still do carbons and weekly trial balances! Cousin Emilia is all for computers. She's got the best money mind in the family, but it's going to take a lot to convince the oldies like Evangeline and . . . well . . . everyone else. I like a goose feather quill and an inkpot as much as anyone, for the right tasks, but have you seen a dot matrix printer? For donkey work, lists of new books, and so on . . . sorry, I'm babbling."

"No," said Susan. "It's good. Good to talk about ordinary things."

"Yes," said Vivien. "I know we've said this before, but we really do lead ordinary lives most of the time. I mean you have seen that in the time since, up until this weekend. Haven't you?"

"I believe you can lead a mostly ordinary life," said Susan. "But I'm not sure that's going to be true for me. I'm not sure I'll be able to lead an ordinary life at all."

"Well, we don't know as much as we would like about demi-mortals—"

"Because you've always killed them," said Susan. "Sulis Minerva warned me about that. And Una was looking at me strangely today, as if I were a threat to be dealt with."

"Una looks at everyone like that," said Vivien, leaning across to hug Susan tightly. "Susan . . . I admit there may be some of the family who might *theoretically* think it is safer to kill you, but if it ever went beyond that, we wouldn't let them. Merlin and I won't let them, or Zoë and Helen, or Audrey, or anyone you know. Evangeline is an old autocrat but she's not like Merrihew and she's a stickler for agreements. You are officially an *ally* of the St. Jacques. A highly valued one. You just saved Merlin for us, for heaven's sake! And me, because I would probably have gone in after him even if I couldn't get your help."

"Thanks," said Susan. She sighed. "But it isn't only that. Or rather that's the lesser of my worries. I *can* see in the dark, you know. I realized last night. It was only me thinking I couldn't that stopped me before."

"It's very handy," said Vivien after the briefest pause. "Even some ordinary mortals have really good night vision."

"And I know metals," continued Susan. "If I want to, I know where they were mined, how they were smelted or refined, everything there is to know. And I think . . . I think if I wanted to, I could push my finger through this car door, or twist a lamppost. Make the metal do my bidding. And stone, too, I think. Or certain kinds anyway, those that exist within or beneath Coniston."

"I can do that, too," said Vivien. "Also handy. And you wouldn't even need to hold your breath. Uh, probably. Now I've said that it might be worth checking on that one. . . ."

"Why do you hold your breath to do your magic?" asked Susan.

"Our right-handed magic costs," said Vivien. "Directed, specific magic, not passive abilities. There's always a price to pay for that, and if you don't specify what it is to be, the magic *will* take something you don't wish to give. So we give it our breath. It's a self-regulating system because if we run out of breath we pass out and the direction stops, therefore the magic stops."

"So I should hold my breath if I want to try out my power over metal?" asked Susan. "I don't remember that from my dreams. . . ."

"Your dreams?"

"I dream about my father's demesne," said Susan. "Extremely vivid dreams of the mountain, the lake, the land about. But mostly the mountain. And I can go within it, through earth and stone, deep, deep down, where the Knockers work. Only

I'm not sure they're literally under the mountain or somewhere else entirely, that you reach via the depths, if you know what I mean. And they treat me like *I* am the Old Man of Coniston. It feels like when my father gave me some of his power when we were fighting Southaw, but more so . . . as if I am becoming him, the Ancient Sovereign that is centered there, and losing myself. Which I don't want to happen."

"You should talk to Zoë or Helen about this," said Vivien. She sounded almost frightened and held Susan more tightly.

"That isn't all," said Susan slowly. She hesitated, then decided that if she couldn't trust Vivien, there was no one in the world she could trust. "Sulis Minerva tried to give me a bronze bracer, a Roman bracer like a centurion would wear on their forearm. My father and some other Ancient Sovereign made it together, long ago, for someone special, I don't know who. It had a bear engraved on it, but a sitting bear eating honey, not a rampant, fighting bear like you'd expect. Only it wasn't a joke, or meant to be humorous. And I knew the bracer would give me greater power, it would strengthen me to be an oath-maker, one such as there has not been for centuries. A High Queen."

"Shit," said Vivien. "Arthur's bracer. You have to keep this to yourself. I mean, you can tell Merlin, of course, but no one else. Not until we figure out what to do. Also, can I see it?"

"I didn't take it," said Susan. "I gave it back. Threw it back, actually. I asked her to keep it for me till later. Uh, really, Arthur's bracer? King Arthur?"

"Not really the one in the legends," said Vivien. "They're

a kind of echo of the real Arthur. He was never a king of any mortal kingdom, but he is the most significant demi-human in the mythic history of this sceptered isle. Also kind of a distant ancestor of ours, and one of the spiritual founders of the whole idea behind what we do. Keeping the peace, patrolling the borders, protecting mortals. All of that. Wow! I wish I'd seen the bracer. But you were right to give it back. For now."

"I knew if I took it I would change," said Susan thoughtfully. "It would be an irrevocable step. Which I don't want to take. I want to be mortal, Viv. As ordinary as I can be. But I suppose I'm a hypocrite because I also like being able to see in the dark. . . ."

"I know," said Vivien. "I understand. And here I was thinking that old stone statue-shifting killer was our biggest problem."

"Thank you for saying 'our.'"

"All for one and one for all," said Vivien. "Which reminds me, did you ever pick up the old sword? The one Merlin had under his bed? Or touch it at all?"

"No," said Susan. "I carried the bag but never handled the sword. Why?"

"That was Arthur's, too," said Vivien. "I wonder what would have happened if you did touch it. Though I guess you didn't have your father's power then. And he didn't make that sword."

"That sword is *Excalibur*?"

"Uh, no," said Vivien. "Arthur wielded three swords. The one Merlin had—gosh I hope he's put it back, come to think of it—is the least of them, though still mighty in its own way. Its name is Clarent, the sword of peace, the defender that protects its wielder from scathe. You know, the more I think about this, the more I think you need to talk to Zoë. I'm sure she can be trusted. Or Helen, though I guess she's still in New York."

"Okay," replied Susan. "I . . . I would like to know what's going on. With the dreams."

"Staying here might help," said Vivien thoughtfully. "If they're not actually dreams."

"What?"

"They might be more than that," said Vivien. "Some form of yourself actually having those experiences. But the wards here will stop that kind of travel."

"You mean it's like astral projection or some—"

"No," scoffed Vivien. "Astral projection is mostly nonsense, all that silver cord rubbish. But it may be your essential self is visiting Coniston, and you perceive it as a dream. . . . Zoë will know more. Can I ask her to talk to you?"

"Yes, I said okay," replied Susan. "But—"

A knock at the car window startled her, but it was only Merlin. Vivien opened the door, and he leaned in.

"Come on! It's nice and warm, there's drinks, and Diarmuid's gone to get some curries in."

CHAPTER FIFTEEN

⊳━◆━○━◆━◁

London, Monday, 12th December 1983

*Cab. A contraction of cabriolet (a little caperer), a
small carriage that scampers along like a kid.*

⊳━◆━○━◆━◁

SUSAN FADED AFTER THEY HAD THEIR TAKEAWAY DINNER FROM TIM'S
Curry Club, an excellent restaurant that was fortunately not far
away up Abbey Road, so everything came hot in both senses of
the word. She went to bed early and alone. Merlin did not ask
to join her, nor did she invite him. Without discussing it, they
both felt they were on duty or that their personal relationship
should continue on hold until their next designated date, on
the coming Wednesday.

He did come into her bedroom later, very quietly, with two
much better suitcases than any she owned, bringing her clothes
and art materials over from her student house as he had promised.
Susan saw him through a sleepy, half-open eye and mumbled
her thanks. He smiled and slid out in an exaggerated tiptoe.

Susan slept so well she didn't get a chance to fully enjoy the admittedly sybaritic bathroom of the safe house with a lingering bath. If she had dreamed, she didn't remember, and she wondered if the warding done by the booksellers had indeed kept out oneiric intrusions or prevented her from communing with her father's wellspring of power or whatever was going on.

At breakfast she met the keeper of the safe house and was reminded of the late Mrs. London. Her new host was also Scottish but had the more likely name of Mrs. MacNeill and was from Fort William, not Glasgow. But she was physically quite similar to Mrs. London, a tall, rather bony woman in her later fifties, who again like her predecessor had presumably once worked for MI5 or SIS before becoming part of Inspector Greene's Section M of the Special Branch. She cooked a fine full English, which was being partaken of in a quite palatial breakfast room by Merlin, several other left- and right-handed booksellers, and Inspector Greene and one of her cohorts, a quiet, prematurely silver-haired stick of a man, probably no more than thirty, who Susan had seen before but had never been introduced to and wasn't now. He was wearing overalls with "GLC" for Greater London Council stenciled on the back, and he had a hard hat under his chair.

"Have to keep this quiet, Mrs. Mac," said Greene, forking up a piece of bacon. "This is so much better than our canteen I'll have everyone in the section coming around."

"And I'll send them straight back out again with nae more than a harsh word, if they're not on the roster," said Mrs. Mac-Neill. "That goes for your folk, too, Mr. Merlin. I've a house to run, not a circus. You'll be eating more than that, Miss Susan?"

"Um, no, I'm already almost late," said Susan, who had only two pieces of toast, a ladle of baked beans, two fried eggs, and a Cumberland sausage on her plate, and was trying to eat fast. "I have to finish my painting today or tomorrow."

"You've got time," said Merlin. He was dressed very ordinarily today, Susan noted, in jeans, a dark-green shirt, and a slightly muddy navy-blue padded anorak, currently on the back of his chair with his favorite tie-dyed bag.

"I don't know this part of London," said Susan. "Where's the nearest Tube station? What line is it? Oh, that's no good is it? You don't want to upset the entities who lurk beneath. It'll have to be the bus. I'm not turning up in that Range Rover with the whole cavalcade along, I can tell you."

"Audrey's going to take us in her cab. It should only take twenty minutes at the most, traffic willing," said Merlin. "Surely even art students sometimes take taxis?"

"Not the ones I hang out with," said Susan between mouthfuls. "But yes. Some people have money. I suppose that's okay. And it will be nice to see Audrey."

It was nice to see Audrey twenty minutes later, and listen to her Cockney patter routine while Susan did her best to ignore that she was accompanied in the cab by Merlin and Diarmuid, and she didn't fail to notice the gold Ford Capri with more booksellers in it following her, nor the fact that Greene and her companion had gone out five minutes earlier and were almost certainly in the GLC van that was oddly always preceding them in the traffic and had suspiciously smoky windows so she couldn't see who was inside.

"I didn't see Vivien at breakfast," she said as they proceeded along Marylebone Road at a pace that was quite exhilarating for central London, approximately fifteen miles per hour with no completely halted traffic lined up ahead of them. "Did she go back to her place?"

"Viv did stay at the safe house last night, but she was up very early. She's looking into some things," said Merlin. He cleared his throat and turned his head, making sure neither Audrey nor Diarmuid could see his slight wink. "We had a brief chat before she went out."

"Right," said Susan. "So where are you lot going to be while I'm painting away?"

"Nearby," said Merlin evasively. "Which reminds me . . ."

He reached into his tie-dyed yak hair bag and pulled out a PF8 radio. He held it out to Susan.

"This is on, but the volume is down to zero. You turn this knob here, and this is the push to talk button. You hold that down while you talk, let it go to receive, okay? We're all on the same frequency, it has a range of a couple of miles, though not if you're right in the middle of a big solid building or underground. If you need us, grab it and call for help, telling us where you are. That's the most important thing. Straight off give your location and then if it is safe, any other details."

Susan took the radio and wondered where to put it. She started to open her art satchel, but Merlin shook his head.

"Stick it in your inside pocket," he said, "You might be separated from your bag."

"I think I'll be safe enough inside an art school," protested Susan. But she unzipped the West German Army surplus field coat she was wearing and slipped the radio into an inside pocket. Under the jacket she was wearing a leather waistcoat borrowed from her mother over a coveted red-and-blue bullseye The Jam band T-shirt, with slightly flared Wrangler jeans and her ubiquitous burgundy Doc Martens. Her CND beanie was in a pocket of the jacket, along with a very optimistic pair of Ray-Ban Wayfarers with green lenses in a black frame.

"We'll be close by," repeated Merlin. "What time will you finish today?"

"I guess I could be done by five," said Susan. "I don't have any actual lectures or anything this afternoon, I'll just be working on my painting."

"What about lunch? Do you go out?"

"I usually bring something, but I ate a lot at breakfast so I'll probably just work through. Or I can grab something at the Union. I don't have to leave as such."

"Okay," said Merlin. "Probably better if you don't. If you do, call us first."

"I'll find a cupboard and radio in," said Susan. She wasn't joking. She was already thinking of a supply cupboard she could hide in to use the radio, if necessary. If any of the other students saw her using it, they would think she was some sort of government spy placed among them to rat out radicals. Her own mother certainly would.

"Gower Street," said Audrey, the taxi accelerating into a right-hand turn. "Be at the Orangeade in half a tick."

"Now you're just making it up," said Susan. "No one calls the Slade 'the Orangeade.'"

"Who's the dialect specialist here?" asked Audrey as she pulled the taxi to the curb. "Get out of me Sherbert Dab and hit the Frog and—"

"Enough! Enough! I'm getting out. Please no more."

"That'd be worth an extra couple of quid if you were a tourist," grumbled Audrey as Merlin and Diarmuid exited first and took up positions that would suggest to casual bystanders that they were thinking about where to go next, rather than looking for potential assailants. "You keep safe, orright, Susan."

"I'll do my best. Thanks, Audrey," said Susan, and climbed out. She headed straight for the open gates that led to the main quad of University College, joining a steady stream of students and staff. She glanced back briefly to see Merlin and Diarmuid idly following her, apparently chatting to each other, and farther back Green's silver-haired offsider in the GLC overalls now had his yellow hard hat on and had parked himself by the front gate and was unfolding a set of plans and peering at the footpath.

They didn't follow her all the way into the studio, and as she got on with her work Susan managed to mostly forget about her guards until the lecture on "Interpreting Art Through the Lens of Artifice" at eleven o'clock, where she saw Diarmuid in the second back row of the theater, though not Merlin. After the lecture, which she didn't really understand but was not worried because no one else did either, she returned to her painting and the comfortable silence interspersed with occasional utilitarian comments about borrowing paints, brushes and the like, peppered with personal reactions to how the work was going, which varied from sighs of dismay and groans of despair or even sobs to smug *sotto voce* comments like "that is good" or surprised laughter at something turning out different but better than expected.

Susan did skip lunch, as predicted, and by the time five o'clock rolled around she was very hungry. She hurried to the Gower Street gate, into an already dark night and a steady drizzle. There were still a lot of people about, mostly students hurrying out. Carried along by the general tide, Susan found herself almost past the gate before she slowed down and edged out of the pedestrian traffic. She was wondering if she could just sidle up to the wall of the gatehouse and surreptitiously use her PF8 to call Merlin when a nearby man lifted his umbrella and it *was* Merlin.

"Ready to go?" he asked, raising the umbrella over her head. The rain fell on his straw-colored hair and made him look even more windswept and interesting, if that were possible. Several students—men and women—slowed to stare at him as he shook the raindrops off and smiled at Susan, before he took her arm and they reluctantly looked away.

"Yes," said Susan, noting the looks. She wondered how long it would be before her new friends at the school and probably perfect strangers as well started to quiz her about Merlin. She'd kept him very separate up until now.

Audrey's cab was stopped about fifty yards down the street. Merlin walked her towards it, with Diarmuid joining them a few steps behind on the other side. The GLC van with the smoky windows crawled past them and pulled over halfway to the cab, and the booksellers' gold Ford Capri, which Susan now recognized instantly, started an illegal U-turn in the one-way street, blocking anyone from following, resulting in a blare of car horns and insults shouted out of windows and helpful calls and pointing fingers from pedestrians on the footpath trying to communicate to the driver that they couldn't go that way. As if slowly getting the message, the Capri started to turn back, but in two incompetent kangaroo hops and then its engine stalled, so it was still effectively blocking the street.

Vivien opened the cab door as Susan hurried in, closely followed by Merlin, though Diarmuid went somewhere else. Susan couldn't see where with the drizzle and the flaring headlights of all the stopped cars. As soon as Merlin was in, Audrey took off with the characteristic swift acceleration of a London cab heading homewards while avoiding passengers in the rain, which would have made anyone else have an accident folding the umbrella, but Merlin managed to do it while falling backwards into the seat next to Susan as if he'd meant to all along.

"All okay?" asked Vivien, who was on the fold-down seat opposite Susan.

"Secure," said Merlin. "No signs of anyone or anything

taking an interest in Susan. Untoward, Old World–type interest, I should say. There is one chap in your painting studio I think would like to know you better, Susan. The guy three easels across with the ponytail and the fondness for Prussian blue. In fact I'm not sure he was using anything else. He kept looking over in your direction."

"Oh, that's Gryf," said Susan. "He's just hoping I stuff up my painting. In his mind I'm a competitor for some prize or other that's coming up next year."

She frowned and added, "How did you see him? I never saw you in the studio."

"I am a master of disguise," said Merlin. "A mistress of disguise, too, for that matter. Besides, you were an admirable study of an artist intensely focused on her work. I doubt you would have noticed me if I'd poured a jug of ice water over your head. Now, this Gryf—"

"Forget him!" said Susan impatiently. She was hungry and tired. "Does the fact that I remained perfectly safe all day mean you can cut back on the royal protection treatment?"

"Not until after the winter solstice," said Merlin. "But it presumably means all the Ancient Sovereigns have come to the party and agreed to keep Gwyre out of London."

Vivien cleared her throat.

"Ahem. There has been a slight hitch in that regard."

"What?" asked Merlin and Susan together and then Merlin continued hotly, "Why haven't I been kept up-to-date? You know how important—"

"I'm telling you now because I've only just been told," said Vivien patiently. "All the significant powers have agreed, bar one. Great Fire. It's always very slow getting any message to that Old One and receiving an answer, his ambassador or representative is quite difficult, so at first Theo—he's the right-hander doing the negotiations—thought it was just that. But after a lot of slow backwards and forwards, it turns out Great Fire won't agree to bar Gwyre until its representative has met Susan."

"I hate that little bastard," said Audrey, glancing back over her shoulder.

"Who?" asked Susan in puzzlement.

"Great Fire's messenger or valet or whatever he is. The Golden Boy of Pye Corner, in Smithfield," replied Audrey, turning right and expertly inserting the cab into an almost nonexistent gap in the line of traffic heading north on Tottenham Court Road. "Nasty little cherub who's meant to mark the extent of the Great Fire, as far as it got. The original one, I mean, in 1666. But he's a bleeding pyromaniac, and I bet he doesn't properly take messages to Great Fire anyway."

"Who is Great Fire?" asked Susan. "I remember the others you told me about and where to stay clear. The Beast of Camden, That Beneath the Tower, and London Stone—come to think of it, that last wouldn't be a natural ally of Gwyre's, would it?"

"No," said Vivien. "London Stone is generally benevolent. And also quite dozy. It has agreed, as have those you mentioned and the Primrose Lady and Oriel. There was some discussion about even needing to approach Great Fire, but it was decided to be necessary because it has a very broad demesne, which was greatly expanded by the Second Great Fire during the Blitz, in 1940. It has been largely quiescent since the last V-2s fell in 1944, and it shouldn't rise unless there is a really major conflagration, so its only current point of contact is via the Golden Boy of Pye Corner. Who despite Audrey's suspicions is definitely some sort of herald for Great Fire. Anyway, the Boy won't pass on our request unless he meets Susan in person. Curiosity, it seems, like Sulis Minerva. Or it might simply be the Golden Boy enjoying being difficult, making us take you to him."

"What does that involve?" asked Merlin. "I've never had any dealings with the Golden Boy or Great Fire but—"

"He'll want a fire before he manifests," interrupted Audrey. "In front of him. We had to light up a garbage bin full of paper last time before the little git would answer our questions."

"When was this?" asked Merlin, frowning. "I don't remember hearing anything particular about Great Fire or the Golden Boy."

"A couple, no, three years back, bit of a sideline investigation into the Denmark Place nightclub fire," said Audrey. "Merrihew wanted to rule out any involvement from our neck of the woods. Or maybe Southaw did, I mean in his persona as Holly, I don't know. Anyway, eventually we got the gen from Great Fire, via the Golden Boy."

"Was an entity involved?" asked Susan. She vaguely remembered seeing the TV news about that fire. "A lot of people were killed, weren't they?"

"Thirty-seven," said Audrey. "But no, it was an ordinary

human tragedy. The coppers got the bloke who did it."

"I remember the fire," said Merlin. "I didn't know we'd been asked to investigate."

"Merrihew kept her cards close," said Audrey. "Particularly if it was something for Southaw."

"Do we have to go and see this Golden Boy?" asked Susan wearily.

"The higher-ups think it would be politic," said Vivien. "It should be safe enough. The Golden Boy isn't particularly powerful; he wouldn't dare cross us."

"Can I have dinner first?"

"Certainly," said Vivien. "It's going to take some time to prepare, because this time the Golden Boy wants the full ceremony. A fire in a garbage bin isn't going to cut it."

"Oh no," groaned Audrey.

"So I'm guessing the full ceremony is *really* going to be a pain?" asked Merlin.

"Yes," agreed Vivien. "Back to the Blitz. We have to get a World War Two fire appliance, be dressed appropriately, and fight a full-on incendiary bomb conflagration while talking to the Golden Boy. Look on the bright side—before the Second Great Fire we'd have to be all seventeenth century and working a bucket brigade."

"I don't understand," said Susan. "Do we go back in time?"

"Not exactly," said Vivien. "Great Fire's locus is that night of December 29, 1940, but it is a kind of copy, a snapshot of the time and place. For it to revel in the fires. Over and over again."

"Like Gwyre's garden?" asked Susan. "But leaving the original in place?"

"In a way," said Vivien. "It's a different order of magic and not done intentionally. Great Fire was quiescent, asleep deep down, when it was woken again by the blitz and the resulting fires. Its demesne, which was the extent of the Great Fire of 1666, was transformed and extended by the fires of the newer disaster. Fortunately, it isn't the sort of entity that actively tries to expand its influence and power, or there'd be far more fires in London than could be rationally explained, and we'd have to sing it down like we did Southaw."

"So where are you getting a World War Two fire engine?"

"Appliance," said Vivien. "Got to speak the lingo. We've got one, but it has to come down from Manchester on an artic. It won't be here until about midnight. We've got all the other stuff at the New Bookshop, but we'll get it brought over and gear up at the safe house. Kickoff will be about one a.m."

"And we have to fight a fire?" asked Susan. "With old World War Two equipment? Does anyone even know how to do that?"

"You won't have to hold a hose or anything," said Vivien. "You'll be talking to the Golden Boy. And three of the aunts were in the Auxiliary Fire Service in the war. They'll be joining us, so we'll be all right on that score. Aunt Druetha even got a George Medal for some amazing rescue in 1941."

"Oh right," said Susan weakly, suddenly reminded of the booksellers' long and often complicated lives. "So, one a.m.? So much for getting back to my normal life in London. Where do we have to go anyway?"

"Smithfield. Pye Corner is on Giltspur Street, right next to St. Bart's."

Susan shook her head.

"And we're going to drive up in a World War Two fire engine dressed all 1940s and hope no one notices? Even at one a.m. there'll be people around the hospital!"

"You'd be surprised by what people don't pay attention to," said Merlin, who while he'd been listening kept watch, constantly looking out the windows. "If anyone asks, we'll say we're practicing for a reenactment or a film or something. Besides, once we summon the Boy, we won't be there. I mean, we will, but we won't. No one in the here and now will see what happens. In a way it's easier than lighting a fire in a garbage bin, because that would attract real attention."

"You're telling me," said Audrey. "We had to put on this whole act that we hadn't seen who put it there and lit it, we'd just stopped to put it out, being good citizens. Who just happened to all have fire extinguishers. Greene's predecessor, Albert Jacklin, had to come and get us out of that bit of Barney Rubble."

"Jacklin," said Merlin. "Where did he go? He make Chief Inspector in some quiet regional force like he was always talking about?"

"Nah," said Audrey. "Afraid not."

Merlin didn't ask what had happened to Inspector Jacklin, and neither did Susan or Vivien. The answer was in Audrey's tone and choice of words, and Susan remembered Torrant's comment about the police officers who headed up Section M.

"Almost back to the rat and mouse," said Audrey. "Home

sweet home. What are you lot having for supper or dinner or whatever you call it?"

"Mrs. MacNeill was working on a boeuf bourguignon pie when I popped in earlier," said Vivien. "Said she'd lay on dinner this once as Susan was special, first resident in the house and so on. Huge thing, crust the size of a tablecloth. Guess she expects a few extras."

"I might deign to grace you with my presence in that case," said Audrey, suddenly sounding not at all Cockney and disturbingly like the Queen Mother. "Here we are."

The gold Capri had somehow got ahead of them, which might have reflected badly on Audrey's knowledge if she hadn't let them nip in ahead at the last turn. Diarmuid and another left-handed bookseller got out and wandered in different directions up the cul-de-sac, and Merlin didn't open the door until they had signaled, and the house door was opened by another left-hander, whose shadow slid into the street, long and angular and threatening. To others, but a welcome to Susan and company.

CHAPTER SIXTEEN

‑‑‑◆‑O‑◆‑‑‑

London, Tuesday, 13th December 1983

Fire. (Anglo-Saxon, fyr; Greek pur.) I have myself passed through the fire; I have smelt the smell of fire.

‑‑‑◆‑O‑◆‑‑‑

FIVE HOURS LATER SUSAN WAS CRAMMED IN THE CREW BENCH SEAT of a very well restored or possibly long maintained Bedford Heavy fire appliance between Merlin, Vivien, and Diarmuid, with Aunt Druetha in the driver's seat, accompanied by Aunt Ceridwen and Aunt Patricia, none of these three looking a day over forty-five and all utterly convincing as Auxiliary firefighters of 1940 in their well-fitting blue woolen coats, rubberized trousers, and tin hats with the red line around the brim. They even looked as if they'd all just had their hair done, cut short, waved, and set to look good under their helmets. This was because they had; they were laughing about it and reminding each other of fires they had fought more than forty years ago, and the people they had served with, the personal losses and tragedies an acknowledged, if unspoken, presence behind the cheerful reminiscences.

By comparison, the others did not look so convincing. Susan's uniform coat was too long in the sleeves and her helmet was too big. Even Merlin didn't look quite right, though he had spent a hasty ten minutes hemming his trousers up before they all had to embark in Audrey's cab to head to the rendezvous with the firefighting aunts and their vehicle.

"Are the aunts right- or left-handed?" asked Susan into Merlin's ear, hoping the women's own conversation and the very noisy motor of the fire engine would keep them from hearing her inquiry, or would at least let them pretend they hadn't heard. As everyone was wearing heavy leather gauntlets of the requisite era on both hands, she couldn't tell.

"Druetha is one of the even-handed. She's actually in charge of our Crawley Tunnel Library in Edinburgh. She flew down earlier tonight," whispered Merlin. "Ceridwen and Patricia are right-handed. They only had to come up from Thorn House."

"When you say fly down, do you mean in a plane?" asked Susan. Druetha had fierce eyes, rather like a bird of prey, and made Susan think of her somehow jetting through the sky under her own power.

Merlin frowned. "British Caledonian to Gatwick. You mean is she a pilot with her own plane?"

"No," said Susan, regretting her joke.

"Quite a lot of us *are* pilots," said Merlin seriously. "The left-handed particularly."

"Okay, we've got the high sign," said Druetha suddenly, going from conversational to operational voice. Greene had signaled from the top of Giltspur Street that police under her direction had blocked the road just south of Cock Street, and her officers at the north end had opened the gate that usually blocked vehicular access from the big Smithfield roundabout. They would close it behind the appliance after it went through.

The Bedford made even more noise as it got underway, with Druetha's grinding gear changes attracting fondly reminiscent remarks from her companions in the front seat about the skill it took to drive the appliance, and the general namby-pambiness of modern vehicles with synchromesh and other such devices made to sap the vigor of the true driver.

Luckily there was no traffic ahead, thanks to Greene's diversions, though some ambulance staff drinking tea and smoking outside the station stared as the vintage fire engine lumbered past in a series of jerks and accompanying barks of the exhaust and headed down Giltspur Street.

"Okay, Susan, remember the Golden Boy's demesne is quite small, probably only fifty or sixty yards around the actual statue that is his locus," said Vivien. "That's the cherub that sits in a niche on the corner of the building at Cock Str—yes, Diarmuid, we know it got its name from the brothels that were once there—"

"I didn't know," said Susan. "Really?"

"Yes," said Vivien. "As I was saying, the statue is in a niche on the corner of Cock Street and Giltspur, above head height. Now, we don't have a formal safe conduct as the Boy never gives one because of the intrinsic uncertainties of fire. His word could be unintentionally broken by an ember landing on you or whatever. So if for some reason things go pear-shaped, run north on Giltspur Street and you should get out of his little piece of World War Two and Greene will be there, along with some of our people for backup."

"I'll stay close to you," said Merlin. "Vivien and Diarmuid have to help the aunts."

"There'll be a lot of smoke and noise and fire; it will be pretty terrifying," shouted Druetha from the front. "We'll take care of any immediate fire threat but stay close to the appliance, and whatever happens, do *not* go inside a building. Understood?"

A chorus of "yeses" answered her from the back seat.

A hospital porter on the street outside the St. Bart's arched pedestrian entranceway farther down the street was lighting his pipe as they approached, sneaking a surreptitious smoke in the early hours. A sudden, enormous flare from his match made him drop the pipe and stumble back, followed by a double take as he saw the Bedford trundling in his direction. He was old enough to have been alive in World War Two.

"The Boy's awake," said Druetha. "Ring the bell."

Ceridwen reached up and pulled vigorously on a handle, swinging the bell on its mount above the cab. The bell's *ding-ding-ding* sounded sharp above the roar of the engine. Druetha swung the appliance to the right and pulled up with the screech of not very good brakes and the alarming sensation the vehicle might not stop in time, just in front of the corner of the building where the Golden Boy looked down from his niche. She wrenched the handbrake on and put the engine in neutral.

"Crew, stand by pump and run out hose!" she snapped, flinging the door open and leaping out. Everyone followed her lead.

As Susan jumped down, the world changed. From the relative quiet of modern London in the early morning, it was suddenly astonishingly loud. There were explosions all around, from bombs and anti-aircraft fire, so many they almost merged into a shocking symphony of ear-shattering sounds. Susan felt the ground lurch and the air shiver. The smell of smoke was everywhere, a horrible, industrial, acrid stench, a haze all around, lit within by the horrifying, ever-present red glare.

Not all the noise was from explosions. There was a constant rumble, too, the hungry, terrifying roar of the fire itself. A sound somewhat like a jet taking off, if you were too close, and it was far worse because it didn't stop, it didn't fade away into the distance. If anything, it only got louder.

Susan scuttled around to the front of the appliance, feeling herself shrink inside her coat and helmet, as if she might become a smaller, safer target. A sudden, closer, and much more distinct explosion, accompanied by the shrill scream of ricocheting shrapnel from a falling anti-aircraft round, made her dash forward, and she almost fell but managed to steady herself against the radiator grille.

She looked up and saw the Golden Boy in his niche, a little cherub with folded arms. He uncrossed his arms and waved. Small, bright-yellow wings—incongruously like a Brimstone butterfly—emerged and spread from his shoulders and he launched himself out and fluttered down to hover in front of Susan. His wings seemed barely sufficient for the task to hold him aloft, beating so fast they were a blur.

Merlin came up close behind Susan. She tried not to flinch as something blew up not far behind them, the red light strengthening. She felt the radiant heat intensify on the bare back of her neck. Metal rain fell on the cobbled street, more shrapnel from anti-aircraft shells, bomb casings, downed aircraft. Druetha was shouting orders, the pump on the appliance was adding its own distinctive beat to the cacophony, and there was a snarling hiss as the hoses were put in action and water fell on flames, though it was nothing compared to the triumphant roar of the fires.

"I greet you, Daughter of Coniston," said the Golden Boy. He had a surprisingly adult, old-fashioned voice for a little toddler statue. He wobbled closer on his odd wings. "And I—"

He suddenly darted forward like a wasp, one pudgy little hand outstretched. Merlin lunged to intercept him, but he was a fraction of a second too late. The Golden Boy touched Susan's shoulder—and everything changed.

"I tender my apology for what I have done, and must do," continued the Golden Boy, retreating upward to flutter out of Susan's reach.

The stench of smoke was still all around, but it smelled different, less oily and metallic, more like woodsmoke. The red glare and the roaring of the hungry flames was the same, but there were no constant explosions, no rattle of falling metal. Susan stared around her, taking in her new surroundings. The Bedford pump engine was gone, and the booksellers. The street was different, much more indifferently cobbled and very dirty, with an open drain that stank of sewage so strongly it almost overcame the smoke. The building with the niche for the statue was entirely different, Elizabethan half-timber above roughly plastered stonework.

"I could not gainsay the Lady Gwyre," said the Golden Boy apologetically. "Despite I know well the ire of the St. Jacques will be severe, and I will suffer for it. Alack!"

"Why couldn't you gainsay her?" asked Susan angrily. She unbuttoned her heavy uniform coat and reached inside for the folding knife and silver cigarette case in the pockets of her leather waistcoat. Vivien had okayed that garment, as it dated from well before the war anyway, and Merlin had insisted she continue to carry knife and salt at all times.

"Grinling Gibbons wrought this form, but it was his daughter Everilda who woke Great Fire in it," said the Golden Boy. He fluttered still higher, backwards towards the ledge that preceded his later niche. "In a sense, I am as much a child of Everilda's as her daughter. So Gwyre is, in a sense, my stepmother. Familial obligations must be answered, no matter the cost."

Susan's response was to open the folding knife, but before she could do anything more she was grabbed from behind, two cold arms fastening around her middle. She pushed back, trying to reverse headbutt whoever it was and smash them with her tin hat, but her helmet flew off, and when she tried to simply fall backwards, she couldn't budge whoever held her. It was like heaving against a wall.

Effortlessly, she was lifted up, turned about, and flung over the shoulder of a grey-white Purbeck marble statue of a medieval saint, a seven-foot-tall figure of indeterminate gender in a belted robe with Roman sandals, who had possibly once had a crown but it had weathered to become a ring of odd little knobs like growths around its temple. A rosary and cross thrust through its belt had fared better and were still recognizable.

The stone saint immediately started to head south at a swift walk, along the smoke-wreathed Giltspur Street, past a bucket brigade of sooty, startled, seventeenth-century people who screamed and crossed themselves and fainted and started praying aloud, save for one burly fellow who raised his ax and came after them shouting about the devil.

"No, don't!" shouted Susan as he ran after them, ax held high. The ax couldn't do much to the statue, but he was all too likely to hit her. She squirmed around, trying to get free, but one of the saint's arms was wrapped around her middle and might as well have been a loop of immobile stone.

The axman came on, still bellowing about the devil, until suddenly all the smoke and fire and noise snapped off as if someone had flipped a switch. The red light was gone, replaced by the cold radiance of modern streetlights.

They had left the Golden Boy's demesne and were back in 1983. Three uniformed police officers were just ahead of them, standing by a gently swaying line of police tape that had been stretched across the road. They stared at the sudden apparition, stunned, and lost valuable seconds as the statue sped past with Susan wriggling about on its shoulder, parting the tape as if it had won a running race.

"Call Inspector Greene!" shouted Susan. "And keep your distance!"

One officer bent her head to her radio handset and the other two followed, drawing their truncheons. The statue paid them no heed, continuing its fast walk, its heavy feet clattering like horse hooves in the night. It went straight across Newgate Street, and Susan blessed the lack of traffic, though a bus did need to slow down to avoid hitting them, and a car going the other way pulled over for a moment before seeing the pursuing police officers and continuing on its way. Susan heard sirens starting up behind them, almost certainly Greene's vehicles, hopefully now containing Merlin and the other booksellers in hot pursuit.

The statue could easily have crushed Susan and killed her, so she figured this was a kidnapping, not an attempted murder. She was briefly tempted to see where it took her, as it might lead them to Gwyre. But that thought went out of her mind as she saw the police officers following suddenly stop and split up, crouching low as they sought cover. Hanging over the back of the stone saint, she couldn't see why, but a few seconds later two very loud, booming gunshots told her the reason.

Susan put the cigarette case in her mouth, gripping it hard enough to make her teeth hurt, and drew the ridiculously sharp blade of the folding knife across her palm. It cut deeper than she intended and she almost cried out and dropped the case. More shots rang out, and a bearded man in overalls and a thorny rose Masonic apron, wielding a seven-foot-long double-barrel punt gun, ran past and took up a position behind an ornamental hedge outside a modern office building. He fired again, both barrels, at the first in line of the police vehicles that were screaming down Giltspur Street, with lights and sirens.

The statue jigged sideways into a narrow lane, too narrow for cars to follow. Susan craned her head and saw it was now being led by another aproned Mason, who ran ahead constantly beckoning as if the statue needed guidance to know where to go.

Cursing herself for not practicing this, Susan swapped the knife to her bloody left hand, almost dropping it, and clicked open the cigarette case. She almost dropped that as well, but managed to pour a quantity of salt over the bloody knife in her left hand. Closing the case again, she put it back in her mouth, and took the salty, bloody knife back in her right hand.

After that, Susan hesitated for a full minute, knowing this was yet another step towards becoming something other than human. But the statue ran on, with the Mason leading it, and who knew where?

There were many cracks and crevices in the aged stone. Susan found one high on its back and thrust the knife in, sliding it backwards and forwards at an angle so the salt and blood mixture spread across and into the smooth, shell-patterned grey marble.

"You will serve me! I am your master!" she mumbled over the cigarette case in her mouth. It sounded like "Yush shush mer imma yermasher."

Nothing happened.

Susan snatched the case out of her mouth and tried again,

investing her words with grim determination.

"You will serve me! I am your master!"

The statue shivered as she spoke, and the bloodstains on its back shone red, like a stormy sunset. Susan suddenly could sense the entity inside, a small, fierce, entirely instinctual being who was caught in a trap. It wanted to fight or flee, but it couldn't do either.

"I am your master," said Susan again. There was no doubt in her voice.

She *was* the master.

The thing, the spirit, or whatever it was, flinched with every word. Susan could sense it giving in, becoming subservient. It was not much of an entity at all. It was only a very limited, tiny part of something far greater, a piece of Gwyre the Stone Lady.

Susan could see into its very rudimentary mind. It had only been lifted to the low level of sentience it possessed a few days before. She experienced its first awakening, spreading itself through the statue, learning how to make the stone move. This had taken place in a dark cavern, with the Crone. The statue had been brought in by half a dozen Masons, or rather pushed along some sort of rolling conveyor, and it had woken still lying on it. It had climbed off the rollers and been led back up a tunnel alongside the conveyor by a Mason, to a lorry, walking up a ramp of planks that bent and groaned under its weight. There was complete darkness for a time in the back of this vehicle, then it followed the Mason from the lorry to a narrow boat on a river or broad section of a canal. The gangway there did break under the statue's weight, but only as it stepped off.

Later it was offloaded on a shaly river beach, recognizably on the Thames, the statue landing so heavily when it jumped off the bow, the Masons had to help dig its feet out. Then they went into a sewer outfall, the stone saint easily tearing away the iron bars that blocked the way, and marched along a neatly bricked Bazalgette main sewer to an almost disastrous emergence in Cock Street, the metal rungs of the Victorian ladder bending, but not quite breaking, as the statue climbed out. From there it hid in a doorway, awaiting the Golden Boy's call only a half hour later.

Behind these recent memories of a programmed drudge, Susan found a tiny thread leading back to a greater intelligence. Gwyre was keeping watch over her servant. But the connection could work both ways.

Susan mentally reached for the thread and imagined herself pulling on it, dragging the Old One forcibly back to this cast-off piece of its essence. The thread grew tight, and with it came a sudden sense of amazement, a feeling of shock that this could be happening. Gwyre was quite a long way away, Susan felt, and confident in her own power. The Stone Lady's essence was anchored in a massive weight of Purbeck marble, the Crone locus, but despite this Susan was pulling her out of it, bringing more of Gwyre into the statue. It might even be possible to subject the Ancient Sovereign to her will. It would be very difficult, but perhaps it could be done.

Blood and salt and steel. Her father's power, and whatever the Copper Cauldron had granted her. It was enough. She hoped.

"You will serve me."

The weak, cast-off entity inside the statue wanted to obey Susan. It wanted to serve a new master. Its capitulation resonated along that narrow thread. Gwyre felt it and was suddenly afraid.

She did the only thing she could. She abandoned the fraction of herself in the statue of the saint and cut the cord.

Susan felt the connection sever. The little fierce, stupid entity within the statue did not immediately comprehend what had happened, as if it had taken a mortal but not instantaneously fatal wound. The statue slowed like a battery-operated toy on Christmas night as the animating power ebbed away. It took one more step and stopped. It was still holding Susan over its shoulder, one arm encircling her, but it was now nothing more than stone.

Susan redoubled her efforts to slide out from the statue's grasp and get off its back.

"What have you done!" screamed the Mason who had been leading the way. He doubled back and came around to swear at Susan, at the same time fumbling in his pocket for a revolver. The pocket was too narrow and the hammer was caught, and he was in a frenzy, eyes wide in panic.

"Make her come back! Make her come back or I'll—"

There was a shot, incredibly loud and close. The Mason looked down at the massive, spreading stain on his thigh where he'd shot himself. He sobbed and fell whimpering to the ground, hands pressed to the wound to try to stop the effusion of blood, to no avail.

"Sorry, Mistress. I'm sorry, sorry," he muttered. "Not my fault, please, please . . ."

Susan undid more of her coat and managed to get her arms out and slither backwards until she fell down the front of the statue in a tangle with the discarded coat over her head. She heard footsteps approaching and panicked, fighting to get the coat off, certain she was about to be attacked.

Flinging the coat free, she saw a middle-aged, very nattily dressed man leaning against the wall. He was clearly very drunk or out of it on drugs, staring with bright but unfocused eyes at the statue; at the bloodied, now almost unconscious Mason on the ground; then at Susan in her waistcoat, rubberized trousers, and with one bloodied hand clutching a silver cigarette case. The knife was still stuck in the statue's back.

"What do you call it?" slurred the man. He had a French or maybe Belgian accent.

"What?" asked Susan. She looked back along the lane. Blue light was reflecting down it and she heard shouts above the sirens.

"The art, the work," said the man, gesticulating. "The installation. It is very impressive. I had thought the exhibit did not open until tomorrow and was . . . over there."

He pointed vaguely and laughed at himself.

"What?" asked Susan again, just as Merlin burst into the lane at speed, with Diarmuid a few steps behind, both of them still in their vintage fire uniforms, complete with red-ringed Brodie helmets. They had their pistols drawn and ready, Merlin his .357 Smython and Diarmuid a Browning Hi-Power. They slowed as they saw Susan, the statue, the Mason on the ground, and the man behind.

"Armed Police!" they shouted in seconds-apart stereo, raising their weapons. "Do *not* move!"

The man leaning on the wall staggered upright and took a step towards Susan.

"There is more?" he said. "A theatrical component?"

"No!" shouted Susan to the man. "Seriously! Don't move!" She turned to the booksellers. "He's a civilian! Don't shoot!"

The man staggered forward again, one step left, one step right, and wavered between the statue and Susan.

"Do not move!" Susan repeated, investing her words with every ounce of command, telling herself she was the child of an Ancient Sovereign, she had authority and power and must use it. He was at most a second away from being shot and killed.

The man stopped, wavering in place.

"I have perhaps misunderstood," he said sadly, staring down at the pool of blood that was widening near his feet. "Not art, not theater. Life. And death."

Holding the statue, he doubled over and threw up.

A few seconds later, Merlin and Diarmuid were there. Diarmuid took control of the vomiting art critic, handcuffing him, while Merlin swept past to watch the other end of the lane, with a quick glance at Susan. The Mason who'd shot himself was clearly dead.

"You okay?" he snapped. "How bad's your hand?"

Susan lifted her hand and watched the blood trail down her wrist.

"Just a cut," she said. "I did it myself. Salt and blood and steel, to bind Gwyre to my service. But there was only a kind of, I don't know . . . fragment or particle of her in this statue. She was connected, but she managed to withdraw before I could . . . before I could try to dominate her."

"You did the right thing," said Merlin. He took the knife out of the statue and cleaned the blade with his handkerchief. "They might have got away with you otherwise."

There were more sudden footsteps, and the arrival of a multitude of police, led by Greene, and more booksellers, led by Vivien. The lane filled with people, there was much talking on radios, the art critic was taken away, and an officer bent to double-check the Mason in an act of optimism, given the vast pool of blood beneath him.

Vivien took Susan's elbow and led her back to the street and into the Bedford, which looked very out of place surrounded by modern police cars and two ambulances, *and* a contemporary Dennis appliance of the London Fire Brigade that had just turned up. Druetha, Ceridwen, and Patricia were chatting with the firefighters. From what Susan heard in passing, they were pretending to be the middle-aged daughters of themselves, engaged in a reenactment to honor their parents' service, the firefighters too interested in their equipment to wonder why they were doing this in the middle of the night.

Vivien quickly went to work on Susan's hand using a thankfully modern first aid kit filched from one of the ambulances.

"Sorry that didn't go according to plan," she said, cleansing the wound with gauze and some sort of burning alcohol. The fine cut was beginning to really hurt. "This isn't too bad; you don't need Sipper spit. You used your power? You bound the entity in the statue to your service?"

"I tried," said Susan. "It was a kind of *piece* of Gwyre. A puppet, given just enough smarts to follow basic orders. But she was watching over it, and she knew when I took control. If she hadn't broken away, I think I could have got her. Maybe. The remnant or whatever it was didn't survive the shock of separation."

She winced as Vivien started to fix a dressing on the wound.

"I guess in a way I killed it. The sad little servant in the statue. It really had no idea what it was doing, save to obey Gwyre's will."

"How do you feel about that?" asked Vivien.

"It had to be done," said Susan grimly. "It was Gwyre's. I saw a little into what passed for its mind. It was taking me somewhere, to keep me until the solstice, for Gwyre in her Crone shape to hunt me down."

"Somewhere?" asked Vivien eagerly. "Do you know where?"

Susan shook her head slowly. She didn't want to think about it.

"Somewhere . . . somewhere . . . underground."

She stopped, drew a shaky breath, and continued. "I saw the Crone. When she was making the statue come alive."

"What did you see?"

Susan shuddered.

"A statue of Purbeck marble, all grey and mottled. A massive old woman, all hunched over, with a *shell* coming out of her back. Like a snail, a massive shell three times her height, and she was six or seven feet tall, or would be if she stood straight. Her arms were very long, too. I mean, *twice* as long as they should be, and she had hooked hands. I'm not sure if she even had fingers, just these massive hooklike fists. I don't think she had legs either, just a . . . a long, rubbery mass that moved and glistened, the marble sweating. What do you call that in a snail?"

"The foot," said Vivien.

"And her eyes were on stalks," said Susan. She put her hand over her mouth. "I think I'm going to be sick."

She opened the door and leaned out, gasping, but didn't throw up. She panted heavily, sucking in fresh, cold air. After a few minutes, she sat back up straight and shut the door.

"I'm okay," she said.

"Good," said Vivien soothingly, in the tone of someone who didn't really believe that assessment but wanted to. "Here comes Merlin. We should get you back to the safe house."

Merlin climbed in. He looked at Susan with concern, and handed back her folding knife, all clean.

"Are you all right?"

"Yeah," said Susan. She slipped the knife back into her pocket, gritted her teeth, and nodded again. "Yeah. I'm okay."

"What happened with the Golden Boy?" asked Merlin.

"He took me back to the first Great Fire," said Susan. "Apparently Grinling Gibbons made him. The statue I mean, which is his locus. And Grinling's daughter, the wizard Everilda, she woke him up, whatever that means. So the Golden Boy thinks they're family. He said Gwyre was sort of his stepmother. So he had to help her. The statue was waiting and it grabbed me and took off."

"I felt the change, but I didn't know what it was," said Merlin, who was clearly upset. "You and the Boy vanished. The fires blazed up and we had to get out, back into our time and place, and Greene came running up to tell us you'd been abducted."

"Again," said Susan. "And like last time, I rescued myself, thank you."

Merlin nodded, shamefaced.

"I've failed you—"

"No!" exclaimed Susan. "No. I'm joking. I know you would have rescued me. I just got there first. And I still needed your help. I will need your help. In fact, can you exercise your powers to get us out of here? Because I really want to have a quick shower and go to bed."

"Una and Evangeline expect a debriefing. They'll want to deal with the Boy—"

"They can bloody well wait," said Susan.

"I guess I can fill them in . . ." Merlin started to say.

"No," said Susan firmly. She reached over and took his hand. "You're coming to bed with me."

"But it's only Monday. I mean Tuesday morning. Not Wednesday yet."

"I don't care," said Susan. "Now, can we go and find a vehicle that will get us back to that ridiculously luxurious safe house at more than ten miles an hour?"

"Yes," said Merlin. He jumped out and held up his hand for Susan, who took it before jumping down. "Let's go."

Vivien, left alone in the back seat of the Bedford, emitted a weary sigh.

"Guess *I'll* go and tell Evangeline and Una everything they want to know, then," she said to the empty cab. "Shall I?"

CHAPTER SEVENTEEN

➤—I—◆➤—◦—◅◆—I—◅

London, Tuesday, 13th December 1983

*To take the cake. In ancient Greece a cake was the
award of the toper who held out the longest.*

➤—I—◆➤—◦—◅◆—I—◅

IN THE EVENT, SUSAN'S DEBRIEFING DID NOT TAKE PLACE UNTIL THE afternoon. Despite several requests, she refused to visit the Old Bookshop before going to the Slade, and spent the day finishing her painting, which judging from Gryf's reaction ended up working out very well. She ignored the security arrangements, though she did wink at Merlin when she passed him in the corridor outside the studio. He was telling several interested third years that he was indeed available to be drawn, nude or clothed, at somewhat more than the usual rate, but not immediately.

Leaving the Slade went as smoothly as it had the day before, with the extra input of the other two St. Jacques black cabs instead of the Gold Capri, the drivers lining up side by side to exchange insults about some imagined fare stealing, effectively blocking any pursuit. Not that there was any pursuit in evidence.

Vivien had not managed to tell Una and Evangeline everything they wanted to know, because they wanted to know more than Vivien could tell them. Consequently they did not wait any longer for Susan to come to see them but came to see her at the safe house. Or at least that was their excuse, rumors of Mrs. MacNeill's excellent cooking possibly having already spread through the bookshops. Susan had only just walked in through the front door when Mrs. MacNeill told her she had visitors waiting in the library, the "higher-ups" as she referred to them.

Susan sighed, put her satchel down, and went to the library, followed by Merlin.

"Did you know they were here?" she asked outside the door.

"No," said Merlin. "I'd have told you."

Susan opened the door. She'd had a quick look in the library before, and seen a pleasant, light-filled room with tall windows on the left-hand wall, and floor-to-ceiling bookshelves on the other three, including around the doorway in the south wall. It had a couple of comfortable leather club chairs of likely 1920s vintage, and a low table of ebonized wood with gilt edges that Susan suspected of being late Victorian, of the Aesthetic Movement.

But it had been transformed. There was now an enormous corkboard leaning against the shelves on one side, its surface covered with most of the same exhibits from the incident room at the Empire Hotel, plus new ones, so many they overlapped each other and spread past the sides of the board. The black and gilt low table was gone, replaced by a much longer folding table with a white plastic top. This was surrounded by very utilitarian plastic chairs of modern ugliness, and these chairs were filled by booksellers (and Inspector Greene), all occupied having a late-afternoon tea, while also reading books that had been chosen from the shelves, judging from the gaps.

Susan took in this surprising sight as the books were laid down upon her entry, most of the readers being reminded by her arrival to drink their tea or coffee, or take another piece of Mrs. MacNeill's lemon drizzle cake.

Una's book was *The Worm and the Ring* by Anthony Burgess, who Susan only knew for *Clockwork Orange*; Zoë, who was in her wheelchair at the head of the table, had a large old-looking volume called *Book Repair and Restoration* by Mitchell S. Buck propped up in front of her; Clement's book Susan couldn't identify as it was open flat on the table, but he was looking at a photo section in the middle of it, black-and-white photographs of castles or of one particular castle; Vivien was reading *Red Moon and Black Mountain* by Joy Chant, a hardcover with a very simple but fabulous blue-and-red dust jacket. It had to be the American first edition as Susan didn't know it, and she immediately coveted it. Evangeline, who was closest to the door, had laid her book down faceup so Susan could easily read its title, *Origins of the English Parliament* by Peter Spufford; and next to her, Prahdeep was reading *Pet Sematary* by Stephen King, which had only been out for a few weeks.

Inspector Greene was also reading, a pocket-sized paperback, but she slipped it inside her jacket as Susan came in, so she couldn't identify it.

"Ah Susan, welcome," said Evangeline. "You have a very nice library here. Better than I expected, the inventory not having passed my desk as yet."

This last was obviously a dig at somebody, but no one reacted. They were too busy securing the last pieces of lemon drizzle cake, correctly interpreting Merlin's sudden acceleration as an attempt to seize one for himself.

"I'll bring in the other cake," announced Mrs. MacNeill from behind Susan. "And a fresh pot of tea. And coffee."

"It's not my library," said Susan, taking a seat and the cup slid towards her by Vivien. "But I'm glad you like it."

Merlin sat down next to her, looking daggers at his relatives, who all had their mouths full.

"That other cake had better be lemon drizzle, too," he muttered.

Evangeline ignored him. Taking up her teaspoon, she tapped the side of her cup.

"I call the meeting to order," she said. "Maybe I should have a gavel?"

"You don't need a gavel," said Una scornfully. "Can we get on with this? I have a lot to do. Christmas sales are up fifteen percent on last year and we aren't getting the reorders out on the shelves as quickly as I'd like."

"I meant more permanently, not just right now," said Evangeline. "In any case, this meeting has been called to ensure everyone is up to date on Operation Stone Crack, as I have chosen—"

Crumbs sprayed as the other booksellers couldn't repress their giggles. Susan looked around amazed; she had not seen them so lighthearted before. Even Una was laughing.

"Or perhaps not," said Evangeline stiffly. "If it will provoke the more juvenile among us. Zoë, I am surprised that an even-handed bookseller of your seniority would find the term 'crack' so amusing—"

"I think it is the cake," said Zoë diplomatically. "So delicious, so redolent with citrus, it's making everyone feel zesty."

"I don't know about that," said Evangeline dubiously. "I will have to come up with another name—"

"We already have one," interrupted Greene. "And everyone's been using it. Operation Garganey."

"Garganey?" asked Evangeline, her nose wrinkling. "That's a kind of duck. It has no relevance to Gwyre, or stone, or Purbeck—"

"That's the point!" said Greene, obviously trying but not succeeding in hiding her exasperation. "It's chosen at random from a list so anyone who isn't supposed to know about it can't immediately work it out."

"Garganey," said Evangeline, sounding it out. "Very well. Operation Garganey continues promisingly. First of all, Clement has identified the original location of Alphabet House, which is being searched for the Crone shape as we speak by a crew under Cameron, from the Small Bookshop."

There was a polite round of applause for Clement. He inclined his head.

"It was relatively easy once I got access to the books of the Kennet and Avon Canal company, where the tariffs paid for the passage of the Purbeck marble were recorded; and we obtained access to the architect Joseph Gwilt's papers last night. He had enciphered his diaries, but not, of course, sufficiently well to keep us from reading them."

He sat back, very self-satisfied. Looking directly at Merlin, he popped the last fragment of cake from his plate into his mouth and chewed slowly.

"So where is it?" asked Susan.

"Between Bradford on Avon and Staverton," said Vivien quickly, after a glance at Clement, who hadn't answered because he was trying to swallow his last, too big mouthful of cake. "There's nothing there now, only a wood that was probably part of 'Wolf Wood' on the map, and a large sunken field where the house was, with faint traces of a ditch that was the extension of the canal."

"Gwilt refers to the place's destruction by a 'most surprising cataclysm' in 1821, though it is not clear what he meant by that," said Clement, who'd managed to get the cake crumbs down. "The house and gardens would have completely disappeared from the foundations up when it was removed from this world, so perhaps he thought there was an earthquake or something. He was very disappointed, as he worked on it for five or six years from 1814 and had hoped it would become well-known and earn him future commissions."

"If the Crone form is there, it will be found," pronounced Evangeline. "In any case, since we now have the agreement of all significant Ancient Sovereigns, she cannot enter London, so you are quite safe, Susan."

"Speaking of agreements with Ancient Sovereigns, I'd like to hear more about what happened with the Golden Boy, Susan," said Una rather coldly.

Susan told them what had happened, including her binding of the statue, and her vision of the Crone.

"How fascinating!" declared Zoë. "Could you draw it for us?"

"If I have to," replied Susan reluctantly. "Oh, you mean right now? I'll get my satchel."

She went out and got her satchel, returning to draw a quick sketch of the Crone. This was passed around the table, with various booksellers commenting.

"Not a very agile form," said Una. "Two or three of us with crowbars would finish her off easily enough."

"This is fascinating," said Evangeline. "Her shell is of the *Viviparus* water snail."

"Naturally enough," said Clement, with a sniff. "Purbeck marble is a fossilized limestone, composed of tightly compacted snail shells laid down in the Early Cretaceous—"

"I know, I know," interrupted Evangeline testily. "That is what I was going to say. The inherent nature of the stone has been reflected in the carving. I wonder if it was intentional on the part of Frances Gibbons or—"

"*Frances* Gibbons?" asked Susan.

"Yes, yes, we'll come to her in a minute. When we're finished with your debriefing. What else did you learn from your connection with the statue? Besides seeing the crone?"

"She was underground somewhere," said Susan. "In a cavern, but a human-made one, an old Bath stone mine, I think. I didn't really see much, the connection was fleeting. As soon as I bound the fragment, Gwyre severed the connection—"

"This is what disturbs me," interrupted Una. "You bound an entity to your service. Do you want to do it again? Or bind others, not necessarily entities?"

It sounded and felt like an attack.

"I was trying to stop an animated statue from running off with me to be used as a sacrifice!" snapped Susan. "The serial killer Ancient Sovereign you're supposed to have tracked down and dealt with by now. And it wasn't a complete entity, anyway. I don't even know if I could bind anything more powerful."

"I don't dispute you may have needed to take action in this case," said Una. "But it is the future I am concerned with. We used to kill your kind specifically because you *could* bind others to your will, including us! Now you've actually done it, and you might do it again—"

"What do you mean my kind?" interrupted Susan angrily. "I'm just like you if we get down to it. You're made what you are by inheritance and a cauldron you call the Grail. I am the same, even if my power comes more directly! Why would I be more untrustworthy than a bookseller? Look at Merrihew! She was in charge of you lot and she couldn't be trusted at all!"

"A fair point," said Zoë. "Una, I think you have been looking at this far too narrowly. Tactically, not strategically. Susan is an ally who has proven herself and her integrity multiple times. I believe that matter is closed."

"But Mum . . ." Una started.

"Closed," said Zoë firmly. She ignored Susan's swift look between the two booksellers and back again, finally catching on to the resemblance, which was mostly in their eyes. "And it is not the point of this meeting. We are here to discuss the murderer Gwyre and what must be done to put a stop to her activities."

"Here's the second cake," announced Mrs. MacNeill from the doorway. There was a momentary stillness, then rapid movement to clear space for it, everyone obviously wanting the cake put down in front of them. It *was* another lemon drizzle cake, roughly the size of a small bicycle wheel.

"Now, now," said Mrs. MacNeill sternly. "No seconds until Merlin and Susan have had some."

"Or thirds," added Merlin, with a suspicious glance at Clement. Mrs. MacNeill put the cake down in front of him, carefully cut two slices, put them on plates, and handed them to the two new arrivals. It was an exquisitely moist lemon drizzle cake that had apparently been drizzled in something other than lemon after the baking. Even Susan could smell something seriously alcoholic.

"This is delicious," mumbled Merlin between mouthfuls.

"With a secret ingredient, I think?" remarked Susan. The

cake was even more alcoholic than her mother's fruitcake.

"Yes, dear," beamed Mrs. MacNeill. "A bottle of Cedratine in and on every cake. It's only a cordial, nothing like so strong as whisky. I use it for the flavor. I'll be back in a moment with the tea and coffee."

"A bottle of Cedratine!" remarked Vivien after Mrs. Mac-Neill had exited. "That stuff is *exactly* as strong as whisky!"

"Do you think *in* and *on* means there are *two* bottles in every cake?" said Merlin, in awe.

"Pass me another piece," said Evangeline, her request immediately echoed by almost everyone else.

There was a long hiatus for everyone to eat cake and drink the fresh pots of tea and coffee Mrs. MacNeill brought in, before the meeting resumed.

"Now, where were we?" asked Evangeline. "Ah yes. The binding of the entity or partial entity in the statue of Saint Jordan of Bristol."

"Is that who it was?" asked Susan.

"Yes, we've identified it," said Evangeline. She looked at Greene, who took a last sip of cake-washing-down tea before speaking.

"It was originally in a church near Bristol, Holy Trinity at Westbury on Trym, but got shifted during the Civil War and has been in the possession of the Bristol Museum and Art Gallery for at least the last hundred years. It was in a storage annex, not on display. It was reported stolen three days ago, but may have been gone longer than that, given it was in a row of statues and the dozy watchman isn't sure he would have immediately noticed the gap. The great minds there took a while to work out that their own forklift wasn't used to shift it, either, so it's been a puzzler to them. They settled on it being a prank by the engineering students from the uni, with the statue likely to turn up somewhere amusing. It should have been reported to Torrant as being an exotic crime, and got to us before anything happened with you, but because they'd flagged it as a student thing, Torrant didn't get to hear about it."

"Incompetence," sniffed Una.

"It does suggest that Gwyre had no other suitable stone figures to animate anywhere closer," said Evangeline. "Which is good news, now that London is finally closed to her creatures. We have also confirmed the identity of the wizard, and of her daughter. Prahdeep?"

Prahdeep fussed about with some papers in front of him, almost knocked his cake plate off the table, and endured another one of Una's sniffs before he got going.

"Yes. Grinling Gibbons did have an illegitimate daughter, we've located the parish record of her birth and some correspondence. It was Everilda Gibbons, as previously suspected. She was born in 1702, and while there is no record of her death, we have several references to her in our own archives from around 1760 to 1821. She was a known practitioner but believed to be innocuous. There was certainly nothing about her relationship with an Ancient Sovereign or any other entity. Her daughter we think is one Frances Gibbons. She is much more obscure, but if it is her, she was born in 1719 and had some repute as a "carver of grotesquery" much later in the eighteenth century. There are few references; she did not have a high profile. One interesting fact is that she apparently could sculpt or carve with great skill but chose not to—"

Zoë had made a noise as if about to speak, but as Prahdeep paused she waved for him to go on.

"Uh, yes, there is a letter from a collector, Henry Blundell himself, lamenting this fact. He mentions she is Grinling Gibbons's granddaughter and says 'she has all Grinling's skill but a twisted nature that is brought forth in her works.' It isn't clear what that means."

"Is she also a wizard?" asked Susan. "Or displayed, I don't know, powers?"

"We have no records of our own concerning Frances Gibbons," said Prahdeep.

"Yet we know she is a demi-human," said Una. "And must possess magic herself. Are you sure we have no record of her? Nothing?"

Prahdeep spread his hands and shrugged to indicate this was the case.

"This does suggest Frances Gibbons may have had nothing to do with the murders," said Greene. "If you have no record of her misusing her magic through her lifetime—and she was close to a hundred years old before her two mothers froze her in time or whatever they did—then she can't even be considered an accessory."

"She carved the three statues: Maiden, Matron, and Crone," said Evangeline. "She basically made useful bodies for Gwyre, who had previously only been a great lump of stone."

"But she didn't necessarily know what use Gwyre would make of them," argued Greene.

"I think she did," said Zoë quietly. Her voice, as always, had great authority. "We can see it in the heraldic statues. I consider it very likely she began to carve those statues when she knew she had cancer, their grotesqueries a representation of the growth inside herself, and in fact were a means of prolonging her life by displacing the energy of the cancerous growth into the stone she worked. This is a known technique, utilizing the law of contagion. But it is, of course, limited if you cannot cure the primary tumor. So she had the power to perform that particular magic. She, Everilda, and Gwyre must have hatched the later plan to keep Frances out of time when it became clear the displacement into statues would not be enough to keep the cancer at bay. Clearly Frances was desperate to stay alive and had already engaged in a magical process to do so. It is interesting that Everilda did not have the same determination to live, given that in the normal course of things a wizard can extend their lifespan to three or four hundred years. But she gave up her life to the spell that took Alphabet House out of time and held her daughter in stasis. Either she truly loved Frances very much or she was coerced to design and initiate the ritual."

"By Gwyre?" asked Susan.

"Oh no," said Zoë. "I doubt Gwyre is a very sophisticated

entity. It, or she if you prefer, was lifted into wakefulness by Everilda for her own purposes, and Frances carried that on. The splitting of her locus, that central stone, into the three shapes will have diminished her intellect as well, and it was probably done to reduce any chance of rebellion against the Gibbonses. No, if any coercion occurred, it would have been by Frances. I am very confident she is not an innocent in this, Inspector Greene."

"We can't know for certain unless we can question her," said Greene. "And Gwyre, if that is possible. But your plan is to simply eliminate both."

"It is the safest course," said Una impatiently. "It is not merely Susan's life at stake—"

"Merely?" asked Susan. "Come on—"

"We cannot risk another demi-mortal usurping or abrogating her powers," continued Una, speaking more loudly. "It's no different than a judicial hanging. Gwyre and Frances have murdered twenty-six people!"

"Apart from the minor detail that there'll be no trial beforehand and we got rid of the death penalty in 1969," said Greene.

"*We* did not get rid of the death penalty," snapped Una.

There was silence around the table. Greene sighed, and sat back, and stared at her hands.

"What about the Golden Boy?" asked Susan, to change the subject. She did not want to talk about the booksellers killing demi-humans.

"He has been dealt with," said Una ferociously. "He will not revel in his fires for many a year to come."

"That isn't what I meant," said Susan, swallowing nervously. "Was he really made by Grinling Gibbons and woken by Everilda? That's what he told me, why he set up the trap. He said he was effectively a stepsibling of Frances and owed them family loyalty."

"Oh yes, he was made by Grinling Gibbons," said Prahdeep. "He has the peapod on the sole of his foot."

"What?" asked Susan.

"The peapod," said Prahdeep.

Susan sighed and wished there was more alcoholic cake.

"I don't know what that means either, Prahdeep," said Merlin.

"It was in the briefing notes we put together earlier," protested Prahdeep. "The page on Grinling Gibbons. He worked mostly in wood, like the Boy, who was gilded later, and he generally carved a peapod somewhere on his work."

"I must have missed that," said Merlin.

"I never even got a copy!" said Susan crossly. "Considering I am the one under threat—"

"That isn't how it works," snapped Una.

"You can read my copies," whispered Vivien as Susan drew breath for an angry retort.

"I think perhaps we are straying from the matter at hand," said Zoë.

"Which is that everything is under control," said Evangeline with satisfaction. "We simply need Susan to stay here until after the winter solstice and the problem will resolve itself."

"I'm going back to my mother's house on Friday," said Susan

determinedly. "Or Saturday at the latest."

"That would be most unwise!" exclaimed Evangeline.

"We cannot allow it," added Una. "Until the Crone form has been found and neutralized, you need to stay in London. Ideally, you wouldn't leave this house until after the solstice. We have already accommodated you going to the Slade, something I still consider a serious risk."

"There really are advantages to being here, Susan. Safety-wise, I mean," added Vivien. "Like we were talking about before."

"I told Mum—" Susan started to say, then she subsided, realizing that Vivien was talking about the dreams of Coniston. Which she had not had here at the safe house. "Yeah. Okay. I'll think about it."

"I believe we're all caught up," said Evangeline. "I am returning to the New Bookshop. The search team at the Alphabet House site should be finished by tomorrow morning, and their report will be circulated as per usual. We will reconvene here tomorrow at five for a situation assessment. Vivien, please tell Mrs. MacNeill we would be delighted if she bakes more cakes."

"I'm working tomorrow afternoon," said Susan. "At the Twice-Crowned Swan."

"This is foolishness," said Una, her mouth tightening in displeasure.

"Evangeline just told me I'm perfectly safe!" exclaimed Susan.

"Safe from the creatures of the Old World," said Una. "Provided all the Ancient Sovereigns of London continue to do as we have asked. And we still do not know if Gwyre has more mortal followers. The Masons of the Thorny Cross may have more lodges than the one we found in Chippenham. Why can't you just stay here in the house? Read some books? Have a holiday?"

"Because I need my job," said Susan. "It was hard enough getting two weeks off over Christmas."

"Oh, very well!" snapped Una. "If you will insist on making *our* job more difficult we will simply have to rise to the occasion. Merlin, you have command of this detail. Keep me informed."

She pushed her chair back, got up, and strode out. Evangeline followed, with Prahdeep close behind, clutching papers.

"Guess I'll be off, too," said Inspector Greene. "Sergeant Hiss will be here on duty tonight. I'll see you at breakfast."

That left only Zoë, Susan, Vivien, and Merlin and a lot of cake crumbs.

CHAPTER EIGHTEEN

⊱━◈━◦━◈━◦◈━◈━⊰

London, Tuesday, 13th to Tuesday, 20th December 1983

Swan. Swan, a public-house sign, like the peacock and the pheasant, was an emblem of the parade of chivalry.

⊱━◈━◦━◈━◦◈━◈━⊰

"WHO'S SERGEANT HISS?" ASKED SUSAN.

"You know, silver hair," said Merlin.

"He was never introduced," said Susan. "I don't think I've ever even heard him speak."

"Yeah, he doesn't talk very much," said Merlin. "He's okay. Reliable. Been with Section M longer than Greene."

"I wonder if I might have a few words with you alone, Susan," said Zoë. "Concerning your dreams."

Merlin looked at Susan, who nodded.

"Guess I'll take a bath and get changed," he said. "Though typically Heather didn't bring over the clothes I requested, or fold them properly. I think she simply grabbed everything off the rack closest to the door and stuffed it all in a suitcase. I'll be ironing for hours!"

"And I have an assignment to finish before Friday," said Vivien. "See you later, Susan."

They left together. Zoë gestured for Susan to move around to sit next to her at the head of the table.

"Vivien has told me a little of your dreams," said the even-handed bookseller. She was wearing fancy gloves today, pale leather trimmed with folded-back lace, that looked very seventeenth century, though otherwise she wore what Susan had always seen her in, a white pantsuit that was rather like a navy tropical uniform. "But if you wouldn't mind telling me directly, in more detail? When did they begin?"

"I'm not sure," replied Susan hesitantly. "I think I was having them long before I realized, I just wasn't remembering them when I woke up. That started to happen about a month ago."

"Tell me of the dreams since then," said Zoë.

Susan told her as much as she could remember, right up until her first night at the safe house, when the dreams stopped.

"That is indicative," said Zoë. "It does suggest these are no mere dreams but a form of preparation."

"Preparation for what?" asked Susan.

"They are not nightmares?" asked Zoë, avoiding this question. "You are not frightened by them?"

"No," said Susan. She hesitated, then added, "Quite the reverse. I enjoy what I'm doing. It's exciting to be able to move through stone and hold molten metal as if it's water, and to know the minds of others. But it's too attractive, if you know what I mean. I know it will change me."

"Perhaps not as much as you fear," said Zoë.

"And you didn't answer my question. A form of preparation? For what?"

"I would guess a readying of the vessel."

"That doesn't sound good," said Susan. "I'm not a vessel! I'm a person!"

"My poor choice of words. I should rather say that I suspect your father is planning to pass some significant part of his power to you," said Zoë calmly. She thought for a moment, then added, "Perhaps there is also some authority he wishes to relinquish."

"Some authority?"

"Even among Ancient Sovereigns the Old Man of Coniston holds a high place. He is a High King, an entity who cannot only bind others to his will but can make freely given oaths binding, even beyond death. But I do not think he has always had that power, for he is also known as a maker of objects of power, a great worker of copper, gold, and silver, even iron. The two do not usually go together. As always, it is very difficult to ascertain the extent and history of an entity's powers, but I suspect your father took on the oath-maker's magic from someone or something else. A long time ago, certainly, perhaps a thousand years or more. Though that is not long by how he might measure time."

"And he wants to give that power to me?" asked Susan. She almost added something about the bracer Sulis Minerva had tried to give her. Arthur's bracer. But she didn't. Even telling Vivien had made it seem more concrete, as if it was something she had to accept. Sulis Minerva had warned her the booksellers would want it, and Zoë had the academic curiosity all the right-handed shared, to an extreme degree. She would want it to see it even more than Vivien had and would not necessarily be held back by concerns of friendship.

"He has already done so, a little of it at least," said Zoë. "Then there is your interaction with the Copper Cauldron. This also prepared you to receive greater powers. Enlarged you, in a sense. I suspect your father has begun to grant you more of your inheritance far earlier than might otherwise be the case."

"But I don't want it!" protested Susan.

"Don't you?" asked Zoë. "None of it?"

Susan started to answer, then fell silent. She did want it, but not at the cost of losing her humanity.

"In any case, that is what I think is happening," said Zoë. "I could be wrong. I believe your father said he would wake at the turn of the year?"

"Yes," muttered Susan. "I . . . I'm planning to go to Coniston then."

"I do not think there is anything you can do about this until you meet with him," said Zoë. "Even going to Coniston earlier would not help, if he has not risen. In any case, while you are here, within the wards, the dreams cannot reach you."

"Would you recommend I accept whatever my father wishes to give me?"

Zoë hesitated.

"It must be your choice. I cannot advise you. Other than to

say that no power, particularly mythic power, comes without cost. Consider what you are willing to pay."

Susan did not dream that night. Merlin was with her, but she went to sleep immediately when her head touched the pillow and did not wake until he brought her a cup of tea at half past seven, and then it was a rush to get ready, have breakfast, and get to the Slade in the already familiar routine with Audrey in the cab and several accompanying vehicles.

With her painting and artist's statement done, and no other classwork, lectures, or tutorials, it was clear to Susan that no one took the message of staying until Friday very seriously. In fact, half the staff and a greater proportion of students had already obviously taken off and would not be back until 1984 rolled around.

By five o'clock she was at the Twice-Crowned Swan on Cloudesley Road, transported there by her security detail, with Merlin and Darren (Diarmuid was working at the Old Bookshop that day) going in first to check everything out. Susan also noted that Sergeant Hiss, in a blue factory worker's coat, was already inside, a freshly drawn pint of London Pride in his hand.

Only Mr. Paul was working that night. His partner, Mr. Eric, was away.

"He's run off to the bloody circus," said Mr. Paul with a grin. As they were both former circus strongmen, this was not as unlikely as it sounded. Even so, it took several snatched partial conversations through the evening for Susan to discover that Mr.

Eric had in fact gone to help out his sister for a week or so. She was ringmaster of a small circus that was currently wending its way down the east coast. This naturally led to Mr. Paul asking whether Susan might in fact be able to delay her departure to Bath and work, if possible, up to Christmas.

Until that point, she had been undecided. Her mother would be disappointed, she knew, but not that much given that she would have several friends staying. As long as Susan made it for Christmas itself, she could delay. It galled her that she had to do the booksellers' bidding, even more so because it was the sensible course. But Mr. Paul's hopeful face settled the matter, and so Susan agreed to work the afternoon and evening shift every day until the 23rd, the day after the winter solstice.

Part of her decision-making came down to the dreams. If she could avoid them for as long as possible, she was also avoiding whatever change was coming. Possibly, without the dreams, she might not be ready for whatever her father planned. She hoped this was so.

Susan could still see in the dark and was reminded of this in the cellar of the Twice-Crowned Swan, tapping a keg. It wasn't until she came out she realized she hadn't turned the light on. This was also a reminder that she was already changed, even in this small but helpful way.

Vivien came in about nine, to order a gin and tonic and loiter at the bar. It wasn't very busy, but there was still a lot to do, so it wasn't until an hour later and close to last drinks that the pub was quiet enough for her to tell Susan the afternoon briefing had not been consequential and everyone was annoyed because Mrs. MacNeill had made some sort of healthy Scottish oatmeal cake entirely devoid of alcohol. The upshot of it was that the Crone form had not been found, and there was nothing underground at the site of Alphabet House. However, there were a great many underground sites in the general area, and investigating them would take a lot of time and personnel and be very visible to the general public.

"All of which the higher-ups begrudge," said Vivien. "Both our lot and Inspector Greene's, Inspector Torrant's at Avon and Somerset Police, and Torrant's equivalent at the Wiltshire police. The general thinking now seems to be that if we keep you safe, we don't even need to find the Crone. Gwyre fails to get you, the spell unravels, Alphabet House and Frances Gibbons cease to exist, and Gwyre, too, because the Wild Hunt will sweep them all up. Without causing Evangeline et al. any budget upsets. Other than the cost of protecting you, of course, which she was complaining about."

"Really?"

"Not seriously, they're not going to cut back or anything. Just general complaining. It's nothing compared to searching all the mines and so forth around Alphabet House. That would take weeks, hundreds of coppers and scores of booksellers, who are all flat strapped with the Christmas trade before we even talk about our other work. Plus the army and so on, because there's a lot of old defense establishments there."

"Okay," said Susan. "It's annoying but also comforting. I

really don't want to be kidnapped and taken away to be hunted down by that ghastly half-snail woman."

"Yeah," agreed Vivien. She hesitated, then was unable to stop herself adding, "I was wondering about that aspect. The Crone would not move fast, so how could she hunt? She has to do it personally for the spell. I mean, the Maiden or the Matron, obviously they had legs, and could run fast. But a snail in pursuit? She'd have to hobble her prey or something—"

"Vivien! Don't," snapped Susan, shuddering.

Unfortunately the image prompted by Vivien stayed with her. That night she did dream. It was a perfectly ordinary nightmare of being chased by the Crone, strangely through central London. There were Beefeaters involved, and the lions from Trafalgar Square, and the Golden Boy of Pye Corner flitting along continually apologizing to her until Susan woke hyperventilating and sat up, choking down a scream.

"Nightmare?" asked Merlin. He was already sitting up in bed, reading *Eight Days of Luke* by Diana Wynne Jones in the half-dark. A thin shaft of moonlight came in the window, illuminating the pages. "Or one of your other dreams?"

"Nightmare," gasped Susan. "My other dreams don't scare me. It was something Vivien said at the pub, about the Crone needing to hobble her victims, because otherwise she'd be too slow to hunt them. Horrible."

Merlin put down his book and held her close. Susan rested her head against his silk pajama–clad shoulder, and her breathing slowed. He stroked her stubbled head, and within a few minutes she was asleep again. But Merlin didn't move or pick up his book. He stopped stroking her head and just held her, watching the moonlight slowly move across the room.

As predicted, Jassmine was both pathetic and cross for about a minute about Susan not coming down, before she forgot to be, and as two of her friends were already at the house and all three were engaged in something Susan couldn't quite hear but sounded suspiciously like "smoking ceremony," the conversation was quickly terminated.

The rest of the week was surprisingly normal after that. Susan returned to the Slade briefly on the Friday to appear as if she'd been there the whole time, making a point of saying hello to her painting tutor who was working on something of her own and seemed very surprised to see any student at all. Apart from that, she lazed around the safe house, reading, watching television, and making a series of sketches of Mrs. MacNeill at work. In the afternoon, she went in Audrey's cab with various disguised escort vehicles—her favorite was an orange VW camper van with badly painted maps of Australia on the doors and a kangaroo on the front—to the Twice-Crowned Swan, and returned around eleven.

After the disappointment of the oatmeal cakes, Evangelina and Una and company did not return to the safe house, and the scaled-down incident room was relocated to the New Bookshop. The library was returned to its original state. Susan was kept updated by Vivien, who confirmed her previous opinion that there was no longer any serious search for the Crone. Everyone expected it all to naturally conclude on the night of the solstice.

Merlin, however, was very serious about keeping Susan safe and did not let this laissez-faire approach on the investigative side affect the protective detail. In fact, as the solstice approached, he became even more cautious, and Susan got used to waking up to find him standing by the curtains, watching the street, already dressed and with his tie-dyed bag over his shoulder.

Inspector Greene also did not slacken. She and Merlin met before breakfast every morning to go over Susan's planned movements and check rosters and the deployment of various booksellers and police officers. The meetings tended to go over into breakfast, and Susan would sleepily sip tea as her two protectors drew pencil lines on maps and called people on radios and Mrs. MacNeill gave up calling them to the telephone and simply put one with a long extension cable on the table next to the toast.

Whether their caution deterred any incidents or there simply weren't any, by the evening of Tuesday the 20th it seemed the plan was going to work. Gwyre had not gotten to Susan, and without the hunt and the sacrifice, the spell would fail.

Susan was feeling more relaxed, too, after more than a week of *not* dreaming about Coniston, and no encounters with the Old World. She'd even gotten quite used to being taken everywhere by Audrey or one of the other left-handed cab drivers, and escorted by booksellers and police. She had also enjoyed being with Merlin, having given up trying to ration her contact, as it were, though she knew that he also felt there was change coming and that their time together might be limited, so they had to make the best of it. Mrs. MacNeill had also been unable to resist cooking far more than breakfast, so Susan had eaten better in the last week than in her past six months.

Curiously, while Mrs. MacNeill baked every day, whenever the senior booksellers dropped in, there was only ever the honey oatcakes for them. The alcoholic lemon drizzle cake did make a reappearance but only "for the workers." Mrs. MacNeill announced this socialist decision when delivering the cake to a rather surprised small group one evening, and she delivered a short diatribe about how Mrs. Thatcher was somehow ultimately responsible for the Harrods IRA bombing that had happened the previous Saturday, only to immediately shut up when Inspector Greene quietly mentioned a friend of hers had died in the blast. The drizzle cake had been eaten in silence after that, Susan thinking about how all the terrors and awfulness of the ordinary world went on, yet she seemed so far away from it right now. Cocooned in her safe house, waiting for the winter solstice to be over. But what then? There was the New Year, and her father's waking, and whatever he intended for her. Could she ever only have one world to worry about, one world to live in? Surely that was enough?

But those thoughts and worries disappeared under the stress of hard work. The Twice-Crowned Swan was very busy, particularly for a Tuesday. Susan was collecting glasses as Mr. Paul called time when two men who she instantly thought were police officers came in, rain glistening on their coats. It wasn't just their short hair, it was the cheap suits and the way they moved, shoulder-first as if pushing aside an invisible crowd. One was fortyish, red-cheeked and cold-eyed, you wouldn't ask him for directions; the other was much younger, with anxious eyes trying to pretend otherwise, very much in the slipstream of the older. The older man had a photo in his hand, passport-sized. He held it up to Susan, and she saw herself.

"This you, luv?" he asked. "Miss Susan Arkshaw?"

"Depends who's asking," replied Susan. She set two pint glasses she'd just picked up back on the table and looked over to Diarmuid, who had put his newspaper down and stood up and back from his high table. Sergeant Hiss had already moved to the door and was looking outside. Susan knew Merlin was about somewhere; he always came with the pickup detail half an hour before closing.

"Police," said the older man, flicking a warrant card open and shut in front of her face too quickly for her to read it. "You need to come with us, please."

"What's this?" asked Mr. Paul, moving around from behind the bar with a swiftness that often surprised people. It was like a battleship suddenly turning on speedboat performance. He was six-foot-six and weighed eighteen stone. The younger police officer took a step back, but the older one didn't.

"We need Miss Arkshaw to assist us with a serious inquiry," he said easily.

"It's okay, Mr. Paul," said Susan. She had seen Hiss gesturing for her to go outside before he immediately slipped out. "I'll go along. There's not much left to clean up. You be okay?"

"I suppose so," said Mr. Paul suspiciously. "What station are you two from? I don't know you."

"Detective Sergeant Price and DC Duggan from West End Central," said the older man. "Come along please, Miss Arkshaw."

"Okay," said Susan. She started for the door. Diarmuid beat her to it, opening it up and bowing her ahead.

"After yers, me beauty, yer honors," he slurred, suddenly extremely Irish.

Susan stepped out into light rain and winter chill, and shivered. Her coat was still inside, but she didn't think she'd be outside for very long. Nor would she be going anywhere with the two police officers, if that's what they were.

"The blue Vauxhall, there, please, miss," said the constable, pointing to a car parked about four spaces farther along the road.

Susan started towards it, then spun around as she heard sudden movement.

The two men were already down. Diarmuid was kneeling on the sergeant's back, twisting his arm back to be handcuffed with an ease that evidently amazed the man, who probably thought of himself as strong. The constable was on his knees, with Hiss already locking the handcuffs on him.

Merlin got out of a British racing green Daimler Double-Six that was parked directly in front of the pub in a no-parking zone. He was shrugging a police traffic vest on, luminously blue and white under the streetlight. Another left-handed bookseller, similarly attired with a police traffic vest but also a fluorescent hijab, also got out and walked a little way to the corner so she could watch in several directions. There were people around; some had stopped to watch. Merlin waved at them and called out cheerfully, "Police operation! Nothing serious. Move along, please."

He turned back and came over to the two prisoners.

"Hiss, you want to do the honors?"

Hiss shook his head.

"Oh all right," said Merlin. He opened his warrant card, bent down low and held it front of both captive men's faces in turn.

"I am an officer of MI5, and I am arresting you on suspicion of attempting to pervert the course of justice, and treason—"

There was a bellow from the sergeant and some violent back-arching to no avail, and the constable started to stammer something.

"Quiet please," said Merlin. "You know this bit. 'You do not have to say anything if you do not wish to do so, but anything you do say may be used against you in a court of law.' Okay, search them. Greene is on her way. She'll take them to Paddington Green. Hmmm, never said that aloud. How appropriate she should be based there."

"What are you going on about!" croaked the sergeant. "We're police officers! We're picking up a suspect."

"Are you?" asked Merlin. He expertly searched the sergeant, eliciting a snarl. The wallet and a plaited leather cosh—certainly not police issue—he laid out next to the man's head, while he examined the warrant card and a business card that was in the same wallet.

"Detective Sergeant Rick Pastin from Romford," he said. "More than a little off your manor, aren't you, Sergeant? And who's your little helper?"

"Bastard, I'll fucking—"

Whatever the sergeant was going to say was lost as Diarmuid's left hand gently came down and pinched his nose shut and forced him to take a breath through his mouth instead.

"Constable William Rowntree," said Merlin. "No business card. Also of Romford, Constable?"

"Yes, sir," mumbled the young police officer. "I didn't know what this was about! Sergeant Pastin told me I had to come along!"

"Those aren't the names the sergeant told Mr. Paul," said Susan. "And he said they were from West End Central."

"Well, well. You can explain all this to Inspector Greene," said Merlin. "Of Special Branch. And a judge, in due course. And hark, I think an inspector calls, to paraphrase my Priestley."

Sirens were coming closer, resolving out of the general noise of the city and the heavy beat of the rain.

"You should get back inside, Susan," said Merlin. "Diarmuid, go with her, in case this is a feint. Discourage your mountainous employer from coming out, Susan. I can hear his heavy footfalls approaching the door."

When Susan came out five minutes later with her coat on, the two Romford police officers were sitting in the back of a marked

Rover, the sergeant staring defiantly ahead, the constable with his head down, utterly crushed. Inspector Greene was talking to Merlin, both of them ignoring the rain and the cold, though Susan noticed Greene had given in to the elements enough to put a raincoat over her ubiquitous leather jacket.

"More Masons, it looks like," said Greene to Susan. "Not thorny rose ones, just the regular sort. Someone high up asked the sergeant to pick you up 'as a favor,' but he won't say who it was. Yet. The constable probably doesn't know anything. I'll interview them immediately. I'll let you know whatever turns up, Merlin. Hiss will be with you till eight, but I've also put Singh and Palmer on; they'll be at the safe house."

"Right," said Merlin. He was quite drenched, but unlike a normal person, he did not look woebegone and miserable, more as if he'd intentionally gone swimming in his clothes, and had a great time and would do it again. "Let's get home."

He took his PF8 out from under his traffic vest and said into it, "The game's afoot!" before ushering Susan to the Daimler. Diarmuid went around to the driver's side, while Merlin got in the back with Susan.

"Not really afoot, since we're driving," he said cheerfully.

"Where's Audrey and her cab?" she asked. "Or one of the other taxis?"

"Got a fare to Heathrow," said Merlin.

"So much for my priority," said Susan, feeling faintly miffed.

"I'm joking," replied Merlin, surprised she'd taken him seriously. "We're just changing it up. She's parked a hundred yards down the road, she'll join up as we pass. Here's Sabah."

The woman who'd been watching the corner got in the front and waggled her fingers at Susan.

"Hopefully that was Gwyre's last hurrah and nothing more serious is waiting in the wings," said Merlin as they sped away. "I'll be very glad when we're past the solstice."

"Me too," said Susan. "Will those two really be charged with treason?"

"No, they'll get kicked out of the force, and it'll be left at that, I'd say," said Merlin. "To keep it quiet. I hope Greene can find out who ordered them to pick you up, though."

Susan nodded wearily. She was usually tired after a shift at the Twice-Crowned Swan, but she felt particularly weary now. She leaned against Merlin and shut her eyes.

A moment later, Susan was standing atop the Old Man of Coniston, the very top, her feet on the cairn that marked the summit. It was snowing, but the snow swerved in a circle around her, spinning and tumbling away. She did not feel cold, but rather invigorated, no longer tired. She could feel power filling her up, rising from the ground beneath, all the way from the deeps so far below. She started to raise her arms, reveling in it, and suddenly—

Was back in the car again, awake. Merlin was shaking her, a look of surprise and alarm on his face.

"I fell asleep," mumbled Susan. "I was atop the mountain. The Old Man."

Merlin nodded grimly. He bent close and whispered, "You

started to fade. I could see a snowstorm through you. You were physically translocating there!"

"Is that possible?" Susan whispered back.

"Yes," said Merlin. "Theoretically, at least. Though usually some sort of portal is involved, like a pool to enter Silvermere."

"All okay back there?" asked Diarmuid. There was an uncertainty in his voice, a tone Susan had not heard before. Susan looked up and saw he was darting glances in the rearview mirror, and Sabah was watching, too, her dark eyes concerned.

"Yes," said Merlin. "Let's just get back to the safe house."

"I won't fall asleep again," Susan whispered. Merlin nodded, and extended his warm, human right hand. Susan took it and gripped it tightly, so tightly the still-healing cut on her palm burned like fire, and she willed herself to stay awake.

CHAPTER NINETEEN

The Winter Solstice,
London and to the West, Thursday, 22nd December 1983

Break. *To break out of bounds. To go
beyond the prescribed limits.*

SUSAN SLEPT IN THE NEXT MORNING, AND WAS SURPRISED WHEN SHE
woke up to find it was already almost eleven o'clock. It was raining
very heavily outside, beating down on the roof and windows, and
it felt super luxurious to be lying in a very comfortable double
bed within the large bedroom of the safe house, rather than in
her own narrow bed in a room not much larger. Not that she
should get used to it, she told herself. She would move back to
her student accommodations tomorrow, and if the dreams came
again, or even if she was translocated to Coniston, she would
deal with that, too. Or so she told herself sternly, pressing down
the fear that was bubbling up from deep down, that once she
went to Coniston she would never return.

A soft knock at the door preceded Merlin poking his head
around.

"You're awake," he said. "Want breakfast in bed? Mrs. Mac has weakened and allowed it just this once."

"Yes, please!" said Susan, sitting up and dragging another pillow behind her. "Two soft boiled eggs and toast please, and tea in a mug."

"Coming up," replied Merlin. "I'll probably have to bat away a kipper and fend off several other items as well. Sure that's all you want?"

"Definitely," replied Susan. "And please thank Mrs. Mac-Neill profusely. She has looked after me so well. I'll miss her when I'm gone."

Merlin nodded and exited, shutting the door.

"When I'm gone," muttered Susan to herself. "Poor choice of words."

Merlin returned quite quickly with the promised breakfast, which Mrs. MacNeill had managed to keep to Susan's order, or else any extras had been discarded along the way. There was also a copy of Tuesday's *Time Out* on the tray.

"I thought we might go see a film tomorrow," said Merlin, tapping the magazine. "There's a screening of *Local Hero* at the Odeon in Swiss Cottage. Want to see it again?"

"Definitely," said Susan. "What about going today?"

Merlin shook his head. "Better not. The winter solstice is tricky at the best of times, and there's already a lot of other things going on. We've got a full shift here, but if there was real trouble, I'd have difficulty getting help."

"What are the other things going on?"

"There are powers and entities that rise near to wakefulness at the solstices," said Merlin. "And there are rituals that can only be performed on this day, so of course there are people who will try them, usually with dire results. We have to keep a lid on it all."

"Powers like the Wild Hunt?" asked Susan. "What is that, exactly?"

"Good question," replied Merlin evasively. He hesitated. "It's best not to talk about it too much, particularly today. There are mythic forces that do not appear as individuals, they are not single entities, and cannot be reckoned with in the same way. The Wild Hunt is quite literally a force of nature."

"So if the Wild Hunt does rise, what do you do?"

"We try to make sure it doesn't, in the first place," said Merlin. "Which is why Everilda and the Crone's spell is so dangerous, trying to leech off a little of the Hunt's power. But if it does . . . the only thing to do is get out of its way. As swiftly as possible."

"What happens if you don't?" asked Susan.

"For the Hunt, there is only the hunt and the hunted," said Merlin. "Have you seen what happens at the end of a fox hunt? I mean if the fox doesn't get away?"

"The hounds tear the fox to pieces," said Susan.

"There we are," said Merlin.

"But it is possible to escape the Hunt?"

"I don't know," said Merlin. "Likely if anyone does, they have been chased so far and through such places that they can't find their way back anyway. Like I said, best not to let the Hunt rise, and if it does, keep out of its way."

"I guess I'll be staying in, then," said Susan. She looked at the water streaming down the window. "I might draw these windows, I think, with the rain. Or even a painting . . . I haven't done anything with watercolors for a while."

"Sounds like a good idea," said Merlin. He turned his head back to the open door behind him. "Hmmm. Someone arriving in the street. Jaguar, V-12. Probably Greene."

"I'm still sort of amazed you can hear anything over the rain," said Susan. "I shouldn't be, I suppose. I'd better get up."

"I'll take your tray down," said Merlin. "See what's what. It *is* Inspector Greene."

"How can you tell?" asked Susan as she slid out of bed and headed for the bathroom.

"Her footsteps," said Merlin. He arranged the mug and plates and orange juice glass into safer positions on the tray and lifted it up to balance on top of his left hand, in approved waiterly fashion. "Cuban heels. Hopefully she's found out who was behind our friends from Romford."

Inspector Greene had found out, but she had only arrested the senior officer concerned a few hours before because it had taken most of the night to get Sergeant Pastin to reveal his name. A Superintendent Pike, who was a Freemason, which gave Gwyre's thorny rose Masons a point of contact, but he had only agreed to do what they asked in return for a bribe, made in gold. So it was much more a case of corruption than a Freemason favor.

"Ten thousand pounds," said Greene, her generally hard face

looking even more iron-set than ever. "A thousand for Pike to organize, and two thousand pounds each for the officers carrying out the two jobs."

"Two?" asked Merlin. They were in the library, Greene stalking backwards and forwards by the tall window and Susan and Merlin sitting in the comfortable armchairs. "So as well as the attempt on Susan—"

"Two other officers, not Masons this time but long suspected of being bad 'uns, arrested a young woman early this morning," said Greene. "Her name is Megana Ageyo."

"Ageyo?" asked Susan, jumping up. "An A name. You mean Gwyre is simply starting the spell over again, without me?"

"That's what I'm guessing," said Greene. "I called it in to the booksellers. I haven't heard back. They've got some sort of flap going on. We haven't tracked down the two officers concerned as yet, so all I know is what I got from Superintendent Pike half an hour ago. Ageyo is a medical student, they were to pick her up as she left her night shift at King's College Hospital, just after seven. We have to presume they did, as she isn't at home and has not been seen elsewhere. Pike didn't know where his two men were to take her—they were to meet a contact outside the hospital—but they were told to have a fueled up non-police vehicle. We've got an alert out for their own cars, their homes have been checked, close connections, and so on. They're probably using a stolen vehicle and driving the girl somewhere."

"To the Crone," said Susan quietly. "To be hunted tonight, and sacrificed. But I don't get it. Starting the spell over again won't save them from the booksellers."

"It might," said Merlin somberly. "If Gwyre also stays in Alphabet House, outside of our time, with the map, then we might not be able to find another way in. It will give them seven years' grace, and a chance to try again in another hundred and sixty-two years. For you, or for someone like you."

"One hundred and sixty-two years!"

"All being well, you'll still be alive," said Merlin. "And one hundred and sixty-two years is not long for an Ancient Sovereign. They take a very different view of time to mortals."

"We can't let Gwyre murder someone else!" said Susan. "Is the search for the Crone shape being stepped up?"

"I'm doing what I can," said Greene. "Torrant's trying to get extra help, and Inspector Danziger from the Wiltshire force. But we need booksellers, and I haven't heard back from Evangeline or Una. We also need Evangeline to pressure the Home Office, to get more people on the job. Do you know how many bloody quarries and mines and caverns are around that neck of the woods? The place is like a honeycomb, all the Bath stone dug out of there over centuries. We need MOD support, too, because a bunch of those places were turned into subterranean lairs and ammo stores, and a big bolt-hole for the politicians."

"I can find her," said Susan quietly. She was leaning forward in her chair, thinking furiously, her chin resting on her hands. "When I saw the Crone, the stone saint had been moved to her on a kind of conveyor belt. No, not a belt, just the rollers, that ran down the side of the tunnel. That must be a clue. But more than that, I think the earth would speak to me, the stone beneath. If I was close enough, I think I could tell where the Crone is."

"Bloody hell!" said Greene. "A roller conveyor? It must be one of the CAD Corsham depots. They used conveyors to shift shells up and down in the war. There's four or five depots, I think, mostly decommissioned in the sixties. But that's still hundreds, maybe thousands of miles of tunnels. I need to call Torrant and Danziger, and the army. I hope there isn't a new liaison officer. And we'll have to get you out there as quickly as possible. There's no time to—"

"No," interrupted Merlin. "Maybe that is Gwyre's plan after all. To lure Susan in, draw her out of safety here."

"Merlin! I have to go. The poor girl—"

"My orders are very clear," said Merlin. He stood up and brushed some lint from the lapel of the jacket of his elegant vintage 1950s Hardy Amies grey suit, which he was wearing with a purple shirt and a surprisingly floral tie, which somehow worked. "You are to stay here until after midnight."

"Orders!" scoffed Susan. "You forget them readily enough when you want to. And if we don't rescue Megana, then Gwyre will still be around and will have the chance to kill another twenty-five more people and maybe *me* in a century and a half, and it will be all your fault!"

"It won't be my fault!" snapped Merlin. "Look, let me call and see what's going on with the search. They probably don't even need you. We can tell them it's one of the old ammunition depots. That'll narrow it down—"

"Not enough," said Greene. "There are far too many underground sites to search quickly. It would take a thousand of us a week or more and we'd probably still miss them. Surely we can keep Susan safe *and* have her help us find Gwyre and her hostage?"

"I don't . . ." Merlin started. Susan was staring at him, fury in her eyes, and his voice faltered. "I don't want to risk your life, Susan."

"You'd risk yours, wouldn't you?" said Susan. "I mean you have, many times. You risked your life to save *me* in Highgate, just a mortal woman you'd never met before. Now there's someone else just like me at risk and I have the power to help her."

"Damn," said Merlin. He sighed. "Look, let me talk to the higher-ups and see what the situation is."

"And then we'll go," said Susan.

"Maybe," said Merlin, but she knew he had accepted she was right. He tilted his head, listening. "Vivien's here."

Vivien burst into the room at high speed.

"Gwyre's got hold of a girl to start her spell all over again!" she gasped. "And Merlin, have you still got the sword?"

"We know about Megana Ageyo," said Merlin. "What's the sword got to do with it?"

"Susan needs it," said Vivien. "*Have* you got it?"

"Not exactly," said Merlin. "I can get it, though. What do you mean Susan needs it? Have you had a vision—"

"No! I just know she does," said Vivien. "So what's the plan? We going to go rescue the girl?"

"I still think Susan needs to stay here," said Merlin. "But she says she can locate the Crone—"

"I bet she can," said Vivien strongly.

"And it could all be a trap," resumed Merlin. "That's what worries me. I need to talk to Una and Evangeline."

"You know what they'll say," said Vivien.

"Even so, I still need to call," said Merlin.

"Me too," said Greene. She grabbed the telephone on the stand. "And I bags this one. You'll have to use the hall phone."

"Okay, okay," muttered Merlin as Greene started dialing. He loped out of the room, calling over his shoulder. "I'll be back."

"I'd better get changed. Again," said Susan, who was wearing "lounging around a well-heated London luxury house" clothes—basically an oversized Jethro Tull T-shirt, tracksuit pants, and slippers.

"Merlin must be getting old," said Vivien. She was already dressed for a cold, rainy winter day expedition, in a bookseller's blue boiler suit, Fair Isle jumper, and a navy mackintosh. "They'll tell him you have to stay here."

"And he'll obey?" asked Susan, turning back from the door. "I mean, force me to stay?"

"Oh no," said Susan. "But there will be unpleasantness. You should change quickly. We need to get going before someone senior turns up to stop us."

Susan ran upstairs and, after a moment's thought, donned her own blue boiler suit, making sure the cigarette case was full of fresh salt and the folding knife was in her pocket, plus the candle stub and matches. She added some sharpened pencils and a small plain paper notebook. She hesitated over the PF8 radio, before unplugging it from the charger and taking it as well, putting it in the pocket of her West German Army surplus coat. Slippers replaced with heavy socks and her Docs, she was ready.

Back downstairs in the library, she found Greene still talking on the phone, often in exasperation. Vivien was looking at an Ordnance Survey map of Corsham in Wiltshire. Merlin was not in evidence, and Susan hadn't seen him in the hall.

"Merlin's gone to get the sword," said Vivien. She did not need to explain to Susan which sword she meant, it had to be Clarent, King Arthur's sword. "And to reborrow Emilia's Range Rover. He tried to get a helicopter but no dice, particularly as Una has said under no circumstances are you to leave here. Which means we need to be going right now, since I'll bet she's already on her way to make sure we completely understand her instructions."

"I can't get a helicopter either," said Greene, slamming down the phone. "Not from anyone: police, army, air force, or Fleet Air Arm. Rain's too heavy, apparently. Or maybe it's the wrong sort of rain. Where's Merlin meeting us?"

"Layby on the A40 about a mile past the Hanger Lane Gyratory, or he'll radio if he's behind," said Vivien, folding up the map. "Diarmuid's bringing the Daimler around, and we'll have Sabah along, too."

"Are they okay going against Una's orders?" asked Susan.

"I don't think Merlin asked," said Vivien. "But I'd say once they know where we're going and why, it will be okay."

"I'll lead, take Singh with me in the Jag," said Greene. "Lights and siren. You lot next, and Palmer will follow in the patrol car. With Hiss, if he gets here on time. We're going to rendezvous with Torrant, Danziger from the Wiltshire force, and the MOD liaison at MOD Corsham. The traffic is absolutely terrible, the M4's a car park, and there's some local flooding. Wish we could have got a helicopter. Anyway, you ready to go?"

"Yep," said Vivien.

"Rock 'n' roll," said Susan, making the devil's horns with her fore- and little finger.

"What?" asked Vivien. "Don't do that! Not today!"

"Oh, sorry," said Susan. "I mean, okay, let's go. Is that really—"

"No, I'm joking. The sign alone won't do anything. Come on."

Susan stopped as she stepped outside. Not because of the sudden impact of the cold, or the rain that was so heavy it was splashing back and hitting her even while she was under the portico. The street, the Daimler with Diarmuid opening the door, Vivien hurrying into it, all this vanished and she saw the blue expanse of Coniston Water ahead, with the rain pockmarking the surface right in front of her, as if she stood on its shore. She felt a sudden, electric sensation that something was about to happen and she took a step forward and the cold rain on her face brought her back. There was the car again and she dived in and Diarmuid slammed the door behind her. He sloshed around the car to the driver's door, and Sabah rushed over from the other side of the street, where she'd been standing guard, towards the passenger side.

"You froze," said Vivien. "What happened?"

"Coniston," said Susan, shivering. "The lake. It was right in front of me. And I felt this jolt, this incredibly strong sensation as if everything was going to change. I stepped forward, and the rain brought me back. The world was normal again."

"It's the winter solstice," said Vivien. "We feel it, too. The Old World is closer, and there is a feeling anything might happen, because it can. But I don't believe you can be transported anywhere if you don't want to go. Even half asleep, if you resist, you will remain here. And asleep, only your dreaming self will venture away, to return when you awake."

"I do half want to go," whispered Susan. "That's the problem. But I know if I do, that will be the end of me. Or at least the end of ordinary me. And I don't want that."

Diarmuid and Sabah got in the front, both expressing disgruntlement at how wet they were, despite raincoats, and the big V-12 engine roared into life and the heater, which actually worked, began to blast welcome warm air.

Even with police vehicles ahead and behind using lights and sirens, it was very slow getting out of the city. The heavy rain did not let up, the traffic was snarled, and matters were not helped twenty minutes in when they were barely past White City and Una started barking over the radio telling them to turn around and come back, until Merlin broke in to instruct Diarmuid to change to the "previously agreed" frequency.

"Aren't you going to get in a lot of trouble?" asked Susan.

"Nah," replied Diarmuid. "It's all on Merlin. He led us poor unsuspecting types astray, right, Sabah?"

"For sure," agreed Sabah, who had adopted a storm-grey hijab today, rather than the fluorescent traffic-warning one of the night before, with a very elegant Burberry trench coat in RAF blue. The silenced De Lisle commando carbine she held across her knees was rather at odds with her overall elegance.

"Okay," said Susan dubiously.

Sabah turned around to look at her.

"Una isn't like Merrihew," she said. "She'll rant a bit, but she'll come around. Provided we can rescue this young woman, and not lose you, of course. But if we fail in that, I doubt we'll be around to face Una's ire anyway."

"What about Evangeline's ire?" asked Susan.

"We've gone operational. It's a left-handed matter," said Sabah.

"Evangeline's out of the reckoning for now, anyway," said Vivien. "She had to go to Scotland this morning. Something stirring in the waters."

"Loch Ness?" asked Susan curiously.

"Oh no, there's nothing much *there*," said Vivien. "She's headed for Loch Maree. I bet she got a helicopter, come to think of it. Anyway, some would-be druids have woken the *Muc-sheilch*, and it has to be convinced to rest once more. Preferably without eating anyone other than the druids."

"Other than the druids?"

"It already ate them, so yes," said Vivien. "They misunderstood the nature of the raising. The *Muc-sheilch* would have thought they offered themselves. Evangeline had to go because she's talked to the entity before, which always helps."

"Gods but I hate this super roundabout," said Diarmuid as they approached the Hanger Lane Gyratory. "It gets worse every bloody year. I don't even understand what they've done now, and I can't see a single bloody lane marking in this rain!"

"Just follow the flashing blue light, my child," said Sabah.

Greene had clearly deciphered the new gyratory system in advance, or her simple confidence won out, because they made it through without colliding with anything, or having to go around again, as so many other cars seemed to be in the process of doing.

A mile past the horrendous intermingling of roads, the radio pinged and Greene warned they were approaching the layby.

"I see the so very bright silver Range Rover," she said. "Merlin, that you? You see us?"

"Affirmative." Merlin's voice crackled over the radio. "I'll drop in after Diarmuid in the Daimler, if that's okay."

"Do that," replied Greene. "Hiss, you got any burrs hanging on your rear?"

"No, we're clear," came a very faint response. The previously unheard voice of Sergeant Hiss, who had obviously made it in time to get aboard the police Rover SD-1 that was bringing up the rear, invisible in the rain except for a blurred and impressionistic jumble of flashing blue light and bright headlights.

"'Diarmuid in the Daimler' sounds like a children's book for toffs," said Sabah.

"You should write it," said Diarmuid amiably. "Here comes Merlin."

They flashed past the layby. Susan caught a glimpse of Emilia's metallic silver Range Rover accelerating out of it to cut in behind them.

The rest of the journey was one of stalled traffic, stop-start annoyances, dashes up the hard shoulder, and continuous blinding rain. Susan found herself almost nodding off and jerked up and pressed her thumbnails into her forefingers hard to keep herself awake.

"You okay?" asked Vivien.

"I mustn't sleep," said Susan.

"I do think you'll be okay," said Vivien. "If you don't want to go to Coniston, you won't. Tell yourself so, repeat it a few times."

"Maybe," said Susan dubiously. "Did Merlin tell you I almost faded away in the car last night?"

"Yes, he told me," replied Vivien. She had an odd expression on her face. She looked almost guilty, thought Susan.

"The thing is," Vivien continued, "this might be my fault. I mean, I talked to Zoë again about your whole situation. . . ."

She paused, looking at Diarmuid and Sabah in the front seat.

"It's okay," said Susan. "I think if I can't trust present company, I'm up the creek anyway."

"So I talked to Zoë, and she said that getting you to draw the translocation picture that got us out of Alphabet House might have stirred you up, woken your mythical self," said Vivien. "I mean it would have happened later, but not until you were already with your father. So you would have more guidance."

"I had to help Merlin," said Susan. "And my dreams started weeks ago. I reckon Dad's waking up earlier than he said. Before the New Year."

"It's possible he might consider the winter solstice marks the true New Year," said Vivien, troubled. "The Venerable Bede wrote that the Anglo-Saxons, or some of them, would have it so, the new year starting when the sun begins to return."

"I've put it out of my mind for now," lied Susan. "I have to concentrate on finding the Crone, and rescuing Megana Ageyo. Do you know anything else about her? I thought she needed some connection with the Old World to be a suitable sacrifice for Gwyre."

"Ageyo has that," said Vivien. "Greene said she has worked part-time at G. Baldwin & Co., the herbalists, since she was seventeen, and has an interest in alternative medicine. There is a considerable overlap between the medicinal and mythical qualities of herbs."

"Does her family know she's been abducted?" asked Susan.

"I don't think so," said Vivien. "Greene didn't want to tell them. If we can rescue her before the news gets out, that's better all around."

"Yeah," said Susan. "If we can."

The rain eased somewhat as they progressed west on the M4, but the traffic remained terrible and there were several accidents blocking the shoulder so they couldn't easily get past, but they had to crawl along with everyone else.

While the rain had lessened, it now looked like it might turn to sleet. It was cold enough, though Susan had to ask Diarmuid to turn the Daimler's heating down. She needed it to be colder to help her stay awake. Despite Vivien's reassurance, she still felt that if she slept she might fade out of the car and reappear atop the Old Man of Coniston.

CHAPTER TWENTY

>‑┤◆►‑O‑◄◆┠‑◄

The Winter Solstice,
Corsham and Monkton Farleigh, Thursday, 22nd December 1983

*Diggings. Come to my diggings. To my
rooms, residence, office, sanctum.*

>‑┤◆►‑O‑◄◆┠‑◄

THE RAIN AND THE TRAFFIC PROBLEMS MADE THE TRIP SO MUCH
slower than usual it was almost five o'clock and fully dark by
the time they turned on to the Bath Road from Chippenham,
which would take them to Corsham. All the snow of the previous week was gone, long washed away, and there was a lot of
standing water by the sides of the road. Down in the Somerset
Levels there was already widespread flooding.

The radio pinged again as they neared the Corsham turnoff.
Susan had just seen the sign appear for an instant in the beam
of the Daimler's headlights.

It was Merlin calling.

"Susan, do you have any sense of where the Crone is yet?"

"No," called out Susan from the back seat. "I have to touch
the ground. I think."

Diarmuid relayed this.

"Okay," said Merlin. "We're meeting up with the police and the army liaison outside the main entrance to MOD Corsham. Follow Greene. Stay in the vehicle, Susan, until we're sure everything is okay. Diarmuid, Sabah, you know what to do."

"Hang on, Merlin," said Diarmuid. "Are we official now? Una hasn't pulled the plug? Because it would be good to know there's at least the possibility of some backup. Over."

"We've spoken," replied Merlin. "Una is . . . reluctantly . . . on board. She's coming down, too, probably an hour behind. And the Small Bookshop has sent a team. Out."

"That's a relief," said Sabah. "Apart from Una coming down herself."

Corsham was like any other small market town of the area. Susan looked out the window as they drove down Park Lane, but it wasn't until they'd turned onto Westwells Road and gone a mile or more that there was any aboveground evidence of the defense establishments that lurked beneath the normality of a country town. A characteristic ten-foot fence with concrete posts and alarmed top wires ran alongside the road, and behind it were dull, obscure buildings that looked of 1950s vintage and robust, bombproof construction.

A little farther on, they emerged from the unlit road to a floodlit expanse around the main or at least public entrance of a defense site that had numerous names, having once been Basil Hill Barracks, then the Central Ammunitions Depot Corsham, and now MOD Corsham. It incorporated outlying parts all reputedly connected underground, including RAF Rudloe Manor and the Central Government War headquarters, known by the codewords "Burlington," "Chanticleer," "Site 3" and others, a Cold War bolt-hole for the Prime Minister and their chosen four thousand to survive a nuclear strike.

The entrance looked innocuous enough, a guard block and gate, manned by RAF Regiment troops. Several guards stood about the gate, their SLRs slung, while they pretended not to be interested in what was going on in the car park in front of them. This was outside the gate and off to the left, presumably for civilian day workers and the like. It was currently occupied by an army Land Rover and police vehicles from the Avon and Somerset and Wiltshire forces, a small host of patrol cars, Land Rovers, Range Rovers, and a minibus. Almost everyone was inside their vehicles, staying warm and dry, but Susan saw the very recognizable Inspector Torrant and a couple of other senior-looking police officers gathered around the army Land Rover talking to an army officer. As they drove in, Susan saw it was a woman.

Diarmuid parked the Daimler away from the other cars, facing out, for a quick exit. He and Sabah opened their doors a few inches but did not get out. The fresh, cold air was welcome, as was the harsh light from the floodlights on the high concrete poles above. Susan suddenly felt very awake.

"At least it's stopped—" Sabah started to say, before she was shushed by everyone else. If the fatal last word had been uttered, they all knew the heavens would open once again. Right now it was merely cold and damp. There were puddles all over the car park, and the drain by the side of the road was running high, taking water down the hill.

Merlin got out of the silver Range Rover as Greene exited her Rover 3500, the two of them immediately going over to the huddle with the army officer. After a few minutes, Merlin stepped away and called out towards the Daimler.

"Susan, come over, please," he shouted. He was wearing his hunting tweed jacket again, but with a kilt in the simple blue and green Hamilton hunting tartan, instead of plus fours, and vintage hobnailed boots with long socks and leather gaiters. Instead of his usual tie-dyed bag he had a khaki Brady Severn fishing bag over his shoulder, the leather straps undone for quick access.

Susan got out and walked across the car park, with Vivien beside her. Diarmuid and Sabah also got out but did not follow. Sabah stayed on the left-hand side, the door open, her silenced carbine on the seat. Diarmuid wandered around to the boot, opened it, and took out a bag very similar to Merlin's, though it was olive green. Putting it over his shoulder, he closed the boot and leaned against it, watching.

"Should I be worried about something?" asked Susan softly as they walked over. "I mean, in particular here?"

"They're just being careful," said Vivien. "Speaking of which, look who's over there."

She inclined her head. Susan looked across. Three people who had been hidden behind one of the Somerset and Avon Police Land Rovers were now visible, the team from the Small

Bookshop: Cameron and Stephanie, the left-handed booksellers, and Ruby the right-handed bookseller. Stephanie was, as always, in a track suit, this one a relatively subdued green and red. It was hard to tell what Cameron was wearing because over it he had an enormous double-breasted black greatcoat with a huge astrakhan collar of black-dyed lambswool, and on his head he wore a very high-crowned charcoal cowboy hat that would have suited Tom Mix in a western but here looked very eccentric. Ruby, in contrast, was in a tweed skirt suit under a white Burberry coat, held a furled umbrella, and looked as if she was just off to church or a meeting of the local conservatives.

They waved, and Vivien and Susan waved back, but the Small Bookshop team didn't come over to join the command group by the army Land Rover.

Torrant greeted Susan with a nod. Merlin made the introductions to the others. The woman army officer, up close, had a puzzled expression as if she couldn't quite grasp what was going on. A lieutenant-colonel in DPM camouflage, she wore a dark blue beret with a Royal Army Ordnance Corps badge.

"Susan here is a consultant to MI5," said Merlin. "Susan, this is Colonel Leraigne, who oversees the former ammunition depots in this region. You know Inspector Torrant, and this is Inspector Danzinger, who has the same role with the Wiltshire Police."

Susan nodded to the two she didn't know. Inspector Danziger was a white, very short, brown-haired woman who looked close to retirement age, in her early sixties, but she had sharp black eyes and seemed at ease with the booksellers. Like Torrant, she was in uniform. Unlike the other inspector she wore her pistol openly, holstered outside her raincoat.

"Good afternoon," said Leraigne stiffly. "I admit I am now even more puzzled about what is going on here. What kind of consultant are you?"

"I'm not allowed to explain," said Susan.

"And yet you, or someone, thinks one of our subdepots has been compromised," said Leraigne. "As I've just been explaining, all the entrances outside of the controlled area here have been sealed for ten years or more, and we inspect them regularly."

"Where would we find a very long inclined tunnel with a conveyor along the side?" asked Merlin, ignoring her statement. "The conveyor minus its belt, only rollers."

"There are a number of locations with various conveyor systems for moving ammunition," said Leraigne stiffly. "The rubber belts were removed from all of them in the middle of last decade."

"Susan?" asked Merlin.

She looked at Merlin. "Um, I can't tell anything just standing here. Can I . . ."

She pointed at the ground.

"Yes, go on," said Merlin.

Susan knelt down and put the palms of both hands flat on the asphalt.

"What on earth is going on? Your circus troupe—"

"Quiet, please," said Merlin. "You've had very specific orders, haven't you? In writing. Do you need them reiterated? I can get General Troughton down here if you insist. I doubt he'd be pleased and the delay would have very serious consequences."

Colonel Leraigne muttered something but said no more.

Susan shut her eyes. She felt nothing more than the rough imprint of the car park surface at first, but as she concentrated, she had the sensation that she was sinking into the ground. There was reinforced concrete beneath the asphalt, but under that was good soil, quite a depth of it, before she came to rock. Unsurprisingly, this was Bath stone. Susan felt it rather than "seeing" it, a warm glow that her mind translated into the honey-colored stone. She could feel how far it extended, and also she began to become aware of how much it was hollowed out. There were tunnels and caverns in all directions around, many of them now reinforced with concrete and steel beams and pipes and tubing, which she felt like splinters in her skin, noticeable and unwelcome intrusions. There were machines, too—electric wires and telephone lines, air-conditioning units, generators, heaters, dehumidifiers—all manner of machinery for keeping subterranean bases in good shape. But farther out these were quiescent, often no more than hulking piles of rust, unused for many years.

Susan sank deeper, spreading her awareness wider. She could sense groups of people almost directly beneath her feet, obviously in some still-operational installation, perhaps the "Burlington" government bolt-hole. She couldn't separate them into individuals, but she could tell there were fifty or sixty people present.

There was another smaller group not that far away, people who were still in the business of quarrying Bath stone. She could feel the rock being cut.

Deeper, far deeper, there were Knockers, like but unlike the ones she knew from Coniston. They felt her touch and fled from it, frightened and suspicious. There were other things, too, which Susan recoiled from as soon as she felt them, knowing they were best left undisturbed.

She came back from the depths, back up to the human workings, and tried to reach out farther, not deeper.

Finally, she felt the presence of the Crone. The hideous snail-woman statue was about five miles away, and three hundred feet underground.

Even as she detected that presence, Susan felt a sudden magnetic tug. Coming from much farther away, to the north. A mountain, beckoning. The Old Man of Coniston. Susan felt it loom higher and higher in her consciousness, and an unseen force began to pull upon her hands, drawing her into the ground, down to the deep ways far below any human delving, there to be taken northward to her birthright.

"I've found her," said Susan, jerking her hands away as if they had been stuck to the ground with glue. She stood upright, gasping for breath.

Colonel Leraigne goggled at her, eyes bulging, and Torrant and Danziger looked perturbed.

"Your hands," stammered the army officer. "They went . . . they sank into the . . . but there's no hole!"

Susan looked down. The asphalt was unmarked.

"Never mind that," said Merlin, with a swift glance at Susan. "Where is she?"

Susan swung around and pointed.

"Almost five miles that way. About three hundred feet down."

"What's there?" asked Merlin forcefully, fixing his gaze on Colonel Leraigne. "Pull yourself together!"

"Uh, it must be the Monkton Farleigh depot you mean," said the officer. Taking a deep breath, she added, "The long corridor with the conveyor will be the Main West Tunnel. But the access—Main West Entry—is really blocked off, a new wall of Bath stone was built in front of the concrete plug about three years ago when the building above was demolished. Or partly demolished."

"A new wall? Why?"

"I don't know," said Leraigne. "I wasn't here. I presume it's because we're gearing up to sell the site, to be used for records storage or the like, and it looks better."

"Bath stone," said Vivien. "Was the work done by local stonemasons? From Chippenham, perhaps?"

"I don't know," said Leraigne. "Maybe."

"It doesn't matter now," said Merlin. "We need to get over there and take a look. Can you lead us there, Colonel?"

"Uh, yes, I suppose so," said Leraigne dubiously.

"We'd better take a look at a map first," continued Merlin. "If there's more Rosy Thorn types involved, they might be defending the entry."

"Rosy Thorn?" asked Leraigne.

"Armed terrorists," said Merlin shortly.

"Terrorists!"

"The ones we've met so far haven't been very good shots," said Torrant soothingly. "But I've got a Land Rover full of holes that makes me uneasy about just driving on over."

"We're not going to just drive over," said Merlin testily. "Are there any fixed defenses? From when it was operational?"

"There *are* two pillboxes guarding the entry, from the early 1940s," said Leraigne. "They don't have rear doors, but otherwise they're basically intact. If there are terrorists in them . . . look, I think I need to report this and seek further orders—"

"Your orders are to completely follow my instructions, are they not?" asked Merlin. "Let's look at the map. I expect we'll assemble short of the target. Sabah, Diarmuid, Cameron, and Stephanie can go ahead to deal with the pillboxes and scout out the entry. There shouldn't be any risk to you, Colonel."

"It's not personal risk that concerns me," said Leraigne, clearly offended. "I was in the Falklands last year, you know, clearing mines among other things. But we need to raise the threat warning here if there are terrorists nearby—"

"Okay, you can do that before we go. Who has a—"

Vivien offered her map. Merlin took it and walked around to the bonnet of the Land Rover, unfolding it and laying it out, the others following.

"Leraigne?" asked Merlin. "Show us the location and how to get there."

"The quickest way is to get on the Bradford Road, turn right where it crosses the A365, continue almost to Bathford before turning left into Prospect Place, which becomes Farleigh Rise, then the entry road to the subdepot is here. There is a locked gate at the intersection. Obviously I can get the key—"

"That won't be necessary," said Merlin. "Don't worry about your paperwork. Any damage will be sorted."

"Main West Entrance is here, about two hundred and fifty yards from the gate," said Leraigne. She took out a pencil and drew a cross on the map, and then two very small squares. "There is a pillbox about twenty yards north, here, and another the same distance south. They were built to each house a Vickers machine gun, and I'd say their fields of fire are about so."

She drew two overlapping triangles.

"I hope they don't have any bloody machine guns," muttered Torrant.

"Our team will avoid a direct approach," said Merlin, studying the map. "They can circle around and come in behind. What's the terrain like?"

"Immediately around it is all fields, with some copses of oak, beech, blackthorn," said Leraigne. "Open land, hard to cross unseen if the moon comes out—"

"It'll stay dark," said Merlin. "I doubt this cloud will clear."

"Do your people have night vision gear?" asked Leraigne curiously. "The latest from the Americans?"

"Yes," said Merlin. Torrant and Danziger exchanged a glance that fortunately Leraigne missed. "How many other entrances into Monkton Farleigh are there?"

"There are four," said Leraigne. She indicated points on the map, surprisingly far away from the first she'd drawn, all of them at least half a mile apart. "They're all permanently closed. Concrete plugs, as I said."

"And is there an underground connection from your base here?" asked Merlin.

"No," replied Leraigne.

Vivien held her breath for a moment and touched the colonel's arm. The officer flinched back.

"Yes there is," said Vivien, exhaling.

"What on earth? Yes, I suppose technically there is a slope that joins to the subdepot, but it is closed at the far end, and on this end is very heavily guarded. Besides, it comes out almost on the opposite side to the Main West tunnel. You'd have to make your way through a very complicated series of passages to get there. It would take hours and hours, even if I could get permission to let you through."

"So the straightforward approach is, if not best, quickest, which is necessary. We'll assemble along the road some way back. This car park here, for Browne's Folly," said Merlin decisively, tapping the map. "My left . . . my people will go up on foot to check out the entry gate and make sure it's not guarded or deal with it if it is, and then swing around on either side, horns of the impi style, and approach those pillboxes from the rear. Once they've secured them and the entry, we'll drive up and see what's next."

"You think four of you can successfully attack well-positioned terrorists?" asked Leraigne. She looked Merlin up and down. "I can call on our ready reaction force. We have a platoon on standby, RAF Regiment. I mean, I don't want to be . . . but you are wearing a kilt and that man in the cowboy hat—"

"Irregular troops for irregular actions," said Merlin with his most charming smile. "Susan, do you think you'll be able to tell if the Crone moves?"

"Not unless I'm touching the ground," said Susan. "Which I'm loath to do again unless it's really necessary. Coniston is calling to me. Very forcefully."

"Who or what is the Crone? And Coniston?" asked Leraigne. "Are they code names?"

"Uh, the Crone is the terrorist leader," said Vivien. "You don't need to know about Coniston."

"Okay, let's get everyone together and go over the plan, such as it is," said Merlin. He looked around and circled his hand over his head, summoning everyone in. "Vivien, there's a box of PF8s set to the bravo frequency in the back of Emilia's car, can you hand them out to our army and police friends? They won't have much coverage without a base station, but we should all be fairly close and it will put us on the same net."

He looked at his watch.

"It's six fifty," he said. "We should aim to be at the assembly area by seven twenty, so we've got about fifteen minutes to get all kitted out here. We'll leave Emilia's Range Rover and the Daimler, ride in Torrant's Land Rovers, if that's okay, Lucy?"

"Sure," said Torrant. "Though I hope we can avoid breaking any more of them. I've got a stack of paperwork six inches high to do for the one that got bowled out."

"Do I need to be armed?" asked Leraigne. "I'll have to sign a pistol out from the guard post, it might take more than fifteen—"

"We'll lend you a Browning Hi-Power," said Merlin. He pointed at the group of left-handed booksellers, who were sauntering over. "Diarmuid will sort you out. That reminds me, everyone will need a crowbar or hammer as well as firearms. We've brought plenty."

"Why?" asked Leraigne.

"A precaution," said Merlin. "That reminds me, I need to give you my cricket bag, Susan."

"Your cricket bag, why . . . oh," said Susan, catching on. Merlin had used his cricket bag to transport swords before. The sword Clarent must be in it.

"I'll give it to you before we move off again," said Merlin.

"Thanks. Uh, Colonel, speaking of going, is there a toilet here I can use?" asked Susan, precipitating a general desire to use the facilities in the guard post, as everyone was reminded of the need, made more urgent by what dangers might lie ahead. But she got in first.

CHAPTER TWENTY-ONE

>─┤◆>─O─<◆┤─<

The Winter Solstice,
Monkton Farleigh, Thursday, 22nd December 1983

*Moon. The moon is called "triform" because it presents
itself to us either round, or waxing with horns towards
the east, or waning with horns towards the west.*

>─┤◆>─O─<◆┤─<

THE LEFT-HANDED BOOKSELLER ASSAULT FORCE LEFT THE BROWNE'S
Folly car park like ghosts, the four of them fading into the brush
and stunted trees of the wood that straggled around the slope.
The folly itself—a nineteenth-century tower—was somewhere
farther up Bathford Hill. The car park had been empty when
they arrived, and extremely muddy. Now it was full of parked
police and army Land Rovers, all quiet, all dark.

"This shouldn't take long," said Merlin. He and Torrant
occupied the front bench seat of Torrant's vehicle; Susan, Vivien,
and Danziger sat on the rear bench. The Land Rover smelled of
mold, and there were little pools of water under the doors, testa-
ment to it leaking. "It's the worst part, in some ways, waiting."

"What do we do once the entry is secure?" asked Susan.

"Go down, smash up the Crone, and rescue Miss Ageyo. Or is

it Dr. Ageyo? Do third-year medical students get called doctor?"

"No," said Torrant. "My second daughter, Karen, she's a doctor over at St. Michael's, the maternity hospital."

"Um, there were a lot more . . . of your people needed to deal with Southaw," said Susan. "Isn't Gwyre as dangerous?"

"Oh no," said Merlin. "Far less powerful. I think we'll be able to handle her. Though Una is on her way, as I've said, with reinforcements."

A moment later, the radio handsets pinged and someone, probably Diarmuid, said, "Road entrance is clear. Not contested. Proceeding."

They sat in silence after that, tense and waiting. Susan looked out the window, still surprised by how well she could see at night. A few cars went by on the road, which was a lane of about the same level of importance and repair as Drifton Hill near her home—that is to say, a single lane at best, crumbling at the edges, and very muddy on the verges. The police officers Torrant and Danziger had brought with them did not get out of their vehicles, nor did Leraigne and her driver. The army vehicle was parked next to Torrant's. Susan could see the sergeant asleep, his cheek pressed against the window and she had to resist an urge to tap on her own window and wake him up. Partly this was because it was so quiet, with all the engines off. It was also cold, without the heating.

"The Crone won't just kill her, will she?" asked Susan, after what felt like half an hour but was probably five minutes. "I mean, kill Megana?"

"Probably not," said Merlin after a moment's hesitation.

"She will want to preserve her for the ritual, up until the last possible moment," said Vivien. She looked at her watch. "Three hours fourteen minutes to midnight."

"We will have to move swiftly," said Merlin. He shifted uneasily. "The closer to midnight, the greater the danger."

"I feel it, too," said Vivien softly. "Things without names are stirring in their sleep. This will be a solstice to remember, and not fondly. The sooner we get done here, the happier I'll be."

"Well, that was a confidence booster," said Susan. "Things without names! What the hell does that mean?"

Everyone's PF8s pinged at once, and they all jumped. Diarmuid's voice crackled loudly out of Merlin's radio, which was the only handset with the volume turned up.

"Merlin. Pillboxes are secured, two aprons down, no ouches on home team. You are clear to proceed. There is a passage in the new wall and the concrete plug has been cut through to allow access to the tunnel. You want us to hold here or go down? Over."

"Hold and watch," said Merlin. "We're on our way. This is Merlin to everyone, my vehicle will take point, moving to site now. Go! Out."

There was a sudden commotion as the vehicles started.

"Lights and siren?" asked Torrant as the Land Rover eased forward, churning up the mud as it moved out of the car park onto the road.

"Might as well now," said Merlin.

Torrant flicked two switches, and nothing happened. She repeated the process and the blue dome light above started to flash, but the siren only gave an asthmatic whoop and died. However, the police vehicles behind made up for it, with a sudden cacophony of slightly different sirens and many oscillating and blinking lights illuminating the road and the hill behind with lurid flashes of blue.

The whole cavalcade moved off down the single-lane road and came to a halt fifty yards on as an ancient Austin coming very slowly up in the other direction did not move off the road, the elderly driver apparently unawed by wailing sirens and flashing lights.

"Heaven save us from the wonderful British public," muttered Torrant. She drove off the road and went around the offending vehicle, spattering it with mud and dirty water.

"Danziger, have someone arrest him and get the car off the road," said Merlin. "He's probably unconnected, but you never know."

Danziger lifted her PF8 and snapped some orders into it. Susan looked behind and saw that while most of the other vehicles followed Torrant's offroad circumvention, one of the Wiltshire Police Land Rovers had stopped in front of the Austin, and constables were getting out.

The gate to the defense site was open, the chain cut or snapped by a left-handed bookseller. The convoy raced up the access road, which to Susan looked like any other farmyard track. There were only fields around them, nothing to indicate what was underneath. Fifty yards on, they bumped over old railway tracks, and roared past an old pillbox, one of the two that guarded the site. There were no lights, only the headlights of the approaching vehicles, but Susan could see well enough, in the strange grey-tone vision she'd gotten used to having at night.

There was a single building ahead, a kind of long railway shed that had obviously been part of a larger construction. There was still a steel skeleton of pillars and beams extending from the partially roofed section, and a concrete railway platform ran the length of the building on the left-hand side.

A flashlight snapped on at the far end and was swung in circles. Diarmuid came on the radio.

"My light. Entry way is behind me. Over."

"Got it," said Merlin into his radio. "All vehicles, park up in an extended line with headlights towards the building. Disembark but await orders to move. Merlin out."

Torrant drove into position and swung the Land Rover around, the headlights illuminating the interior of the partially demolished railway shed. The concrete floor sloped down at a twenty-degree angle, so the far end some hundred feet away was below ground level and it was faced with a wall of Bath stone, which had a rough door-shaped hole in the middle, with a dark tunnel beyond. Diarmuid and Stephanie were on either side of this entrance, but standing back a bit, like cats watching a mousehole.

The bodies of two Thorny Rose Masons were laid out on the railway platform, at the end closest to the new arrivals. Susan did not look at them.

"Stay near me," said Merlin to Susan. He hopped out, the

fishing bag on his hip and a crowbar in his left hand. Everyone followed, Torrant and Danziger flicking on their big Maglites to add to the illumination from the headlights of the parking vehicles. One of the Wiltshire Land Rovers also had a spotlight, which was being swiveled around.

Susan had just stepped down when there was a massive rumble, like a close thunderclap. The ground shook beneath her feet, and she stumbled and almost dropped the cricket bag. A second later a huge plume of dust roared out of the tunnel and across the approaching personnel and vehicles. Merlin pulled Susan down to the ground just before it hit.

"Cover your eyes!"

Susan pressed her face into her sleeve. She felt the wave of dust pass over but did not move for another four or five seconds, then slowly lifted her head. Merlin was propped up on his elbows next to her, blinking furiously and watching. Both of them were covered in fine honey-yellow dust.

Merlin spat out some dust, stood up, and shouted, "Diarmuid! Steph! You okay?"

There was no answer for a moment, then a shout came back out of the settling cloud of dust inside the shed.

"Yes!"

"Stay down," said Merlin to Susan. He got up and ran forward.

Susan stayed down. She had to resist the temptation to place her hands upon the concrete apron under her, to try to sense what was going on. But she knew if she did, the mountain would call to her again, and this time she might not be able to withstand its summons.

Vivien crawled over next to Susan and croaked, "I think that confirms Gwyre has given up on you. And this is not a trap to lure you in."

"Why?" asked Susan.

"Well, I suppose her Masons could have stuffed up, but collapsing the tunnel with you on this side suggests Gwyre is sticking with Plan B. Or maybe that should be Plan A, for Ageyo."

"Is that what happened? They blew up the tunnel?"

"I'd say so," said Vivien. "Guess we'll find out shortly."

"Why do you think I need the sword?" asked Susan.

"I don't know," said Vivien. "It's a feeling. Have you touched it yet?"

"No," said Susan. "I have my own feeling, that it might be the straw that makes the camel go to Coniston, if you know what I mean. When I looked into the earth before, to find Gwyre, I was almost taken away. Like being sucked back in a wave, taken out to sea, only this would be to take me by deep ways to my father. It was hard to resist."

"But you did," said Vivien. "We can stay at the Small Bookshop tonight, by the way. It's warded, so you won't dream. Everything should be easier once the solstice is past."

"I hope so," said Susan. "Oh look, Merlin's waving us in."

They got up and brushed themselves off. Other dusty individuals were doing the same. Torrant and Danziger were issuing orders, deploying armed police officers around the perimeter, Maglite beams flickering all around like infant World War Two searchlights that couldn't reach to the sky. Susan picked up the cricket bag and walked into the shed. Most of the roof was missing at this end, and she could see the moon starting to edge out from behind the clouds. To her surprise, the sky was clearing, clouds parting and drifting away, seemingly in several directions, despite the weather forecast for continuing rain and little wind.

The tunnel entrance was still visible, but about ten feet past the doorway it was almost completely full of new rubble. Colonel Leraigne and her sergeant were examining the rockfall, with Merlin, Cameron, Stephanie, and Diarmuid conferring nearby. Ruby came running after Susan and Vivien. She called out to them before she caught up.

"Vivien! Can you feel it?"

She pointed at the patch of sky visible through the holes in the roof. Vivien looked up, as did Susan. Though it was only a minute since she'd last looked, the clouds had completely vanished from a huge swathe of the sky directly above them. The moon was completely visible now. It was waning gibbous, only a few days past full, a bright circle with its shadowy face distinct. A ring of ice was forming around the disc, something Susan had only ever seen once before.

"I can't feel it yet," replied Vivien, obviously shocked. "But I can see it. We need to tell Merlin."

She broke into a run, Ruby and Susan at her heels, and they dashed to the far end of the railway shed. Merlin turned towards them, raising his crowbar, but he let it fall as he saw they were not pursued.

"What is it?" he asked. "I take it something bad?"

"Fimbulwinter!" snapped Ruby. "Summoned a few minutes ago. It will come fast, this night."

"Wizard's work," said Merlin heavily. "How long?"

"Minutes, not hours," said Vivien. "Is the way entirely blocked?"

"Close enough," said Merlin, gesturing at the two soldiers who were now examining the jagged ceiling of the tunnel. "Leraigne says commercial high explosive, gelignite or similar, placed in boreholes. She can't say how much of the tunnel is collapsed, it's probably only twenty feet or so given the expense and time to emplace the demolitions. But that's enough."

"There's some space at the top," said Susan. "Could we crawl through?"

"It's completely closed a bit farther on," said Merlin. "We'll have to shift it by hand. But that will take hours, take us dangerously close to midnight. I suppose it's moot now. The two of you can't break the Fimbulwinter?"

"Not on the winter solstice," said Ruby grimly. "We'd need a full circle."

Vivien suddenly exhaled. She'd been holding her breath, her right palm held up like a traffic policeman stopping cars.

"It's coming faster. We have to get out of here before it really takes hold. Back across the road. That's Roman. It will be boundary enough. Frances Gibbons must have opened a way from Alphabet House. She's definitely a wizard, and strong. Her parentage, I guess. I would not have thought the Fimbulwinter could set in so quickly."

"What is Fimbulwinter?" asked Susan. She made no move to turn around, even though the others were already looking back.

"Like the worst midwinter cold snap ever," said Vivien. "And it will wake entities best left undisturbed and draw them here. This whole area will be basically uninhabitable till dawn. We should be grateful it's still a military area or every farmhouse nearby would be full of frozen and dismembered people by morning."

"What about Megana?" asked Susan. She looked straight into Merlin's eyes, challenging him. "Are we just going to abandon her?"

"We can't reach her in time now," said Merlin, avoiding her gaze. "Even we cannot stay here under the Fimbulwinter. Can't you feel it? I'm sorry, but I've totally stuffed this up. Una's going to go spare."

It was much colder and getting worse by the minute. Susan's breath came out as a swirl of fog as she looked around. The moonlight was strong now, bathing everything in icy light, washing out the yellow beams of the car headlights and the police torches. The sky glittered, as if ice were forming in the air.

"Back to the vehicles, everyone!" shouted Merlin. "Count everyone in and drive out, form up on the far side of the road!"

He raised his PF8 and repeated the instruction. People started to run, the sudden, biting cold sparking fear, as did the uncanny, icy moonlight.

Susan did not run. She dropped the cricket bag marked with Lord Peter Wimsey's initials (it had been a present to Dorothy Sayers from Merlin's grandmother and had come back to her at the author's death, and thence to her grandson many years later), opened it, and took out Clarent. It was sheathed in its ancient, heavy leather scabbard, banded and tipped in greenish bronze, but Susan drew it swiftly free, the ivory-inlaid grip steady in her hand. The sword felt completely right to Susan, as if she had wielded it before.

She knew its balance, it knew her.

Susan raised Clarent above her head and felt as if she had grown taller with it, or the others had shrunk.

"Susan . . ." Merlin cried out, and reached for her, but Vivien held him back and he did not struggle.

"The Crone and Frances Gibbons are *not* going to sacrifice Megana," declared Susan. She turned on her heel and strode towards the blocked tunnel. Leraigne and the sergeant came running back the other way. There was already ice in their hair and on their camouflage jackets, and their eyes were wide with fright.

Susan started climbing up the rubble. She could feel the cold, too, but at a distance. The sword kept it at bay. The heat was familiar to her, the forge fire of the Knockers contained within the steel, even though no flames licked along the blade, and it did not shed light.

"Susan!"

She turned to look. Merlin was standing in the tunnel entrance, Vivien and Ruby at his side. Behind them, everyone else was fleeing for the vehicles, and some of the cars were already turning away, engines racing.

"Come back!" shouted Merlin.

Susan nodded, knowing he did not mean now. The booksellers spun about and ran, too, boots cracking the new sheets of ice that spread across the concrete floor like a time-lapse film of a freezing pond.

Leading with the sword, Susan crawled into the narrow gap between the top of the rubble and the tunnel ceiling and began to squirm her way forward, willing the stone to move away, to shift to allow her passage, and not fall upon her.

CHAPTER TWENTY-TWO

Near Midnight, The Winter Solstice,
Thursday, 22nd December 1983

Ice-brook. *A sword of ice-brook temper. Of the very best quality.*

THE TUNNEL WAS BLOCKED FOR MUCH FARTHER THAN TWENTY FEET, and it was very slow going for Susan to twist and slide and squirm through the rubble. The broken Bath stone did answer her, but it was not like when she ghosted through Coniston shale, she couldn't simply move through it, she had to make it shift out of the way, willing it to clear a passage for her. She didn't know how it worked, but if she concentrated, the rock would shift ahead of her, though it fell in again behind.

She could feel Coniston calling to her, too, though not so strongly. She sensed Clarent helped her resist it, or perhaps the fact that she was not moving into the stone, but forcing it aside. It still took effort to resist the call.

It was all mentally very tiring, and after a while Susan began to wonder what would happen if she became too exhausted to go on. She'd be stuck in the rubble then, possibly even smothered by it. She banished this thought, but she was physically tired, too, from the effort of twisting and slithering. Her arms burned from holding Clarent out in front, even though she switched the sword from hand to hand every five minutes or so.

Time was slipping away. She couldn't draw her wrist back to look at her Swatch. It was impossible to tell how close to midnight it was already. Surely, Susan told herself, she hadn't been making her slow way through the collapsed tunnel for more than an hour? It shouldn't be past ten o'clock. But maybe it was.

Finally, rubble fell away ahead and there were no more rocks beyond. Susan saw the tunnel clear in her strange grey-toned night vision. It continued on as far as she could see at a slight downward grade, curving gradually to the right. The conveyor was on the left side, a continuous line of metal rollers about two feet wide and waist high, the end closest to her mangled and crushed by the rock fall.

The tunnel itself was easily fifteen feet wide and ten feet high, and the original raw face of the Bath stone mine had here and there been faced with concrete, and there were steel reinforcing beams at intervals.

Susan slithered down the face of the rubble and very slowly stood up, feeling aches and pains in every joint. A few more rocks fell behind her, making her jump. When she looked back she confirmed the way was totally blocked again. She'd come through like a worm through earth, creating a passage only for herself, which had closed behind.

It was cold, even with the warmth of the sword, but not so cold as it had been above. Susan sensed she was about a hundred feet down, and fifty or sixty yards west of the railway shed entrance.

She looked at her watch, sighing as she saw the cracked face. Somewhere along the way she must have hit it against the rubble. It was stopped at 11:12, but whether that was mere minutes ago or had occurred much earlier, Susan didn't know.

Susan stretched again, and swished Clarent from side to side, remembering her saber practice at school. Then she started down the tunnel, walking swiftly. The curve became more pronounced as she progressed, so it was impossible to see very far ahead. Without her altered eyesight, Susan knew it would be pitch black and absolutely terrifying. It was scary enough for her even now. There were lights set in the ceiling, but the electric cables between them had been stripped away, probably salvaged or stolen for their copper.

The tunnel was very long, and though the incline was not steep, it went very deep. Even without touching the ground Susan could feel the weight of the rock all around and above.

It was also very quiet, the only sound Susan's own footsteps and her breathing, which to her sounded as if it was getting louder and louder. She had sped up without active thought, her swift walk turning into a jog. Susan had to find Megana before midnight, though she wasn't at all sure what she would do once she did.

She was almost running when she saw the body lying on the floor ahead. For a moment she thought it must be Megana, already dead, before she took in that it was a man. Slowing down, she approached warily. It was a Mason, thorny rose apron over overalls and duffle coat. He wasn't dead but deeply unconscious, and there was blood coming out of his ears and nose. He had what Susan thought was a large round pill container in his hand, but when she prized his fingers open and unscrewed it, it contained unusual matchsticks where the head was a full half of the match. Susan realized he must have lit the fuse that detonated the charges farther up the tunnel but had not been able to get far enough away from the blast, which would have been greatly intensified by being compressed in the tunnel.

He was armed with a Webley revolver. Susan took it, snapped it open, and ejected the cartridges before skimming the weapon under the conveyor. The Mason had an electric torch, but it was flat. She took the tin of matches. She was about to continue on her way when she thought to look for a watch. He wore one, but it was also stopped, at two minutes past nine. The time of the explosion.

Susan left the unconscious man and continued down the tunnel, Clarent held ready. She did not run now, more wary than before.

At last, the tunnel ended in a closed blast door, as it declared itself, with "Keep Blast Door Closed At All Times" in letters ten inches high. The letters were probably red, but Susan could not see color without external light.

She frowned at the wording, for a door that had to be kept shut at *all* times was not a door, it was a wall. There was a handle on the right side, so she pulled on it and was surprised when it slid aside on a still well-greased rail. But even so, it was frighteningly loud, the sound echoing all around.

The cavern beyond was huge, a kind of subterranean square where three other tunnels met. The natural pillars made by the stone miners had been replaced by steel and concrete columns, one every ten feet or so, and there were a dozen of these ahead and six to either side. Susan sensed the chamber was square, extending one hundred and twenty feet wide on each side.

Two of the tunnels were closed by blast doors like the one she'd just come through. The third tunnel, directly opposite, was closed by a gate in faux Egyptian style, with two stone leaves.

She'd seen that gate before, in the garden of Alphabet House.

Right in the middle of the chamber, there was a pile of blankets, with a person slumped inside them. The lump moved as Susan began to walk towards it, and a frightened female voice cried out, "Who's there? Help!"

A moment later, the Egyptian Gate opened, and a swathe of bright summer sun shone forth, banishing the grey, revealing the warm honey color of the Bath stone, the cold white-painted concrete, and the red warning signs on the blast doors. Susan was blinded for a moment, but she shielded her eyes with her left forearm and did not falter, breaking into a run.

Megana screamed, stood up, and immediately fell again into the nest of blankets. There was something wrong with her legs or feet. She also shielded her eyes, pressing her face into the sleeve of her white doctor's coat.

Frances Gibbons appeared in the Egyptian Gate but did not cross the threshold. She wore a scarlet robe embroidered with thorny roses in rich gold, and leaned heavily on a blackthorn staff. She did not seem so aged as she had when Susan had seen her in the bed, in her nightgown. She was old, not ancient, and she reeked of power.

But it was not only the wizard's power that Susan felt. There was a fluttering inside her, an almost electric sensation that ran through her whole body, the sense that something was about to happen. There was magic all around, deep magic, rising up like an inexorable spring tide overtopping the dykes that sought to keep it back.

"Do not interfere, Daughter of Coniston!" shouted Frances. "I admit my folly, I acknowledge your power! I no longer wish you any harm!"

Susan ignored her. Reaching the shocked young woman in the blanket nest, she crouched down by her side.

"I'm here to help, Megana," she said. "My name is Susan Arkshaw."

"I don't understand," sobbed Megana. "I don't understand!"

"Leave me the girl," called out Frances. "We are kindred spirits, you and I!"

Susan saw Megana wore a watch. She grabbed her wrist, turning it to read the time, even as the other woman screamed and tried to pull away.

It was a digital watch.

The time was 11:57.

"I'm trying to help you," snapped Susan. She did not look

at the young woman but kept her gaze on the wizard. It was too late to get away, but she knew it was necessary for Megana to get up, to show she was *not* running. "Can you stand up?"

"No," sobbed Megana. "They broke my ankle."

"Hold on to me," said Susan, hauling her up. "No, my left side! I have to keep my sword arm free."

"We must have the girl!" screamed Frances. "Mother!"

Megana looked past Susan's shoulder, screamed, and tried to hop away. Susan nearly fell over the twisted blankets, but she steadied herself and gripped Megana around the waist.

"No!" she shouted. "You mustn't run!"

She understood Megana's fear. The Crone had slithered up out of some unseen shaft in the far corner, her long, hooked arms pulling her forward as the grotesque "foot" extended up and out, the shell riding high behind the female torso.

Gwyre slid across the concrete floor towards them. As she moved, Susan heard the first faint call of hunting horns. Distant but closing, and from behind came the ominous toll of a bell.

The bell in the clock tower of Alphabet House.

It was the first stroke of midnight.

"Mother!" shrieked Frances. "Faster! There is no *time*!"

The Crone's hook hands struck sparks as she used them to propel herself forward, her long foot reaching and contracting as she humped ahead, faster and faster. Her eyes rose up out of her face, long tendrils supporting human-shaped eyes the size of oranges. Megana tried to fling herself away again, but Susan held her in place.

"We stand!" shouted Susan.

Some unknown sense made her turn, using Megana as a pivot. Clarent blurred through the air, batting away the stone roses Frances threw at her, and then she spun around again. The Crone was terrifyingly close. Hook hands sliced at Susan, only to be parried by Clarent's swiftness, the sword striking off splinters of stone.

The bell tolled again, and the hunting horns grew closer and more strident. There were hoofbeats now as well—many, many hoofbeats that did not sound quite like they came from normal horses. Beneath the raucous cry of the horns there were shouts and eager cries, but these did not sound even remotely human. They were more like whale song, but much deeper, stranger, and more frightening, a sound that was felt as much as it was heard. Susan's muscles twitched and shivered in answer and she felt an almost overwhelming urge to run.

Almost overwhelming, for she resisted.

The Crone struck again, and again Susan parried. Clarent moved swiftly in her hand, and the blade cut through the Purbeck marble where it had splintered before, and the steel took no scathe. Gwyre hissed as her blows failed to land and her prey did not run.

If the prey did not run, there was no hunt, and the spell would fail.

The bell tolled again, and the inhuman roar of the Wild Hunt drew closer.

"Run!" screamed Gwyre at Susan, her voice high and horrible, like a chisel screeching on stone. "Run!"

Megana flexed galvanically, desperate to flee, but Susan wrestled her down to the ground and crouched above her, swinging Clarent to block more blows. A stone rose thrown by Frances almost hit her but was parried away, and the wizard screamed in frustration, for the roses were spelled. Susan sensed the fell magic in the stone missiles. Clarent was truly named the Defender. If any of those roses touched her skin, they would slay her with even a glancing touch.

The bell tolled for the sixth time, and Frances Gibbons's screams changed from anger to fear. The Wild Hunt was imminent, and the cavern was now lit not only with the sunshine from Alphabet House pouring through the gate but also the glow of red fire, and the scent of burning pine from hundreds of torches was strong in the air.

The Crone put her long arms down and reared back, her awful foot a great mass of living Purbeck marble that stretched forward as she readied herself to smash down on Susan. But she was too much the snail, too slow. Susan rolled aside, dragging Megana with her. The massive statue crashed down on bare concrete, cracking the floor.

Susan quickly stood again, keeping Megana trapped between her legs, and struck where Gwyre's female torso joined the snail shape. Clarent sunk deep and stone cracked.

"We are not running!" shouted Susan, hacking at the Crone's head, stone chips flying. She could hardly hear herself, the sounds of the Hunt were so close. "We stand!"

"Mother! It's too late!" Frances screamed in anguish, her

shout almost lost amidst the cacophony of the Hunt and the tolling of the bell. She dropped the blackthorn staff and tried to step forward, but she bounced off the open gateway as if she had collided with unseen glass. She stood back, held out her arms beseechingly, and cried again, "Mother!"

Gwyre lurched forward, towards the gate, leaving Susan and Megana behind. Her shell was cracked and one of her hooked hands shorn completely off, but her foot still stretched and contracted, propelling her to her daughter.

"Oh no, oh no, oh no," muttered Megana, over and over again. She tried to crawl away, but Susan crouched again and held her tight, drawing her close.

"Shut your eyes," she soothed. "Everything will be okay."

Susan did not shut her own eyes. She lifted her head and shouted, "We are *not* running! We stand!"

The sound of the Hunt grew even louder until it overwhelmed everything else, even the tolling of the bell. The light of their fiery torches joined and grew to become the light of a vast sunset, and the cavern seemed to open wide to the sky, and there was the moon with its icy circle and stars brighter than Susan had ever seen. The Wild Hunt roared past and over her, an avalanche of blurred color, indistinct figures that she could not properly see, she could not tell whether they rode mounts or were the mounts, or were something else again beyond her comprehension. All she knew was the furious energy of their chase, and the relief that they had found someone other than her for their prey.

Gwyre made it through the Egyptian Gate and Frances Gibbons fell into her embrace as the bell tower struck twelve. A moment later the Hunt came down on them like a great wave, and Crone, wizard, gate, and all of Alphabet House were swept away.

Suddenly it was dark, cold, and quiet.

Susan let out the breath she didn't know she'd been holding, only to inhale again sharply as the silence was broken.

She heard the strange, slow hoofbeats again. But this time it was a clearer, quieter, more defined sound. A single mount, coming closer at a walk, not with the hurly-burly rush of the massed Hunt.

A lone rider drew near, a shadowy figure Susan could not properly make out even with her night vision. It was as if they were sketched in broad charcoal strokes, with no sharp lines, nothing for her mind to fasten on to. Their mount was also indistinct, but Susan somehow knew it definitely had horns like some great deer, even if she couldn't see them.

The rider halted their mount by Susan. She looked up and nodded, but did not otherwise react. She set Clarent gently down on the ground and rummaged in her pockets. Finding the stub of candle, she lit it and cupped it in her hands.

"You're safe now," she said to Megana, holding the candle close, so they were both enveloped in its soft light. "Wrap yourself up warm."

Megana slowly sat up. She was still shaking, but she dragged blankets up and wrapped them around herself. Either she couldn't see the rider and the horned mount because they were outside the ring of light, or she couldn't see them anyway.

"Rescuers will come soon," said Susan. She slipped the tin of fuse-lighting matches into the pocket of Megana's white medical coat. "Here are some matches, and I'm going to set the candle down over here."

"You aren't staying with me?" asked Megana very shakily. "Please, please—"

"The police will be here when you wake up," soothed Susan.

"I can't possibly sleep—"

"You will," said Susan. She reached out and rested her palm on Megana's forehead. "You will sleep without dreams, and you will only remember that the men who brought you here were foolish criminals who thought you were someone else, and they did not harm you. It was all a mistake, an unlucky mistake. Sleep now, and all will be well. Sleep warm and safe, and wake when the rescuers are here."

She spoke not as Susan Arkshaw but as the Daughter of Coniston. Megana's head drifted forward, and Susan gently lowered her to the floor, making a pillow with another blanket. The medical student sighed and sank into a restful sleep.

Susan dripped some wax on the floor and set the candle down. It wouldn't last more than an hour, and it would take longer than that for Merlin and the others to get down here, but she was confident Megana would stay asleep and be all right.

The rider waited patiently, their mount also, but they made slight movements that Susan found comforting. She had had her fill of statues.

For a moment she considered leaving Clarent, but that felt wrong. So she picked the sword up.

"I will go with you to Coniston, nowhere else," she said clearly. "To arrive before this coming dawn, not in some other time."

The rider nodded, and Susan saw them more clearly, the abstract figure coalescing into definite shape. The rider, like the mount, had horns. She held up her left hand, but the rider did not take it. Instead, the mount knelt on its forelegs so she could clamber up. There was no saddle, but Susan had no difficulty taking her seat, even though she held Clarent by her side.

The mount rose.

The rider raised a horn to their lips and blew a single peal, and then they were gone.

Merlin and the other rescuers arrived four hours later, covered in dust and weary from the backbreaking work of shifting stone. They found Megana asleep in her blankets but not on the cold concrete floor. She lay on a patch of rich spring grass, dotted with wildflowers, and a tall candle still burned where it was set upon a cleverly chiseled block of shale, not Bath stone.

When woken, Megana knew only she had been brought to that place by two men who were sorry they had got the wrong person and had apologized for leaving her there.

She had no memory of the Masons, of the Crone, of Frances Gibbons and the Egyptian Gate, nor of Susan Arkshaw.

Of Susan herself, there was no sign.

EPILOGUE

MERLIN ATE THE LAST FRAGMENT OF THE SLICE OF CAKE OLD MRS. Parment had given him, along with a lecture about succumbing to a cold if he insisted on fishing in the brook when anyone could see it was going to snow again and he wouldn't catch anything anyway.

He threw a few crumbs in, but no fish rose to eat them, and they swiftly swirled away.

"I know you're there," said Merlin conversationally. "The least you could do is send a fish my way."

The brook guardian did not reply, but its presence gave Merlin hope, as did the lurking entity who had moved along the hillside and was now up the slope behind him; and the ravens had abandoned the massive chestnut to haunt the willows on the opposite bank, across from the island where

Susan's rocky throne rose out of the water.

Merlin's float bobbed, which might have been a response after all, but he didn't lift his rod. In truth, he didn't want to actually catch a fish. It was just an excuse to be standing there, and there was no bait on his hook. If he really wanted to go fishing, it would be with flies, and in Scotland, not this course fishing in a small stream.

Mrs. Parment was right about the snow, Merlin thought, with a glance at the sky. The clouds were drifting lower and looked full. It was only three in the afternoon, but it was already quite dark.

He had come every day to the island in the brook since Susan's disappearance. Vivien had gone up to Coniston, but there was no sign of Susan there, and her father had not responded to any attempt to contact him.

Una had said quite openly that the Wild Hunt must have taken Susan, and this was for the best. Evangeline was not so sure, but she also seemed to think this was a reasonable and not unwelcome outcome. Of the senior-most booksellers, only Zoë and Helen had commiserated with Merlin, and Vivien, too, for the loss of a lover and a friend. Inspector Greene had greatly surprised him by giving him her pocket edition of *The Power of Positive Thinking* by Norman Vincent Peale, and a brisk assurance that Susan would indeed be back, Greene was sure of it.

"I do think she'll come back," said Merlin to the frosty air. It was a clean, crisp cold, unlike the fearful bone-biting chill of

Fimbulwinter. But in an hour or so, he would welcome the warmth of the Aga in Jassmine's kitchen, and she would also reassure him once again that Susan would come home soon. Though she had no powers he knew of, Merlin wanted to believe her.

"Who'll come back?" said a voice across the stream.

Susan's voice.

Merlin dropped his fishing rod and fell in, rising from the brook to stumble across to the island, water streaming down his face, his blue Cornish smock black and sodden, and the pockets of his corduroy trousers filled with wriggling minnows, a humorous gift from the guardian of the brook.

Susan stood on her throne, Clarent held in both hands, the point resting on the stone. She was dressed as Merlin had last seen her, but her clothes were not dusty and torn, and she looked beautiful to him, healthy and full of life.

"Won't be a moment," she said, and pushed the sword down into the stone, as easily as a knife into cheese. When only the emerald on the pommel was showing, she stood on it, until that too disappeared.

Susan stepped off the throne, and they embraced, ignoring Merlin's extreme dampness.

"I hoped you would come here," whispered Merlin, after one very long kiss. "Some of the others thought you were taken away by the Wild Hunt."

"Not exactly," said Susan, holding him tight. They kissed again before she continued. "I went to my father, as I had to do. He wanted me to . . . become him, basically."

"What?"

"He was tired, being imprisoned by Southaw wearied him, and . . . I don't really understand this . . . but he could go somewhere else, become something else," said Susan. "Only then I would need to be him."

"The Old Woman of Coniston," said Merlin. "But you're not an Ancient Sovereign, I know you're not. You couldn't be here to start with, and you're, you're still *you*."

He kissed her again, as if to make sure of what he had just said.

"I am still me," said Susan smugly, coming up for air. "But that's how I got out of it. I told him I wasn't old, and I didn't want to take on his power and majesty, that I needed to live my mortal life. I could not be the Old Woman of Coniston until I am actually old, in human years."

"And he—"

"He accepted it, quite readily," said Susan. "Was it you or Vivien who told me that Ancient Sovereigns do not consider time as mortals do? I asked for a delay, and he granted it, as if we were deciding to do something tomorrow instead of today."

"How long?" asked Merlin anxiously. He held her even tighter.

"A hundred years," said Susan. She laughed and hugged him tighter still, so close he could barely breathe. "A hundred years! And he took back the powers he had given me! I'm an ordinary human again!"

"Really?" asked Merlin skeptically. His left hand came to rest on her shoulder; she could feel the warmth of his fingers through the glove and her own clothes.

"Well, I kept being able to see in the dark," said Susan. "And maybe a few other odds and ends. How's Mum? Is she okay? I wanted to come back earlier, but . . . it's easy to lose time in the deeps."

"Jassmine is fine," said Merlin. "*She* told me you'd be back. And she's made Christmas puddings. A *lot* of puddings."

ACKNOWLEDGMENTS

My parents, Henry and Katharine, made me a reader by their own example, by giving me books, and by always supporting my access to books. This was, of course, a prerequisite to becoming a writer, the necessary apprenticeship that has continued throughout my reading life.

My parents have also been incredibly supportive of my writing career, from the very beginning when I was a small child and wrote extremely brief short stories that I made into books, through my early days as a "one book wonder," and then beyond, to the more recent halcyon days of being described as "prolific" and "long established."

This is the first of my novels that my father, Professor Henry Nix AO, will not get to read, as he passed away on 2nd February 2022 at the age of 84. I owe both my parents a great deal, for many reasons, and I am very sad my father will not get to devour this book in a single sitting, as he liked to do.

My agents are invaluable business partners, supporters, and eternal encouragers. I thank Jill Grinberg and her team at Jill Grinberg Literary Management in New York; Fiona Inglis and the gang at Curtis Brown Australia; and Matthew Snyder and his associates, who look after film/TV for me at CAA in Los Angeles.

My publishers help me in many different ways to do my job. They make beautiful books and market and sell them superbly, and I am honored to be on their lists. Thank you to Katherine Tegen and the HarperCollins crew in the USA; Eva Mills and everyone at Allen & Unwin in Australia; and Marcus Gipps and Gillian Redfearn and their team at Gollancz in the United Kingdom. I have also been very lucky to work with fantastic audiobook publishers, at Listening Library/Random House, Bolinda, and Gollancz. In addition, I am very grateful to the translators and publishers who publish my books in languages other than English.

Booksellers have been absolutely essential in my own reading life (along with libraries), of course, and I am also grateful to all booksellers, not just for supporting my own books but for everything you do to connect people and reading.

I am very fond of Bath; it is one of my favorite towns (or small cities). I first visited Bath in 1983 in my not very trusty Austin 1300 with the gold flame stripe down the bonnet, which made it go so much faster, and have been back many times since. I have taken some liberties with the reality of Bath and environs in this book, and with its inhabitants, in keeping with this being a slightly alternate world. Similarly, there are many fine book-shops and wonderful booksellers in the real Bath, but I have made up those in this story. I hope the real booksellers of Bath do not mind me using "sinister" in connection with them. Of course it only refers to left-handedness. Nothing else. Honest.

Many thanks are also owed to my wife, Anna MacFarlane, who not only manages a very busy career as a publisher but also our family; and to our sons, Thomas and Edward, who are very understanding of their father's foibles and limitations, so often related to at least half my mind being absent in a book. Our dog, Snufkin, also deserves mention for dragging me away from writing to take him for walks, which so often helps me work out what I am supposed to be writing.

RETURN TO THE OLD KINGDOM

Special anniversary editions celebrate the first three novels in the Old Kingdom series with original artwork by Leo and Diane Dillon!

KATHERINE TEGEN BOOKS
An Imprint of HarperCollins Publishers

epicreads.com